PRA...
SPINE-TIN...
AND GRIPPING ROMANCE OF
ANDREA KANE

THE SILVER COIN

"The Silver Coin leaves readers wondering what Andrea Kane can do next. . . . The action-packed story line never eases up."

—*Affaire de Coeur*

"The tension and suspense remain at a high level throughout the book, punctuated by the escalating romance and passionate love scenes."

—Bookbug on the Web

THE GOLD COIN

"Kane's engrossing plot and her quick-witted, passionate characters should make readers eagerly await this novel's companion. . . ."

—*Publishers Weekly*

"A superb novel. . . . The story line is nonstop and loaded with romantic tension and intrigue."

—*Affaire de Coeur*

"Kane has seamlessly combined a beautiful romance with an intriguing mystery. . . . *The Gold Coin* should please readers who like their romance spiced with adventure and danger."

—*Old Book Barn Gazette*

"Andrea Kane has created a fast-paced adventure that is sure to make these hot summer nights even hotter."

—CompuServe Romance Reviews

THE THEFT

"Kane has created another exciting mystery complete with a spirited heroine, a dashing older hero, and plenty of dark secrets. There are lots of good plot twists cleverly woven into Regency mores and styles to keep readers intrigued and entertained."

—*Publishers Weekly*

"Secrets, villains, and the danger [the hero and heroine] each present to the other's heart make this a rousing romance and a titillating thriller. Ms. Kane writes like no other. . . . A book that will steal your heart."

—*Romantic Times*

"The magnetism between the protagonists is contagious; it simmers and sizzles with sexual tension."

—*Rendezvous*

THE MUSIC BOX

"*The Music Box* is a trip to Wonderland, full of adventure and mystery with a magical romance to warm readers' hearts!"

—*The Literary Times*

"Breathtakingly brilliant! Andrea Kane ... has taken intrigue and passion to new heights."

—*Rendezvous*

"Ms. Kane's mystery/romance will ... bring a sparkle of love and laughter to your life."

—*Bell, Book & Candle*

"Ms. Kane has worked her special magic with this delightful story. . . . *The Music Box* is simply enchanting. Don't miss it!"

—CompuServe Romance Reviews

Books by Andrea Kane

My Heart's Desire
Dream Castle
Masque of Betrayal
Echoes in the Mist
Samantha
The Last Duke
Emerald Garden
Wishes in the Wind
Legacy of the Diamond
The Black Diamond
The Music Box
"Yuletide Treasure"—Gift of Love Anthology
The Theft
The Gold Coin
The Silver Coin
Run for Your Life

Published by POCKET BOOKS

ANDREA KANE

RUN
FOR
YOUR
LIFE

POCKET BOOKS

New York   London   Toronto   Sydney   Singapore

This book is a work of fiction. Names, characters, places, and incidents are products of the author's imagination or are used fictitiously. Any resemblance to actual events or locales or persons, living or dead, is entirely coincidental.

An *Original* Publication of POCKET BOOKS

POCKET BOOKS, a division of Simon & Schuster, Inc.
1230 Avenue of the Americas, New York, NY 10020

ISBN: 0-671-03656-4

First Pocket Books printing November 2000

10 9 8 7 6 5 4 3 2 1

POCKET and colophon are registered trademarks of Simon & Schuster, Inc.

Cover art by Lisa Litwack

Printed in the U.S.A.

To Brad,
who adds new depth and dimension
to the word "partner"—with
all my love and thanks

Acknowledgments

There are a number of people who helped me provide the detail needed to make *Run for Your Life* all it could be. I deeply appreciate their assistance:

The Society of Competitive Intelligence Professionals (SCIP), especially Mitchell Audritsh, the New Jersey chapter coordinator, for helping me accurately weave the exciting profession of competitive intelligence into Zach's character.

Dennis Horner, an expert in electrical systems, who offered his knowledge patiently and on a moment's notice.

IBM, for providing details on Smart Card technology and how it integrates with their desktop computers.

The staff at the Plaza Athénée, for their gracious hospitality.

John Malabre, born-and-bred New Yorker and tour guide extraordinaire, for an insider's view of the greatest city in the world.

Andrea Cirillo, a great coach, there from inception to delivery—encouraging, supporting, and occasionally flogging me into producing the book she knew I could create.

Caroline Tolley, my greatest champion for more than a decade.

Wendi Kane, for fashion design, brainstorming, and emotional input.

And last, but always first—to Brad, Wendi, and Mom and Dad, for sharing, caring, and understanding. My love and gratitude abound.

RUN
FOR
YOUR
LIFE

1

Central Park, New York City
Saturday, April 15
6:15 A.M.

They were closing in on her.

She could feel it.

Like a hunted animal she whirled around, backing away from the danger that threatened. Her eyes darted around furiously. Cowering in the shadows of the trees, she searched the path, terror vibrating through her.

Nothing.

She ran. Sweat drenched her body. She staggered and nearly fell. Regaining her balance, she sucked in short bursts of air, her burning lungs unable to get enough oxygen to satisfy her racing heart. She stopped, unable to go on, gasping as she stumbled down the footpath.

Not a second to waste.

Daylight was beginning to overtake night, the New York City skyline coming into focus.

Detection would soon be a certainty.

Even the oncoming rainstorm wouldn't be able to conceal her. They'd followed her. They knew just where to look, and what to look for. Her bright yellow robe beckoned like a bull's-eye. They'd find her. They'd punish her. She was terrified of that. But she was more terrified of what was happening to her.

She was desperate. She needed help. Now. Before it was too late.

She had to get to her sister.

A few raindrops fell, a welcome chill against her over-heated skin. The relief was short-lived. The droplets intensi-fied to a steady drizzle, dampening her robe and causing it to cling to her skin.

Her teeth began to chatter.

Her limbs faltered, and her knees buckled.

Reeling, she grabbed a tree trunk for support. She fought the nausea and the dizziness, blinking as she tried to clear her head and regain some strength.

It was no use. Her body was losing its fight. Her heart was bursting out of her chest. She had no energy left to run. And nowhere to run to.

Her sister. She was her only chance.

Why isn't she here yet? she thought, scanning the park with eyes barely able to see. *Where is she?*

The path was deserted. The rain was coming in a thin, steady stream now. Maybe she'd stayed in bed. Maybe the rain had dissuaded her. Maybe this entire reckless attempt had been for nothing.

In that case, it was over. The desolate park grounds would make it easy to find her. To catch her. To imprison her for good.

They'd be here any minute now.

Hysteria bubbled up inside her.

Nearly blinded by dizziness, she staggered down the path, no longer certain where she was going, but propelled by the will to live.

A twig snapped in the distance.

Her head jerked up.

Rhythmic footsteps sounded from around the bend. *Plod. Plod.* Definitely footsteps. She hadn't imagined them. Not the rapid strides of one in pursuit, but the mea-sured gait of a jogger. The tempo drew nearer—not from behind her, from ahead. It continued to approach, the strides close enough now to be accompanied by the metered pants of someone dedicated to his or her run.

God, let it be she.

Black spots were dancing before her eyes. Her heart rate had accelerated to the point where she couldn't regulate her own breathing. Her body was shaking uncontrollably. Please, she prayed silently. Please.

A flash of color.

Red. A red jogging suit with a white stripe down the pants legs—the gift she'd given her sister for her last birthday.

Thank God.

She lunged forward, determined to be seen. Her limbs failed even as she did. The ground rushed up to meet her. She felt its impact slam against her shoulder, then her back. A stick jabbed into her arm.

Raindrops struck her face. A gentle hand wiped them away.

As if from a great distance, she heard the familiar voice calling her name. She opened her eyes, but, try as she would, she couldn't see anything. Only the blackness.

Her lips moved, and she heard her own broken gasps. Or did she? She was speaking. Then why couldn't she hear herself?

Again she tried. Her mouth formed the numbers.

But, like a suffocating blanket, the darkness choked them into silence.

2

Victoria Kensington had almost ignored her alarm clock that morning.

It had been an exhausting week at work. Three new clients, all matrimonial cases, all emotionally distraught women exploited by their husbands.

She'd heard their stories more times than she cared to recall. There was Faye Larimore, the victim of her husband's drunken rages. Then Marlene Scallery, an emotionally abused thirty-two-year-old who'd finally worked up the courage to take her two small children and leave. Finally, Doris Webster, a classic case of a middle-aged woman who'd devoted thirty-five years to her husband and children, sacrificing her identity to stand behind her husband during his successful corporate career, only to have him dump her like yesterday's garbage and take off with their bank accounts and his twenty-three-year-old assistant.

The world might be more sophisticated, but people never changed. Especially scum like these men. They only got worse.

Each new client had required hours of consoling before Victoria could even broach the issue of her legal rights. Those were hours she willingly gave and would never bill for, no matter how badly her fledgling legal firm needed the money. She, Megan Stone, and Paul London were in full agreement on that. It was one of the reasons they'd started this practice—to represent people whose cause meant something to them, regardless of the opportunity for financial gain. They'd planned for years, talking about little else all the way through law school and after. Even when they'd each taken jobs at separate firms and were working grueling hours to establish their reputations, they'd meet every week for a drink at Hurley's, where they'd map out their partnership on the back of a cocktail napkin.

It was an altruistic dream, they well knew. But it was a dream they were determined to transform into reality.

Now, after three years of conforming to the system, they'd saved enough money, acquired reputations, and secured enough clients to go out on their own.

The law practice of London, Kensington & Stone had opened its doors last autumn. Their offices were modest—one level of a small brick building just north of Midtown that they'd rented at a steal just by being at the right place at the right time. Modest-sized or not, they attracted a respectable number of cases. The firm was beginning to hold its own—just barely, perhaps, but enough to provide a small amount at the end of the month that allowed for each partner to scrape by.

She, Paul, and Meg each had specific types of clients to whom they were particularly sympathetic.

Paul's were struggling entrepreneurial companies whose principals had grand ideas and empty pockets.

Meg's were elderly people whose fears and questions outweighed the size of their estates.

And hers?

Hers were emotionally crippled women.

It didn't take a therapist to figure out why.

Not if one knew the way she'd grown up.

After last week, it wasn't a surprise that her sleep had been restless, broken by unpleasant dreams. She was weary, her mind preoccupied with the plights of her new clients and how best to address them.

With so much to think about, her ritualistic jog would probably be the best thing for her. She ran every Tuesday, Thursday, and Saturday; she had since her days at Columbia Law. Running cleared her mind and renewed her in a way sleep never could.

On the other hand, she really needed sleep. Saturday had finally arrived. The office was closed. *And* it was about to rain. The ugly gray clouds gathered outside her window told her that within the hour, it would go from overcast to wet. By the time she finished her two-mile jog and returned to the apartment, she'd be drenched.

The arguments in favor of sleep were compelling.

Except that she wasn't sleeping. She was awake—wide awake—lying in bed, debating whether or not to get up.

She might as well put her energy to good use.

That decided, she'd turned off her alarm, yanked on her running clothes and shoes, and headed out.

She left her brownstone at 5:45 A.M., same as usual. The quarter-mile walk to Central Park was early-Saturday-morning quiet, quieter still because of the weather. Only a spotty dose of traffic trickled down East Eighty-second Street. On the sidewalks, an occasional determined patron hurried along, stopping to buy his or her newspaper or dashing in for a first cup of much-needed coffee. Mixed among the patrons were dog owners, taking their overly exuberant canines for morning walks. The owners tapped their feet impatiently as their pets stopped to sniff every tree, hydrant, and sign. No one lingered; everyone hurried along, obviously eager to get home.

And with good reason.

The skies were about to open up.

A fine mist was already falling when Victoria reached the Seventy-ninth Street entrance to the park. She didn't waste time on a full warm-up. She just stretched a few stubborn muscles, then broke into a jog.

It didn't take long to find the rhythm that worked her

body and relaxed her mind. Slowly, all the fragments of yesterday's meetings, which had been plaguing her, seemed to fall into place, the actions she needed to take becoming clear. Her tension began to dissipate, washing away with the first sizable drops of rain.

She was just rounding the first bend when a flash of yellow caught her eye.

She stopped in surprise as a woman wearing a lemon-colored hospital gown teetered toward her, tumbling to the ground just fifteen feet away. The woman's hair was tangled about her face, and she made a painful sound, arching upward and reaching out her arm as if trying to grasp Victoria. Then her arm fell to her side and she lay still.

Victoria rushed forward, bending over the woman's form and brushing the hair off her face. A sharp cry lodged in her throat as she saw who it was. "Audrey!"

Everything inside Victoria went cold and numb. Audrey—how could it be? Audrey was in Italy. No, this woman couldn't be Audrey. And not only because she was here in New York. But because she looked different, almost eerily so. This woman was oddly bloated, her complexion mottled, and her eyes glazed, open but unseeing.

Victoria stared at the woman's face, and a sickening realization struck, settling like lead in the pit of her stomach. This woman's features were distorted, yes. But it was definitely Audrey. Something was very wrong with her, something physical that was warping her appearance. Her breath was coming in unnatural pants, her chest rising and falling with each unsteady intake of air.

Fear gripped Victoria's gut.

"Audrey." She touched her sister's cheek, wiping raindrops from her skin.

In response, Audrey's lips moved slightly. "Fi . . . fi . . . five . . . oh . . . four . . . oh . . . oh," she rasped, her tone as unnatural as her appearance. "Dan . . . ger."

She slumped back, unconscious.

Panicked, Victoria threw back her head and scanned the area, hoping against hope she'd see someone who could help.

There was no one.

Cursing softly, she made two attempts to lift her sister, both of which failed. Judging from Audrey's erratic breathing, there was no time to waste. She needed immediate medical attention.

Leaping to her feet, Victoria cupped her hands over her mouth and called for help. She waited, praying someone would respond. But the area remained deserted.

She gauged her whereabouts, deciding the best thing she could do was to find one of the policemen who patrolled the park. She hated leaving Audrey, even for a few minutes, but she had to get an ambulance. The public phones were too far away, and besides, they never worked.

She cast one quick, worried glance at her sister, then ran off to get help.

It took ten minutes to find a cop, and five more—given her overwrought state and far-fetched story about a sister who'd appeared out of nowhere only to collapse unconscious—to convince him that she wasn't insane or some wacko looking for attention. Finally, he accompanied her back to the spot on the footpath where she'd left Audrey.

It was deserted.

"There's no one here," the policeman announced pointedly, as if Victoria couldn't see that for herself. She would have told him as much, but she was far too stunned and worried to pay attention to his annoyance.

Where was Audrey?

She darted about, searching the immediate area.

Nothing. Not a sign that anyone had been here a few minutes ago.

"Look, lady, I don't know who you saw—"

"She was here." Victoria whipped about, her jaw set.

"Fine. Well, she isn't here now. So she must have felt better, gotten up, and gone home."

"She was unconscious." Victoria slid her hand beneath the clip that held back her mane of sable hair. She rubbed the nape of her neck, blindly scanning the grounds, the anxiety in her gut intensifying. "There's no way she could have gotten up, much less gone home."

The cop's eyes narrowed suspiciously, and he studied her face with an expression Victoria recognized only too well.

"I'm not on anything, Officer," she informed him firmly. "I'm an attorney. My name is Victoria Kensington. And I'm telling you that my sister collapsed right here at my feet in this very spot. She was unconscious when I went to find you."

Evidently, the officer was satisfied with the first part of her story, if not the last. "You're sure it was this spot?"

"Positive. I know Central Park like the back of my hand. I run here three times a week—same time, same course."

"With your sister?"

"No. Alone. She knew that. She must have come to meet me." Victoria fought back her rising panic. "With all due respect, I have to find her. If you're not going to help me, I'm going to scour this park on my own."

He scratched his head. "If it was your sister, why don't you check her apartment? She probably went home. Especially if she's feeling as sick as you say."

Victoria bit back her explanation. There was no point in telling him that Audrey couldn't have gone home, that home wasn't even in New York and hadn't been for years. And there was certainly no point in elaborating that she'd been dressed in what looked like a hospital gown and that she'd looked odd and distorted, not just sick. It would only convince the cop that she was either lying or completely nuts.

And it would waste time. Time she could use to search for her sister.

"Thank you, Officer. I'll do that."

She turned and dashed off.

*   *   *

Two and a half hours later, Victoria let herself into her apartment. She was soaked to the skin, her teeth chattering from the cold. She'd combed what seemed to be an endless stretch of Central Park, and there had been no sign of Audrey. Then she'd gone to the local police precinct and begged for their help.

Even those officers she knew from court appearances had eyed her skeptically. Two of them had offered to call the local hospitals now and later to conduct a search of Central Park—*after* the weather had cleared up.

The second part of their offer was pointless. She'd checked everywhere on the park grounds within a half-mile radius. And hours from now? By then Audrey could be anywhere. But as for the first part of their offer, calling the hospitals, that she'd taken them up on.

They'd phoned every medical facility within ten miles of the park. Not one of them had an Audrey Kensington listed as a patient.

Where had she disappeared to? What in the name of heaven was going on?

Victoria slammed her front door shut and headed for her bedroom. She paused only to yank open the linen closet, grab a towel, and wrap it around her to absorb the rain. She really needed a bath and a change of clothes, but that would have to wait.

She went straight to her telephone and dialed her parents' private number at their home in Greenwich, Connecticut.

Her mother's sleepy voice answered. "Hello?"

"Mother, it's me."

"Victoria?" A faint note of concern. No one ever called this number before 10 A.M. When Victoria had lived at home, she'd made sure of it, turning off the ringer so her mother wouldn't be disturbed. Everyone thought Barbara Kensington just slept fashionably late. Victoria knew better. Her mother was sleeping off the effects of a late-night brow-beating and the liquor needed to dull the pain and fill the emotional void created by her husband.

The drinking had eased. The pain and emptiness hadn't.

"Victoria?" her mother repeated. "Is everything all right?"

"I don't know," she replied. "Mother, where's Audrey?"

"What?" Barbara Kensington paused, and Victoria could almost see her delicate brows knit in puzzlement. "What kind of question is that? You know where Audrey is. She's in Florence, painting."

"Are you sure?"

"Victoria, you're starting to frighten me. Of course I'm sure. What is this about? It's not even eight-thirty in the morning. Did you hear something on the news that upset you? Is that what's prompting this call?"

"No, nothing like that." Victoria watched puddles form at her sneakered feet. She studied them idly as she tried to decide how much to tell her mother. Her first instinct, as always, was to protect her. There was no point in alarming the poor woman unnecessarily—especially since Victoria didn't have all the facts. On the other hand, she had to do something to find Audrey.

She chose a most distasteful detour.

"Is Father home?" she tried, wondering how long it had been since she'd actually *wanted* to talk to her father. Years, probably. But in this case . . . well, if anyone knew Audrey's whereabouts, it would be he. He was the one who paid her expenses, kept tabs on her, sent her cash when she needed it. Not out of love. Victoria knew better. It was another one of her father's ways of controlling others, particularly members of his family. He was a master at the fine art of domination.

"Mother, is Father home?" she repeated. "Or did he go to the office?" She found herself praying he had. Park Avenue, where the elite law firm of Waters, Kensington, Tatem & Calder was located, was a lot closer than Greenwich.

"It's Saturday, dear," Barbara reminded her, as if that in itself were explanation enough. Which, actually, it was. Walter Kensington spent every Saturday morning on the golf course.

"He can't be teeing off today," Victoria protested. "It's pouring outside."

"Well then, he's probably inside. He met a client at the club. If their game was called off, they're probably chatting over breakfast. What has all this to do with Audrey?"

This conversation was going nowhere. Obviously, her mother had no idea that Audrey was in New York, much less that she was ill and missing.

"I was sure I saw her this morning when I went out for my jog," Victoria supplied carefully. Not a lie, just a partial truth. "It startled me."

"Well, it couldn't have been your sister. She's still abroad." A hopeful silence, like a puppy anticipating a treat. "Did you want to leave a message for your father? I'm sure that would please him very much."

Please him? Only if that message meant giving in, agreeing to exactly what he wanted.

Victoria nipped that particularly distasteful thought in the bud.

Her mind raced, latched on to another idea—hopefully one that would preclude the need to involve her father. "No, Mother, there's no message. At least not yet. I need some facts I thought he might have. But I have another source I can check. If I can't get what I'm looking for, I'll call him back later."

"That would be lovely, dear. I'll tell him the minute he gets in."

A hard swallow. "Fine. Now go back to sleep, Mother. I'm sorry I woke you."

"Don't be silly. Your father will be so glad to hear you asked for him. Good-bye, dear."

A click that was as fragile as she.

Victoria winced. But she didn't allow herself to be side-tracked. The instant she heard the dial tone hum in her ear, she began wracking her brain for the right digits.

Five, five, five—oh, four, oh, oh. That's what Audrey had been trying to say. Obviously, a phone number. It was the only answer that made sense. Her sister had been urging her to call that number—for what reason, Victoria had yet to learn.

But she intended to rectify that fact right now.

She dialed.

Two rings later, the connection was made.

Silence.

"Hello? Hello—is anyone there?" she demanded.

Ten seconds passed. Then a computer-generated voice replied, "I'm sorry, but you have the wrong number."

A click, then a dial tone.

Victoria stared at the phone in disbelief. Without hesitating, she dialed again. "I'm looking for information on an Audrey Kensington," she blurted out the instant she heard the receiver lift. "She gave me this number. I'd appreciate anything you could tell me—"

Again, the computer voice droned, "I'm sorry, but you have the wrong number."

The line went dead.

Wetting her lips, Victoria gripped the phone more tightly. Someone or something had answered her call, then hung up.

Well, she wasn't going to accept that.

She redialed the number.

This time, she began, "Look, I know someone's there. I'm not trying to harass you. I just need to find Audrey Kensington. She's ill. She gave me this number. I have nowhere else to turn—"

The same message interrupted her, playing woodenly in her ear. Then—dial tone.

Furiously, Victoria called back. The instant the connection was made, she began pressing the keypad, trying to recall every possible combination of voice-mail access codes she could remember.

Nothing.

She made one last attempt, this time just waiting for the connection to be made, then punching random keys as fast as possible.

The detached computer voice interrupted her, indifferently advising her that she'd reached the wrong number. Then, a definitive click.

No, she thought bleakly, hanging up the phone. I've got the right number. But I don't know how to use it to find Audrey.

She sank down on the edge of her bed, dropping her head in her hands. Something was wrong. She was more convinced of it now than ever. And she had no idea how to find out what that something was.

Audrey was dressed in a hospital gown. She was unconscious and needed medical attention. She couldn't tell anyone that she had a sister, much less how to contact her. She'd said something about danger—God alone knew what that meant. Was someone trying to hurt her? Did that same person take her from the park? To where? Why? To do what?

Victoria's nails dug into her skin. Audrey needed her, but Victoria couldn't get to her to help. She couldn't even get a human being on the other end of the phone. Just a goddamned computer.

At that very moment, elsewhere in Manhattan, another computer completed its programmed function.

A rapid whirring sound. Two beeps.

Information processed.

A security warning flashed on the screen. A window popped up, displaying Victoria's name, address, and unlisted telephone number.

The attendant monitoring the station acted immediately.

He lifted the telephone receiver and pressed the appropriate buttons.

Minutes later, the disinfection team was dispatched.

3

Walter Kensington leaned back in his tufted leather chair, steepling his fingers in front of him and staring intently at the intricately detailed model Jaguar on his desk.

Rising, he crossed over to the window and rotated the wand that controlled the vertical blinds. He opened them just enough so he could gaze out over the manicured grounds of his Greenwich estate.

He remembered when he'd bought this place, twenty-five years ago. He'd just been made senior partner. At thirty-eight, he'd been the youngest senior partner of what was now Waters, Kensington, Tatem & Calder. It had been fitting that he'd moved to an appropriate home. And the shrewd real estate agent the firm had hired, dollar signs glittering in her eyes, had skipped over the other listings, taken him straight here.

He'd bought the place on the spot.

He, Barbara, and Victoria—then three years old—had moved in a month later. Audrey had been born the following summer.

Since that time, he'd added the stables, doubled the size of the swimming pool, and converted the tennis courts from clay to composite. He never did like clay. Too many flaws, leaving too much to chance.

Chance was totally unacceptable. One had to control life, not the other way around.

That brought his mind back to Victoria. She had a will of iron. She'd been born with it. Even at three, she'd already earned his respect. She had backbone, spunk. She was intelligent, confident—a leader. She was her father's daughter. Audrey, on the other hand, was shy, unsure of herself, filled with silly dreams. An artist's soul, Barbara used to say about her.

Well, he had little use for artists or their souls. Audrey's painting classes and nonsensical retreats where she bonded with nature were something for Barbara to deal with, just as she dealt with the staff, the running of the house, and the social calendar.

Important matters were his to manage.

He frowned, considering the problem at hand. Solving it was more than important—it was crucial.

A knock on the door interrupted his thoughts.

"Yes?"

"Excuse me, dear." Barbara eased the door partway open, hovering uncertainly on the threshold. "I wanted you to know that Victoria called while you were out. Twice. She asked to speak to you. Something about information she needs. It sounded urgent. Maybe she's working on a case and wants your advice." A bright smile.

"Really." Walter turned, smoothing a hand through his impeccably groomed salt-and-pepper hair. "When was this?"

"The first time was early. Before nine. She thought you might not be playing golf, since it was raining. The second time was around noon. She was obviously eager to—"

"So you said," Walter interrupted. "Did she mention anything else?"

Barbara shifted nervously. She hated it when her husband used that militant tone. It meant he was on edge. "During the first phone call, she said something about seeing a person who reminded her of Audrey. I think that was just an excuse to speak with you. She's too proud to admit she needs your help. The second time she was more direct.

She just asked if you were back yet. When I said no, she left a message for you to return her call."

Walter pursed his lips, hands clasped behind him. "Is she at home or at that place she calls an office?"

"Home." His wife interlaced her fingers tightly. "Walter, please—don't insult her law firm. I know you hate the idea of her devoting herself to something inferior. But she's finally reaching out to you. If you aren't diplomatic—"

"Enough." With a curt nod, Walter waved her away. "I don't need you to give me lessons in talking to my daughter. I'll call her now. In private, if you don't mind."

Relief flooded her face. "Of course." She hesitated, just long enough to say what she had to. "Before I go, just a reminder. You invited Clarissa and Jim over for drinks. They'll be here at seven."

His brother and his wife. He'd forgotten.

Tensing, Walter spared a quick glance at his Patek Philippe. It was three-thirty. He relaxed. He had more than enough time to call Victoria, resolve his loose ends, shower and change, and read today's *Times*—all of which he intended to do before receiving company.

"Fine," he replied brusquely. "Have Robert check the liquor cabinet."

"That's already been done. Robert brought up a new bottle of Maker's Mark from the basement, and two bottles of that excellent Bordeaux—the '80 Lafite Rothschild Pauillac— that Clarissa enjoyed so much the last time they were here. Also, if the two of them decide to stay on, there's sliced filet mignon marinating in the fridge. We can barbecue, if the rain lets up."

"Good idea." Walter wasn't even listening. Barbara was the ideal hostess. She never made a mistake, not when it came to entertaining. It was one of her better qualities. Besides, he was eager to make his phone call.

Sensing her husband's impatience, Barbara retreated into the hall and shut the door.

Walter sat down at his desk and stared at the phone for a long, thoughtful minute. Then he picked it up and dialed.

"Hello?" Victoria's voice was taut with anxiety.

"It's your father. I hear you've been looking for me."

"I have."

"A specific case of yours, your mother said. Do you need advice, or to borrow some reference books—the kind your firm can't afford?"

Victoria bit back her anger. "Neither. I made up that excuse for Mother's sake. My calling you has nothing to do with a case."

"I see." Walter gave her no opportunity to explain. Instead, he steered the conversation in the direction of his choice. "Does this mean you've given more thought to my offer? That you're finally going to come to your senses and join my firm? You'll be coming in as a junior partner, Victoria. It took quite a few strings for me to manage that, but I happen to think you're a damned fine attorney. So I—"

"Father, stop." Victoria spoke with quiet control, although her fingers gripped the receiver so tightly her knuckles turned white. "This has nothing to do with my career. As I've told you a dozen times, I'm happy where I am. I don't want to work at Waters, Kensington, Tatem and Calder. I don't want you to use your influence to get me a partnership, junior or otherwise. I want to practice the kind of law, with the kind of partners and the kind of clients I choose. I realize you don't understand that. But it's my decision to make, not yours."

Walter's hand balled into a fist. "You're being a fool."

"That's your opinion. I don't happen to share it." She drew a calming breath. "I don't want to argue. The reason I called you was to ask when you last spoke with Audrey."

"With Audrey? Last evening."

"Last evening?" Victoria's heart started pounding. "Where was she?"

"In Florence, where she's been for the past six months."

A chilly pause. "Is there a reason for this particular inquisition?"

Victoria began pacing back and forth across her room, twisting the phone cord around her finger. "Yes, a good reason. I saw Audrey this morning. She was in Central Park, not Florence."

"Excuse me?"

"Audrey. She's here in New York."

Walter fell silent. When he spoke, there was censure in his tone. "Victoria, I don't know who you saw, but it wasn't your sister. Audrey called me collect an hour or two before we sat down to dinner last night. She needed money, as usual, which I wired her, as usual. When we hung up, she was on her way to bed. She planned to be up at dawn to paint the sunrise—using supplies she paid for with the last of the allowance I sent."

Last night? Victoria shook her head, denying her father's claim. There was no way Audrey could have still been in Italy then. Their parents ate dinner at eight o'clock. A few hours before that meant the call would have had to come through around six-ish, making it midnight in Florence. There was no direct flight from Italy that would have gotten Audrey into Kennedy Airport in time to place her in Manhattan at dawn.

Something was out of whack.

Either Audrey had lied to their father, or their father was lying to her.

"Victoria?" Her father's voice was impatient. "Are you still there?"

"Yes, Father, I'm here." She gritted her teeth and braced herself for the storm she was about to instigate. "I'm here—and so is Audrey. Not in my apartment, but in Manhattan. I didn't see someone who resembled Audrey, or someone who reminded me of her. I saw *Audrey*. She was wearing some kind of hospital gown. She looked terrible, all puffy and distorted. Obviously she's sick—*very* sick. She collapsed at my feet, muttered a few words, then lost consciousness. I went to get help. When I got back, she was gone."

Victoria paused, the silence at the other end positively ponderous. Either her father had decided she'd lost her mind, or he was trying to think of an appropriate response.

"Father?" she pressed. "Are you sure it was *last* night that Audrey called you? And if so, are you sure she was in Florence? Couldn't you just have assumed she was there?"

"No, Victoria, I couldn't." Her father's tone was glacial. "The overseas operator connected us. The call was made from Florence. And I might be sixty-three, but I'm not senile yet. Audrey called *last night*. Whoever that poor woman you saw was, it wasn't your sister."

"You're wrong."

Another silence. "I'm beginning to think working in that office of yours is starting to get to you. Audrey was always the scatterbrained one. You I could count on to be level-headed."

"I *am* level-headed. Which is why I know what I saw, and what I heard."

"What did this person say to you?"

Victoria wished her father were easier to read. Was he trying to placate her or grill her for information? And why would he grill her unless he knew there was an element of truth to what she was claiming?

"She said something about danger," Victoria replied, trying to gauge his reaction. "And she mumbled some numbers. The way she said them—three digits, then a pause, then the other four—I'd be willing to bet it was a phone number."

"Ah. Let me guess. Knowing you, you called this phone number."

"I did."

"And? Did they give you any answers?"

"No. I got a computerized message. It told me nothing. That's why I called you back. I was hoping you could tell me something." Victoria stopped pacing, bluntly coming to the point. "Father, I'm aware of what Audrey's like when she's depressed, what she's apt to resort to." She leaned against the bedpost, gripping the phone tightly in both hands. "I'm also aware of your feelings on the matter. But she's my sister. I love her. I want to help. So if you're keeping something from me, don't. If Audrey called you from New York, if you know something about her state of mind, I have to know. I won't tell a soul, not even Mother. But she's in trouble. I'm sure of it. She's scared and she's sick—too sick to contact us. I need to find her, to know who took her away and why. I need to see for myself that she's being cared for, and that she'll be all right. So, please, tell me the truth."

"There's no truth to tell." Her father spoke in terse syllables, his words as unyielding as his tone. "Victoria, I've never heard you like this. You're irrational. Maybe it's *you* who should see a doctor. You've been working round the clock to get that firm of yours off the ground. Maybe the strain is catching up with you."

Frustration churned in Victoria's gut. "I'm fine—physically *and* mentally. I just—" She broke off, realizing she was banging her head against a wall. Her father either couldn't or wouldn't tell her what she wanted to know. Fine. She'd get at the truth another way. How, she wasn't sure. Her options seemed to be vanishing before her eyes. But she was determined to find her sister. "What number do you have for Audrey in Florence?"

"I don't have one. She didn't give it to me. She never gave me any of her phone numbers over the past three years." Abruptly, her father changed the subject, attempting to placate her in a way she found more maddening than his anger. "Uncle Jim and Aunt Clarissa are coming over for drinks this evening. I'm sure they'd be delighted to see you."

He paused, and Victoria knew he was well aware that this was one invitation she'd be tempted to accept. It was hardly a secret that she felt close to her father's younger brother and his wife. What she found ironic was that her father was using that, of all things, to distract her. Knowing how strongly he disapproved of her bond with Jim and Clarissa, he must be even more eager than she realized to divert her from her search for Audrey.

Which made her more convinced than ever that he was hiding something.

"Jim and Clarissa will be here around seven," her father was continuing, clearly taking for granted that she meant to accept his invitation. "I'll send a car to pick you up."

"I'd love to, but I can't." Victoria felt a sincere pang of remorse. She could use Jim and Clarissa's calming presence about now. On the other hand, maybe it was just as well she didn't seek it out tonight, when she still had so much to sort out. Besides, she'd rather see them alone than with her parents. When the whole group of them were together, the tension was so thick you could cut it with a knife.

"I'm having dinner with Meg tonight," she explained.

"Discussing your extensive client list?" Walter asked with pointed sarcasm.

"Developing it."

"I doubt the restaurant stays open late enough to make headway on a project of that magnitude."

Victoria ignored the barb. "Good-bye, Father. Give Mother my love." She placed the receiver in its cradle, her uneasiness intensified rather than diminished.

Clearly, her father was being evasive. He couldn't have spoken to Audrey last night—at least not in Florence. Which meant that either he had spoken to her in New York—in which case he knew of her predicament and was trying to sever communications with her so as to protect his damnable reputation—or he hadn't spoken with her at all and was trying to convince Victoria she'd never seen her for the same reason.

Either way, he was blocking Victoria's attempts to get at the truth.

And either way, it wouldn't work.

4

At 7:40 that evening, Victoria walked down Third Avenue, lost in thought as she agonized over Audrey.

She should have sensed her sister was in trouble. But how? In the past, Audrey's relapses in her constant struggle with bulimia were always preceded by bouts of depression or self-doubt. She hadn't sounded depressed in her last few letters. Then again, it was hard to tell. Audrey's letters were always a mixture of wonder and melancholy—her artist's soul, as she described it. Tidbits of travel adventures were blended in with expressions of either excitement or dejection over the state of whatever painting she was lost in and emotional outpourings on the current man in her life. Victoria had become accustomed to her sister's extreme highs and lows. So it never dawned on her that a relapse was brewing. Particularly since Audrey had been fine since her late teens.

She'd looked so well the last time Victoria saw her, nearly three years ago, on that humid August night she'd taken off for Europe.

"Are you sure this is what you want?" Victoria had asked over the chaotic din at Kennedy Airport's international terminal.

"Positive." Audrey gave her sister a fierce hug. "I need to get away from him, Victoria. You're strong. I'm not. You can't protect me forever—not from Father or myself. I need

to be who I am, to find out who that is. I need to paint, to live on my own. Besides, I'm much better now. Trust me. I have to do this."

Victoria had nodded, feeling the anxiety and protectiveness of a mother hen who was letting her chick fly. "You'll stay in touch."

"I'll write. It's too expensive to call. As it is, Father's paying my way. No sense pissing him off more. Besides . . ." A sad smile. "He wants this to be a clean break. The farther away I go, the longer I stay there, the better an investment this is for him. No chance of my screwups doing much damage from four thousand miles away."

Victoria's guts had wrenched. "Sweetie, if you need me—"

"I'll know where to find you," Audrey had assured her, lips trembling. "Just as I always have."

Recalling those words, Victoria flinched. Yes, Audrey had found her. Now it was up to her to do the same.

With a troubled sigh, she stepped into the thriving pub-like atmosphere of Wollensky's Grill. She scanned the crowded dining room, spotted Megan, and headed over.

Slipping into her seat, she gave her friend a half-hearted wave. "Sorry I'm late. It's been one of those days."

"You look like hell," Megan noted.

"Thanks. That's how I feel." Victoria ordered a glass of cabernet and a burger, grateful they'd picked a casual spot for tonight's meal. And not only because of their limited budget these days, but because the last thing she felt like doing was getting all decked out, putting on heels and makeup. Here, she could be comfortable, dressed in a silk blouse and jeans, her dark hair loose, curling under just slightly in its customary fashion as it grazed her shoulders. Other than a touch of mascara and several brushstrokes of blush to hide her pallor, she was makeup free.

"Let me guess." Megan shot her a half grin as she nibbled at a piece of bread. "Another fight with your father.

This time he's sending in the National Guard to personally escort you to your new job on Park Avenue."

"Cute." Victoria waited as her glass of wine arrived, then took a healthy swallow before she replied. "But only half true. I argued with my father, but not about that. Oh, he mentioned the partnership—he always does. But our fight was about Audrey."

"Audrey?" Megan's brows lifted in surprise. "Why? Did you hear from her?"

Victoria stared off into space, seeing Audrey's bloated face, her glazed eyes. She had to answer carefully, to keep certain personal fears to herself in order to protect her sister. "If I tell you, you have to promise to believe me. I don't think I can stand one more person telling me I'm imagining things."

"That's not a hard promise to keep. You're the sanest person I know. Too sane, in fact."

"Not this time. At least not according to the police and my father."

"The police?" Megan sucked in her breath. "Explain."

Sticking to the facts, Victoria told her about the incident that had occurred that morning when she went running, and everything that had taken place since.

By the time she'd finished, Megan's golden brown eyes had grown wide. "Wow," she said with forced lightness, trying to ease the anguish she saw on her friend's face. "And all I did today was lounge around and review my files."

"Meg, I know it was Audrey." Victoria leaned forward, her brow furrowed anxiously. "The problem is, I don't know how to find her. I've told you what a loner she was. The only one she was close to was me. I called the little art gallery she used to work in down in SoHo. They haven't heard a thing. They reluctantly gave me the phone numbers of a couple of Audrey's acquaintances. No one's heard from her or seen her since she left for Europe."

"You could try 'reverse searching' on the Internet to see

who belongs to that phone number she mumbled to you—although my guess is it's unlisted. You say you checked with all the hospitals?"

"Twice. The first time, the police made the calls. I tried again from home, just in case Audrey didn't get admitted until later. Not only isn't she a patient at any hospital in Manhattan, but none of them uses yellow hospital gowns. It's bizarre."

"But you think your father knows something."

"I'm sure of it." Victoria inclined her head. "Would you like to hear how he changed the subject to divert my attention from Audrey? He invited me over tonight to have drinks with my uncle and aunt."

A wry grin. "That's a first."

"Exactly. Look, Meg, my father has no tolerance for weakness and less tolerance for Audrey. If she's ill, if that illness might result in any social embarrassment for him, he'll pretend she doesn't exist. Which means ignoring any call for help she might have initiated. It's no accident that she found me today. She knows I run that same footpath three times a week. She was looking for me. My father must have cut her off at the knees. So, the way I see it, I could dart around like a rat in a maze and get nowhere, or I could follow my instincts and use my father as the starting point."

"You said Audrey called him collect." Megan drummed her fingers on the table. "If that's true, his phone records will tell you where she called from."

"Not that he'd volunteer those records, but, yes." Victoria took another sip of wine. "Eventually, Audrey's call will show up on his bill. But what good does that do me now?"

"Maybe more good than you think." Megan spoke slowly, gauging her friend's reaction. "You're assuming Audrey just arrived in New York, and last night's call to your father was her first. I don't mean to sound suspicious, but if he's hedging about what he knows, isn't it possible he's also leaving out a few details? Like the fact that Audrey's been here awhile?"

"I never thought of that." Victoria frowned. "I suppose anything's possible. Audrey would definitely have turned to him first. He's cultivated that dependency since she was a child. She runs away from him, yet she turns to him blindly whenever she's in need—financial or otherwise. So if she's been here a few days, or even longer, yes, my father would probably know about it."

"Let's backtrack. Did you try Audrey's number in Florence, see if she'd left, and when?"

"I never had a number for her in Florence. According to my father, neither did he. He just wired her money when she asked, which she picked up at whatever Western Union agent happened to be nearby. I can't dispute that. Audrey's a free spirit. She moved around every few days. She liked to come and go as her artistic muse dictated. So she was never in one place long enough to settle in. She wrote to me sporadically. The last letter I got was dated April fifth. And it was definitely postmarked Florence."

"Fine. Then start there. Sometime during the past ten days Audrey arrived in New York. As for finding out exactly when . . ." Megan cleared her throat, uncomfortable with what she was about to suggest. "That brings us back to your father's phone records. Any chance you can get a look at his last bill without him knowing about it? It won't cover last night, but it might date back a week or two."

Victoria's gaze met hers—direct, unflinching. "It'll take some doing. I'll have to be careful and discreet. But with a bit of cooperation from Robert, maybe."

"Robert adores you. He'd never give you away."

"He also wouldn't knowingly betray my father. So I'll have to tread lightly. I'll do the snooping myself, and just ask Robert to look away." Victoria scarcely noticed the waiter placing her dinner order on the table before her. "Monday morning," she murmured. "My father goes in to work early. Before seven. My mother will be sound asleep. I'll take an early train to Greenwich. I'll do some nosing around, see what I can find out."

She pulled out her Day-Timer and scanned her schedule for Monday. "My first appointment is at ten. It's Faye Larimore. If I'm delayed, will you fill in for me? She'll need a lot of hand-holding if that bastard of a husband dropped in on her over the weekend."

"No problem. I'm a good substitute hand-holder." Megan fell silent, pushing her onion rings around with her fork, but not eating them—an uncharacteristic action for Meg. She and onion rings were like a bear and honey.

"Okay, enough about me," Victoria announced, eyeing her friend. "There's obviously something bothering you. Let's have it—is it a personal or a business problem?"

"Neither. Well, actually it's a personal problem, but not mine. At least, not directly. Only inasmuch as I care about you."

"You've lost me."

Meg put down her fork, abandoning the onion rings altogether. "Victoria, you're going through a difficult time. I hate to add to it, but this is something you're going to find out about anyway. You already would have, if you'd had time to read today's paper. But since you didn't—I'd rather you hear the news from me."

Having just taken her first few bites of food, Victoria paused, chewing slowly. Megan sounded solemn, almost worried, a mood that was unusual for her high-spirited friend. Meg was the one who was always preaching to her to take life less seriously and not to carry the world and all its burdens around on her shoulders. Yet here she was, her pixielike features drawn, her invariably upturned mouth unsmiling.

Whatever this news of hers was, it was serious.

"Just tell me," Victoria urged. "What is it?"

Her friend stopped mincing words. "Zach's in New York." She opened her purse, unfolded a newspaper clipping, and shoved it across the table for Victoria to see. "He's the keynote speaker at that SCIP conference being held in New York the week after next."

Automatically, Victoria's gaze went to the headline: "Zachary Hamilton to make keynote presentation on Thursday, April 27, at the annual conference of the Society of Competitive Intelligence Professionals." It went on to list Zach's credentials: president and CEO of Hamilton Enterprises, Inc., one of the world's foremost competitive intelligence companies, with a long list of clients from the Fortune 100. Education: LL.D. from Harvard; joint M.B.A. and M.S. in electrical engineering from MIT; B.S. in electrical engineering with a minor in industrial psychology from MIT.

The article announced that Hamilton had arrived in Manhattan on Thursday evening after a prolonged assignment in Europe. It concluded by proudly declaring that this appearance at SCIP marked his first formal speaking engagement in several years, and his first trip back to the United States in as long a time.

Beside the article was Zach's picture.

That's what got her.

It wasn't the bio. She knew it by memory and, besides, it was only a bunch of fundamental facts. It was seeing Zach's face, even blurred by poor newspaper quality, that twisted a knife in her heart.

Victoria inhaled sharply, staring at the picture. For a timeless minute she battled a drowning sensation as a deluge of memories washed over her in great untamed waves.

Then she pushed away the clipping. "It had to happen sometime," she noted, keeping her tone as light as possible. "He couldn't stay away forever. Besides, I don't think we need to worry. New York is a very big place. I doubt he and I will run into each other. He's here for the conference. In a few weeks, I'm sure he'll be jetting off somewhere else. That's Zach."

Megan tucked a strand of honey-brown hair behind her ear. She wasn't fooled for a minute by her friend's show of bravado, but she knew Victoria better than to push. "You're okay, then?"

"I'm fine. Thanks for worrying about me, and for telling me. But I can handle it."

"Can you?"

"Yes. It's been four years."

"I know. But you're still not over him."

Victoria stared at her burger, wondering how she could possibly swallow past the lump in her throat. "That chapter of my life has long since been closed."

"Really?" Megan took one forbidden step. "Is that why you've had six dates and zero relationships in four years?"

Shutters descended over Victoria's hazel eyes. "You know very well what I do with my nights. I work. First, I worked to establish a name, then I worked to get enough clients so I could go out on my own with you and Paul. Now, I—"

"Work to forget Zach."

Silence fell between them, made more pronounced by the boisterous conversations and clatter of dishes taking place around them.

It seemed everyone else was celebrating the pleasures of Saturday night.

"Meg, can we drop this subject?" Victoria asked tightly. "I know you mean well, but I'm not up for an interrogation on my social life tonight. In fact, I'm not up for any more heavy discussions at all. Let's just eat, drink, and gossip, like everyone else."

"All right." Meg took the cue, realizing she'd pushed her friend as far as she cared to be pushed. With one of her more customary grins, she handed Victoria the bottle of ketchup. "Start by drowning those fries. Then we'll order a few more glasses of wine each and do some serious damage to our images and our waistlines."

Victoria couldn't help but grin back. "That sounds perfect. Damage it is."

She coated her fries with a healthy blanket of ketchup, determined to give her overtaxed mind a break. No more fixating, not tonight. Not on Audrey. And certainly not on Zach Hamilton.

Downtown, in the FBI's deserted field office at 26 Federal Plaza, Zachary Hamilton leaned back in his chair, skimming the materials he'd been handed.

"Is this everything?" he asked Special Agent Meyer.

"Everything we've got. What comes next is up to you." Meyer propped his elbows on the desk, intently regarding the tall, powerfully built, dark-haired man who was seated across from him. He'd worked with Hamilton before. The man was as cool as they came, and smart as a whip. Oh, Meyer was pretty sure he had his own agenda—he'd read enough about Hamilton's background to know that, and to suspect what that agenda was. But whatever his personal objectives, they did nothing to compromise his work for the Bureau. He was good. Damned good. And in delicate situations like this one, Zachary Hamilton was exactly what they needed.

"I have some initial surveillance tapes," Meyer added, running a hand over his receding hairline. "They should be delivered here by Monday. I'll send copies to your hotel suite right away."

"Good." Hamilton rose, slipping the files into his expensive leather briefcase, then snapping it shut and locking it. "In the meantime, I'll read this thoroughly and come up with a preliminary approach before the tapes arrive. That way I'll be able to assess the data and develop a comprehensive perspective on what we're dealing with. From there, I'll make a final decision on how best to proceed."

"Okay." Meyer came to his feet as well. "Thanks for coming by. Sorry to drag you out on a Saturday night. But this couldn't wait."

"Not a problem." Zach shrugged. "At least not for me. I didn't have any plans. But you—" A quizzical look. "You have a wife and two kids, if I remember right."

Meyer's tough features softened. "Yeah, you remember

right. Two boys. Nine and eleven. Their mom rented a movie for the four of us to watch together tonight. If I know her, the popcorn's probably already in the microwave and my dinner's next to it, ready to be reheated." He patted the slight paunch he was beginning to acquire.

"You'd better get home then."

"I'll be heading out just as soon as I clear off my desk. Fifteen minutes, tops." Meyer stuck out his hand, gripped Hamilton's in a firm clasp. "Until Monday. And, Hamilton—welcome back to New York."

Zach's expression never changed. "Thanks. It's been a long time."

5

Four years. That's how long it had been since they'd seen each other, how long since they'd shouted their good-byes and forever slammed the door on what they'd had.

Victoria threw back the blanket and perched at the edge of her bed, raking both hands through her tangled mass of hair. She didn't need to consult the clock to know it was after three. She was exhausted from tossing and turning, alternately worrying about Audrey and thinking about Zach.

She wondered where he was staying. Probably the Plaza Athénée. It was a particular favorite of his, combining Europe's old-world charm with the pace and flavor of New York. The accommodations were well equipped and spacious, the staff always certain to provide the privacy his work required. As for the elegance and the posh surroundings, those he enjoyed the same way he enjoyed a fine bottle of wine—quietly and with the casual appreciation of one accustomed to the finer things in life.

Although, as he had often teased her, it was she who was born to the Plaza Athénée, not he. Until Hamilton Enterprises took off, his idea of a luxury hotel was one of Boston's local bed-and-breakfasts.

Their first night together had been at the Plaza Athénée.

Victoria could still recall each detail: her favorite flowers, yellow roses, placed on every table and in the marble bathroom; their mutually craved and often shared late-night snack—a bottle of Franciscan Oakville Estate cabernet sauvignon and a huge platter of chocolate hazelnut biscotti—set up on the dining table along with a stuffed Jack Russell terrier named Jackson, a proxy for the real thing she'd always wanted but wouldn't permit herself until her fledgling firm could afford a more conducive office—one that allowed her to smuggle a dog into it.

Then there were the other wonders.

The city's thousand twinkling lights stretching out before them like a sea of glittering stars.

The endless hours in bed.

Dammit.

With a pained glance at Jackson, who was perched on her rocking chair, she bolted to her feet, yanking on a robe and flipping on a few lights as she headed for the kitchen. She'd make some camomile tea. Maybe that would help her sleep. If nothing else, it would divert her energy and force her to stop dwelling on something that was long gone.

Ten minutes later, she carried her cup of tea back into the bedroom, sipping at it as she glanced through the pile of unread suspense novels on her night table. Tonight was a good time to begin one of them. She'd read until she nodded off. Tomorrow, she'd give Uncle Jim a call, see if he and Clarissa were free for dinner one night this week. She'd invite them here. She hated to cook, but preparing a meal would give her something to do and would keep her mind focused on tasks rather than emotions. And she could pick their brains about the situation with Audrey. Carefully. Without saying anything too harsh about her father or openly accusing him of anything. She was always respectful of the fact that, different from her or not, her father was her father—*and* that he and Jim were brothers.

Still, she was determined to know something concrete about Audrey's whereabouts by the time her uncle and aunt came to dinner.

She selected a book and tossed it on the bed. Setting her

teacup on the night table, she squirmed out of her robe and draped it across a chair. She turned, reaching for the switch on her reading lamp.

For an instant, her gaze flickered toward the window.

Something moved outside.

She caught the barest hint of motion, captured by the streetlight, but it was enough to alert her to the fact that someone was standing directly across the street from her building.

Whoever it was shifted into the shadows.

He didn't continue on his way or disappear into a building. He just remained as he was, a faint outline in the darkness, standing as still as a sentry manning his post.

Victoria stepped away from the window, telling herself she was being absurd. It was probably someone out for a cigarette.

But who? She knew all her neighbors. None of them went outside at three-thirty in the morning to smoke. Besides, there was no glow of an ember, no flicker of a match. Only the outline of a man. And this particular block didn't hire doormen.

Casually, she inched forward again, peering across the way.

He'd shifted back into her line of vision.

This time he realized he'd been spotted.

In the space of an instant, he vanished.

Victoria felt a shiver of apprehension go up her spine.

True, this was New York. But her building was in a residential area, one that was pretty quiet at this hour of night. The few people that did venture by walked briskly along, headed home. But this person had just been glued to that one spot, staring up at her building as if he were watching something. Or someone.

Victoria had the oddest feeling that that someone was she.

Badly shaken, she climbed into bed. She pulled the covers up high, feeling like a child seeking comfort—a child who'd learned very young to rely on no one but herself to receive it.

Reading had lost its appeal.

Instead, she stared at the ceiling, asking herself why she felt so certain it was she that the man had been watching.

Who was he? Why would he want to watch her? Could he be stalking her? Was this connected in any way with Audrey? Or was she just letting her imagination run wild?

Danger. Audrey's broken gasp echoed in her head.

What had she meant by that?

Fuzzy images swam into view.

White caps moving about a room that should feel cozy but didn't. A wooden ceiling fan, whirring clockwise, pushing cooling puffs of air on her face. Quiet voices. Sunlight flickering across the bed, blocked by the white caps, then back again.

She moaned softly, wishing she could summon the strength to get up. There was something she needed to do, although what it was escaped her. Her body felt heavy, her mind too hazy to focus.

"She's waking up."

The brisk voice belonged to one of the white caps.

"So I see." A man. One whose voice was familiar . . . very familiar . . .

That triggered a flicker of memory—something frightening and ugly.

But what?

She shifted her legs ever so slightly, and she winced at the resulting pain.

"Good morning." The cap had a pleasant voice. "How are you feeling?"

"Leg . . . hurts . . ."

"I'm not surprised. It's from all that running. It wasn't good for you. You're too weak."

Running. Central Park. Victoria.

With another moan, she struggled to sit up. "Vic . . . tor . . . ia . . ."

"You're becoming agitated again." It was another man's voice—one she didn't recognize. "You can't get well if you're upset."

He was right beside her, fidgeting with a lamp beside her bed. No, not a lamp. A silver pole with a plastic bag hanging from it. A plastic bag that moved when he raised it. Something glistened in his hand, something long and pointed that he rested against the bag for what seemed like forever.

"She's got to eat something solid," the cap murmured.

"She will. When she wakes up again. She'll be calmer next time. Won't you?" The first man leaned over her.

She didn't answer.

She couldn't.

Two sleepless nights and another tension-filled day later, Victoria was at the ragged edge of control.

The mysterious man watching her still hadn't reappeared.

And she'd learned nothing new about Audrey.

She'd spent all day Sunday making phone calls, first to every acquaintance Audrey had known since high school, then to every damned bed-and-breakfast in Florence. Finally, she'd given in to her worst nightmare. She'd called the morgue, her hands shaking violently as she provided them with a description of her sister, then paced and prayed until the attendant returned, assuring her that no one matching Audrey's description had been brought in.

Weak with relief, yet unwilling to rest, Victoria had gone back to Central Park and examined the footpath inch by inch. She didn't find so much as a yellow thread.

Nor did she spot the man who'd been outside her building Saturday night.

By the time Monday morning rolled around, she was half convinced she'd become paranoid.

With an aching head and an intensifying resolve, Victoria left her apartment. She was at Grand Central Station before 6 A.M. and on an express train for Greenwich ten minutes later.

The train arrived at 6:45, and she bought a cup of coffee to kill a few minutes, just to be on the safe side. She wanted to give her father's driver plenty of time to leave Greenwich and get on the road. Then again, not *too* much time. Should her father question her later—if he found out about her visit—she wanted to be able to claim she'd tried to catch him before he left and had just missed him.

The second part wasn't a lie. She would have just missed him—but not by accident.

At 7:05, she caught a cab out to her parents' estate, pulling through the iron gates at 7:15.

Robert opened the door to her knock, the expression on his keen, somewhat lined face showing his surprise at the notion of receiving such an early morning caller. He was even more surprised when he saw who that caller was.

"Miss Victoria." He still addressed her that way. After working for her family since Victoria was in nursery school, it seemed absurd for Robert to switch over to something as formal as Miss Kensington. So, Miss Victoria it stayed.

"Hi, Robert." She gave him a rueful smile. "Sorry to barge in so early."

"Nonsense. Come in." He opened the door the rest of the way, gesturing for her to enter.

She stepped inside, glancing around the tastefully furnished center hallway. "Is my father still home?"

If Robert was surprised by her question, he hid it well.

"You missed him by ten minutes." Robert's forehead furrowed in concern. "Is everything all right?"

"Yes, everything's fine."

Victoria had considered her approach a dozen times

since Saturday. True, Robert was loyal to her father. On the other hand, he was also loyal to her—and to Audrey. He'd never let anything hurt either of them. But to involve him in this—without knowing exactly what *this* was—would be terribly unfair. It would compromise his integrity, placing him smack in the middle between her father and her.

Later, she'd be specific—if she had to be. For now, the less Robert knew, the better.

Still, she wouldn't blatantly lie. Not to Robert. He'd see through it. She had to stick to the truth, but as vague a truth as possible. She had to convey her urgency without divulging the details behind it.

"I badly need some information from my father's files," Victoria explained. "Information I didn't ask him for when we spoke on Saturday." Robert would know about the call. He knew everything that went on in that house.

"What sort of information?"

"It's confidential. But I do need it right away." Victoria met Robert's gaze. In a few swift, definitive motions, she unbuttoned her khaki linen blazer, slipping it off and tossing it over her arm in a gesture that told him she meant to stay. "I'm sure I can find it myself. I'll just need a few minutes alone in Father's office."

She saw the flicker of understanding—and of reservation—in Robert's eyes. "I see. Does your father know about this?"

"As I said, we talked on Saturday. We touched on the subject, yes. But we never resolved it. The missing pieces have been worrying me all weekend."

Robert's expression gentled. "I can see that. You look exhausted."

"Please, Robert." Victoria touched his arm. "It's a family matter. An *important* family matter. I'm not asking you to help. Only to look away. Please."

The word "family" found its mark.

Clearing his throat, Robert plucked an imaginary speck

off his sleeve. "Your mother has been getting up earlier since we turned the clocks. Around nine-ish. Will you be joining her for coffee?"

Relief swept through Victoria as she realized Robert was defining her time restraints. "Unfortunately, I won't be able to. I'll be gone long before then."

"Fine. I'll pour some in a travel mug. That way, you'll have a decent cup on your train ride back."

"Thank you," Victoria said, speaking of far more than the coffee. "I appreciate it more than you know."

"Is there anything else I can do?"

Victoria hesitated, then went with her instincts. "You still pay the household bills, don't you?"

"Other than those your father takes care of, yes. I prepare the checks, your father signs them."

"Including the phone bills?"

"Yes. Those, too."

Hope flared in Victoria's gut. "Think, Robert. When did the last phone bill get paid?"

"I don't need to think. The telephone bills are paid on the twenty-first of every month."

The twenty-first. Today was the seventeenth.

"The current bill, the one you'll be paying on Friday, is it in Father's office?"

A nod. "On the far right-hand corner of his desk, under the small model Porsche, along with the other bills I'll be paying this week."

"Perfect." Victoria was already backing away. "This will take even less time than I thought."

"Good." Robert shot her a meaningful look. "The less time needed the better. After all, you have to get back to the city. I'm sure you'll have a full office of clients waiting for you by then."

"I'm sure you're right." With that, Victoria turned, hastily making her way down the hall to her father's office.

The door was shut but unlocked, probably so the maid could get in to dust.

She went inside and shut the door behind her.

The phone bill was exactly where Robert had said it would be, under one of her father's precious model cars.

She skipped over the local numbers, going immediately to the long-distance section.

Thirty-nine. That was the country code for Italy.

Victoria's eye scanned the listing of calls that began with that number. There were six collect calls in all, each made from a different place. Two from outside Florence. One from Genoa. Two from towns between the two.

The last call was made from Florence twelve days ago.

Of course, the billing period ended on the tenth—a full week ago. So nothing here either proved or disproved her belief that Audrey wasn't in Italy yesterday.

Quickly, Victoria skimmed the last recorded calls—*all* the calls that had been made on the ninth and the tenth. Nothing unusual. At least nothing that jumped out at her. Then again, the bill was too long to analyze here. She hadn't the time.

There was a ready solution to that.

She walked behind the desk and flipped on the copying machine, waiting the few seconds it took to warm up. Then she photocopied the entire invoice. She stuffed the duplicate in her purse and turned off the copying machine. Stepping back over to the desk, she refolded the original bill and replaced it exactly where it had been beneath the model Porsche.

Done.

She drew a huge sigh of relief. Now she'd grab her coffee and get out of here before her mother woke up and started asking questions.

She spent the cab ride on her cell phone, calling all the collect numbers from Italy to see if anyone had information on Audrey's whereabouts. No luck. She then spent the train ride back to the city examining the phone bill more closely and circling every unfamiliar number.

The marked-up bill was hot in her hand when she burst into the white building on the corner of Madison Avenue and 67th Street that housed her law firm. She ran up the two flights of steps and through the door to the third-floor office suite that read London, Kensington & Stone.

It was 9:40. She had twenty minutes before Faye Larimore arrived, and she intended to use that time to start checking into the handful of circled phone numbers.

She nearly groaned when she saw Paige manning her post at the front desk. Their part-time secretary—who spent twenty hours a week at the office and the rest of her time either at NYU pursuing her undergraduate degree in theater, at her agent's office pursuing an audition, or at the city's hottest nightspots pursuing her latest boyfriend—was never in before 11 A.M. Not unless she'd had an especially juicy date and wanted to tell them all about it.

Obviously, this weekend had been worthy of mention. Meg and Paul had probably gotten a full recounting. Which meant that now it was her turn—unfortunately.

Oh, she adored Paige. They all did.

Life with her was never boring.

It was also never without incident or intrusion.

And today was one day Victoria needed her privacy. She also needed to make the most of the next few minutes.

She steeled herself to disappoint Paige.

The nineteen-year-old cute-as-a-button blonde looked up from her desk, her cornflower-blue eyes lighting up with surprise at the sight of her third employer. "Hi, Victoria. Megan said you'd be late."

"Well, as it turns out, I'm not." Victoria shot her a grin, glancing around the waiting area. "Mrs. Larimore's not here yet?"

"Nope." Paige tucked a strand of strawberry-blond hair behind her ear, leaning over a stack of files on her desk to pat a just-opened box of tissues. "But I've got these all ready. Just in case that horrible husband of hers dropped by again this weekend." She frowned, her customary enthusiasm eclipsed by her equally customary compassion. "That man is a monster. I wish they'd lock him up so he can't hurt her anymore."

"Mrs. Larimore hasn't pressed charges," Victoria reminded Paige. "Nor does she want to. All she wants is her freedom."

"Well, I hope she takes him for everything in the divorce." With that, Paige dismissed the subject, her exuberance restored. "Anyway, wait till I tell you about Maurice."

Victoria's brows rose a fraction. "Maurice? What happened to Steve?"

"Steve?" Paige gave a dramatic sigh, accompanied by a wave of her hand. "He's *fini*. I bid him *adieu* after Saturday night. That's when I met Maurice. He's *très romantique*. That means romantic," she supplied.

"Yes, I know."

"He's French," Paige continued, disregarding the dry note in Victoria's tone. "You know, like Maurice Chevalier. No, you probably don't know. Maurice Chevalier was an actor about a million years ago. I'm sure you've never heard of him."

"I've heard of him." Victoria was biting her lip to keep from laughing. "I saw *Gigi* four times."

"Then you know how sexy his voice was. That awesome accent. That's how Maurice sounds when he talks. Oh, and he's a poet. He's writing a poem about me. In French. He's going to translate it into English, then read it to me himself. With that incredible voice." She emitted an exaggerated sigh.

"Paige, I want to hear all about Maurice," Victoria interrupted, inching around the front of Paige's desk and backing toward her own office. "But I've got a couple of calls I've got to make before I see Mrs. Larimore. The minute she leaves, I'll be all ears. I promise. Okay?"

"Okay." An understanding, if slightly disappointed, nod. "I'll give you every detail."

"I'm sure you will." Victoria turned around and hurried off to make her calls.

"You'll regret that promise," Paul hissed as she shot by his office. "The Maurice stories are even harder to take than the Steve stories. And you remember how sickening the Steve stories were."

"Yup. Very well." Victoria chuckled, pausing to give Paul a brief wave. "But I'll survive." She pointed toward her office. "Gotta take care of something. We'll talk later."

Without waiting for an answer, she dashed on, poking her head into Meg's office. "I'm back," she announced to her friend. "Mission accomplished. Some of the numbers need checking out. If I'm on the phone when Mrs. Larimore gets here, will you start for me as planned?"

"Sure." Meg looked up from the legal pleading she'd been drafting, lively curiosity dancing in her eyes—curiosity she visibly squelched. "Do what you have to. You'll fill me in later." Her lips twitched. "After you hear about Maurice." A measured look. "You okay?"

"I'm not sure. I'll let you know." Victoria continued down to her office and shut the door. She didn't even waste time sitting down behind her desk. She just grabbed the phone and began.

She'd recognized most of the Manhattan and Greenwich numbers as those of old family friends or legal colleagues. Uncle Jim's office number in Midtown appeared a couple of times, as did Aunt Clarissa's at Mount Sinai. Nothing unusual about any of that.

There were about a dozen New York City calls to numbers she couldn't place. Most of them, it turned out, belonged to other high-powered attorneys or corporate clients of her father's firm. A few belonged to well-known, affluent individuals whose names Victoria recognized as soon as she heard them—individuals, she learned, who were clients of her father's.

Two of the numbers didn't fall into any of those categories.

In addition, there was one overseas call she hadn't noticed before. A call made *to* Italy rather than *from* it. Now that was odd. Supposedly, her father didn't have Audrey's number at any of the places she stayed. No one in the family did.

She tried that number first.

A background buzz—the hum of an overseas connection. Then the call went through.

The phone rang twice, clicked, and was answered.

A brisk, efficient female voice at the other end said, *"Ospedale de Firenze. Pronto!"*

Florence Hospital?

Victoria sagged against her desk. She didn't speak much Italian, but she certainly understood that. Why in God's name had her father called there?

"Ciao?" the operator repeated firmly. *"È chiunque là?"*

"Sì. Buongiorno." Victoria thought frantically. *"Parlate inglese?"*

"Un minuto, per favore."

She was put on hold for what seemed like the longest minute of her life.

At last, another operator picked up. "Hello," she said, her English punctuated with an unmistakable Italian accent. "I speak English. May I help you?"

"Yes. Please." Victoria's knuckles tightened on the receiver until they turned white. "I need information on a patient."

"Do you know what unit he or she is in?"

"She. I'm not sure. Probably intensive care or some other emergency unit."

The clicking of computer keys. "And when was she admitted?"

"Sometime last week."

More clicking. "Her name?"

"Audrey Kensington."

A few additional clicks—then silence.

"I'm sorry, I have no information on an Audrey Kensington."

"Are you sure?" Victoria pressed, feeling as if she would scream if she hit one more dead end. "I might have the dates wrong. Also, it's possible she was released during the past few days."

"In that case, she would no longer be in our admissions database."

"Couldn't you check——?"

"I'm sorry, *signora.* Anything more specific is considered confidential and is against hospital policy to release."

"But——"

"I'm sorry I can't help you. Good day, *signora.*"

A dial tone hummed in Victoria's ear.

Slowly, she eased the receiver away from her ear, staring at it as if it were a foreign object. She must be getting paranoid. Because she could have sworn that woman was being helpful until she found out who the patient was that Victoria was searching for.

She sucked in her breath, glancing at the clock on her desk. It was almost ten. She had to try the two remaining New York numbers before she saw Faye Larimore. Which meant all speculation would have to wait.

She began to dial.

At Florence Hospital, the English-speaking administrator paged Dr. Antonio Riazzi. In quiet tones, she informed him of what had just taken place and what the caller had requested. Riazzi's mouth thinned into a grim line as he listened to what she had to say.

He hung up and promptly dialed a number in the States.

6

The first local number rang through.

Victoria wasn't paying full attention. Her mind was still preoccupied with her call to Florence. Besides, she didn't really expect these two Manhattan numbers to yield any results. The people at these numbers were most likely her father's colleagues.

She was caught completely off guard when an authoritative male voice at the other end of the line responded, "Aviation Group, Hope Institute."

Hastily, Victoria hung up, if for no reason other than to mask her surprise and gather her thoughts. This was the last thing she'd expected—reaching the aviation division of a private company. What did it mean? What could she say without arousing their suspicions? A better question was, What had her father said to them? Why on earth had he contacted them in the first place?

She checked the length of his call. Six minutes. It hadn't been a wrong number, not for that length of time. And even if this Hope Institute was one of his corporate clients, why would he be in touch with their aviation group?

To arrange for a flight. A flight to or from a company whose aviation group was located in New York. Which had to mean, so was the company itself.

The Hope Institute.

It certainly sounded like a medical facility of some kind.

A medical facility that might have Audrey as a patient.

The call had been made on April 8, the day after the call that had been placed to Florence Hospital. Was that when Audrey was flown to New York?

She'd have to check into it—after Faye Larimore left. For now, all she had time for was verifying the final New York City telephone number. A number that had been dialed on April 10.

Victoria pressed the appropriate buttons.

She nearly jumped out of her skin when a cool female voice inquired, "Hope Institute. How may I help you?"

Two Hope Institute calls? That clinched it.

This time Victoria didn't hang up. Instead, she acted on impulse.

"Is this the Hope Institute medical facility?" she asked in as collected a voice as she could muster.

Evidently, it did the trick.

"It is," the receptionist assured her. "How may I direct your call?"

Finally.

"I'm trying to reach Audrey Kensington. This is her sister, Victoria."

"Just a moment, please."

The onset of elevator music told Victoria she was on hold. Fine. That gave her time to think and to compose herself.

She sank down on the edge of her desk, her relief at having found Audrey marred by the ramifications of that discovery. Her sister was obviously as sick as she'd feared. Worse, their father had arranged to have her hidden away at some private clinic. Hidden not only from outsiders, but from her family.

Why?

"Hello?" The receptionist was back.

"Yes?" Victoria held her breath.

"I'm sorry, but your name is not on our approved list."

"Your approved list?" Victoria's temper was unraveling. "This is Victoria Kensington. I told you, I'm Audrey's sister. Put me through to her immediately."

"As I said, Miss Kensington, I'm not able to help you."

"Let me speak with her doctor, then."

"I repeat, you're not on our approved list."

Victoria's insides gave a frantic twist as the finality of the woman's tone registered. "Don't hang up. Please. At least give me verbal confirmation that my sister is a patient there."

"I can't do that." A phone in the background rang. "I don't mean to be curt, but I have to answer that other line. There's nothing more I can tell you. Good day."

A firm click.

Numbly, Victoria replaced the receiver. Paranoia was no longer a consideration. Not after the way that receptionist had rushed her off the phone. She was getting the runaround—first from her father, then from Florence Hospital, and now from this Hope Institute. Not to mention the call she'd discovered from her father's line to the Hope Institute's aviation group.

Massaging her temples, Victoria wracked her brain for any possibility other than the obvious. She could find none. Her father had clearly made arrangements with the Hope Institute to transfer Audrey from the Italian hospital to theirs.

The next question was, what specific type of medical facility was the Hope Institute?

She intended to find out.

She was thumbing through the white pages when a knock at her door interrupted.

"Yes?" Absently, she inclined her head in that direction.

"Victoria?" Paige poked her head in. "Sorry to bother you. But I saw your phone light go off, so I knew you'd hung up. Before you get involved again, I think you should see Mrs. Larimore. Megan's with her, but she made it pretty clear she wants you. I think her creep of a husband came over yesterday. He upset her pretty badly."

"He didn't hit her, did he?"

"No, I don't think so. It sounded to me like he just threw a fit. But it was enough. She's pretty fragile these days."

"Yes, I know." Victoria rose, folding the phone bill and tucking it in her purse. "Send her in."

Paige's pale brows knit. "Are you okay? You look kind of shaky."

A sigh. "I'm fine. I've just got a lot on my mind. But thanks for asking."

Victoria spent the next half hour with Faye Larimore. The poor woman was more jittery and lonely than she was frightened for her safety. There were too many changes happening in her life at once. Her teenage son was reacting to his father's drunken tantrums with his own rebellion, a rebellion that was hurting his grades and his social life, and tearing at Faye's heart. Her elderly parents weren't well, her brother and sister refused to give her a shred of emotional support, and her estranged husband had indeed come by this weekend to vent some more steam.

Fortunately, that was all he'd done. He'd collected some of his things, hurled a few belligerent insults at her—not to mention making the ludicrous threat that if she went through with this divorce he'd win sole custody of their son—and stormed out of the house. On the plus side, he'd been stone sober and in tight physical control, probably at the advice of his attorney. But still, his appearance, especially after the hell he'd put Faye through, had been enough to push her over the edge.

Victoria calmly reviewed the facts with her, emphasizing the strength of their case and assuring Faye that there wasn't a chance in hell her husband would win custody of their son. Not after his recent behavior, which was atrocious and well-documented. Things being as they were, he'd be lucky to get any unsupervised visitation rights.

It was a much calmer, more heartened Faye who left Victoria's office thirty minutes later.

Of course, Victoria had a lot of experience at soothing women who were intimidated by the men they lived with. Twenty-eight years of experience.

She picked up the phone book and resumed her search. Nothing.

Swearing under her breath, she slammed the book shut and tossed it aside. There was no Hope Institute listed anywhere, not in the white pages and not in the yellow pages under "medical centers" or "clinics." That meant they were unlisted. Knowing her father, they were probably an elite institution guarding their privacy. So how was she going to find them?

She was at her computer searching the Internet's various business directories when Paul leaned into her office, his clean-cut, all-American features tight with concern.

"Victoria?" He adjusted his trendy wire-rimmed glasses on the bridge of his nose. "Do you want to tell me what's going on?"

Slowly, Victoria's head came up. "Hmm?" she asked distractedly.

Paul's forehead creased as he eyed her with keen insight. "Something's up. Paige says you're acting weird, and for once, she's right. I tried asking Meg, but I can't pry a word out of her. Which means that whatever it is, you've confided in her. Care to do the same with me?"

Slowly, his words sank in and Victoria focused on his worried face. "It's personal, Paul."

"Is it your father?"

She started. "What?"

"Your father," he repeated patiently. "Is he pressuring you to join his firm again? Or . . ." He snapped his fingers. "Don't tell me. He's trying to steal one of my prestigious corporate clients."

Victoria managed a weak smile. "Nothing as simple as that. No, this is a real mess."

Paul continued to study her, a brooding expression on his face. "We've helped each other out of more messes than I can count. Let's add one more to the pile."

She hesitated.

"So it's not your father?"

"I . . ." How ironic that question was. Oh, it was her father, all right. But not in the way Paul meant. "No."

A brief nod. "Is it Zach, then? I read he was in town."

"It's not Zach." Instantly, Victoria cut Paul off, touched though she was by his concern. The last thing she needed now was to probe the subject of her lingering feelings for Zach. She had too much else on her mind—too much that was critical.

"Are you sure?" Paul pressed, apparently taking her silence as reluctance to admit the truth. "I know you and Meg always accuse me of being 'an oblivious man,' but I'm not totally dense. I remember what you were like when you and Zach broke things off. You walked around like a zombie for months. So if that's what's getting to you—"

"It isn't," Victoria interrupted to assure him. It wasn't like Paul to be so persistent. "This involves a lot more than my bruised emotions. It involves my family." She made a frustrated sound. "Look. I need to try to resolve this on my own. If I can't, if I decide I need help, I'll come straight to you and Meg. I promise."

Paul shot her a dubious look. "There's that damned wall of yours going up again. How many years do we have to know each other before you lower it for good? We all need to rely on others sometimes, Victoria. Even you." He held up a palm to ward off her reply, fully aware he'd over-stepped his bounds. "Okay, I've said my piece. I won't push you—yet. But I *will* hold you to your promise. If you're still acting like this by the end of the week, I'll be right back in your face, insisting on knowing what's going on and demanding to help."

Another weak smile. "Thanks, Paul. You and Meg are great friends."

"Yeah, if you'll let us be." With a dark scowl, Paul went out and shut the door.

Victoria exhaled sharply, dropping her head into her hands. Maybe she should have told him. But she wasn't ready. To call on Paul—and even Meg to a greater extent than she already had—would mean to tell them everything: why she was so worried, how delicate Audrey's emotional state could sometimes get, and what that emotional frailty often resulted in.

She couldn't do that. Not now. She had to protect her sister the same way she'd protected her all her life, and keep her skeletons hidden.

Until and unless she believed she'd be doing a better job of protecting her by revealing her past rather than by concealing it. If that should happen, then she'd call on Meg and Paul.

A dull ache began to throb at Victoria's temples. She was upset and confused, her mind filled with so many questions.

Stop thinking like a sister, she berated herself. *Think like a lawyer. Begin with the facts.*

Okay. The facts—coupled with the obvious evidence of the phone calls her father had made.

Audrey had been living in Florence. Now she was in New York. She was ill. She'd been dressed in a hospital gown. She was running away.

That was the part that made Victoria's skin crawl.

Why had Audrey been running? Who was she afraid of? Why did she want Victoria to call the number she'd gasped out, and what was the danger she'd alluded to?

Worse, what part had their father played in all this? Why wouldn't he tell her what was going on? Who was he protecting? Who'd recaptured Audrey and taken her back to wherever she'd been—and where she probably was now?

Victoria knew damned well where: the Hope Institute.

She raised her head, staring at the irrelevant details reflected on the computer screen before her. She'd accessed every search engine she could think of. There was no mention of the Hope Institute—no website, no media articles, and no data on them whatsoever—not their board of directors nor their locations . . . nothing.

She *had* to get a lead on this mystery clinic. It was the only way to find Audrey. But she was rapidly exhausting all her conventional sources for answers.

The logical thing would be to go to her father. It would also be the stupid thing. He'd only deny any connection between Audrey and the Hope Institute. That would result in Victoria learning nothing and being forced to tip her hand in the process.

She was too shrewd to allow that. If she'd inherited anything from her father, it was his sharp, analytical mind and his ability to keep one step ahead of the opposition. That and his unsettling poker face. Those traits were probably why she was so effective in court—and why she was the only person who *wasn't* intimidated by Walter Kensington.

Pensively, she considered the way her father's mind worked. If he'd chosen this clinic, it had to be upscale. That meant it would be nearby, either in Midtown or on the Upper East Side. It had to be affluent. And it had to be private—somewhere patients could be transported unobtrusively.

A sudden idea struck, and Victoria grabbed the phone book again. She had more than enough facts. It was time to resort to a bluff.

She flipped to the section of the yellow pages with the heading "ambulance service." There was a half-column list. She chose the companies that offered limousines as well as ambulances—a clear indication that they appealed to a wealthy, privacy-conscious clientele.

There were five such companies.

She began making her calls.

The first two yielded no results. The efficient receptionists, though sympathetic, had never even heard of the Hope Institute.

She got lucky on the third try.

"Select Care. May I help you?"

"I certainly hope so." Victoria carefully assumed just the right tone—the anxiety of a loved one coupled with the haughtiness one expected of a rich snob. "My name is Susan Haines. My grandmother is ill, and I've been staying with her for the past week while my parents are away. They left instructions about how and where to transfer her, should that become necessary."

"And has it?" the receptionist inquired instantly.

"Not yet. But I want to be prepared. I also want *you* to be prepared, since you were recommended by my grandmother's physician. I'm verifying my information now, just in case she takes a turn for the worse. Should she need to be hospitalized, I don't want to waste time on the phone."

"Of course, Miss Haines. I understand." The receptionist cleared her throat. "Please, go ahead."

"For starters, my grandmother's name is Mary Haines. She lives at 987 Park Avenue, between East Eighty-third and Eighty-fourth. Her apartment number is 3F. As for the medical facility she's to be transferred to, it's the Hope Institute. And it's located at . . ." Victoria rustled some papers around, holding her breath while she did. This was the part where, on both previous tries, she'd hit a dead end.

She didn't hit one this time.

"I'm familiar with the Hope Institute," the receptionist interjected.

Victoria's heart gave a wild little leap. *Calm,* she warned herself. *You've got to stay calm. It's the only way you'll sound convincing.* "Of course. I assumed you would be." She paused, rustling her papers again. "Now, where is that address?" she muttered aloud, exasperation lacing her words. "My secretary was supposed to print all the information out for me. But I only see part of it. Here's the Institute's phone number . . ." She rattled it off for authenticity. "But I can't seem to find—"

"It's 105 East Seventy-eighth Street, between Park and Lex," the receptionist supplied, proud that she could recite the address off the top of her head. "We can get your grandmother there in no time. Please be assured, Miss Haines, our company's record is impeccable. We know what we're doing."

Victoria could have kissed her.

"I'm sure you do," she said calmly. "And I can't thank you enough for your patience. I feel much better. Hopefully, my grandmother will hold her own, so I won't need you while my parents are away. But if I do, I feel confident she'll be in good hands."

With that, she replaced the receiver, stood up, and buttoned her blazer.

105 East Seventy-eighth.

She was on her way.

Zach leaned forward on the couch in Suite 1010 at the Plaza Athénée. Intently, he stared at the TV across the room as it displayed the final segment of the videotaped surveillance the FBI had sent over. The audio had been dubbed in from an infrared bugging device, planted near the front entrance of the Hope Institute and monitored by the surveillance team.

To a passerby, the Hope Institute was just a six-story, nondescript apartment building on New York's fashionable Upper East Side. A brick veneer, complete with a green awning overhanging the front, a doorman at the entrance, two potted plants on the landing, and an iron-gated drive on the side. Externally, there was no evidence it had been converted to a clinic.

As for the events revealed on tape, there was nothing unexpected. The past week's arrivals had included only a linen truck and three food service trucks driving up to deliver supplies to the private side entrance, a thin stream of doctors, nurses, and clerical workers walking in and out of the front door, and one or two new, obviously wealthy patients arriving in limos—limos that disappeared beneath the building and into the private underground garage.

Innocuous or not, Zach took note of every detail. He was well aware that any one of them might wind up being significant—either on its own or when coupled with other recorded events. In his business, one needed a sharp eye for detail almost as much as one needed patience.

He had both.

Jotting down a few more notes, he pressed the stop button on the remote control, then clicked off the power. He settled himself more comfortably, sipping at his coffee and reading through his thickening file.

The Hope Institute was doing a damned good job of keeping their existence quiet. And if something illegal was going on inside those walls, the guilty parties were doing an even better job of concealing that.

He shoved a hand through his hair, letting his head drop back against the sofa cushion and shutting his eyes for a moment—partly to think better and partly to give his eyes a rest. He hadn't slept much these past weeks, not since the FBI had contacted him, requesting his help in their investigation into what now appeared to be a worldwide drug-trafficking ring. A series of shipments had been traced to Manhattan and the Hope Institute, implicating the clinic and giving the FBI its first real chance to crack the case wide open.

Now all they needed was proof.

He intended to get it.

Funny how things worked out.

The invitation to deliver the keynote address at the SCIP conference had come at the perfect time. It granted credibility to his visit to New York and at the same time eliminated any potential questions about who his client here was, and what bait had been used to lure him back to the States after four years abroad.

This was one client who had to remain anonymous.

Normally, Zach would be providing competitive intelligence to elite, high-tech companies interested in learning more about specific competitors—their business strategies, new products they had yet to introduce, their approaches to bidding for large contracts. It was all perfectly legal and aboveboard—Zach wouldn't have it any other way. He simply applied his sharp analytical skills to publicly available information, discerning subtle patterns that the inexperienced eye would miss. As for his government affiliation, many of his prominent colleagues at SCIP had spent time in the intelligence community. So it was no surprise the FBI had found him.

It wasn't the first time he'd assisted the government. While in Europe, the CIA would call on him to develop intelligence on various organizations. But it was the first time the case he was investigating hit so close to home. There had been one related case four years ago—the initial matter the FBI had approached him with. That investigation had been prompted by atrocities similar to the one that shaped his past. But this time there was a direct link, not only to the crimes, but to the criminals themselves.

It was more than enough to bring him home.

The feds had been confident he'd jump on the first plane back. And they were right. They knew how badly he wanted those men. They also knew why. His personal history was hardly a secret. More than a few of the now-seasoned agents heading up this investigation had been involved fifteen years ago when Zach's world had been violently shaken, his security and foundation snatched away.

His life had been altered forever that night. The FBI knew it. Just as they knew the magnitude of his determination to see justice done. It was one of the reasons they'd called him.

True, fifteen years was a long time. And, yes, the pain of loss had dulled. But some wounds never healed—not completely. And if he could keep scum like that from hurting anyone else, destroying other lives . . .

Abruptly, he stood, went to the window, and peered out. The sun was bright, glistening off the tall buildings that defined the New York skyline. On the street below, people scurried about in a rhythmic pattern like worker ants, dodging traffic and jumping in and out of cabs.

The growling of his stomach told him it was past lunchtime. Maybe he'd get out of here for a while, grab a bite to eat, then take a stroll through Central Park.

He wasn't usually this restless, not while he was working. This time was different. This time everything seemed much more personal.

For more reasons than one.

He jabbed his hands in his pockets, a different type of emotion—this one not bitter, but bittersweet—trickling through him.

It was odd being back in New York. He should feel detached, a visitor rather than a native. Yet he didn't. On the contrary, he felt more at home here than anywhere else, maybe even Boston, where he'd spent the largest chunk of his life. There was something about Manhattan that made him feel connected, a pulse that reached out to him, beat inside him as well as out.

If he ever wanted to plant roots, this is the city in which he'd choose to do so.

He'd entertained that idea before, four years ago. He'd been all ready to settle down, to make Manhattan his home. It hadn't happened. Instead, he'd ended up in Europe—alone, as was his custom, but this time lonely in a way he'd experienced just one other time in his life.

And empty in a way he'd never known.

He frowned. This was definitely not the direction he'd meant his thoughts to take. Yet hadn't he realized they'd do just that when he set foot in this city, walked through the doors of this hotel and into Suite 1010?

He stepped away from the window, rubbed a palm over his jaw. He needed to shave and to shower. Then he'd get some lunch. After that, maybe he'd stroll around a little, reacquaint himself with this amazing city—a city that somehow still held him in its grasp.

He didn't choose to contemplate why.

7

Victoria crossed the understated lobby of the Hope Institute.

Nodding curtly at the doorman, she marched through to the reception area and straight up to the woman seated at the desk—the woman she'd undoubtedly spoken with earlier.

She wasn't going to be deterred—not this time.

"Yes?" The middle-aged receptionist leveled an unwavering stare at Victoria— not overtly rude, but far from welcoming. "May I help you?"

"I believe we spoke earlier today ... Miss Evans," Victoria qualified, noting the nameplate on the woman's desk. There was no point in denying her earlier call. The receptionist wasn't stupid. And lying would accomplish nothing but getting her tossed out. "Victoria Kensington," she identified herself, placing one of her business cards on the desk.

The tiniest flicker of surprise. "Yes, Miss Kensington, I remember. You called to inquire about a relative of yours. You seemed to think she was a patient here."

"My sister, Audrey. And she *is* a patient here. She called me herself, just after you and I spoke, to ask that I come over and see her. I also checked with my father. Evidently, he'd spoken with Audrey's doctor who now agrees that a visit from me would do her a world of good. So, if you'd kindly direct me to her room?"

Miss Evans didn't react, nor did she miss a beat. She

simply retrieved a computer printout from some discreet hiding place behind her desk and scanned it. "As I told you earlier, Miss Kensington, you're not on the approved list. Nothing's changed since then."

Victoria's chin came up. "Obviously, my sister's physician didn't have a chance to add my name to your list. He'll do so later, I'm sure. But I'm here now. And I'd like to see my sister right away."

Miss Evans leaned forward, her body language more openly confrontational. "The Hope Institute values our patients' privacy just as we do their health." One manicured fingernail tapped the computer printout sheet. "I can neither allow you inside nor confirm whether your sister is one of our patients until I see your name on this list."

"I've just explained—"

"Those are our rules, Miss Kensington," the receptionist interrupted. She picked up Victoria's business card and tucked it beneath a paperweight on her blotter, an I-wasn't-born-yesterday glint in her eyes. "I have your office number. Should I receive an updated list with your name added, I'll call you immediately."

Victoria squelched her anger, fully aware it would buy her nothing except an ugly war of words with a woman she couldn't afford to make her enemy. "All right," she agreed, forcing a tight smile to her lips. "I suppose that will have to do." She inclined her head. "May I take some literature with me? I'd like to know more about the clinic that's treating my sister."

Miss Evans's composure was back in place. "Of course." She reached into her desk and pulled out a paper-thin pamphlet. "That will give you some basic information."

Very basic, Victoria noted, glancing at the expensively printed brochure that amounted to no more than one regular sheet of 8½ by 11 paper folded in three. Four color pictures filled up most of the space, all of bedroom suites and immaculate radiology rooms. There was no mention of the type of illnesses the Institute treated, no glowing success stories, no list of affiliated doctors, and no website address.

Private was sounding more and more like *secret*.

"The photos are lovely," she said aloud. "Clearly, your patients are well cared for. I assume they're also happy here, that they're made to feel at home?"

"See for yourself." Miss Evans waved her arm, indicating the periphery of the room.

Taking in her surroundings for the first time, Victoria realized the walls were covered with photographs. Moving closer, she saw they were a compelling advertisement—no, actually, a photographic testimonial to the Hope Institute. Spaced just far enough apart to be tasteful rather than overwhelming, the pictures were full-color depictions of happy, smiling patients being catered to in the most elegant style, tended to with the utmost care. They were being served gourmet meals in their bedrooms, helped to walk the halls, settled in overstuffed chairs in what looked to be an inviting living room with a big-screen color TV.

Victoria kept her back to Miss Evans for a long time, pretending to contemplate the photos. Eventually, she composed herself enough to murmur a terse but polite good-bye. Keeping her head bowed by feigning interest in the brochure she'd been given, she made her way out of the Institute. She knew that if she turned around, her face would give away everything she was feeling—renewed fear coupled with equally renewed conviction.

Because all the patients in those full-color photos had one thing in common.

Every one of them was wearing a lemon-yellow hospital gown.

Across the street, in the ground-floor apartment the FBI had temporarily taken over, the camera whirred quietly. From its well-placed window angle, it videotaped Victoria's departure in the same way it had her arrival.

*   *   *

Just outside that building, a nondescript man dressed in a herringbone jacket leaned against the brick wall, casually smoking a cigar. No one spared him a second glance, nor would they, since smokers emerged all day long for their much-needed nicotine fixes. Nor did they notice when he reacted to the emergence of a woman across the street by straightening, stubbing out his cigar, and following in her direction, falling into the purposeful strides of a native New Yorker.

Keeping this particular woman in sight was a snap, he mused. Oh, her clothes were subtle enough—all classic lines and subdued colors. But that glossy black hair, that elegant walk, and that drop-dead body made her an easy target. It also made working on this disinfection team a helluva lot more enjoyable.

"An easy target" was putting it mildly. She was so predictable. He'd bet his next two paychecks that she was going back to her office. After that, she'd head home to her apartment, to spend the night alone.

Now *that*, he thought as he turned the corner onto Madison Avenue, was a waste. A stupid, pointless waste.

One he'd be delighted to rectify.

Victoria stopped off to buy a salad. She brought it back to her office to eat, grateful to discover that Paul and Meg were both in court and Paige was on the phone—presumably with Maurice, given her intimate tone and occasional French phrases. It was better this way. Victoria needed time by herself to sort things out.

She went into her office and shut the door, placing her lunch on the desk. Dropping heavily into her chair, she rubbed her temples as she mentally berated herself for her lack of success.

What had she really accomplished by barging into the Hope Institute? Despite her convincing lie, she'd seen no one, found out nothing, and the literature Miss Evans had given her was purposefully devoid of information. The only concrete detail she'd uncovered was that the color of the robes the patients at the Hope Institute wore was the same yellow as Audrey's—and that didn't prove anything, since they could argue that many hospitals and clinics used yellow robes. Even if Victoria pointed out that the Hope Institute was the only facility she'd found thus far using that color, they would declare it to be pure coincidence. And she couldn't argue otherwise. After all, she'd only checked with the major hospitals. There were a variety of private clinics throughout Manhattan, not to mention New York's four other boroughs. Any one of them might use yellow robes.

Worse, she didn't even have anyone to support her claim that Audrey was wearing yellow, or, for that matter, that she'd been fleeing through Central Park at all.

Goddammit. Victoria's hands balled into fists. She had nothing for the police. She didn't have a shred of evidence against the Hope Institute.

She *knew* Audrey was in there. But how could she get back inside to find her, especially with that pit bull patrolling the desk? Even if she bribed one of the delivery men to sneak her in the side entrance, she'd be spotted in an instant. And if that happened, she'd be arrested for breaking and entering, which would greatly curtail her ability to find Audrey.

Flipping open the plastic foam lid on her lunch, Victoria stabbed at the salad with her fork, playing with it but not eating, not even really seeing it. Interesting how Miss Evans had reacted to her introduction, she mused. Surprised, but not stunned. Insistent, but not rude. Definitely prepped for her chance arrival.

Prepped by whom?

Instantly, a possibility presented itself—the most likely and the most unthinkable one.

Her father.

Miss Evans hadn't reacted when Victoria mentioned having conversed with him. The receptionist had shot down everything else Victoria said, but she'd never demanded to know who Miss Kensington's father was, never challenged the implication that he yielded enough power to convince one of the Institute's doctors to bend the rules.

That could be because she already knew he did.

If so, how?

The obvious answer was that the Institute had firsthand dealings with him—dealings that centered around his admitting Audrey as a patient.

The ringing of the phone broke into Victoria's thoughts. At first she ignored the sound, assuming Paige would answer. But that likelihood disappeared rapidly, as the ringing and flashing light continued to intrude while, at the same time, the first line remained steadily lit, indicating that Paige was still in heated conversation with Maurice.

Rolling her eyes, Victoria lifted the receiver. "London, Kensington and Stone."

"Victoria?"

Automatically, her heart lifted at the sound of the familiar voice. "Uncle Jim. Hi."

"Is it a bad time?"

"No." She shook her head. "In fact, I was planning to call you in a few minutes. Father mentioned that you and Aunt Clarissa were due there for drinks last Saturday night. I wanted to join you, but I had plans with Meg."

"We didn't stay long," her uncle replied in that low, comforting tone that soothed even his most distraught psychiatric patients. "We had dinner plans with some friends up in Greenwich. So we drove up, grabbed a quick drink with your parents, and then went on our way. We wouldn't have been able to spend much time with you. That's why I'm calling. I just hung up with Clarissa. As luck would have it, we're both finishing unusually early tonight. We'd love for you to come over for dinner—if you're free."

Victoria almost smiled at his tactful qualification. They both knew she'd been "free" every time he and Clarissa had invited her over—other than the occasional business dinner she'd been required to attend—for the past four years.

"Yes, I'm free," she responded, more grateful for the invitation than she expressed. "In fact, I need to bounce some things off you, if you don't mind."

"You know I don't." Uncle Jim didn't ask for details. It wasn't unusual for Victoria to go to him for psychological advice about her emotionally abused or distressed matrimonial clients. "How would seven o'clock be?"

"Perfect." Her mind was already racing, trying to determine how much she should say. It wasn't a question of trust; she trusted her aunt and uncle completely. But since her suspicions about the Hope Institute involved her father, she'd have to tread carefully. Very carefully. "Seven o'clock it is. What can I bring?"

"Yourself—and your appetite. Clarissa's been worried since the last time we saw you. She thinks you've lost a few pounds."

Victoria grinned. "Then I'll gain them back tonight. Promise. I'll see you later. And Uncle Jim—thanks. To you both. I could really use some company tonight, especially yours and Aunt Clarissa's."

Zach had no idea what prompted him to drop in at FBI headquarters that evening.

It was rush hour. The streets were packed, and it looked like it was going to rain again. But he'd just reached a convenient breaking point in his analysis, and his earlier restlessness hadn't faded. So he ignored rush hour and grabbed a cab down to the field office to check in with Meyer and see if there were any new developments.

Meyer was alone in his office, and he waved Zach in as soon as he spotted him.

"You saved me the trouble of getting this to you," he said

in greeting, angling a remote control at the TV set across the room and rewinding a tape as he spoke. "Come in and close the door." He pressed the stop button and pointed. "This video just came in. It's interesting. Take a look."

"Different from the others?" Zach perched his hip against Meyer's desk, fixing his gaze on the screen.

"Let's say today's tape yielded a new face. A gorgeous one. See for yourself." Meyer pressed the play button and watched intently as the unfamiliar woman walked up the steps of the Hope Institute, paused to throw back her shoulders, then marched in. He fast-forwarded through the intervening time, then hit play again as she exited the facility. "She's never been there before. I have no idea who she is— yet. But I've already got men checking into—"

"Stop the tape and run through it again," Zach interrupted to command. "Then freeze it when she walks out and zoom in on her."

Meyer's head jerked around in surprise, his gaze shifting from the TV to Zach. Hamilton was one of the most inscrutable men he'd ever met. He was always cool, his thoughts and emotions always in check.

He didn't look inscrutable now. He looked stunned, his dark stare glued to the screen, a muscle working at his jaw.

If it were anybody else, Meyer would tease him about being turned on by the beautiful woman visiting the Hope Institute. But it wasn't anybody else, and the fierce expression on Hamilton's face obliterated any notion Meyer had of goading him. Wordlessly, he rewound the tape and played it again, pressing the pause button when the woman emerged, then zooming in for a close-up. "There you go."

Zach exhaled sharply. "Shit."

"You know her?" Meyer inquired, brows raised.

"Yes. I know her." Zach pushed away from the desk. When he turned toward Meyer, his composure was restored, his mask back in place. "She's no criminal. She's a lawyer—an honest one. I don't know why she went to the

Hope Institute, but it wasn't for anything illegal." Another quick glance at the TV screen. "Can you make me a copy of that tape while I wait? I want to take it with me."

Meyer nodded slowly. "Sure. You also want to be the one to talk to her, I take it."

A flash of irony glinted in Zach's eyes. "What I *want* isn't the issue. I've *got* to be the one to talk to her. It's the only chance we have of finding out anything, especially if she's there representing a client. She'll protect that person like a lioness guarding its cub. Trust me, she won't budge an inch."

"Loyal or stubborn?"

"Both."

"But she'll talk to you?"

"I'm not sure. I hope so."

Meyer pursed his lips. "Not to pry, Hamilton, but I'm going to need a few more details. Like this woman's name."

"Victoria." A reluctant pause. "Victoria Kensington."

The agent blanched. "As in Walter Kensington's daughter?"

Zach scowled. "She's not involved, Meyer."

"Not involved?" Meyer leaned forward, his elbows striking the desk with a thud. "Do I have to remind you who Kensington represents? How far back he and Benjamin Hopewell go? What the possibilities are . . . ?"

"No, you don't." Zach's palms flattened on the desk. "But that doesn't mean Victoria's involved. Give me a day. One day. Let me talk to her. If I get nowhere, you can take over. Deal?"

Meyer studied Zach speculatively. "Yeah. Deal."

8

Victoria and her uncle Jim had always had a strong rapport, even before he'd married Clarissa eight years ago. Nine years her father's junior, Jim was a fine man and a brilliant psychiatrist—and one of the few people Victoria had been able to turn to over the years for advice and emotional support.

That entire scenario was yet another bitter thorn in her father's side—not because he needed her affection, but because he hated coming in second at anything, especially to Jim. It wasn't enough that he was older, richer, and more powerful than his younger brother. Walter Kensington had to be superior at everything.

In her father's mind, Victoria's affinity with her uncle meant blatant disrespect toward him. And certain key events had done nothing but feed that belief.

It was Uncle Jim who'd backed her decision to go to Columbia University, then on to Columbia Law. Her father had been incensed, his heart set on her attending his own alma mater, Harvard. Between her brains and his connections, her admission to Harvard was a shoo-in.

Victoria had explained time and again that she loved New York, that she wanted to live there, that the quality of education at Columbia was exemplary. Her explanations had fallen on deaf ears. Walter Kensington was hell-bent on building a legacy—and that legacy included his elder daughter.

Uncle Jim had done the unthinkable: he'd taken her side. He'd actively supported the Columbia option—not to spite his brother, but because he astutely figured out the *real* motive behind Victoria's decision: to be close to home so she could act as a buffer between her father and the rest of the family, to give her mother and sister the emotional protection they needed.

Her father had figured it out, as well.

And he'd seethed.

His punishment had come as one of his typical displays of control. He'd allowed her to attend Columbia, but insisted she remain under his roof—not close by, not in the city, but right there at home. If she was so devoted to her life here, so be it. She could live in Greenwich and commute to Manhattan. After the bad judgment she'd shown by throwing away a Harvard education, he meant to keep an eye on her, so she'd make the right career choice.

And the "right choice" meant taking her place at Waters, Kensington, Tatem & Calder.

Victoria hadn't argued—not then. Wisely, she'd remained silent, knowing she had years to fight that particular battle. Besides, living at home gave her more time to study and a better opportunity to keep an eye on Audrey and her mother, both of whom were becoming more fragile.

Her father's anger toward her had just begun to simmer down when the next brouhaha struck.

Three years ago she graduated from Columbia Law, with honors, and sought the independence she'd deferred until then. Jim and Clarissa had responded by helping her buy the most wonderful graduation present she could ever have imagined: the cozy Upper East Side apartment she now called home. Her father had been livid, insisting that the only way he'd permit her to have her own place was if she came to work for him and, even then, it would be an apartment of his choosing.

Jim and Clarissa had argued that she was an adult, and

entitled to make her own decisions. The apartment was safe, in an ideal neighborhood, and perfect for Victoria's needs. She'd chosen it herself and paid for a portion of it with the trust fund her grandparents left her. The rest she'd stubbornly refused to accept as anything but a loan. That meant signing a mortgage with her aunt and uncle, and making monthly payments.

The apartment had been purchased.

And the game of one-upmanship escalated, as did her father's resentment.

Her proximity to Jim and Clarissa—and their frequent get-togethers—only made things worse.

And that includes tonight, Victoria reminded herself bitterly as she walked the few blocks uptown, *which he'll view as yet another transgression.*

Jim and Clarissa Kensington's apartment was on Fifth Avenue near East Eighty-fourth Street, only a few blocks from the false address Victoria had provided to Select Care ambulance service when she'd posed as Susan Haines.

Their penthouse view was one of the most spectacular and desirable in Manhattan, a striking panorama of celebrated landmarks, famous art galleries and museums, and the lovely section of Central Park surrounding the reservoir. Every time Victoria visited, she marveled at the contrast between the frantic pace of the world outside and the serenity of life inside their spacious two-bedroom apartment.

Much of that contrast, she suspected, had to do with Jim and Clarissa, and the incredibly soothing way they both had about them—a trait that extended to the quiet elegance of their home. All muted tones of beige and brown, the apartment was very much them, particularly the living room, which boasted a sprawling sofa, every imaginable electronic component for Uncle Jim's sound system, and an entire windowbox of lush, green plants.

The plants were all Clarissa's doing. A brilliant doctor

dedicated to medical research at Mount Sinai, she also had a skilled green thumb. Her touch made all flora thrive, and she tended the plants with the same meticulous care, the same gentle respect she gave every form of life. Victoria always suspected her aunt would have preferred to lavish that attention on children. But for whatever reason, the personal nature of which Victoria respected, children hadn't entered the picture. Pets weren't an option, given Jim's and Clarissa's long hours and demanding careers. So, plants had become her passion.

Too bad plants couldn't talk, Victoria mused broodingly as she reached her destination. From their vantage point in that sprawling windowbox, they might very well have seen Audrey tearing through the park on Saturday morning. God only knew, she could use a few witnesses.

The doorman, Leonard, was an outrageously vocal man of middle years whose bluntness bordered on audacity. He kept his job only because he made his residents laugh, because his twinkling eyes and portly belly made him a natural at playing a Fifth Avenue Santa Claus each Christmas and—perhaps the most compelling reason of all—because he made it his business to know every resident's most intimate secrets.

Now, he smiled at Victoria and tipped his cap. "Good evening, Miss Kensington." He held open the door. "Hurry. It's really beginning to come down hard."

"Hello, Leonard." Victoria blinked, becoming aware that her lightweight spring jacket had droplets of water on it. "I didn't even realize it was raining." She scooted into the building just in time to avoid the steadier downpour, combing her fingers through her damp strands of hair and inspecting the damage to her black linen slacks and cream silk blouse. "Wonderful. I look like a drowned rat."

He shot her a disbelieving look. "You've got to be joking. You look gorgeous."

A rueful grin. "Thanks. But I know better."

"Clearly not." Leonard leaned forward, speaking in a hushed, confidential tone. "Most of the women in this building pay thousands to have themselves lifted and tucked, and they still don't come close to looking like you." He rolled his eyes. "You wouldn't believe the stories I could tell you. Anyway, you've got nothing to worry about. You're a knockout."

"I've heard some of those stories." Victoria couldn't control her laughter. "But I appreciate your vote of confidence."

He pushed open the inner door. "My pleasure. I'll take you to the elevator. Both Doctors Kensington are expecting you. And that rack of lamb your aunt brought home looked unbelievable. I hope you're hungry."

"Very." Victoria stepped into the elevator and waited while Leonard leaned in and pressed the button for the penthouse.

"Have fun," he called, tipping his cap again as the elevator doors closed. "And remember," he added in a hiss, "other than Dr. Kensington, you're the best-looking woman in this building."

"I'll remember," Victoria hissed back.

What a character, she thought, still chuckling. He'd almost succeeded in taking her mind off Audrey.

Almost.

Her smile faded as the elevator reached the top floor and the doors slid quietly open. Tonight's issue loomed just ahead. She wished she could think of a subtle way to broach it. Close or not, this wasn't going to be easy.

She walked over to the apartment and rang the bell.

Her aunt opened the door, a welcoming smile on her lips. Stunning as always in a pale green silk dress, Clarissa Kensington was willowy and blond, ethereally lovely, and looked a decade younger than her forty-three years. She greeted Victoria affectionately, taking both her hands and giving them a squeeze.

"I'm so glad you're here," she said warmly. "We both are." She glanced over her shoulder and called, "Jim?"

"Victoria." Her husband appeared instantly, hugging his niece. "It's so good to see you."

She returned the hug. "It feels like a year, not a month." Smiling back at her uncle, she thought for the millionth time that except for his imposing height and probing hazel eyes—the latter of which she'd inherited—there was no likeness between her uncle and her father.

Uncle Jim, now fifty-four, was as soft-spoken and easy-going as her father was sharp and intense. He was lanky, his body language relaxed, and he had a wonderful, calming smile and just a few flecks of gray in his wavy dark hair. Even his manner of dress was casual; tonight he wore a camel-and-black crewneck sweater and camel slacks.

"Come in and sit," he instructed her. "I'll pour you a glass of cabernet."

Victoria complied, feeling her uncle's deep, searching gaze linger on her for an extra moment before he went off to get the wine. She knew very well what that look meant, just as she knew her uncle. And the insightful way he'd just studied her meant he'd concluded there was something big on her mind—although, in his customarily patient fashion, he would wait for her to bring it up.

She'd better come up with a way to broach the subject of Audrey, and fast.

It took an entire dinner and two glasses of wine for Victoria to take the plunge.

Sighing, she settled herself on the sofa after finally accepting Clarissa's staunch refusal to let her help clear the dishes.

"You keep Jim company," her aunt had advised. "I'll get the dessert and coffee. We'll have it in the living room."

With a decisive wave, she'd disappeared into the kitchen.

"Aunt Clarissa's being wonderful," Victoria murmured, tucking a strand of sable hair behind her ear. "And I don't only mean that fabulous meal, either. Although," she added, grinning as she tugged at the waistline of her pants, "she can stop worrying. She's definitely succeeded in helping me regain those pounds she was afraid I'd lost."

Jim smiled, joining Victoria in the living room. "She is an amazing cook. As for being wonderful, she's worried about you. We both are." A pointed glance.

"It's been a difficult few days," Victoria admitted quietly.

"So I gathered." He lowered himself into the armchair directly across from her, interlacing his fingers and falling silent.

Victoria arched a brow. "You're in professional mode— sitting across from me, waiting for me to speak. I hope I didn't frighten you enough to pencil me in for a formal session."

Jim chuckled. "Hardly." He leaned back, crossing his long legs at the ankles in a decidedly more relaxed pose. "Sorry. Force of habit, I guess."

"No apology necessary—now or ever." Victoria rubbed her palms together. "The truth is, I do want to talk. I'm just not sure where to start, or what to say. This is important, but it's also awkward."

"Maybe I can start for you," her uncle surprised her by saying.

Her startled gaze lifted to his, and his smile gentled.

"You've made it clear I'm not to be in therapist mode. So I'm in uncle mode instead—and uncles are allowed to jump the gun." His smile faded. "Actually, I'm not just jumping the gun, I'm overstepping my bounds—big-time. But since I suspect this is a very significant issue for you, I'll take that chance. If that's all right with you?"

Victoria's heart was drumming loudly in her chest. Could her uncle possibly know about her search for Audrey? Would her father have mentioned something about it Saturday night? That idea had never occurred to her. Her father didn't confide in anyone, ever, least of all his brother, and certainly not about a matter that would paint him as a hard-hearted control freak. Still, it was rare for her uncle to assume such a forward role in discussing her problems. So maybe . . .

Slowly, she nodded.

"Okay," Jim responded. "Here goes. I read in the newspaper that Zachary Hamilton is in New York. I remember a time when he meant a great deal to you, probably more than you actually admitted to me. Does his visit have anything to do with your frame of mind?"

Zach. Uncle Jim thought this was about Zach.

The irony of his deduction was eclipsed by that familiar knot in Victoria's gut—the same knot she felt every time Zach's name was mentioned. She shouldn't be surprised by the conclusion her uncle had drawn. He was a very intuitive man. He and Clarissa had spent more than one evening with her and Zach. And, as Meg used to tease her, only a dead man could avoid getting scorched by the flames that leaped between them.

"Victoria?" her uncle pressed. "Have I offended you?"

"No, of course not." She shook her head. "And no, this isn't about Zach, although I *was* taken aback when Meg showed me that article. Actually, I probably would have dwelled on it a lot more if it weren't for what *is* bothering me."

Jim looked perplexed. "Then what is it?"

She met his gaze squarely. "I saw Audrey Saturday morning. Here, in Central Park, while I was out running."

Her uncle's jaw dropped. "What?"

At that moment, Clarissa walked out of the kitchen and placed a tray of fruit on the cocktail table, then returned to the kitchen for the coffee and cake. That done, she glanced from her husband to Victoria and, having decided that whatever was bothering Victoria required additional time alone with Jim, she went tactfully to the windowbox and began misting the plants.

"I appreciate what you're doing, Aunt Clarissa," Victoria said. "But I really wish you'd join us. I'd like your input, both

personal and professional. I'm hoping you know something
about the private medical clinic I'm about to describe."

Clarissa's pale brows knit, but she nodded, coming to sit
beside Victoria on the sofa.

"Private medical clinic?" Jim was gazing steadily at her.
"Is Audrey in trouble?"

"Yes," Victoria said without hesitation. "She is." Her
uncle knew about Audrey's bulimia. He'd "talked" with her
unofficially when his brother had refused to let anyone outside the family be privy to their problems. And eventually,
when unbiased counseling and medical attention became
essential, Uncle Jim had convinced his brother to let him
refer Audrey to his most trusted colleague—his longtime
partner and closest friend, Elliot Osborne.

Abruptly, it occurred to Victoria that Audrey might have
sought out her uncle and Dr. Osborne when she returned to
New York. But, no. One look at Uncle Jim's face told her he
was utterly stunned by the news that Audrey was back.

"I'm not asking you to violate patient-doctor privilege,"
Victoria assured him. "But is it safe to say you had no idea
Audrey was in New York?"

"No idea at all."

A nod. "She's ill, Uncle Jim. And she's missing."

"You'd better explain."

Sticking to the facts, Victoria relayed exactly what had
happened in Central Park—what Audrey had looked like, how
disoriented and bloated she'd been—and all the events that
had occurred since then. The only spots Victoria stumbled
over were the ones involving her father. And not only because
of Uncle Jim's loyalty to his brother, but because putting her
hunch into words was harder than she'd realized. Suspecting
her father of deliberate cruelty was one thing; speaking her
suspicions aloud was quite another. It made them more than
mere possibilities. It made them accusations.

You could have heard a pin drop in the room when she'd
finished.

Clarissa and Jim both stared at her, stunned.

Her uncle spoke first, his tone so uncharacteristically hard, she flinched.

"Victoria, I don't need to tell you the seriousness of what you're claiming. I realize Walter is less than tolerant when it comes to Audrey's emotional fragility. But to blatantly keep her from you? To lie about bringing her here? Why would he do that?"

"I don't know." Victoria made a helpless gesture. "To spare his reputation is the only reason I could come up with."

"But that still doesn't explain why he'd hide Audrey from you," Clarissa mused, glancing at Jim and keeping her own voice gentle, as if trying to neutralize the tension. "If anything, you're the most calming influence she has. You've been her lifeline at times. And your father certainly knows how discreet you are. If he were trying to avoid embarrassment, he'd simply insist you keep Audrey's presence confidential, then prevail upon you to go to her and help keep her calm."

"I agree." Jim came to his feet, clearly agitated by the conversation. "Your father has his faults, Victoria. We both know that. But if Audrey really was frightened and trying to escape from wherever she'd been placed, he wouldn't ignore that. She's his daughter. He'd want her safe. There are ways to avoid a scandal without locking away your own child against her will."

"I know," Victoria managed. "I've thought of all that. But I can't get past certain facts, like: Why did Father contact Florence Hospital? And why the calls to the Hope Institute?" She inclined her head at her aunt, a hopeful look in her eyes. "Please tell me you've heard of it."

Clarissa frowned, rubbing the nape of her neck. "I don't think so. But that doesn't mean anything. My field is medical research. I'm not aware of every private health-care center in Manhattan."

"Uncle Jim?" Victoria gazed pleadingly at him.

Slowly, he shook his head. "I'm not familiar with it, no.

But I can certainly do some digging, if that would help." His lips thinned into a determined line. "But not without mentioning it to your father. I won't go behind his back like that, Victoria. I'd feel dishonest."

"I know you would," she replied in a wooden tone. "I don't feel much better. But I *know* that woman in the park was Audrey."

"I'm not doubting you on that score," her uncle responded. "If you say it was Audrey, then it was Audrey. I'm as worried about her as you are. My guess is that Walter's worried, too. He's just in denial. It's far easier for him to think of Audrey as safe in Florence than to imagine her frightened and alone in Manhattan." Jim stared off toward the window, uneasily pondering all the unanswered questions. "Maybe Walter did make long-distance arrangements to admit Audrey to Florence Hospital. Or maybe she admitted herself and then contacted him. As for the calls to the Hope Institute, your father could have made those as precautionary—just in case Audrey needed to be transferred."

"Then how did she get here?" Victoria pressed. "If Father didn't help her, if he has no idea she's in New York, how did Audrey manage to pay for the flight? Every dime she has, he wires her."

Jim's shoulders lifted in a frustrated shrug. "She could have borrowed the money from a friend. I don't know. But I refuse to believe Walter is involved in some elaborate kidnapping scheme."

That made the hair on Victoria's neck stand up. "I'm not suggesting anything as sinister as that."

"Aren't you?"

Victoria wet her lips with the tip of her tongue. "I'm not sure what I'm suggesting. I only know I have a very uneasy feeling about Father's involvement in all this. I hope you're right. I hope I'm overreacting and condemning him without basis. I hope the whole situation is as innocent as you say.

But the pieces don't fit. Maybe it's the attorney in me, or maybe I've just become too much of a cynic." *Or maybe I just know my father,* she silently added.

Looking from her uncle's unsettled expression to her aunt's anxious one, Victoria wished she hadn't allowed things to go this far. She should have followed her instincts to stick to the basic facts and leave her father's part in all this out of the discussion.

The problem was, this whole ugly mess tied together, like the tangled roots of a tree. And Walter Kensington was one of the main roots.

"I'm very tired," she told her uncle and aunt quietly. "And very worried about Audrey. I need a night to sort things out. I'll call you tomorrow, Uncle Jim, when my head is a little clearer and I've come to some decision about how I'm going to handle things. If I do take you up on your offer to help, I'll accept it on your terms. But, I'd want to be there when you talk to Father."

"Fair enough." Jim regarded her steadily. "And if you decide not to turn to us?"

"Then I'll leave you out of this completely. All I'd ask is that you keep what I've told you in confidence."

"In other words, you wouldn't want me to tell your father we had this conversation."

"I suppose that's what I'm saying, yes." Victoria swallowed. "I'm not out to hurt him, Uncle Jim. He's my father. But his agenda and mine are very different when it comes to Audrey. I've got to get at the truth. Even if doing so risks exposing a family skeleton. The Kensington name will survive. But Audrey . . ." Her voice trailed off. "This whole argument might be moot. If I can't find her on my own or make any headway with the Hope Institute, I'll have no other choice but to go back to Father. Regardless of how deep his involvement is. Because he's the only one with the answers."

9

Zach paced around the hotel suite, swallowing his second glass of bourbon.

He had to stop. Getting drunk wasn't the answer. He needed a clear head to review that tape one more time, and afterward, to plan his strategy.

Besides, no amount of liquor could burn away the memories evoked by seeing Victoria.

He walked back to the VCR and pressed the play button.

He knew the sequence by memory. Twelve minutes from start to finish. First she approached the door, glanced around, steeled herself for whatever she intended to accomplish. Then she walked in. Eleven minutes later, she emerged, glancing over a Hope Institute brochure—or pretending to.

He hit the pause button and scrutinized her face.

He knew that look. Her brows were knit, her bottom lip caught between her teeth. Something was bothering her. She wasn't concentrating on the pamphlet. She was mulling something over. But what? Whom had she gone to see?

Most important, what connection did this have to his investigation?

Knowing Victoria, anything was possible. She could have a client who was a patient there. She could have come upon the name of the Hope Institute in one of her pleadings and decided to poke around.

The only thing that wasn't possible was that she was part of whatever her father was involved in. She couldn't be working with him. Not on this.

Not on anything, he remembered, a corner of his mouth lifting. Even in her second year of law school, Victoria was already battling her father about joining his firm. He was adamant, but so was she. On this issue, she wasn't going to bend.

Walter Kensington was not Victoria's idea of what an attorney should be, at least not as far as his motives were concerned. Zach had to agree. Kensington's brilliance was indisputable. He was a veritable legal genius, but his priorities were sickening—as were his scruples.

Victoria, on the other hand . . .

Zach could still remember the first time he'd laid eyes on her. He was a guest lecturer at Columbia, explaining competitive intelligence and how it was practiced within moral and legal boundaries.

She'd approached him afterward and asked some pointed questions.

He'd noticed her even before that.

The lecture hall was large, but she'd arrived early and sat in the front row. She'd crossed her legs, turned on her tape recorder, opened her notebook, and stared fixedly at him for the entire hour he spoke, as if she were trying to absorb every word. Occasionally, she'd nodded, jotted down a few notes, and once or twice she'd raised her hand to ask for clarification on the relatively new and exciting field of competitive intelligence.

He'd be lying if he claimed not to have noticed her looks. They were impossible to miss. By anyone's standards, Victoria Kensington was beautiful; delicate features, expressive hazel eyes, masses of shiny black hair, and a figure that could take a man's breath away. So, yes, he'd noticed her appearance.

But he'd *kept* noticing her for her intelligence, her depth of perception, her insightful questions, that thirst for knowledge he saw in those keen hazel eyes, the compassion in her voice when she spoke her mind.

And she spoke it often.

His lips curved as he remembered their heated debates—debates that had begun that cold January afternoon and continued for the next five months. It wasn't so much that they disagreed as that they enjoyed matching wits. Or perhaps they were just enthralled by the sparks they generated, sparks that flew between them whenever they came together—intellectually, emotionally, physically.

That first day they'd met, things had stayed purely intellectual. They'd argued ethics over coffee, legal loopholes over dinner, and sleazy courtroom tactics over a late-night drink. Zach couldn't remember ever being so absorbed in another person that he lost track of time and place.

Their first date had led to a second, and a second to a third. His projects in New York were supposed to take him a few months; he'd done nothing to bring them toward closure. In fact, for a man who typically worked eighteen-hour days, he was suddenly working half-days, driving over to Columbia at dusk and picking her up, taking her to dinner, driving her home to Greenwich.

For a man who was totally self-reliant, who'd never been seriously involved, not even in an enduring friendship, much less something deeper, he suddenly found himself falling head over heels in love.

He didn't believe in magic.

She mesmerized him.

He didn't believe in fairy tales.

She made them come true.

He certainly didn't believe in forever.

But he wanted it. And he wanted it with Victoria.

She was equally consumed by what was happening between them. He knew even before she said the words, not out of arrogance but because he was aware of everything she was feeling. He was also aware she was fighting those feelings. And the more he came to understand her, the more she trusted him with pieces of her past, the more he understood why.

She wasn't someone who bared her soul easily. She was as loath to do so as he. And, for an incredibly beautiful and independent woman, she was surprisingly naive about men. He soon realized why.

There hadn't been any.

Not until him.

Zach swore under his breath, drained the last drops of bourbon, and gazed broodingly around the suite.

Their first night together had been here. He'd planned to go slowly, to weave a sensual spell around her, to relax her with cabernet and biscotti, vases of yellow roses, and that cute stuffed Jack Russell terrier.

The food had waited, the gifts gone unnoticed for hours.

And they? They'd scarcely gotten their clothes off in time, they'd been so frantic for each other. They'd fallen into bed as if they were starved, made love with an urgency Zach never knew existed. Again and again, they'd joined their bodies, insatiable with a need that seemed to have no beginning and no end.

A need that only intensified as the night wore on.

It had been her first time.

And, in some ways, his as well.

That familiar knife twisted in his gut.

Goddammit. He'd been abroad for ages. Long enough for her to perfect her role as the emotional rock of her family. Long enough for her to achieve the independence she was hell-bent on securing. Long enough for her to become the brilliant attorney she'd been on the brink of becoming before he turned her world upside down by offering her a future she couldn't live with.

And long enough for her to forget him.

Then why the hell couldn't he forget her?

He knew why.

He wished to hell he didn't.

He hadn't planned on seeing her again. But fate had made a different decision. Her visit to the Hope Institute had collided with his investigation. It was impossible for him to stay away.

Someone had to go see her about this. Better him than Meyer.

Victoria was relieved Leonard was off duty when she left her uncle and aunt's apartment. She was in no mood for banter. She felt frustrated and dejected and, yes, guilty for upsetting her uncle.

She had a great deal to consider. She had to organize her thoughts, separate emotion from fact, and reason out her best course of action.

And she had to get home to do it.

She turned up her collar, ignoring the annoying drizzle, and began walking. As always, she made her way along Park Avenue to East Eighty-second, then turned to walk the remaining blocks to her apartment.

Part of her had been hoping Clarissa and Jim would have the answer, or would at least have heard of the obscure Hope Institute. They hadn't. A dead end—unless she wanted her uncle to do some discreet digging, which would mean involving her father.

Why did that notion bother her so much? Was it because she knew he'd stonewall her again, or was it something uglier? Did a small part of her believe that, by revealing her hand, she'd be tipping her father off, giving him advance warning that she was getting close to finding Audrey and, as a result, giving him ample opportunity to conceal her even more thoroughly?

But why? Why was she assuming the worst?

And did it really matter? With her options being eliminated one by one, she was headed back to her father anyway.

Lost in thought, she wasn't sure when she became aware that she was being followed.

She stopped, her head snapping around so she could scan the area. This section of East Eighty-second was never deserted. As always, people stepped out of restaurants, hailing cabs to take them home. And a few brave souls like herself were walking home.

No one sinister lurking about. Nothing out of place.

But she couldn't shake that feeling.

Someone was watching her.

Clutching her pocketbook to her side, she quickened her pace, making sure to walk directly under the streetlights and close to the buildings, so she could dart inside if necessary. Crime was rare in this section of Manhattan, but as a woman living alone, she was always prepared.

She arrived home without incident, her key out and ready. Actually, she'd had it in her hand, teeth out, from the instant she sensed that she was being followed. A house key could make an excellent weapon.

Five minutes later, she was in her apartment, her door locked. She frowned, crossing over to her bedroom. It wasn't like her to be afraid.

Impulsively, she let her hand fall away from the light switch without flipping it on. She tiptoed through the darkened bedroom and stopped just before she reached her window.

Slowly, keeping back a few feet, she leaned forward and peeked outside.

That same man was standing across the street, lounging casually under the streetlight. Same height, same build, same body motions. The only addition was the cigar he was smoking.

But he was definitely the same one who'd been there Saturday.

And he was watching her town house.

*   *   *

For the first time, Victoria took a cab to work the next morning.

She didn't get in until late, almost eleven. Then again, she hadn't fallen asleep until after five.

She was exhausted, she was jumpy, and she was furious that someone was doing this to her.

Paige had just sat down behind her desk when Victoria walked in.

"Hi," she greeted her. "I got your message on the machine. Whatever case you were working on, it really must be bugging you. According to the machine, your call came in at five after three in the morning."

Victoria managed a weak smile. "I lost track of time," she said, sifting through the mail. "And I knew I wasn't due in court until after lunch. So I pushed myself a little."

"How come I don't look like you when I push myself?" Paige lamented, studying Victoria's face, then taking in the classic lines of her tweed suit. "When I'm cramming all night for an exam, I look like something the cat dragged in."

Behind the letter she was skimming, Victoria's lips twitched. "No, you don't. You're very pretty, Paige. Exams or not."

"Maybe it's your coloring," Paige mused, scarcely hearing the compliment. "It's so vivid. It's easier to see fatigue lines on a blonde. I read that in *Cosmo*. Maybe that's it. I'm too blond." She sighed, sitting back in her chair. "Who am I kidding? It's your body. What man in their right mind wouldn't drool over it? How did you get such long legs when you're not really tall? Only really tall women are supposed to have long legs. But you're only a couple of inches taller than me, right?"

Victoria was scarcely listening. "I'm five-four," she answered automatically.

"I thought so. That must be it. It's your legs. All the men are staring at them. In fact, you'll probably win your case today with that suit on. The skirt looks amazing. If the judge is a man, you're set. If it's a woman, you're screwed."

Slowly, Victoria lowered her piece of correspondence. "It's Judge Williams. And, Paige, *he* won't be looking at my legs. He'll be listening to my arguments. I'm trying to get custody for Agatha Wilding's kids, not pick up a hot date." She paused, realizing how frayed her nerves were, how close she was to blurting out the fact that not everyone was as obsessed with the opposite sex as Paige was.

The best thing she could do for her secretary was to avoid her.

"I'm going into my office to read over the Wilding file," she said tersely. "Please hold my calls."

She hadn't meant to be that curt, Victoria thought as she headed down the hall. She felt guilty for the hurt look she'd seen on Paige's face. But she couldn't do anything about it—not now. She had too much to contend with, and almost no time to do it in. She was due in court in two hours. Between now and then she was determined to call her uncle with a decision.

Should she mention the man who was following her?

She hadn't done so at dinner last night, simply because she was beginning to think the whole thing was her imagination. She'd seen no sign of him since Saturday.

But last night, he was back. He'd followed her home, and then watched her apartment on and off all night. She'd checked at fifteen-minute intervals. Sometimes he'd be there, sometimes not. But he didn't disappear for good until almost five.

She'd considered calling the police. But what would she tell them? That a man periodically showed up outside the building across the street from hers smoking a cigar, and that she was convinced he was watching her? After the Central Park incident on Saturday, everyone at the precinct was exasperated with her. Oh, they'd grudgingly send someone out. But what good would it do? The man with the cigar would undoubtedly take off as soon as he saw a cop.

No, the police couldn't help. But, dammit, she wasn't

imagining things. That man was definitely watching her. She knew it in her gut.

What she didn't know was *why*.

She shut herself up in her office and paced over to her desk. Scooping up the Wilding file, she perused it briefly. She knew the facts for today's hearing like the back of her hand. Agatha would win. Those two little children would stay with their mother and not be subjected to their father's midlife crisis, which was prompting him to bring home a different, barely-at-the-age-of-legal-consent bedmate each night.

She was just getting her papers in order when the knock sounded.

"Victoria?" Paige poked her head in. "Court was just canceled. Judge Williams had some kind of personal emergency. You're rescheduled for Thursday."

"Fine." Victoria tossed the file on her desk, half disappointed, half relieved. Maybe it was better this way. True, she wanted the whole mess over with for Agatha's sake. On the other hand, sure thing or not, she intended to give the case her all. And today her all was pretty pathetic.

Frowning, she massaged her throbbing temples. "Paige, do me a favor? Call Mrs. Wilding and tell her. She'll be okay with the delay; she knows this one's in the bag. I just can't talk to anyone right now. And forgive me for being so sharp with you. I guess I'm more tired than I realized."

Paige's good nature prevailed, and she gave Victoria a sunny smile. "No problem. We all have those days. Take as much time alone as you need. Oh, and don't worry about Mrs. Wilding. I'll take care of her." She ducked out.

Okay, so now she could devote herself to resolving her own personal crisis. Should she ask for her uncle's assistance, or was there a better way to go about finding Audrey?

And how should she deal with the fact that she was being followed?

Reflexively, Victoria walked over to the window and

peeked down at the street, wondering if he'd tracked her to work, too.

Why was he watching her? It had to tie in to Audrey's disappearance. The timing was too coincidental. Had the Hope Institute sent him? Worse, had her father? Why was he so eager to keep her from Audrey? What threat could she possibly represent?

Behind her, there was another purposeful rap on her door.

She ignored it, hoping Paige would take the hint and go away.

No such luck.

The knob turned, and the door swung open.

"Paige, please." Victoria's tone was fraught with tension. "I thought you understood. I really need some time alone. Whatever it is, can't it wait?"

"I'm afraid not."

The deep baritone, quiet and composed, sliced through her like a knife.

She froze, every muscle in her body going rigid. Then she turned around slowly, as if she were on autopilot, feeling a dazed sense of unreality as she did.

Zach was standing there.

"Hello, Victoria."

This couldn't be happening. Not after the roller-coaster ride she'd been on the past few days. It was simply too much for her to contend with. Zachary Hamilton couldn't be standing in her doorway.

But he was.

Victoria said nothing for a long moment, just stood very still, struggling for the composure she was so famous for.

He hadn't changed.

That same powerful height and build. That same square, uncompromising jaw. And those compelling eyes, so dark they seemed to see clear through to her soul.

There were a few subtle differences. His blue, European-cut suit and Italian silk tie were less conservative than he might have worn four years ago. And he looked—*older* wasn't the right word—more seasoned, with a few more lines etched on his forehead and around his mouth. He was thirty-five now. It was hard to believe. Harder to believe was the effect he still had on her, even now, after four long years.

"Zach." She managed to sound fairly normal, although she leaned forward to grip her desk for support. "I—I didn't expect to see you."

A corner of his mouth lifted in that crooked smile that was the only boyish thing about him. Everything else was hard. His features. His mind. His body.

Her mouth went dry.

"You cut your hair." He shut the door behind him and leaned back against it, his dark gaze unreadable.

"I—" Her hand went reflexively to her shoulder, where her hair curled under. The last time he'd seen her, it had been inches longer. "Yes. Last year."

He nodded. "Don't blame your secretary, by the way. I told her I'd show myself in. She tried to stop me, but Meg told her to let me go in."

Victoria swallowed. Meg. Of course. She should have guessed. "I see." Finding some semblance of control, she pointed to the chair across from her desk. "Have a seat."

He waited, and she abruptly remembered how polite he was—a gentleman in a world where few existed. She'd always marveled at how he could treat her as an equal and yet always make her so acutely aware that she was a woman.

She sat down behind her desk. He lowered himself into the chair she'd indicated.

"Can I offer you anything?" The words, uttered countless times to countless people, seemed painfully intimate to her ears. "Coffee?"

"No." Zach shook his head. "I'm fine, thanks."

A nod. "How was Europe?" Unconsciously, her gaze

shifted to his left hand. She shouldn't give a damn. Even so, she felt an incredible surge of relief when she saw his ring finger was bare.

In Zach's case, no ring meant no wife. Marriage to him meant the works, a joining in every sense of the word. And that included the symbols that signified the joining—two rings, hers *and* his.

"Europe was busy." If Zach noticed her fleeting inspection, he didn't react. Instead, he glanced around the office, then gave an approving nod. "Your dream—you, Meg, and Paul made it happen. You started your firm. Not that I doubted it. I'm happy for you."

"Thank you."

Abruptly, Zach leaned forward. "I'm sorry if my barging in here startled you. You probably didn't even know I was in town. I'm speaking at a conference. I'm also working on a project for one of my New York clients. And that project has brought me to you."

Victoria's brows shot up. This was even more unbelievable than his being here. "What kind of project? And who's your client?"

A hint of amusement. "Still firing questions. I pity your courtroom opponents."

"That doesn't answer my questions."

Zach stared at the floor for a moment. "My client prefers I not mention his name or discuss the nature of my work. But the stakes are high. So I have to ask you a few questions, and those questions have to be kept confidential."

"Another covert assignment," she couldn't help but remark in a bitter tone. The painful memories resurfaced far too easily. It was one of those very assignments that had been the proverbial straw that broke the camel's back for them. "Some things never change." She folded her hands on her desk and got her emotions in check. "You have questions. Go ahead, ask."

"What were you doing at the Hope Institute yesterday?"

It took every ounce of self-control to retain her poker face. "Are you having me followed?"

He sucked in his breath. "No, of course not."

"Are you sure? Because someone's been following me." Even as she spoke, she wondered if her pronouncement was an accusation or a confidence. Either way, her nerves must be more frayed than she'd realized.

Zach's head came up like a wolf scenting danger. "Who? Why?"

"I don't know." Victoria feathered a hand through her hair. "It's probably my imagination. And it's not your problem. Let's get back to what you asked me. It's interesting you should bring up the Hope Institute. No one else seems to have heard of it. How is it you have?"

"That's a responding question, not an answer."

"Fine. My visit to the Hope Institute was personal."

"Personal—how?"

"I . . ." Victoria fought the urge to fall back on old habits, to share her worries with him and ask for his help. Was she insane? It had been a lifetime. She didn't even know the man anymore. He'd come to grill her on behalf of a client. And here she was, about to spill her guts.

But she felt so strung-out. He'd picked the worst time to approach her. And the worst subject to approach her on.

"Victoria." Zach had been studying her. He looked concerned, his voice gentling. "I'm not the enemy. Something's obviously wrong. What is it? Why do you think someone's following you? And how does this relate to your visiting the Hope Institute?"

Her gaze met his. "There's something shady about that clinic, isn't there?"

Zach didn't look away. "Yes."

"Oh, God." Victoria could feel her hands shaking as she covered her face. "If Audrey's hurt, if they've done something to her—"

"Audrey?" Zach jumped on her words. "Why would

Audrey be there?" He started to reach for her, then thought better of it. "Talk to me."

Victoria's mind was racing. She knew who Zach's "anonymous" clients were. And not only because she'd been in his bed when he took phone calls from them, but also because those very clients had, by feeding Zach's demons, played a crucial role in shattering their love to bits.

Slowly, her head came up. "What is the Hope Institute involved in?" she demanded. "Are they a front for something? Are they holding people against their will, hurting them in some way?"

Silence.

Victoria's patience snapped. "Zach, I can't just give you some terse, factual answers and send you on your way. This is a terrifying situation for me—and a personal one. My sister's health and safety are at stake. So I have to know who you're working for. Or is that a stupid question? It's the same as always, isn't it? The government? The FBI?"

Zach's expression never changed. "Yes." He half rose from his seat. "You're the only person who knows. To be blunt, you're the only person who's ever known anything about my dealings with the FBI—then or now."

"That's why you came to my office—to drive home that fact?" she asked incredulously. "To make sure I plan to keep your government assignments a secret?"

"No. I came to your office because you walked right into my investigation and I had to find out why."

"*What* investigation?"

Zach drew a slow, thoughtful breath. "For a number of reasons, it would be stupid to play games. As we just said, you know about my business relationship with the FBI. And you're already more involved in this whole mess than you realize. So I'll tell you outright. But not a word can leave this room."

"I've never told a soul about your work," she assured him quietly. "I don't intend to start now."

"I believe you."

Something about the tone of Zach's voice alerted Victoria to the fact that he was referring to more than his faith in her discretion.

What did he mean, he believed her?

And how was she more involved in this mess than she realized?

"I'm helping the FBI break up an international drug syndicate. After years of painstaking work, the feds have uncovered a major distribution point in Manhattan."

"Manhattan." Victoria swallowed. "More specifically, the Hope Institute."

"Yes." He rose the rest of the way, elbows planted on the desk, looming over her like a panther about to spring. "Now tell me about Audrey."

"Wait a minute." Victoria stiffened, the meaning behind Zach's declaration of faith clicking into place. "You knew I was at the Hope Institute, which means the FBI has some kind of surveillance going on there. Now you're here, asking questions, telling me I'm involved, stressing the fact that you believe me. That implies someone else doesn't." Her eyes narrowed. "What exactly does your *client* think I've done? Where do I fit into this investigation of theirs?"

This time Zach didn't smile at her rapidly fired questions. "You're not under suspicion. The FBI just wants to know why you were at the clinic. But they *do* intend to get an explanation. They're not going to be put off by a vague allusion to some personal matter. You can talk to them directly, if you prefer. I thought you'd rather talk to me. If I'm wrong . . ." He shrugged. "You have till tomorrow to decide. After that, it's out of my hands."

"So you came to make things easier for me." The irony was almost too much to bear. After the painful way they'd parted, how could seeing him again make things easier? It was like reopening a wound that had finally stopped bleeding.

"Honestly? Yes, I did think it would make things easier."

It was apparent he wasn't feeling the same emotional wrenching she was.

"Fine." She managed to sound aloof rather than anguished. "So you're here to find out what I know about the Hope Institute. And I take it the concern you expressed for Audrey was your way of getting at that information." Even as she spoke, Victoria knew that dig was unfair. Zach was too decent a person to manipulate her into providing the details he needed.

Clearly, he agreed.

For the first time, his composure slipped, anger simmering beneath the surface. His jaw tightened, and sparks glinted in his eyes. "Don't insult me. And don't insult what we once meant to each other. I'd never use you. I made no secret of the fact that I came here for information. I had no idea your visit to the Hope Institute was tied to Audrey. Now that you've set me straight, of course I'm concerned. I'm even more concerned about your being followed. How can you believe otherwise?"

There was no rebutting that argument. "You're right," she admitted in a tight, dignified voice. "You didn't deserve that. I'm sorry."

Zach's anger banked, but that fierce light still burned in his eyes. "I didn't have to fake interest in your problems to make sure you cooperated," he reminded her. "I could have demanded my answers and walked out of here. Better yet, I didn't have to come at all. I could have let the FBI do its job. I chose not to, for reasons I thought were obvious. It seems I was wrong. Tell me, Victoria, have you completely forgotten what we once had together—other than how the FBI intruded on it?"

Victoria's lashes lowered, and she stared at the corner of her desk. It hurt too damned much to think about the past, much less to be looking into Zach's eyes when he referred to it.

"I haven't forgotten," she managed at last. "It's just that I . . ." She cleared her throat, the compulsion to pour out what was worrying her too strong to resist. "I'm worried sick about Audrey. She's disappeared. My instincts tell me she's at the Hope Institute. But the receptionist there won't tell me anything. Everywhere I turn, I run into another wall."

Zach's mental wheels were turning. Even without looking, she could sense it. She could even guess where his thoughts were going. Just as she was the only one who knew intimate things about him, he was the only one who knew intimate things about her.

During those months when they'd been so close, she'd allowed herself to lean on him in a way she'd never done with another soul. She'd confided in him—her fears, her sense of responsibility to her family, especially her younger sister. He knew just how bad Audrey's bulimia was. He knew how emotionally abusive her father was, how he dominated her mother and destroyed Audrey's self-image.

And he knew the pain all this caused her.

Slowly, Victoria lifted her gaze, met Zach's intense expression. "I saw her on Saturday, in Central Park," she said. "According to my father, she's still in Florence. He says I'm imagining things. But I'm not. She's here, and she's sick. She was bloated, her eyes were glazed. She could scarcely speak. She collapsed at my feet. I ran to get help. When I got back, she was gone. I haven't seen her since. But I . . . checked into a few things. Every indication is that she's at the Hope Institute. She was even wearing one of their yellow hospital gowns. But I can't get a single answer. Not from anyone. And now I'm being followed."

Zach looked grim. "I don't like the sound of this."

"But you don't sound shocked. Why?"

A flicker of discomfort.

"Zach, tell me what you're thinking."

Again, his jaw set. "Those things you checked into. Did they bring you to your father?"

Victoria stared, an unpleasant sense of foreboding form-ing in her stomach. "Why?"

"For once, just answer me. Did the details you pieced together come from your father?"

Warning bells sounded in her head.

Whatever Zach was pumping her for involved a lot more than her father's callous attempt to protect his family name. It involved something illegal. She had to tread carefully, to remember who Zach was. He was no longer her lover. He was a virtual stranger—one who worked for the FBI. Conversely, her father was still her father. Anything she said about him might be more than emotionally revealing. It might be incriminating.

Whatever uneasy feeling she had about her father's actions, she had no reason to suspect he was committing a felony. She wouldn't give the FBI fuel for a fire that might not exist.

"Victoria," Zach prodded. "You found out about the Hope Institute from someone. They're unlisted. There's no information on them anywhere. That leaves word of mouth. We have proof your father's aware of their existence. Did he discuss the clinic with you?"

"No" was her honest reply.

She saw the comprehension in Zach's eyes, watched him weigh his options. "What if I were to promise that whatever you said stayed with me? Would you talk to me then? Not just for my sake—for yours. Yes, it's my investigation. But it's your sister. I might be able to help you get to the bottom of her disappearance."

Damn him for doing this to her. Damn him for being one of the few people she'd ever turned to, maybe the only one she could count on in this case. They both knew he was in possession of facts that no one else had, and that he had the power to use those facts to her advantage.

He could help her find Audrey.

But at what cost?

The decision was pivotal. And it was hers to make.

"Victoria," he added pointedly, reading her thoughts. "Have I ever betrayed your trust?"

There was no argument there.

Wavering, she chewed her lip. She could feel the scales tip in his favor. Still, she was determined to state her position loud and clear so there would be no misunderstandings.

"Whatever I have is circumstantial and off the record," she clarified. "I have nothing to say to the FBI."

A flicker of admiration—and acceptance. "Understood. The question is, what have you got to say to me?"

10

Victoria sucked in her breath and took the plunge.

"The details I put together on the Hope Institute did come from my father, only not directly." *And not willingly* hung in the air as clearly as if she'd said the words aloud. "When I called my father about Audrey, I had the feeling he wasn't telling me everything he knew. So I looked at his phone records. He made two calls to the Hope Institute, one of them directly to their aviation group. And, before that, he made a call to Florence Hospital. My suspicion is that Audrey got sick, he flew her home, and he's trying to save face by keeping her hidden."

"It might be a lot more than face he's saving," Zach muttered.

"Meaning?"

"Meaning it's very possible your father's involvement with the Hope Institute extends far beyond Audrey. He might be up to his corporate neck in their illegal activities."

"Illegal activities." Victoria spoke each word slowly and distinctly as Zach's accusation sank in. It wasn't unexpected after what Zach had told her, but it was painful, nonetheless. "Are you basing this entirely on what I just confided in you?"

"Of course not." He pushed away from the desk, paced to the back of his chair, and faced her. "Your instincts are right. About the Hope Institute, and about your father. I don't know how deep his involvement is. That's part of what I'm working on. But let me fill in a few pieces. The Hope Institute is a private medical facility. It used to be part of a larger corporate conglomerate, a health-care organization that owned hospitals all over the world. But the Institute was sold off several years ago. It seems that its parent company had made several acquisitions. Proceeds from the sale of the Hope Institute were used to reduce the debt that financed those acquisitions. At the time of the sale, everything was aboveboard, and the Hope Institute was legitimate."

"But now it's not." Victoria inclined her head in question. "Who was the parent company?"

"Hopewell Industries." Zach paused and gauged her reaction. "You're familiar with it?"

A slow nod. "Benjamin Hopewell's company. My father has represented Mr. Hopewell, personally and professionally, for thirty years." Victoria chewed her lower lip, trying to make sense out of all this. "Who did Mr. Hopewell sell to?"

"That's just it. The buyer was a Swiss holding company. That's all we know. Who's at the helm is a mystery, but whoever it is, they're using the facility to distribute drugs."

"Were all ties severed between Hopewell Industries and the Hope Institute after the sale?"

"Nope. The Institute buys surgical supplies and services from Hopewell. That was part of the deal."

Victoria tucked a strand of hair behind her ear. "So the FBI thinks Benjamin Hopewell still has a hand in this, that he only sold on paper, so he could branch out into this dirty operation but make it look like his hands were clean."

Zach didn't avert his gaze. "It's possible, and if so, his legal counsel is probably just as dirty."

Odd. Victoria felt more sickened than shocked. Maybe she wasn't convinced. Or maybe she wasn't surprised.

"You said there was someone following you," Zach pressed. "When did this someone first appear?"

"Saturday night. I first noticed him around three in the morning. For all I know, he'd been following me all evening. I didn't see him again until last night. He tracked me home from Uncle Jim and Aunt Clarissa's. Then he hovered around my apartment all night."

"We both know the Hope Institute sent him." Zach shot her an astute look. "And you have a pretty good idea what prompted them to do so."

"Not an idea, a suspicion." A pointed arch of her brows. "Unless, of course, it's the FBI, not the Hope Institute, keeping tabs on me."

"It isn't." Zach's response was immediate and definitive. "The FBI didn't even know who you were until their surveillance tape picked you up walking in and out of there yesterday." A pause. "You have my word."

She nodded.

"So what do you think provoked the Institute to tail you?"

Victoria chewed her lip, then blurted out her suspicions. "Audrey managed to say a few words to me. Before she lost consciousness, she mumbled what I believe to be a phone number, 555-0400. She also said something about danger. They must realize I know something. Either they overheard her talking to me, or they're aware I—"

"—dialed the number," Zach finished for her.

"I didn't tell you that."

"You didn't have to. I know you."

Self-consciously, she cleared her throat, wishing he wasn't right, wishing he didn't know her as well as he did.

Wishing he didn't have the ability to render her so off-balance.

"A recording told me I'd reached the wrong number," she acknowledged. "I tried a couple of times, but I couldn't get through to a person."

"Where did you make these calls from?"

"My apartment."

"Did you mention this to your father?"

An uneasy nod. Obviously, Zach's thoughts had zoomed off in exactly the direction she'd expected them to. "Yes."

His scowl deepened. "Then the powers that be at the Hope Institute either heard it from him, or they got it from their computer system." At Victoria's questioning look, he elaborated. "When you dialed in to that 555 exchange, I'm sure their computer logged a record of your phone number. If your father didn't tell them you'd made that call, the computer did. It doesn't matter. Either way, they realized you were digging. They must have felt threatened. They sent someone out to make sure you weren't getting too close to anything—including your sister."

"Are they keeping her prisoner?" Victoria demanded.

"Not in the way you mean. The clinic really does offer groundbreaking medical treatment. Its staff is primarily honest, dedicated, and unaware of the fact that their facility is involved in illegal activities. The patients they treat are acutely ill, suffering from advanced stages of their diseases, with enough money to pay for luxurious, private health care. I'm sure that's why your father chose it for Audrey. From your description, it certainly sounds as if her illness took a turn for the worse."

"So Audrey's getting proper treatment. I'm thankful for that. But that doesn't explain why I'm being kept from seeing her or why she ran away."

"My guess is that someone involved in the illegal operation is arranging to keep you two apart because Audrey found out something they wish she hadn't. It frightened her enough to run away and try to warn you."

"By 'someone,' you mean my father."

"Yes." Zach answered with his customary frankness. "Think about it. The only scenario that makes sense is that Audrey spent enough time with your father to figure out he's involved in something ugly—something that ties in to the Hope Institute."

"*If* he's involved," Victoria corrected. "It's possible my father is guilty of nothing more than stashing Audrey away in a low-profile facility where no one can learn about her illness. That makes him callous, but not criminal. You yourself just said the computer could have recorded my calls. There's no proof implicating my father in all this. Or Benjamin Hopewell, for that matter. Even if he did retain ownership of the Hope Institute and my father helped him accomplish that. In fact, the two of them may have created this secretive corporate structure for some legitimate purpose—perhaps even to shield the Hope Institute and their privacy-conscious clients from harassment by the media. It's all pure speculation on your part, and on the part of the FBI."

"Fine. Let's assume you're right. If your father's innocent, why would Audrey run to you?" Zach countered. "Why not run to him? He certainly has more power and influence than you do. What's more, if he's the one who brought her to the Hope Institute, she wouldn't have to run any farther than the telephone in her room. So why did she risk leaving the facility to find you?"

Victoria had no rebuttal for that logic.

"We can argue about your father later. Right now what's bothering me most is that whoever's running the show is focused on you and what you know." Falling silent, Zach rubbed the back of his neck, and another inadvertent pang shot through Victoria as she recognized the familiar gesture. It meant he was mulling things over.

An instant later, he proved her right.

"What does this guy tailing you look like? What can you tell me about him?"

"Why? Do you think it's someone on your list of suspects?"

"I doubt it. I'm sure I've never heard of him, much less seen him. He's low man on the totem pole in an operation like this one. Just the same, I need a description. First, so I can take another look at that FBI surveillance tape and see if he's on it. He's been watching you since Saturday. That means he followed you to the clinic, too. If we're lucky, I'll catch a glimpse of him, but even if I don't, it'll be easier to spot him again if I know what we're looking for."

Victoria blinked. "Are you saying you'll ask the FBI to keep an eye out for him? How can you do that without reporting what I told you in confidence?"

There was that crooked smile again. "I can't. I'd have no basis for requesting an FBI lookout without explaining the full extent of what you found out and who it implicates. What I'm saying is that *I* intend to keep an eye out for him."

She fought the surge of relief Zach's pronouncement brought. *He's just searching for a link to solve his case,* she reminded herself. *He's not doing this to protect you.*

Still, she couldn't deny her gratitude that he would be on top of things. Zach was unbelievably good at what he did. That's why the FBI sought him out so often.

"I've only seen this man in the dark," she supplied. "He looks to be of average height, on the slender side. His movements are fluid—as if he could take off at a moment's notice if he had to. The way he subtly appears and disappears, I get the feeling he's done this kind of thing before. I couldn't tell what he was wearing, but last night he was smoking a cigar." She frowned. "I know that's not much to go on."

Again, Zach shrugged. "It's about what I expected. The cigar is a plus. Guys paid to tail people usually try to blend into the woodwork. If he was a six-foot-three linebacker, he'd be remembered. I'll run through that surveillance clip again."

"I'd like to watch it with you. If he's there, maybe I'd recognize him." Victoria couldn't believe she'd just made that request. If Zach agreed, she'd put herself in the unthinkable position of being alone with him—and not in her office, but somewhere private. On the other hand, her self-consciousness in Zach's presence was secondary to her need to find Audrey. So she wouldn't retract her request.

Zach was watching her, his expression again unreadable. "All right," he concurred. "Where and when?"

The ball was back in her court. God help her.

"I'd like to see the tape as soon as possible."

"I agree. The sooner we figure out who's following you, the sooner we'll be able to stop him—and find out who's paying his salary."

"Where are you staying?" Victoria forced herself to ask, bracing herself for the inevitable reply.

"At the Plaza Athénée."

A heartbeat of silence hung between them.

With a terse nod, Victoria made an on-the-spot decision. There was no way she could walk into that hotel and take the elevator up to his suite—to his room—surveillance tape or not. If they had to screen this thing somewhere private, let it be somewhere that didn't scream with memories.

"Can you bring the tape to my apartment?" she inquired, keeping her tone as casual as possible. "I'm not all that far from the hotel."

Zach considered the possibility, displaying no emotion whatsoever as he mentally ran through his previous commitments. "It would have to be late. I've got appointments all afternoon, and a six-thirty meeting over drinks that will probably run into dinner."

"I've got a dinner meeting myself," Victoria replied, thinking of the weekly Tuesday night catch-up sessions she, Meg, and Paul held at that great little Chinese restaurant two blocks from their office. "It should run until nine."

"How's ten o'clock then? Too late?"

Victoria smoothed her skirt and rose gracefully to her feet. "No. I'm too wired to sleep. And I've got to get to the bottom of this. It's the only way I'll find Audrey." She met Zach's gaze. "I'm at 170 East Eighty-second."

"I'll be there at ten."

11

The orderly, late-afternoon hum at Waters, Kensington, Tatem & Calder was that of a well-oiled machine—one that emanated great power and success. Its elegant atmosphere, from decorum to demeanor, contrasted starkly with the affable chaos found at London, Kensington & Stone.

Walter Kensington's firm, which occupied the entire fourteenth floor of 280 Park Avenue, was the epitome of conservative affluence. Voices were subdued, talking minimal. Attorneys interacted briefly with their associates only to issue instructions, then disappeared quietly behind the heavy wooden doors that separated the private chambers from those areas accessible to all.

The furnishings of the outer office were understated Park Avenue; the equipment, state-of-the-art. The men wore conservative suits; the women—three-quarters of whom were paralegals and secretaries—wore tasteful dresses or equally tasteful suits. It was only in the last two decades that the dress code for women had relaxed a bit. Secretaries had been permitted to give up the practice of wearing gloves to work and were now allowed to wear appropriate pants suits rather than dresses—although casual slacks and skirts more than a few inches above the knee were still frowned upon. It was also during this period that women had been grudgingly allowed to join the firm as attorneys, although only four of the twenty-three junior partners and one of the eight senior partners were female.

The hierarchy was clear. Top-notch secretaries of the senior partners labored behind partitioned cubicles that afforded the privacy and respect due women associated with men of rank and power. In contrast, the younger secretaries ranged anywhere from politically savvy, ambitious legal assistants who sought jobs with the "right" up-and-coming attorneys, to task-oriented secretarial school graduates who typed up briefs, made coffee, and screened the constant flow of incoming calls.

The most powerful senior partners were easily recognized by the size and location of their inner sanctums.

Walter Kensington's domain boasted massive dimensions, an engraved gold nameplate on the door, and the most coveted location. It was isolated from the rest of the firm by one large cubicle belonging to Miss Hatterman, Walter's secretary of thirty years, who guarded her boss's office like a vigilant pit bull.

The office was accentuated by two walls of floor-to-ceiling cherry bookshelves filled with reference texts and—the most prominent and impressive fixture in the room—a massive semicircular cherry desk. Kept locked at all times, the desk held all of Walter's personal files. The surface was fastidiously clean, containing only his personal computer and his most immediate and pressing case notes, plus four different model cars that were his particular pride and joy.

As a final, enviable touch, along half the periphery of the room ran wide-paned windows, heralding a panoramic view of the canyons of Park Avenue.

At that particular moment, Walter wasn't interested in the scenery.

Thoroughly riled, he shut his office door, listening to the retreating footsteps and pondering all the facts he'd just been given.

He didn't like being threatened—especially by someone who was so important to his success.

It wasn't his first warning. The Hope Institute's CEO had

been furious since last Saturday morning, when Audrey had succeeded in escaping and making contact with Victoria. Walter had winced through that entire phone call, then solemnly promised things would calm down.

They hadn't. Instead, they'd intensified. Victoria had spent the past few days snooping around, chipping away pieces of information from the impenetrable legal fortress he'd built around the Hope Institute, as a result making things worse than she could possibly imagine.

Goddammit. Why couldn't she keep her nose out of this?

Walter turned away, running a hand through his hair, knowing his answer even as he asked the question.

Audrey.

Victoria had protected her from the day she was born. It didn't matter how hard he'd tried to separate them, how firmly he'd shown Victoria that her nurturing was futile, that Audrey was weak, an embarrassment to him and all he stood for.

Nothing deterred Victoria. She was her mother's and sister's self-appointed savior. And she wasn't about to stop now. Especially since she was convinced Audrey was in trouble.

He crossed over to his desk, staring down at the gleaming wood and idly fingering the model Rolls Royce near his phone.

It was bad enough she'd grilled him and called the hospital in Florence. Now, not only was she making prying phone calls, she'd actually visited the Hope Institute, trying to get in and see Audrey. She was leery of Audrey's treatment, wondering what danger her sister had been alluding to when she'd accosted her in Central Park.

And suspicious of his part in it all.

He'd been ordered in no uncertain terms to control his daughter. The question was, how?

He knew the answer to that.

There was only one way Victoria would believe her sister was safe. She had to hear it from Audrey herself.

Very well. That's precisely what she'd do.

With grim determination, he reached over and picked up the phone.

The attendant at the Hope Institute entered the audiotape room at 5 P.M. sharp. He fitted the key in the lock of the double cabinet and opened the doors, scanning the neatly stacked rows of tapes until he found the two labeled "Kensington, Audrey."

The first tape in her set was the one he'd been instructed to retrieve; the one marked "introductory session." He removed it, tucked it carefully into his inside jacket pocket, then relocked the cabinet and left the room. He had his orders. The audio engineer was waiting to do what had to be done. It had to be completed quickly for its seven-thirty transmission.

He strode briskly to the editing room.

Victoria arrived home at 9:15, totally worn out.

Her dinner with Meg and Paul had included a half-hour of dodging questions about Zach. She couldn't blame them for their curiosity; they'd been there when the entire relationship unfolded four years ago, and they'd been there throughout the painful aftermath. Not that she'd gone to them—or anyone—for comfort. The truth was, she'd scarcely spoken a word about the breakup, other than to say it was over and Zach was leaving for Europe. There were some things that were just too intimate, too emotionally wrenching, to discuss.

But neither of her friends was stupid. They knew she hadn't been involved with another man since Zach left. So they were not only curious to know why he'd visited, they felt protective because of the effect his sudden reappearance would have on her.

She'd said very little, partly because she couldn't breathe a word about Zach's investigation, and partly because she didn't want to even think, much less talk, about how she felt about seeing him again.

The rest of dinner had been spent going over current cases, but even then Victoria couldn't concentrate. Nor could she eat. And not because of Zach.

Her gaze kept straying to the restaurant window, scanning the street to see if the man following her was outside.

Nothing suspicious.

Finally, after intercepting the twentieth worried look between Paul and Meg, she'd excused herself, claiming extreme fatigue, and taken a cab home.

Still no sign of her tail.

She locked her door, slipped off her suit jacket, and headed for the bedroom. She had forty minutes to change and prepare herself for Zach's visit and the viewing of the FBI surveillance tape. She prayed that the bastard following her would be on it. Knowing he was out there somewhere, watching her every move, was really starting to rattle her.

Passing by the answering machine in the hall, Victoria noticed the flashing light and glanced at the LCD display. Two messages. Fine. She'd listen while she changed.

Turning up the volume, she pressed Play as she unbuttoned her blouse, slipping it off in the bedroom doorway so she could listen.

"Hi, Victoria. It's Uncle Jim," came her uncle's even tone. "I'm sorry I didn't return your call sooner. It was one of those days. It's after six, and I haven't even eaten lunch yet. I'm going to grab a sandwich and head home. Give me a call whenever you get in. I'm interested in hearing your decision."

Victoria winced. Her decision. She'd placed that call to her uncle right after Zach left her office that morning, although she'd been more confused than ever about what to say. The only solution she could come up with was to try to buy herself more time. She certainly couldn't share the FBI's suspicions about her father. Nor could she pretend to dismiss the whole matter of Audrey's disappearance as if it were no longer of paramount importance. Uncle Jim knew how she felt about Audrey. He'd expect her to continue her search.

He'd want her to go to her father. Which, it seemed more and more likely, she would end up doing. But what would she say once she got there? There was much more at stake now than just their family secrets and finding Audrey. There were criminal acts involved—major ones. How much was her father mixed up in? Was he merely covering up Audrey's whereabouts or something even more devious?

She'd have to discuss her strategy with Zach. She owed him that much. He was keeping her revelations in confidence; she had to do the same with his investigation.

Damn, she was in an awkward position.

She wriggled out of her skirt just as the beep on her answering machine sounded, heralding the onset of the second message.

"Victoria?" She froze at the sound of Audrey's voice. "Father told me how worried you are. Please don't be. I'm fine, really. I had a bad relapse. The people here are helping me get better. But I'm not allowed any visitors. That's part of my treatment. It's very intensive. I'm not even supposed to be calling. But I didn't want you to worry. I'll let you know as soon as I'm well enough to talk—I promise."

Click.

"Message received seven-thirty-one," the electronic voice on the answering machine reported. Then: "End of final message."

Victoria's heart was thudding in her chest. She walked over and replayed Audrey's message, listening carefully to every word.

There was no fear in her sister's voice. She sounded wooden, emotionless—the total opposite of the hysterical state she'd been in on Saturday. Presumably, she was trying to calm Victoria, to assuage her sister's apprehension rather than express her own.

Definitely not Audrey's style.

Had someone forced her to make that call? She didn't seem to be under duress. Could she be on medication? That was certainly possible.

It was also possible she'd been ordered to make that call by someone who wanted Victoria off his back and the back of the Hope Institute.

Someone like her father.

Leaning against the wall, Victoria began sorting out all the possibilities, then decided it didn't matter. She knew what she had to do.

It was time to confront her father.

Audrey's message had made it clear he knew where she was, and why she was there.

What else did he know?

And how much was he willing to admit?

The jingling of the phone reminded Victoria that she was standing in her bra and pantyhose and Zach was due in ten minutes.

She snatched up the cordless phone and carried it with her into the bedroom. "Hello?" she said breathlessly.

"Victoria. Did you just come in?" It was her uncle's voice.

"Yes, Uncle Jim, I did. I just finished dinner with Meg and Paul."

"Ah, that's right. It's Tuesday. I was just getting a little concerned because it's nearly ten o'clock and I hadn't heard from you."

"And you're wondering what I decided." She paused at the closet, yanking down a pair of coffee-colored jeans and a cream-colored, short-sleeved knit sweater. As she scrambled into her clothes, she realized Audrey's call had made her handling of this conversation easier.

"Frankly, yes. I was very troubled by your reaction last night. I was hoping you'd had time to think about it."

"I have." Victoria zipped up her pants and slipped on some casual, lower-heeled shoes. "I don't like secrets, Uncle Jim. Nor do I like the feeling that I'm betraying my father. So I've decided to go to him and discuss the entire matter."

She could actually hear her uncle's sigh of relief. "I'm glad."

"Me, too." She thought quickly, then decided it would look too suspicious if she didn't mention that Audrey had contacted her. "There's something else, something that eased my mind a lot. I got a call from Audrey."

"You spoke to her?"

"No, I was out. She called here a couple of hours ago. She left a message, saying she's fine, but that her treatment requires seclusion. She didn't want me to worry." Victoria felt uneasy, as if she were telling her uncle a half-truth by implying that Audrey's call had conjured up nothing but weak-kneed relief, when in fact it had evoked mostly suspicion. But she wasn't going to make the same mistake again. Until she had something concrete, she wasn't going to unnerve her uncle and upset him with her misgivings about her father.

"That's wonderful. I feel much better knowing she's safe and getting the care she needs." A pointed pause. "You'll tell your father about this, of course."

"Absolutely. Although I'm sure he already knows. Audrey said that Father was the one who told her I was worried. He must have suggested she call."

"So he did make these hospitalization arrangements." Uncle Jim sounded more pensive than surprised. "I guessed as much, given your father's priorities. I know you don't share them, Victoria, and I'm not saying I do either. But please try to listen when he explains his motives. It's the only way you're going to get past this."

"I will." Victoria ran a brush through her hair, thinking there were some things one never got past. She wished she had more time alone to analyze Audrey's call before Zach arrived. But time was growing short.

As if on cue, the downstairs door buzzer sounded.

"Uncle Jim, I'm going to have to hang up now. Someone's here."

"At your apartment?" His voice became very paternal. "It's very late, Victoria. I don't mean to pry, but is it someone you know?"

She swallowed. "Yes. It's Zach. He dropped by my office today and I invited him over for a cup of coffee."

"Oh. I see." Her uncle gave a discreet cough—a wordless declaration that he didn't want to overstep his bounds and pursue a subject that was none of his business. "All right, then, I'll let you go. We'll talk later this week."

"Definitely. Give my love to Aunt Clarissa."

She hung up, wincing as she thought about how her uncle must have interpreted Zach's visit. He probably assumed they were catching up on old times—in more ways than one.

Squaring her shoulders, she walked into the hall and pressed the intercom button. "Yes?"

"It's me. I'm a few minutes early."

She wet her lips. "Come on up." She released the intercom and pressed the entry buzzer.

Then she drew a deep breath and marched into the kitchen.

By the time Zach rang the bell, the automatic coffeemaker was beginning to drip.

"Hi." Victoria opened the door and gave him a cordial smile.

"Sorry I'm early," Zach offered at once. "I came straight from dinner." He hovered politely in the doorway, giving her the option of asking him to wait.

He looked tired, she noticed, seeing the weariness etched on his face. He was wearing the same suit he'd had on earlier, which meant he'd been dashing from meeting to meeting all day.

"It's not a problem. I got in a little while ago." She eased the door wider, gesturing for him to enter. "Come on in."

He stepped inside, then stopped, gazing slowly around the apartment and taking in the furnishings: the overstuffed sofa and loveseat that took up most of the dusty mauve and pearl-gray living room, the simple gray lacquer dining room set, and the parquet-floored corridor that led down the hall to the two bedrooms and bathroom.

"Nice," he said in a deep, approving tone. "It suits you." He cleared his throat. "Do you live here alone? Or do you have a roommate?"

Victoria wondered if he was fishing, or just curious—curious, but at the same time strained about asking what would be a perfectly natural question coming from anyone but him.

"It's just me," she replied lightly. "I bought the apartment when I graduated law school—with some help from my uncle and aunt. It was a reach, considering I was just starting out. It still is. A huge chunk of my paycheck goes to Uncle Jim and Aunt Clarissa. But I'm never sorry I did it. I love this place."

"It shows." He continued to look around. "Two bedrooms?"

God, why did such an innocent conversation have to feel so intimate?

"Yes. One of them doubles as a den and an office."

A nod. "It's a great investment. This is a terrific location. And you've made the place very charming."

Thankfully, the coffeemaker chose that moment to intercede, spitting loudly as the final drops trickled into the carafe.

Zach's attention was diverted, and he gave a long, appreciative sniff. "Tell me that's coffee I smell."

She couldn't help but smile. Zach used coffee for the

exact opposite reason most people did. It relaxed him, even at night—caffeine and all. "It is. The bad news is, it's decaf. I can't afford another sleepless night. I've got a full day tomorrow."

He gave her one of those crooked grins. "Beggars can't be choosers. Thanks for making it. I'm sure it's the last thing you felt like doing." His dark gaze flickered over her, assessing her, head to toe, in one lightning motion. "On the other hand, I don't feel *too* guilty. At least you had a chance to change. I've been in this monkey suit since seven A.M."

Victoria felt an unwelcome surge of warmth, both at his physical appraisal and at the easy intimacy of their exchange. Why did it seem so damnably natural for them to slip back into this?

"I changed my clothes the minute I walked in," she told him in a tight voice. "More to keep busy than anything else. Otherwise, I just keep looking out the window."

Zach's hard edge returned. "Is he out there?"

A helpless shrug. "I don't know. I haven't seen him. But I keep feeling his presence. Maybe that's just paranoia."

"Or maybe not." Zach reached into his pocket and extracted the tape. "Let's take a look. Where's your VCR?"

"In the living room. Zach, wait." She stopped him with a hand on his arm—a hand she quickly retracted. "There's something I want you to hear. It was waiting for me when I got home."

His eyes narrowed. "All right."

She crossed over to the answering machine and replayed Audrey's message.

Zach listened intently, his expression rapt. He asked Victoria to play it through twice. Then he frowned. "Damned convenient," he muttered.

"I assumed that would be your reaction."

He glanced at her quickly, as if to gauge just how resistant to the truth she was.

She wasn't sure herself, but she had to know.

"Zach, you said we'd talk about my father later. I think later should be now. You've got more to go on than you're telling me. The FBI would hardly suspect someone by association alone. I want to know everything." Her chin came up. "And if you dare tell me it's confidential, I think I'll hit you."

His smile was more tired than amused. "Can I trouble you for that coffee?" he asked, rubbing a palm over his jaw. "We'll run through the tape, see if you recognize the son of a bitch who's following you. Then we'll talk."

Victoria nodded, gesturing toward the sofa. "Make yourself comfortable. The TV and VCR are in the wall unit directly across from there. Set them up if you want. I'll be right in." She paused. "Still black, no cream or sugar?"

He half turned, his eyes meeting hers. "Still the same. Some things don't change."

"I guess not." It was all she could muster. She didn't know exactly how he'd meant that. Nor was she sure she wanted to know.

Retreating to the kitchen, she poured two cups of coffee and placed them on a tray, along with a plate of her favorite chocolate hazelnut biscotti. She stared at the tray for a long time, reminding herself that Zach was here to further his investigation and to help her find Audrey. He was a trusted memory from the past—nothing more. He wasn't going to afford her special consideration, and she wasn't going to spill her guts to him.

Except that she'd already spilled her guts to him, and he'd already afforded her special consideration by agreeing to keep damning circumstantial evidence from the FBI.

For now. But there was a time limit on Zach's ability to run interference for her. Tomorrow. He had to tell the FBI something by then. But if he told them the truth—that she'd been at the Hope Institute looking for her sister—they'd want specifics: How did she know Audrey was there? Who had admitted her? What had led her to the Hope Institute?

The answer to every one of those questions implicated her father. That in itself was upsetting enough. But even more frightening, did it also endanger Audrey?

Victoria's hands balled into fists. She had to get to her sister. And the first step toward doing so was to learn exactly how much the FBI had on her father, and how Audrey's being at the clinic affected their investigation—or was affected by it.

Drawing a deep breath, she picked up the tray and made her way into the living room.

Zach was seated at the edge of the sofa, his brows knit in concentration as he angled the remote control and advanced the tape, bringing it to the exact spot where he wanted it.

He glanced up as Victoria entered, then rose courteously to his feet. He took the two cups of coffee off the tray and waited while she placed the cookies on the coffee table. For a long moment he contemplated the biscotti, the angle of his head making it impossible to see, much less decipher, his expression. Then he glanced up, handing Victoria back one cup and lifting the other to his lips.

"Thank you." He took a deep swallow. "Good coffee."

"Coming from you, that's high praise indeed." Victoria found herself wondering what Zach had been thinking just now. Could the biscotti possibly have conjured up the same intimate memories for him as they had for her?

The prospect was unnerving as hell.

She perched rigidly at the far end of the sofa, leaving a whole cushion of distance between them.

If Zach noticed, he didn't let on. "Okay," he instructed, settling himself again. "Now watch carefully. I'm going to run through the entire segment. If you see anyone who even remotely resembles the guy following you, sing out."

"I will."

They watched the tape through three times. And each time Victoria saw only herself and the stream of people walking up the Hope Institute side of East Seventy-eighth Street.

"Damn," she muttered when Zach hit the stop button for the last time. "None of those people was him."

"That doesn't surprise me," Zach replied. "In order to keep you in his sight, he was probably standing across the street, against the same building as the one our camera's in. Which means he'd be out of our field of view. Thinking he'd be visible was a long shot—one I had to take." His jaw tightened. "I'll find him. You can bet on it."

The severity of Zach's tone was more unnerving than his actual words. He sounded vehement rather than deter-mined—*too* vehement, considering the person following her was a minor pawn in the FBI's case.

It suddenly struck Victoria that Zach's vehemence wasn't tied to his case.

It was tied to her.

Prickles of fear shivered up her spine. Zach wasn't quick to worry. Not unless there was a reason.

"Do you think this man will do more than just follow me?" she asked tentatively.

"No." He gave her a sharp look—and a direct answer. "But that doesn't mean someone else won't. Don't give this guy anything suspicious to report. Stay away from the Hope Institute."

"I've got to find Audrey."

"You will. But marching in there's not the way to do it. You already learned that firsthand. If you keep pushing, you might jeopardize Audrey's life as well as your own."

"But she didn't sound at all frightened on her telephone message. She said—"

"That message was a way of shaking you loose, and you know it. If you didn't, you would have taken my head off when I suggested it."

Victoria set down her cup with a firm click. "Okay, you're right. That message made me uneasy. It was too calm, too soothing to be Audrey. At first I was grateful to hear her voice, just to know she's alive and coherent. After three days, my imagination was starting to run wild. But do I think she made that call of her own initiative? No. And, yes, my thoughts are going in much the same direction as yours." A deep, purposeful breath. "Let's stop dancing around the subject. Tell me what you know about my father."

Zach fell silent, staring broodingly into his coffee.

"Is it that you don't trust me?" Victoria demanded. "Do you think I'll dash off and warn him?"

"No." Zach's head came up. "Trust isn't the issue, Victoria. It never was. Maybe I'm trying to protect you."

"I don't want protection."

"I'm well aware of that," he replied in an odd, strained tone. He turned back to his coffee, finished it, and placed the empty cup on the table. "You're not going to like what you hear. On the other hand, maybe it's better you hear it. It might make you realize why the FBI reacted so strongly to finding out that the woman on their surveillance tape was Victoria Kensington."

"Walter Kensington's daughter."

"Yes."

"You supplied them with my name?"

Zach shrugged. "They would have dug it up in a matter of hours. I spared them the trouble. I also bought some time so I could talk to you first."

"Yes, till tomorrow. After which, if I don't give you something believable to tell them, they're going to haul me down to FBI headquarters and grill me."

"Something like that, yes."

"You said I'm not under suspicion. Why not? Why don't they assume I'm working with my father?"

"Because I told them otherwise."

Victoria blinked. "You vouched for my innocence? Without even knowing the facts? Why?"

"Because I know you."

She felt as if she'd been punched. On one hand, he'd given the FBI her name. On the other hand, he'd demonstrated a blind faith in her that was totally uncharacteristic of Zach. He acted on facts, not emotion.

She wished to God she could separate those right now.

Shaking her head, she muttered, "I don't know whether to thank you or kick you."

"Don't do either. Just hear me out. Keep an open mind. And remember that what I'm telling you is in confidence."

"All right."

Despite his bluntness, Zach looked distinctly unhappy about what he was about to say. "It's true we suspect Benjamin Hopewell of keeping his hand in the Hope Institute *and* its illegal dealings. But even if he's innocent, your father's still heavily implicated. Victoria, he's the attorney of record for the Hope Institute."

She swallowed. "How do you know that?"

"After the FBI traced suspected drug shipments to the Hope Institute, they took preliminary steps. An agent visited the clinic to ask a few routine questions. Miss Evans, that militant receptionist you locked horns with, told him in no uncertain terms that she had nothing to say, that everything pertaining to the Hope Institute was confidential. When the agent pressed her, Miss Evans told him to contact their attorney, Walter Kensington, with any questions he had."

"I see." Victoria was feeling more sickened by the minute. "And did the FBI do that?"

"On what basis? They don't even have enough evidence for a subpoena, much less a head-to-head legal battle with your father. He'd simply deny the charges, refuse them access to the clinic, and deflect any questions, citing attorney-client privilege."

"Especially if the Hope Institute treats the kind of clientele you described," Victoria deduced aloud. "I know the way my father thinks. He'd remind the FBI that the clinic's patients were affluent and well connected, not the kind of people to be taken lightly. Then he'd threaten to call the attorney general, whom he knows personally. And the FBI wouldn't stand a chance." She bit her lip. "Anything else?"

A stiff nod. "Your father's phone records, both home and office, show frequent calls over the past several years to the Hope Institute. The calls you found on his recent bill were just the tip of the iceberg. And while those might very well have had to do with Audrey, the dozens of previous ones didn't."

Victoria stared at Zach, her mind leaping to one surprising, now obvious conclusion. "So this morning in my office, I didn't tell you anything that you—and the FBI—didn't already know."

"Except for what's going on with your sister, no, you didn't tell me anything new." He leaned forward, gripping his knees. "But, Victoria, now that you know just how extensive your father's lies to you were, surely you don't doubt he's the one who arranged for Audrey's well-timed message on your answering machine. He wants to keep you away from Audrey and the Hope Institute. And he doesn't want you to know of his connection to them, personally or professionally."

"In light of everything you've said, no, I can't argue that fact. For whatever reason, my father's working hard to keep me in the dark." Victoria's chin came up. "Zach, I've got to confront him."

"I understand that. I even support it—to a degree. You have to tread carefully. Otherwise, you could blow the FBI's whole investigation to bits."

Something about the matter-of-fact way Zach said that struck Victoria as odd. Abruptly, she knew what it was—and it shed a whole new light on his agenda for being here tonight.

She reacted with anger, not forethought. "You knew our conversation would turn out this way, didn't you? That after I heard what you said, I'd be hell-bent on taking on my father. Of course you did. It was exactly the reaction you were hoping for. After all, it would further your cause. *I* would further your cause. Tell me, am I being given the designated status of outside consultant or mole? Or simply an informant snitching on my own father?"

Those furious glints reappeared in Zach's eyes again. "You've become very cynical, do you know that, Victoria? You never used to jump to such ugly conclusions, certainly not when it came to me. Yes, I knew you'd want to go to your father after we spoke. Yes, I hoped you'd be able to dig up some new information. But, I assure you, my motives were hardly Machiavellian. The more your father reveals, the closer we are, not only to solving the FBI's case, but to finding Audrey. I thought you and I could help each other—and I would have said so, if you'd given me the chance. Which you didn't. But now that you've heard what I have in mind, is there anything unprincipled or self-serving about my approach? Because if there is, say so. I'll be the first to agree with your unflattering assessment of me."

Internally, Victoria winced, not from Zach's barbed comeback, but from the fact that it was justified. What in God's name was the matter with her? Zachary Hamilton was the most ethical human being she'd ever met. And here she was, accusing him, for the second time today, of using her. She was attacking him without giving the slightest thought to whether or not her allegations had merit.

Was she losing all sense of reason?

"I'm sorry, Zach," she said, searching for answers even as she offered them. "I don't know what's come over me. Maybe this whole situation is taking a greater toll on me than I realized. When it comes to Audrey, I feel a little like a mother lioness protecting her cub. It's my responsibility to make sure she's safe, and I'm doing a lousy job. Now my father is suspected of being criminally involved with a drug syndicate. Not to mention that someone's following me."

She swallowed, forcing herself to give Zach the honesty he deserved. "Also, seeing you again has hit me a lot harder than I expected. All those things combined—I guess my nerves are shot and I'm lashing out. And you seem to be the unfortunate target."

He listened to her explanation, then nodded slowly, a kind of wary comprehension coming over him. "Just as long as you know I'm not the enemy."

"I do know that."

A reflective pause. "As for feeling like a mother lioness, it always was that way when it came to Audrey or your mother. As I said, some things don't change."

"I guess not." Victoria's gut clenched, and she digressed in a less unsettling direction. "Getting back to the situation with my father, I'll make a deal with you."

"Go on."

"I'll go to him. I would have anyway, for Audrey's sake. I won't mention the FBI, or anything you've told me about their case. I'll stick to Audrey's message and my own visit to the Hope Institute—all the things Father already knows about or orchestrated. I'll see what kind of answers he gives me. I'll try to finesse him so I walk away with a better idea of just how deeply he's involved."

"And in return?"

"Two conditions. First, you leave Audrey's bulimia out of this. Tell the FBI about my seeing her in Central Park, about my suspicions that she's at the Hope Institute—all that's a matter of public record anyway, after the fuss I made at the police precinct. Tell them whatever facts you need to so they'll understand why I went to the clinic. But don't get into the personal details of Audrey's life. Protect her privacy. That's all I ask."

"And second?"

"We investigate my father independent of the FBI. If he's guilty, I'll turn over the evidence I've negotiated in exchange for leniency."

Zach didn't hesitate. "Consider it done." He leaned forward, extended his hand. "It looks like we have a deal, Ms. Kensington."

She hesitated for a long moment, then wrapped her fingers around his in a firm, businesslike handshake. "Yes. It looks like we do."

12

"Well, Victoria, this is a surprise." Walter Kensington joined his daughter at her window table, nodding at the maître d' and lowering himself to his chair. "When Miss Hatterman told me you'd called and said it was imperative that you see me, I was intrigued—and optimistic. I canceled my original luncheon appointment so we could meet."

"I appreciate that, Father." Victoria kept her features schooled as she counted silently to ten. "Although I'd better tell you up front that this lunch is not about the partnership." *And you damned well know that,* she added silently.

"I see." Her father's poker face was as good as hers, maybe better. He'd had more years to perfect it. "Then what is it about?"

"Audrey."

"Audrey." He repeated his younger daughter's name icily, his expression unchanged. "You're still pursuing that subject?"

"You know I am." Victoria folded her hands on the table, feeling as if she were facing off with the enemy. "I won't be put off again, Father," she said in a tone she rarely used with him. "Not this time."

"So I see—and hear. Remember I'm your father, not opposing counsel. Watch your tone of voice." He picked up the menu, scanning it briefly before making his decision and signaling to the waiter. "Let's order. Then we'll have this unpleasant conversation and put the issue of your sister to bed once and for all."

The last thing Victoria felt like doing was eating. In fact, she wondered how she was going to choke down a bite. But this was supposed to be a lunch. So she ordered a lobster Caesar salad and a glass of sparkling water with lime. If nothing else, she'd sip at the water and play with the salad. It would give her time to ask questions. Lots of questions.

From beneath her lashes, she studied her father as he ordered. If he was nervous about this meeting, he gave no sign. The man was the ultimate pro at concealing his thoughts. As for his emotions, Victoria sometimes wondered if he had any.

"Now then." Having ordered his customary swordfish and a glass of sauvignon blanc, Walter dismissed the waiter with a wave of his hand and fixed his hard stare on Victoria. "What is it you want to say about Audrey that hasn't already been said?"

He was playing this very cool, letting her lead the way and, as a result, letting her show him how much she knew.

Fine. She'd expected as much.

"Please stop pretending," she requested quietly. "I'm aware you know where Audrey is. She called me last night."

"Did she?"

"Yes. She didn't want me to worry about her—which you evidently told her I was doing. So she called to say she was all right."

"Good." Walter's nod said he approved of Audrey's action. "And what did you two discuss?"

Victoria didn't blink or look away. "Nothing. Then again, I can't imagine that surprises you. That *was* the idea, wasn't it—to have her call while I was at my regular Tuesday dinner meeting? That way, she could just leave a message and hang up."

Walter's eyes narrowed. "Is that an accusation?"

Ah. The counterattack. Direct and effective. Reveal nothing but fire a question that would squeeze her, force her to clarify her position.

Time to shift the momentum.

"Not an accusation. A mystery," Victoria supplied, feeling adrenaline pump through her veins. "It does seem strange that you wouldn't mention to Audrey when I'd be home—unless you didn't want me to speak with her directly. I know you're aware of my weekly Tuesday dinners with Meg and Paul, just as *I'm* aware of how thorough you are. Bearing that in mind, it's odd you'd forget to fill Audrey in on something as basic as my schedule—*when* you finally decided I was frantic enough to warrant a call from her, that is."

A frosty stare. "I'm going to excuse your sarcasm as a symptom of your concern over Audrey," Walter informed her in that deceptively low tone that meant he was getting angry. "But I'm not going to remind you again that it's me you're speaking to."

Instantly, Victoria checked herself. Time to put a lid on her offensive tactics. If she didn't watch her tongue, she'd risk provoking her father—which would be a big mistake. She'd wind up leaving here with nothing but hostility.

"I apologize if I've been disrespectful." The words—a show of restraint rather than sincerity—came easily enough. She'd been saying them for years. And they'd always done the trick, since it was the appearance, not the essence, of respect that her father required.

This time was no exception.

"Fine," he acknowledged tersely. "In answer to your question, I finally got Audrey's doctor to agree to let her call you—briefly. He asked when you'd be at home. I told him. I assumed she'd be calling during one of those times. Obviously, he decided she shouldn't make direct contact with you. If you're asking if his decision surprises me—no, it doesn't. Not under the circumstances."

What circumstances? Victoria wanted to scream.

She bit back the long list of aggressive questions she was dying to hurl at her father, instead making it appear that she'd accepted his explanation. "Audrey did say something about not being able to talk to anyone—that it was part of her treatment. But you were both right. I was out of my mind with worry. So, let's forget when she called. Let's talk about Audrey herself, and why you've misled me since Saturday. Why didn't you tell me where she really was, and why?"

"Because I signed papers that specifically forbid me from doing so."

"From telling her *sister* where she was?"

"From telling *anyone* where she was."

"And with whom did you sign these papers—the Hope Institute?"

"Yes," Walter replied calmly. "With the Hope Institute."

Victoria opened her mouth to respond, and was relieved when their meal chose that moment to arrive. She felt like a boxer who needed time between rounds. Her father was a worthy opponent. She had to find new ways to come out fighting.

Staring at her glass as the waiter filled it, she reminded herself why she was here. First and foremost, for Audrey. And then, for her and Zach's investigation. Her job was to find out as much as she could. But she had to do it as believably as possible. She had to continue playing her role as her father would expect—appearing worried and relentless, but only probing into the secrecy surrounding the Hope Institute as it would affect Audrey. She had to keep the focus of this meeting entirely personal, never alluding to the fact that her father was under suspicion of committing a felony.

He was shrewd. Too shrewd to miss anything. If she pressed too hard on something unrelated to Audrey, or glossed over something she'd normally hammer to bits, he'd know.

She had to tread carefully. But she *had* to tread. It was the only way she'd get answers—both the ones her father intended to provide and those he didn't.

"Can I get you anything else?" the waiter asked politely.

"No. I'm fine, thanks," Victoria assured him. She watched her father's standard shake of his head and curt wave of dismissal.

Pausing only until the waiter had gone, she leaned forward, forcing herself to appear very troubled, but not accusing. "You're telling me that the Hope Institute prohibits you from advising Audrey's family of her whereabouts and why she was admitted?"

"Precisely." Walter smoothed his napkin onto his lap. "They also prohibit my discussing the details of her physical and mental condition, or the specifics of her treatment. So I can give you only the bare-bones facts. Nothing more."

"I'm not asking you to compromise yourself, Father." Victoria groped in her pocketbook for a pad and pen. "Give me the name of Audrey's doctor. I'll call him myself."

"I'm the only one allowed to speak with him."

"In other words, you're not going to tell me who he is."

"Right. Frankly, I don't trust you to respect the Institute's policy. If you try to contact Audrey's physician, I'll be liable for breach of contract."

Victoria's pad and pen struck the table with a thud. "Let me get this straight. I'm Audrey's sister. Yet I can't know who's treating her, what treatments he's employing, and for what illness. In fact, I'm not even supposed to know where she is."

"That about sums it up."

"What kind of place is this Hope Institute?"

"The finest private clinic in Manhattan." Walter turned his attention to his swordfish. "With doctors who specialize in acute cases such as Audrey's."

"Acute." Victoria's protective instincts won out. She had

to know how sick her sister was and why. "Father, please tell me—what caused this relapse? How bad is it?"

"Bad." The situation didn't seem to affect Walter's appetite. He reported the critical nature of his younger daughter's health only after several bites of his lunch and an appreciative sip of wine. "She got involved with some two-bit artist in Florence. I don't know the sordid details, nor do I care to, but apparently he used her, left her, and stole whatever cash she had in the process. She fell apart, as she always does. She went on one of her binges. This one aggravated her entire gastrointestinal system, and severely inflamed her esophagus. She stopped eating altogether. Suffice it to say, the damage was extensive. She ended up hospitalized. The hospital got in touch with me. In turn, I got in touch with the Hope Institute and arranged to have her flown home immediately. She's been improving daily since then. End of story." He returned to his swordfish.

End of story?

Victoria felt an almost painful need to see her sister, to hug her and tell her everything would be all right—and then to make sure it was.

"How did you hear of the Hope Institute?" she pressed. "And if it's so wonderful, why hasn't anyone else heard of it? I had to go to great lengths to find the place at all. Also, why did Audrey run away? How do you know they're treating her well? When was the last time you saw her?"

Walter took another calm sip of wine. "Shall I take those in order, Counselor? I learned of the Hope Institute through several clients of mine who placed relatives there. It's highly acclaimed—to those wealthy and influential enough to avail themselves of the Institute's services. It's also extremely private. Superior care is their number-one priority, followed by confidentiality. I should think the reasons for that would be obvious. As for Audrey, she had a temporary setback this past weekend—an unfortunate reaction to her new medication. She panicked. Rather than buzzing for help, she ran away.

Knowing you were nearby and would undoubtedly shelter
her—as you always do—she went looking for you. The staff
found her. It took them a half-hour to bring her around and sta-
bilize her. She's fine now. I saw her yesterday. When I dropped
by, she was calm, her color was good, and her reaction to the
medication had subsided. She was eating a normal meal, and
she was in much better spirits. She scarcely remembers the
whole episode. But she felt terrible about causing you such
distress."

The underlying story was true. Victoria knew her father
was far too smart to fabricate the entirety. It was up to her to
find the variations and embellishments.

"So you see her often?"

"As often as I can get there, yes. Let's see . . . she's been
there for ten days. I've been there four times."

Four times? That was too specific for him to be lying.
Interesting. Victoria wondered how he got in and out of the
building, since the FBI's surveillance tape had picked up no
sign of him at the front door. Probably in one of the limousines that drove directly into the underground garage. Not
that that surprised her. Her father would never allow himself
to be seen walking into the Hope Institute—just in case a
passerby knew of the clinic's existence. And not only to protect his precious reputation. In this case, he'd be more worried about protecting himself. He must know the FBI had
been questioning Miss Evans. After all, she'd named him as
their attorney of record. It followed suit she'd keep him
apprised. So he'd be doubly committed to distancing himself from a clinic that was under investigation.

She had to dig up more.

"What about that phone number?" she demanded. "The
one Audrey muttered before she collapsed? And why did
she gasp out 'danger'?"

Walter dabbed at his mouth with the edge of his napkin.
"The telephone number is a private line to the Hope
Institute. Every patient receives it, along with a four-digit

password, to use in emergencies like the one Audrey found herself in Saturday morning. As for this danger she supposedly mumbled about, my only guess is that she realized she was jeopardizing her health by running away. Her body was telling her so. And she was telling you so—or trying to—in the hopes that you'd bring her back. Thankfully, the clinic's attendants tracked her down before it was too late."

Victoria drew a slow breath. "This sounds very cloak and dagger, Father. I feel as if Audrey is locked away in a fortress—no visitors, no contact with anyone. Are you sure you have enough faith in this clinic to leave her there?"

"As opposed to where, Victoria? Lenox Hill Hospital? They're not equipped to handle your sister's needs, believe me."

"Is it Audrey's needs you're worrying about? Or is it your own?"

You could have heard a pin drop at their table.

Slowly, Walter lowered his fork, his eyes as frigid as glaciers. "Are you suggesting I'd sacrifice my daughter's health to save face?"

"I'm saying your reputation means the world to you."

"I'm not denying that. I worked hard to become who and what I am today. And I'd do a great deal to protect myself, including go out of my way to keep Audrey's damaging setbacks and indiscretions quiet. So, yes, I wanted her at a private facility. But I found the most outstanding clinic Manhattan has to offer, one of the finest any city has to offer. Audrey has twenty-four-hour care and attention— physical and psychological."

Psychological. That introduced another interesting point.

"You didn't discuss any of this with Uncle Jim. Why? You've always kept him in the loop on Audrey's bulimia. And what about Dr. Osborne? He treated Audrey in the past. Why isn't he treating her now?"

A red flush stained Walter's neck. "You spoke to Jim about this?"

Victoria was well aware she was walking into the lion's

den, but she didn't retreat. "Yes. I hoped that either he or Aunt Clarissa would have heard of the Hope Institute. Neither of them did."

"So together the three of you decided I was mistreating my daughter."

"No. Quite the contrary. We never discussed mistreatment, or the prospect that the Hope Institute might be anything but first-rate. As for the possibility of your motives being selfish, I was the one who brought that up. The *only* one. To be perfectly honest, Uncle Jim defended you. He thought I was being unfair. He urged me to take my suspicions directly to you, give you a chance to explain. Which I'd intended to do, even before Audrey's call."

"How gracious of you."

Victoria gritted her teeth. "Father, I'm not trying to antagonize you, or make you out to be some kind of monster. I just don't understand the need for all this secrecy."

"I already answered that question. The Hope Institute has its policies. Period." Walter was obviously ready to end this conversation. Victoria, on the other hand, wasn't. She'd found out nothing. But she couldn't keep going around in circles this way, pressing her father on issues he'd explain away as being outcomes of the Institute's rules on privacy. So how could she get him to tell her more?

"By the way," her father concluded, pushing back his chair. "One of those policies prohibits bringing in outside medical consultants. That includes Elliot Osborne, which explains why he and your uncle weren't told."

"Why would the Hope Institute reject the idea of getting other respected opinions? It's almost as if they're afraid of something." Victoria held up a palm in anticipation of her father's reply. "Don't bother explaining. Privacy."

Walter's lips thinned into a tight line of disapproval. "We could argue this point all day. The bottom line is, you might not approve of the Institute's rigid rules and restrictions, but the results speak for themselves. Audrey is in the best of hands. She's going to get well. And when she does, you're welcome to spend as much time with her as you'd like. Until then, stay away."

Victoria tensed in her chair. Why did that sound disturbingly like a threat?

Her father had already stood, his hard stare scanning the room in search of their waiter. "This subject is now officially closed. I've probably said more than I ethically should have. But I had to put your mind at ease so you'd stop this unwarranted obsession with Audrey and her well-being. She's fine—or she will be if we let the doctors do their job without interfering. Now, I'm paying the check and heading back to my office."

No, you're not! Victoria almost shouted, consciously restraining herself from grabbing his arm to keep him from leaving. *Not yet. I have to find out something before you go back and call the Hope Institute . . .*

Abruptly, she halted, her own thought process providing the solution. Of course. That was her answer.

What was it her father had said, that he'd heard of the Hope Institute through clients of his? Had he meant Benjamin Hopewell, or was there someone else, maybe several someones?

There was only one place she could go to find out—the nucleus where her father kept all his confidential data on clients for whom he was the attorney of record.

His office.

The FBI had no way of getting inside Waters, Kensington, Tatem & Calder so they could search for her father's connection to the Hope Institute.

But she did.

And she had the perfect excuse for doing so: Paul. Paul and the floundering corporate practice he was striving so hard to grow.

There was no time to decide whether or not she was being reckless.

She had to rely on her instincts.

"Before you get the waiter, there's something else I'd like to discuss with you," she heard herself say.

Her father looked more exasperated than pleased. "What now, Victoria—your mother? She's fine."

"No, not Mother." Victoria shoved away her plate, folded her hands crisply on the table. She had to make this businesslike. To appear straightforward, but proud. It was the only way she'd seem true enough to form to convince her father she was sincere, while being compelling enough to pique his interest. "It's about my law firm."

"Really." Her father said nothing more, but she noticed he stopped looking around for the waiter and instead directed his attention to her.

"I'm very proud of what Meg, Paul, and I have accomplished."

A fine start. She sounded self-confident. Even a tad defensive. That's what her father would expect—especially once he heard what was on her mind.

"My partners and I are all dedicated attorneys. We are all good at what we do. Better than good—exceptional. But our firm is new. We're still getting our feet wet." She pressed her lips together. "This is awkward for me. And difficult. Especially after the conversation we just had. I'm sure you're miffed that I questioned your judgment about admitting Audrey to the Hope Institute. I can't help being protective of her. Regardless, that was family. This is business. I hope you're able to view things in that light."

"What things would that be?"

She took a deep, fortifying breath. "I promised Paul I'd ask. So I'm asking. You know Paul specializes in corporate law. If any of your junior associates has an overflow, Paul would be pleased to pick up the surplus."

The barest flicker of surprise crossed her father's face, followed by a more lingering display of interest. "You're asking for my help."

"I'm asking for referrals."

"It's the same thing." Walter gripped the back of his chair, staring down at his daughter—in more ways than one. "Paul London is a novice. His experience is limited. He may have potential, but he's hardly up to handling our level of client. The corporations he represents are too insignificant to even term small."

Victoria didn't blink. "You, too, once had more potential than experience."

"True. And I proved my own worth."

"You had the opportunity to do so," she challenged. "You got a job at a large firm with an existing client base."

"London was in a similar position. He chose to go out on his own."

Her father was enjoying this. Even gloating. Good. That brought her one step closer to where she wanted to be.

She interlaced her fingers more tightly—a gesture she hoped her father would notice. He'd interpret it as emotion. A sign of weakness.

He did.

"I don't often ask you for anything, Father."

Walter's jaw set in hard, reproving lines. "Not only don't you ask, you refuse to accept. Even when what's offered is a golden opportunity—one that won't come along again."

Perfect. Just where she'd anticipated him going.

"You're talking about my joining your firm."

"Not just joining it, Victoria. Coming in as a junior partner."

Victoria fell, very intentionally, silent. She knew just how her father would interpret that silence. It was, after all, the first time she hadn't blown him off at the first mention of the partnership.

Walter reacted on cue.

He reseated himself, sensing a long-awaited victory. "Are you ready to consider my offer?"

"No." Victoria responded quickly, but with less fervor than usual. "I didn't ask for a position. I asked for referrals."

He leaned in, emanating that dominating certainty that made him nearly unbeatable, both in the courtroom and out. "Think about it. You're an exceptional attorney. You're my daughter. You have a bright future ahead of you—*if* you take it. Begging for clients is beneath you. So is living hand to mouth. There's a legacy waiting for you at Waters, Kensington, Tatem and Calder. What's holding you back—pride?"

"Belief in what I do." Victoria's chin came up. She spoke from the heart, but also with the realization that minimizing her commitment to her firm would be stupid. It would alert her father to the fact that her story was phony. "And loyalty," she added. "Meg and Paul aren't just my colleagues, they're my friends. Even if I agreed with your logic, which I don't, I wouldn't turn my back on them. I don't expect you to understand that. I *do* expect you to honor it."

Her father pursed his lips, his mental wheels clearly turning. She held her breath, praying she'd sweetened the pot just enough to lure him over, to give him the opening he needed.

Her prayers were answered.

"Maybe there's a way I can respect your priorities and, at the same time, introduce you to mine," Walter posed.

"Meaning?"

"You said this was business. Well, it is. And in business, there's no such thing as getting something for nothing. You want to settle out of court, so to speak? Give me the proper incentive to do so."

"Go on."

"Here's my proposition. Come work at Waters, Kensington, Tatem and Calder. Not as a partner or even a full-time employee, but strictly 'of counsel' to the firm. Give me two days a week. That will leave you more than enough time to service the clients at your own firm. See which world you prefer. We'll agree to a trial period—say, three months. I'll pay you well, and I'll see what I can do about referring our surplus to London." He inclined his head slightly. "I think that's a fair arrangement. Don't you?"

Fair? Actually, Victoria wanted to shout with triumph. She'd accomplished exactly what she intended—getting through those damned doors and into her father's domain. A domain that held the truth about the Hope Institute.

Outwardly, she remained impassive. Her gaze narrowed thoughtfully, never averting from her father's as he awaited her reply.

"I'd be only an outside counsel," she clarified at last. "And I don't want a salary; I want a contingency. Forty percent of your billings for my time. In a check made out to London, Kensington and Stone."

Walter stared her down. "I'd expect you to give me your all."

"I don't know any other way to work. What's more, you knew that, or you wouldn't be offering me this chance." Victoria raised her chin another notch. "I'll invest the same level of commitment and integrity in your firm as I do in my own. That should produce enough capital to get Meg, Paul, and me off the ground, and give you ample reason to send a few meaty clients Paul's way. But, Father—no manipulation or pressure. No announcements, no business cards, no new letterhead with my name on it. No surprises. I'm a principal of London, Kensington and Stone only. That point is nonnegotiable."

"I don't intend to trick you into joining my firm, Victoria." A brittle smile. "I won't have to. The three months will speak for themselves."

She continued to play hardball. "I can't start until next week at the earliest. I have court tomorrow and back-to-back appointments all day Friday. And even next week is going to be tight. I'll have to check my calendar and see how much time I can spare."

"You do that." An insightful pause. "Not to mention

you'll want ample time to prepare your partners for the bomb you're about to drop."

"It's not a bomb. It's a new client. Waters, Kensington, Tatem and Calder. One that will take a substantial amount of my time. But, yes. I want Paul and Meg to understand what I'm doing and why."

"Very well. Next week, then. Get back to me with your availability." Walter came to his feet, looking like a wolf about to close in on its kill. "In fact, you can give me the specifics tomorrow morning at seven-thirty. I want you in my office for a quick half-hour to meet the people you'll be working with. The senior partners are all in by then. They'll want to see you; it's been ages since most of them have had the pleasure. And by that time, I'll have advised them of your new status with the firm."

Tomorrow morning. This was one curve Victoria hadn't anticipated. That gave her only tonight to talk to Meg and Paul, to plan her strategy, and to try to reach Zach.

"Why the urgency?" she inquired, buying herself a minute to think. "I've already met a fair number of your partners and associates."

"Years ago and in passing. This time you'll be meeting them in an official, professional capacity. There are also many new members of the firm you haven't met at all." Her father shot her a look that was more challenging than it was quizzical. "Why? Is there some problem? You'll have ample time to get to the courthouse. My driver will take you. As for breakfast, Miss Hatterman will order whatever you like. That leaves you all this evening to talk to your partners, and all tonight to prepare for your appearance."

"Which one?" Victoria asked dryly. "The one in court or the one at Waters, Kensington, Tatem and Calder?"

An icy smile. "Take your pick."

"Fine. I'll be there." Victoria put down her napkin and rose. She was well aware she was being tested. Put on the spot to perform up to her father's standards. So be it. He had no idea just how quick on her feet she was. She'd walked into more than one court battle in mid-trial and won with only a night of prep time. She'd do the same here.

Her father was right. Certain golden opportunities didn't come along again.

And this one was hers for the taking.

13

The fan was still whirring.

This time its blades were slicing shadows on the ceiling.

It must be night. But what night? How much time had passed? And why couldn't she form a clear thought?

A rustle from across the room told her she wasn't alone.

She forced her head up, which took a huge effort since it felt like lead.

In the armchair sat one of the caps.

"Head . . . hurts . . ." Audrey managed in a dry croak.

The cap put down whatever she'd been doing and came to her feet. "I know it does." She approached the bed, her expression clear enough to convey concern. "You've been restless. You're running a fever." She pressed a cool palm against Audrey's cheek, which felt as if it were on fire. "Would you like some water?"

"Yes." She let her eyelids slide shut, let the cap anchor her head and press the cup to her lips. She sipped, grateful for the cool sensation of the liquid trickling down her throat.

When she was finished, she cracked open her eyes and gazed around the dark room. "Father . . ."

"Shhh. He'll be here tomorrow."

"No . . . I need to . . ."

"Tomorrow, Audrey," the cap stated firmly. "You'll have solid food and a visit from your father. But now you need to rest." She tucked the sheet and blanket around her, *then fluffed the pillows beneath her head. "Close your eyes."*

Audrey's body seemed to give her no choice.

Footsteps. A purposeful stop in her doorway. A penetrating stare.

There was someone else in the room now.

She could sense it.

But she didn't have the strength to see who it was.

Zach rose when Victoria walked through Lusardi's, the maître d' escorting her to his table.

"Thank you, Marco," she murmured to the beaming, round-faced maître d'.

"My pleasure, Signora Kensington. It's good to see you again. Enjoy your dinner—both of you."

With a knowing gleam in his eye and an appraising glance at Zach, Marco eased away from their table, conspicuous in his attempt to afford them some privacy.

"Subtle," Zach noted dryly, helping Victoria into her seat.

She flushed. "I appreciate your meeting me," she began, trying not to notice the way his dark gaze flickered over her sapphire-blue off-the-shoulder, cap-sleeved dress, trying not to think about how much extra care she'd taken in choosing it.

"Obviously, it was important." Zach returned to his chair.

He looked incredible. Then again, Zach always looked incredible. He wasn't classically handsome, nor even remotely trendy in the way he dressed. He was understated, dynamic, exuding a power and energy that made women of all ages crane their necks when he entered a room. Tonight he wore charcoal gray slacks, a pearl-gray turtleneck sweater, and a black sport coat.

Victoria forced herself not to stare. It was scary, after four years, how attracted to him she still was.

"Victoria?" Zach was watching her closely. "Are you all

right? When I got your message, I assumed that whatever you wanted to see me about had something to do with the meeting you had with your father."

"It does." Victoria pressed her palms together. "My lunch with him was interesting, to say the least." She stopped right there, remembering herself and exercising even more than her usual caution. This was her family she was protecting, not a client. "Did you talk to your associates at the FBI?"

Zach took her wariness in stride. "First thing today. As we agreed, I said nothing about Audrey's medical condition. I confirmed that you went to the Hope Institute to find her. I also said you knew less than we did about your father's involvement in the matter we're investigating." A corner of Zach's mouth lifted. "Did I fulfill my half of the bargain?"

A slight smile. "You did. And so did I."

"I'm all ears." Zach signaled to the maître d'. "First, let's get some wine. You look like you could use it. I assume it's still cab?"

"Um-hum." She gave a brief nod. "As you said, some things don't change."

"True." His voice held that same odd, unsettling quality as it had at her apartment. He cleared his throat as Marco approached, and Victoria considered protesting when, rather than a glass apiece, he ordered an entire bottle of Joseph Phelps cabernet.

"You're going to be drinking most of that," she advised him lightly after Marco had heartily approved of Zach's choice and whisked off to get it. "I have to stand up straight and be coherent in court tomorrow."

"You will be." Zach offered her the basket of warm bread, waited while she took a slice, then ripped off a generous chunk for himself. "What kind of case is it?"

"An ugly divorce and child-custody case. The guy's a selfish forty-year-old going through a hormonal midlife crisis. He abandoned his family, acts like a jerk, and thinks with his—" Victoria broke off.

"I get the picture," Zach assured her dryly. "In other words, you're doing exactly what you always wanted to do—helping women in need."

"You make me sound like some altruistic champion of the oppressed. I do get paid."

"Probably not nearly what you're worth." Zach paused, contemplating his bread. "Then again, you never were driven by a desire for wealth. Otherwise, you'd have chosen a different route. By now you'd be a partner at Waters, Kensington, Tatem and Calder."

Victoria put a dab of butter on her bread. "Funny you should mention that."

Reacting to her tone as well as her words, Zach stopped chewing. "Meaning?"

"That's why I asked to see you tonight." She raised her head and met his gaze. "Tomorrow morning at seven-thirty I'm due at my father's office for introductions. As of next week, I'll be of counsel to his firm."

Zach took in her news, his dark eyes narrowing pensively. "Why?"

She arched a brow. "You just finishing telling me I don't get the compensation I deserve. Waters, Kensington, Tatem and Calder could buy half of Park Avenue and lease the other half. Maybe I just—"

"Victoria, what are you doing?"

A slow breath. "I'm getting in the door. It's the only way I'm going to find out what I need to."

"Explain."

She did, relaying the conversation she'd had with her father at lunch and her subsequent decision to bait him. "It will work, Zach. It has to. The sooner I can figure out what's going on at the Hope Institute, and separate the honest people from the dishonest ones, the sooner I can decide how best to get to Audrey. And I'm praying that what I uncover will exonerate my father of everything except being a hard-hearted control freak and an aggressive attorney who's unknowingly representing a crooked CEO."

Zach was frowning. He remained silent as the waiter arrived to serve their wine and take their order. But his thoughts were racing. Victoria could see that. Even as he sampled the cabernet and nodded his approval, he was pondering her course of action and thinking she was getting in over her head.

When they were alone again, he didn't waste a minute. "I'm not thrilled about this. Your father is a very shrewd man. He's also a ruthless one, when it comes to what's his. Especially his law firm. If he guesses what you have in mind, he'll chew you up and spit you out."

Victoria acknowledged that truth with a shrug. "You're right. He would. But he won't guess. He has a one-track mind when it comes to his law firm. He can't imagine any sane, intelligent person, particularly his daughter, turning her back on what he views as a once-in-a-lifetime opportunity. He's convinced I've finally started coming to my senses, that he's made some kind of breakthrough. I won't do anything to make him think otherwise. Besides, to be honest, London, Kensington and Stone really could use the money we'll get out of this. And Paul could use the referrals. Neither he nor Meg have ever suggested I go to my father for help. Still, I have a feeling they'll be thrilled with the jump start. Especially Paul. He's starting to look pretty grim these days."

"You have a feeling . . . Then you haven't talked to them about this new arrangement yet?"

"No." She shook her head. "They were both out of the office all afternoon at client meetings. I left them each a voice-mail message, asking them to meet me in the office at six-thirty tomorrow morning. I stressed that it was important."

Zach swirled the wine around in his glass. "What are you going to tell them?"

"The truth. Part of it," she clarified, just in case he was concerned about her mentioning his investigation. "The personal part. Audrey. Her disappearance. Meg already knows some of the details anyway. And Paul's been popping his head into my office, asking a million questions and looking worried. They both know something's wrong. So I'll tell them where Audrey is, and that I'm pretty sure my father put her there. As for my affiliation with Waters, Kensington, Tatem and Calder, I'll let them know this is only temporary—until I find my sister and bring a few extra dollars and additional clients into the firm."

"Sounds like a plan." Zach lifted his glass. "Shall we toast to it—and to how carefully you'll execute it?" he added pointedly.

"All right." Victoria raised her glass, as well. "To bringing this whole ugly mess to a happy conclusion."

"Amen." Zach paused, his dark gaze sweeping over her in the same appreciative way it had when she walked in. "And to renewed acquaintances. It's good to see you again, Victoria, regardless of the circumstances." A weighted pause. "You look beautiful."

Her heart did a rapid nosedive, and she wondered how one acquired the sophistication necessary to deal with emotions such as these. She'd spent four years hardening herself to what she felt for Zach. She'd finally managed to build a wall around those feelings. She wasn't stupid enough to believe she'd stopped caring, only that she'd stopped believing that caring could lead anywhere beyond a cache of poignant memories. And now here he was, chipping away at that wall.

Okay, fine. So his presence affected her. As did his openly admiring appraisal and his frank compliment. She couldn't help that. She was drawn to him. That would never change. But anything deeper, more serious than attraction, was impossible. They'd determined that four years ago when they were slapped in the face by the realization that their goals were irreconcilably different. No compromise. Not with them. It was all or nothing. Well, all was out. That left nothing.

Bottom line? It was over. And no amount of wine and nostalgia could change that.

"Victoria?" Zach's tone commanded her attention. "We made a toast. We're supposed to clink glasses and take a sip of wine. Instead, you're clinging to your glass as if it were a lifeline. Stop. I haven't threatened those damned defenses of yours. I told you you were beautiful. You are. In fact, you haven't changed a bit in four years, other than your hair being a couple of inches shorter and your eyes a little more serious. Now accept the compliment and drink."

There was the blunter side of Zach. The tell-it-like-it-is man who spoke his mind. A stark contrast to the sensitive, romantic lover she so vividly recalled.

Quickly, she squelched that line of thought. "Yes, sir," she quipped, wishing she could be as stoic as he. Determined to try, she steadied her fingers and clinked her glass to his. "Thank you for your kinds words. Oh, and it's good to see you, too."

"There." A satisfied twinkle. "Was that so hard?"

"The truth? Yes." She brought her glass to her lips, happy to devote her attention to drinking the cabernet. "Mmm. Very nice. And you were right. I needed it." She took another sip.

"I can see that. Apparently even more so with me than with your father."

That did it. She set down her goblet with a firm thud.

"Zach, please, stop baiting me. If you want to debate politics or philosophy, I'm more than up for it. But I'm not good at this kind of banter—at least not when it comes to us. Let's stick to topics that are less raw."

"It's raw to me, too," he corrected. "Don't confuse candor with flippancy."

"Fine. I'd still like to change the subject."

"All right." Abruptly, his tone gentled. "How's your mother?"

Victoria rubbed the stem of the glass between her fingers, not even bothering to duck the question or give a half answer. She knew what Zach was really asking. He was aware of her upbringing, of her family's frailties. She'd told him about them herself—during one of their lazy, intimate dinners in his hotel suite.

"Better. She doesn't drink herself to sleep anymore. Now it's just occasional antidepressants prescribed by her doctor. And weekly therapy sessions." She glanced up and met Zach's compassionate gaze. "She's surviving. Not happy, just surviving. Then again, I suppose that's all any of us can hope for in life. Status quo."

"Is it? You and I both know there's more."

Again, an intimate twist on the subject. It was the last thing she needed—or wanted.

"Do we?" Victoria heard herself ask, her tone harsher than she'd intended. "Maybe that 'more' is either an illusion or a temporary high. Maybe spurts of happiness are all any of us is granted." She stared at her glass. "And maybe I *have* become cynical, just as you suggested."

"Or badly burned." His voice was low, and she could feel his gaze on her. "I'm sorry if I did that to you."

"You didn't." It was her turn to be frank. "Life did. I'm four years older, wiser, and less angry than I was when you left. I've come to understand that certain things are nobody's fault. They just are. And not only regarding broken hearts. Regarding broken lives, as well."

"Quite a realization."

"Um-hum. One that breeds cynicism, at least for me. People like my mother and Audrey are far from unique. I see that every day the longer I practice law. There are so many victims out there."

"And you want to save them all."

Victoria shot Zach a quick, scrutinizing glance, trying to

see if he was being sarcastic. But the expression on his face was without meanness or artifice.

"I wish I could," she replied. "However, wishing doesn't mean I'm naive enough to believe it's possible. I would have settled for saving my mother and sister. But the more time passes, the more I see there's only so much I can do. I can protect them, but I can't make them fight back. That decision has to come from them." A soft sigh. "Uncle Jim would be pleased. He and Aunt Clarissa have been telling me for years to let Audrey and my mother find their own paths. Maybe I'm finally starting to listen."

"How are your uncle and aunt? Still working hard?"

"Yes. They're the two most dedicated people I know. I can't begin to say how much I admire them, more as the years pass and I realize how rare they are." A pang of guilt. "Uncle Jim was none too thrilled by my hints that Father could be hiding Audrey from us. He and Clarissa have such an ingrained commitment to family. It makes me feel like a snake." Victoria gave a humorless laugh. "Talk about life's dark realities. Here I am, supposedly the backbone of my family, spying on my own father."

"You *are* the backbone of your family. No one knows that better than me. Except maybe them. As for your father, you're not spying on him. You're searching for the truth. And you're hoping that, by finding it, you'll clear him of anything more serious than guilt by association."

"That makes me sound infinitely more noble," Victoria commented dryly. "I wish it made me feel better."

Abruptly, Zach's words inspired another, much different thought—one she held until the waiter delivered their meal. Then she leaned forward, studying Zach intently. "Something just occurred to me. If an FBI agent already visited the Hope Institute, then my father must have been advised of that visit by his contacts. Is there any way those contacts can tie you to the feds?"

Calmly, Zach cut a slice of veal. "Offhand, I'd say no.

But you and I both know that no setup is leak-proof. Is it possible your father will find out I'm working with the FBI if he chooses to dig deep enough? Sure."

"Great." Victoria twisted around, peering toward the front of the restaurant and trying to see out onto Second Avenue. "He might already have made the connection. And here I am having dinner with you, right out in the open where anyone can see us together."

"Yes, you are, aren't you?" Zach continued eating his meal. "Is that so surprising, under the circumstances?"

She turned back to face him. "*What* circumstances?"

"Your father knew you were seeing me four years ago. I drove you home often enough. And we had dinner two or three times with your aunt and uncle. So our relationship wasn't a secret."

Victoria swallowed, thinking about what her uncle had asked her the other night. "No, it wasn't."

"Good. Well, I'm back in town after four years abroad. It's only natural that we'd catch up on old times, get together for dinner, drinks, conversation. Right?"

Her fork clinked against her plate. "You want us to pretend we're involved?"

The word "pretend" hovered in the air like an explosive.

"Not involved, seeing each other," Zach corrected without averting his gaze. "And I think it would be a wise precaution, yes."

"Precaution was never our strength," Victoria muttered under her breath.

"No, it wasn't. Then again, I didn't give a damn. Did you?"

Victoria's insides gave another sharp wrench. "We're not talking about our relationship, Zach. We're talking about making believe we've resumed it in order to throw suspicion off your . . . *our* investigation."

"And?"

She picked up her utensils and began slicing her chicken marsala. "I'm not sure I can pull it off."

"Too far-fetched or too painful?"

Her fork and knife paused. "I think you know the answer to that."

"I think I do, too. But I want to hear it from you."

"All right." Abandoning her utensils, Victoria looked him squarely in the eye. "Both. Too painful for me to face and too far-fetched for me to believe."

Without warning, Zach's hand snaked out and caught her fingers in his. "I understand the painful part. But far-fetched? Uh-uh. Not in the ways that are visible to the world."

His thumb caressed her palm, sending a sharp, involuntary jolt of sensation spearing through her—a physical awareness as vivid as it was alarming. This was one memory she was determined *not* to resurrect.

Zach felt the jolt, too. Victoria could see it in the slight darkening of his eyes, feel it in his barely detectable start of amazement.

No. This was impossible. This shivery, languid feeling couldn't be so easily rekindled. Not after four years apart. Not even by Zach.

But it was.

Zach's gaze fell to their joined hands, his thumb continuing its feathery motion, his grip tightening so she couldn't yank her hand away.

So far, she hadn't tried.

"Is it really so hard for you to imagine, Victoria?" he asked in the rough, husky voice she'd spent endless nights trying to erase from her memory. "Or is the problem that it's too damned easy?"

She inhaled slowly, forcing herself to see the big picture rather than drown in a maelstrom of physical sensation. "Don't do this to me, Zach," she said with quiet dignity. "Don't toy with my emotions, or twist my words to suit your purpose. When I said that pretending we'd picked up where we left off was too far-fetched an idea to pull off, I didn't mean in bed. I'm sure we could pull that part off quite nicely. But if you remember, our relationship had a bit more to it than hot sex."

"Yes, I remember. I remember everything." He released her hand, that guarded expression back in place. "And I wasn't twisting your words. I was merely pointing out that our attraction to each other is too intense to deny, or to conceal. Which is all that anyone, including your father and his contacts, will draw their conclusions from. The scars, as you well know, are worn inside. We just have to do an effective job of hiding them. Can you manage that?"

The irony of Zach's question almost made Victoria laugh aloud. Hide her scars? A piece of cake. She'd been doing it since he left New York. So well that, until now, she'd half convinced herself she was actually healing.

No such luck.

"Yes." She gave a terse nod. "I can manage that."

"Good." Zach resumed eating. "And stop looking so worried. Your father will probably never figure out my connection to the FBI's investigation. As for you, I doubt he's overly interested in your social life—unless it were to interfere with your climb to senior partner at Waters, Kensington, Tatem and Calder."

Victoria couldn't deny that. "You're right." She sipped at her wine. "He's going to be single-minded once I walk through those doors. His goal is to keep me from walking out."

"Mention me."

Again, her head came up. "What?"

"I said, mention me." Zach was regarding her with a touch of wariness. "It might ease his mind to think you're concentrating on something other than Audrey, at least during nonworking hours."

"In other words, lull him into a false sense of security."

Zach's lips curved into that crooked grin. "I think that's a bit dramatic, don't you? I'm just stating the obvious. Your father is unhappy about your preoccupation with Audrey and where she's recuperating. Whether he feels that way because he's a control freak or a calculated felon, we don't know. But we do know he'd relax a bit if he believed you had other interests besides the Hope Institute."

"True." Victoria chewed a piece of chicken. "And just how would you suggest I drop your name into the conversation?"

Zach's eyes twinkled. "Oh, let's see. You could look tired, yawn, and act distracted. I'm sure your father knows you're on your game with a max of four hours' sleep. When he comments on that, tell him you only had three—thanks to me. That should make a big hit."

"Cute. Now be serious."

A chuckle. "Okay. Just keep holding yourself at arm's length, the way you have been. Tell him you had to reschedule your entire previous afternoon and evening to get to his office for that seven-thirty A.M. meeting. You had to move your appointments around, set aside time to talk to your partners, and cut short your dinner with an old friend so you'd have enough time to prepare for court. Drop in my name as the old friend. If he's curious about when I came back into the picture, let him know I'm in town on business, and say we've been catching up. That should be enough."

Victoria glanced at her watch, surprised to see it was almost nine. "Speaking of court, I'd better head home to prepare."

"I'll take you." Zach tossed down his napkin and signaled the waiter.

Again, Zach the gentleman.

A tiny surge of warmth accompanied that memory. Zach, who saw her safely to her door in Greenwich. Zach, who worried about her jogging the streets surrounding Columbia, despite the high level of campus security. Zach, who insisted on picking her up at the end of her day of classes, even if it meant leaving his hotel only to drive them directly back there for the evening.

It didn't matter how much she protested. Zach's values were as fundamental to him as his intensity.

Still, that was then. Things between them now were dramatically different. She couldn't allow Zach's chivalry to enter into the picture.

"You don't have to escort me," she assured him, easing back her chair. "Manhattan's my home. I'm no longer a commuter, or a student. I've managed by myself for a long time."

That last statement hung heavily between them, more heavily than Victoria would have liked. She'd thought only to remind Zach that she was self-reliant. Instead, she'd somehow shoved their breakup back into the spotlight, and at the same time, clued him in on just how alone she'd been these past years.

Neither result was what she'd had in mind.

His silence didn't help.

Self-consciously, Victoria rose, determined to clarify her position. "I'm a big girl, Zach," she said lightly, forcing herself to meet his gaze, uncertain and more than a little uneasy about what she'd see there. "You stay. Have your coffee. I'll go home, prepare for court, and catch a few hours' rest."

He didn't look pensive or brooding or even mystified, as she'd expected. He looked torn. He *was* torn, she suddenly realized. Rather than pondering the implications of what she'd just said, he was having an internal battle over what to do. She knew it as surely as if he said it. He was torn between his parents' decent, old-fashioned teachings about how a woman should be treated and his attempt to respect her independence.

"Victoria . . ." He came to his feet, gripping the edge of the table and leaning toward her.

She had to take a stand—now.

"I tell you what. You pay for dinner," she quipped lightly, tucking a strand of hair behind her ear. "That will appease your unnecessary feelings of guilt. It'll also do a lot more for me than your seeing me to my door. My legs are as functional as yours, but you're richer than I am."

His tight-lipped smile told her he'd picked up on the fact that she was putting a lighter slant on the conversation—and that he didn't like it. "If you prefer it that way, fine. Dinner's on me."

"Thank you." She averted her gaze. "Good night." Scooping up her purse, she turned toward the door.

"Victoria?"

She glanced back questioningly.

"Let me know how it goes tomorrow."

"I will." She walked away, feeling Zach's penetrating stare bore through her and wondering whether he was thinking about the investigation, or about the unresolved personal issues they'd both assumed had been put to bed long ago but that seemed destined to keep resurfacing.

She stepped outside, already scanning the street for a taxi. It was late, she was worn out and confused, and she wasn't up for the half-mile walk to her apartment.

That's when she saw him.

He was standing diagonally across the street, partially concealed by shadows. But she saw the glowing ember of his cigar. And she felt his penetrating scrutiny.

He was still following her.

14

Without missing a beat, Victoria pivoted and weaved her way back through the warm, bistro-like tables at Lusardi's, not slowing down until she could see Zach.

He was ordering coffee, but when he saw her, he stopped and held up a detaining palm to the waiter. "What is it?" he demanded as she reached the table.

"Mr. Cigar." She kept her voice low. "He's outside. Across the street."

"Got it." All in one motion, Zach came to his feet, instructing the waiter to cancel the coffee and reaching into his pocket. He peeled off two hundred-dollar bills. "I apologize for the inconvenience," he told the waiter. "This will more than cover dinner. The rest is for you."

Their waiter beamed. "Grazie, signore."

Zach was already guiding Victoria toward the door. "Did he spot you?" he asked quietly.

"He must have. He was watching the restaurant entrance when I walked out."

"Then he'll assume you saw him, too, and that you went back inside to get help. Or worse, call the police."

"So he'll disappear?"

"Only from view. He's probably hanging out inside another building, waiting to see if a cop shows up. If not, he'll get brave again." Zach opened the door and eased them both outside, casually adjusting his collar while scanning the area. "Is he still there?"

"No. He's gone."

"Not gone," Zach corrected. "Just out of sight." He angled himself to face Victoria. "Listen to me and don't argue. I'm going to walk you home. We're not going to take a cab, because that would defeat the whole purpose. I want him to feel safe. I want him to follow you. I *don't* want him to know he was spotted. Let him think you went back inside to see where I was. In the meantime, you and I are going to walk to your apartment hand in hand, chatting and acting like we're close friends. Understand?"

She nodded.

"Good." He reached down, took her hand in his, and interlaced their fingers. "Let's go. Slowly. And having easy, intimate conversation."

Like we used to, flitted through Victoria's mind as she fell into step beside him.

They headed up Second Avenue toward Eighty-second Street.

"Your hand is cold," Zach murmured. "Are you frightened?"

"A little. More shaken, actually. I'm also freezing. It was warm when I got dressed. Now I wish I'd worn a coat."

Zach released her hand and shrugged out of his sport coat. "Here." He wrapped it around her shoulders, then draped an arm around her to keep it in place. "Better?"

That depended on how one defined "better."

Enveloped in Zach's coat, Victoria was instantly accosted by his scent—the fresh, woodsy aroma of his Armani cologne and the clean, masculine scent that was just plain Zach.

Her body reacted as if to a caress, and a hot tremor shuddered through her.

"Victoria?" Reflexively, his palm rubbed the chill from her arm. "Are you warmer now?"

"Um-hum." She stared at the sidewalk, dimly aware of the throngs of people walking around them. Everything seemed surreal, as if she were reliving a treasured moment from the past. Except that it wasn't the past, and Zach was only walking her home to protect her from the wacko who was following her.

She tensed, wondering if Mr. Cigar was one of the seemingly innocuous people moving up and down Second Avenue, or whether he was hovering in the shadows, watching her head for home and creeping along behind her.

Zach paused at the corner of East Eighty-second Street, glancing about nonchalantly as he waited for the light to change. "I don't see him," he murmured, his breath ruffling Victoria's hair.

She nodded.

The light changed.

They crossed over, heading west toward her apartment. Zach tucked his coat more fully around her, eased her closer against him, and Victoria had to fight the insane urge to lean into him.

"Tell me about your life these past years." His abrupt request jarred her out of her sense of unreality.

Victoria's head whipped around, tilting back so she could see him. "Excuse me?"

Shadows danced across his features, hiding his expression from view. "We're supposed to be talking. So tell me about your life since law school. Surely you've done more than protect your family and start a practice."

"Yes. I busted my tail for three years at a private firm that was a lot like my father's. I hated it. I couldn't wait to get out."

"And did you?"

"Did I what?"

"Get out."

"You know I did."

"I don't mean work. I mean men."

This time Victoria stopped dead in her tracks. "You're asking about my social life?"

"Keep walking. And, yes, I'm asking about your social life. I might as well know how many of the images I tortured myself with were real."

She ignored his command to keep walking. In fact, she scarcely heard it. Her mind was on overload, her breathing fast and unsteady, partly from angry disbelief and partly from the hazy state she'd been fighting when this absurd conversation began.

"I see." Her voice was as raw as her emotions. "And which did you want to hear about first—the lengthy, serious relationships or the short, hot affairs?"

A muscle worked violently in Zach's jaw. "Was that meant to be amusing? Because it wasn't."

"It was meant to be a brutal reminder that what I do, and who I do it with, is none of your business."

"Goddammit, don't you think I know that?" he muttered roughly. "Don't you think I tried to drum that into my head every damned day?"

It happened too fast to predict, much less to prevent.

One minute they were standing there, glaring at each other.

The next minute, they were in each other's arms.

Zach pulled Victoria close, braced her against him. His hand groped beneath her hair, tightened around the nape of her neck, and lifted her mouth to his.

Their breath mingled, their mouths came together, and the world came apart.

There was nothing tentative about the kiss. No tender brushing of lips, no slow, incremental explorations. It was hot, open-mouthed, frantic. They were locked together, their bodies straining to be closer, their joined lips separating only long enough to allow for short, harsh gasps of air before fusing again. Zach's coat toppled to the sidewalk, forgotten, a crumpled pile of wool at Victoria's feet.

Neither of them noticed.

Oblivious to passersby, to anything and everything but the wildness that was taking place between them, they sank into the moment, Zach's tongue taking Victoria's in deep, plunging strokes, one hand tangled in her hair, the other wrapped around her waist, crushing her against him. Victoria's fists knotted in his sweater, then slid up to encircle his neck, to hold him as tightly as he held her.

Neither of them knew how long they stood there.

Nor had they any idea how much longer they might have gone on doing so had two carloads of teenagers not driven by, honking repeatedly and shouting encouraging, if embarrassing, pointers out the windows.

They broke apart, staring incredulously at each other as they tried to catch their breath, to collect their thoughts and regain their equilibrium—in more ways than one.

"Victoria . . ." Zach began hoarsely.

"I dropped my purse." Victoria's voice sounded high and thin, and she stepped away from Zach, combing her fingers through her hair and searching the sidewalk.

The purse was nestled atop Zach's sport coat.

"And they say New York is unsafe," Victoria commented shakily, scooping up the purse and slinging the shoulder strap over her arm. "I just gave any thief the perfect opportunity to—"

"Victoria." Zach caught her elbow, forced her around to face him. "Stop it. Stop running."

Her insides felt hollow and, at the same time, racked with turmoil. She felt more like collapsing than anything else. "Actually, I think running might be a very good idea about now. I can't deal with this. I can't think about it, much less discuss it. These last few days have been . . ." She broke off, her hands trembling as she felt herself slip one notch closer to losing it. "I have to get out of here."

She took off.

Moving as fast as her high heels would allow, she literally ran the remaining distance to her building. She groped in her purse for her keys, yanking them out as she reached the town house. Instinct told her Zach was not far behind, whether to force her to talk to him or to ensure her safety, she wasn't certain.

Nor did she intend to find out.

She needed to be alone.

She was still shaking when she let herself into the apartment. Shutting and locking the door, she sagged back against it, her heart racing. She just stood there, staring into the darkness. She felt numb, void of any reaction other than shock.

So she was surprised when, minutes later, she tasted the warm, salty wetness of her own tears, and realized how hard she was crying.

This was like a goddamned soap opera, the man thought, watching his gorgeous target dash up the street and storm into her apartment. Whoever the guy was, he'd obviously tried something she wasn't ready for. What was it with women? What had she expected after a kiss like that? She'd done everything but drop bread crumbs marking the path to her bed. And now she was playing the injured virgin.

Well, at least she was playing. Until now, he'd begun to wonder if she *ever* cut loose. It was home to office, office to court, court to dinner, dinner to home. Her big night out was a visit to her aunt and uncle's place. Boring. And except for that one trip to the Institute, no threat whatsoever. He wondered why he was still watching her. But orders were orders. The whole disinfection team remained on alert. The target could become a real problem, the team leader had said. Well, he sure as hell didn't see it. But then, he wasn't the one making the decisions—or paying the bills. So he'd make sure she tucked herself in like a good girl and went to sleep. Oh, he wished he could join her, show her a few things to do in bed besides sleep. He'd be glad to distract her, take her mind off the Institute.

He glanced around, saw no sign of that tall guy she'd blown off, and lit his cigar. Puffing lightly, he eyed her bedroom window, waiting for the light to go on.

It didn't.

Now that was weird.

He was about to cross over and check things out, when he heard a quiet thud. Then another. Deliberately muted, but audible—at least to his trained ear.

Footsteps.

Going deadly still, he located their source. Shit. It was that tall guy again.

He ground out his cigar and vanished into the night.

Dammit.

Zach cursed silently as the glowing cigar ember disappeared. He'd been so close. But his shoes had made enough noise to alert Mr. Cigar and send him running.

He closed the distance anyway, searching the area. Victoria's description was accurate. Mr. Cigar was unobtrusive and nondescript. Average height, reedy, fluid of motion. He was also light on his feet and fast as hell, with sonarlike instincts to warn him.

Yeah, he'd done this kind of work before.

Frowning, Zach took out his pocketknife, pulled out the small blade, then squatted. He stabbed at the still-smoldering cigar stub, spearing it with the knifepoint. He looked it over without touching it. Doubtful there were any clear fingerprints. Still, he'd give it to Meyer, just in case. Maybe they'd get lucky. *If* the prints were readable, and *if* the guy had a record, maybe they could get a handle on him.

Zach angled his knife toward the nearby streetlight until he could make out the lettering on the paper band of the half-smoked cigar. No help there. A common Mexican brand—the kind thousands of people smoked. Trust this bastard not to make it easy.

Who the hell was he? Did he work for Victoria's father? And, if so, why was he still following her? Did Kensington doubt his daughter had believed his story about Audrey? Did he suspect Victoria had an ulterior motive for joining his firm? Or had he just not had enough time to call off his dogs?

And where was Victoria?

Zach had seen her dart into the building. But there was no light on—not anywhere in her apartment.

He knew she was reeling from that kiss they'd shared. So was he, for that matter. He also knew she needed time alone. But right now he didn't give a damn. Her safety came first.

He crossed the street and pressed the buzzer.

It took three long rings for her to respond.

"Yes?" Her voice choked.

"It's me. He was out here. Let me up."

Silence.

"Victoria, I'm coming up there. Either buzz me or I'll find another way in."

The buzzer sounded.

Zach took the steps two at a time.

Victoria opened her front door as he reached it. She looked pale but composed, her hazel eyes veiled, slightly damp. "I just looked out my bedroom window. I didn't see him."

"He was across the street. He took off when he saw me." Zach stepped inside, shutting the door behind him and holding up the speared cigar. "Do you have a plastic bag? One that seals?"

Victoria's gaze widened. "His?"

"Yup. I'm no expert, but there might be fingerprints. I'll take it to the FBI and have them check."

She nodded, went into the kitchen, and returned with a small, resealable plastic bag. "Here." She held it open until

Zach had shaken the stub free, let it drop into the bag. Then, she sealed the bag and handed it to him.

"I'll take it in first thing in the morning." He placed it carefully on her counter, then tossed his sport coat onto a chair.

Realizing he meant to stay, Victoria gave a hard shake of her head. "I'm not up for conversation, Zach. You saw me to my door, so to speak. I'm fine. You scared that man off, for which I'm grateful. Now, please, I need to read over my case and get some sleep."

"Go right ahead. I'll take the sofa."

"You'll take the . . ." Her jaw dropped as his meaning sank in. "You're not staying here."

"The hell I'm not." He took one step closer, but fought the urge to reach out and shake her. "This isn't about us, Victoria. This is about you. Your safety. Mr. Cigar's not here to shop for an apartment. He's stalking you. I thought after your talk with your father, this would end, but it hasn't. Why? Until I know the answer to that, you're not staying alone. So you have two choices: either pack a bag and move in with me at the Plaza Athénée, or throw me a pillow and go do your work."

She just stared at him for a moment. Then she exhaled with a sigh, rubbing the back of her neck and looking incredibly tired. "Fine. I don't have the energy to argue with you." She walked away, returning to toss him a pillow and a blanket. "It's almost eleven o'clock," she announced. "I'll be leaving at six A.M. for my meeting with Meg and Paul. So the lights, the coffeemaker, and the hair dryer will go on at five."

Zach acknowledged her pointed warning with an equally pointed statement of his own. "That works out well. My hotel is three blocks from your office. We'll get a cab and I'll drop you off. You're not walking." With that, he retreated to the living room and began making up the sofa.

Victoria didn't take that too well. She marched into the living room, her chin tipped up angrily as she faced him. "Don't push your luck," she advised him. "You're catching me with my reserves down. That doesn't mean I'm always so malleable. I won't have my life arranged for me. I won't be told what I can and cannot do. And I won't let you be my self-appointed knight in shining armor. That approach might work with your European women, but, if you recall, it doesn't work with me."

Zach went very still. He tossed down the bedding, inclined his head in question. "My European women?"

She caught her lower lip between her teeth, but she didn't flinch. "A random, if poor, choice of words—not an inquiry."

She'd become quite the master at hiding her emotions. But Zach wasn't buying it. Nor was he willing to let her off so easily. Painful or not, it was time for them to talk.

"I see," he replied, holding her gaze. "Then tell me, what happened between us a few minutes ago—would you also describe that as a 'random, if poor, choice'?"

She lowered her lashes, stared at the floor. "A *very* poor choice, yes. Random? No." For a long moment she said nothing. Then she raised her head, and Zach could see her struggling for composure. "I don't know what happened out there. Memories. Attraction. Both. I'm not sure. I'm not sure of much since last Saturday. My whole world is out of whack. But one thing I *am* sure of. I can't have an affair with you. And not only because of what I'm going through with Audrey. I just can't."

There were a hundred things Zach wanted to say. There was one thing in particular he wanted to do. But she was at the end of her rope. He wouldn't push her further. At least not tonight.

"Let's call it a night," he said lightly, returning to his bed making. "You have work to do and you're falling off your feet. I tell you what. I'll put up the five A.M. coffee. I'm closer to the kitchen than you are. And I drink twice as much coffee as you."

A tired, strained smile. "Thanks." She ran her fingers through that beautiful, glossy black hair. "Good night, Zach." A brief hesitation. "I really am grateful for your concern and your help. I just don't think we should misconstrue what's happening here."

Zach's gaze was steady. "We're not."

15

Thursday, April 20
6:02 A.M.

Like every meeting at the Hope Institute, this one was cloaked under the protective veil of attorney-client privilege.

The last member of the disinfection team hurried toward Conference Room A. He had an important tidbit to report today. A tall guy had been hitting on Victoria Kensington. The guy's appearance was a mixed bag. Hopefully, it would keep her occupied with something other than the Institute. On the other hand, it would be a helluva lot harder to tail her with her new boyfriend showing up at odd hours, hoping to get laid.

Well, he'd leave the decision on how to handle things to the powers that be.

He edged into the room, nodded at the rest of the group, and shut the door behind him.

"You're late," the team leader pronounced. "And put out that cigar. I'm not going to remind you again. This is a hospital."

6:30 A.M.

Victoria had assumed she'd be the first one in.

She was the last.

As she approached the door of London, Kensington & Stone, she could see a shaft of light shining from beneath it.

And, when she inserted her key, it was to find that the door was already unlocked.

Obviously, Meg and Paul had gotten her message. And just as obviously, they were worried—worried enough to get here before dawn.

Sighing, she stepped inside the office, massaging her aching temples. She wished she hadn't opted to skip her morning run. The adrenaline rush might have done her some good. But she'd never have gotten by Zach to take her jog alone, so the whole idea was out.

How she was going to pull off this day was anyone's guess. First the meeting here, then the one at her father's office, followed by a court appearance—and then Zach.

All when she was running on empty.

True, she didn't need much sleep, but last night she'd gotten none. She'd been too wired from dinner, from being followed home by Mr. Cigar, and from whatever temporary insanity had occurred between her and Zach. Then, to top it all off, he'd spent the night in her apartment, sleeping on her sofa.

Just knowing he was out there had made falling asleep an utter impossibility. Victoria had gotten up at four and was showered and dressed by the time five o'clock rolled around. Still, she hadn't beaten him to the kitchen. True to his word, he'd brewed a pot of coffee and was sipping a cup when she walked in.

They'd hardly spoken. He'd looked worn out and rumpled, as if sleep hadn't come easily for him either. And the shadow of a beard on his face had brought too many memories tumbling back to her—memories of other, more intimate mornings spent together.

They'd left the apartment by six.

Zach had hailed a cab, escorted her to work, and made arrangements to meet her at the end of the work day for a drink. He wanted to hear about any information she'd picked up at her father's office, and discuss a convenient time to show up at her apartment.

To sleep on her sofa again.

Boy, was she going to need that drink. This time, she might just polish off the whole bottle.

"Victoria, is that you?" It was Meg's voice, coming from inside the conference room.

"Yes," she called back. "It's me. Is Paul with you?"

"Yeah, I'm right here." Paul stepped into the outer office, frowning as he studied Victoria. "Are you okay?"

"Fine." Victoria locked the front door behind her. Not that she was expecting anyone at six-thirty in the morning. Still, this conversation was going to remain private, even from the maintenance staff.

She made her way through the narrow outer office to where Paul was standing in the doorway of the room that doubled as their library and conference room.

"Come in and talk." He gestured for her to precede him.

Victoria walked inside the spacious conference room, pacing about because she was too antsy to sit down.

The room's decor was simple and sparse—plain tweed carpet, a long oak table, eight matching chairs, and floor-to-ceiling bookcases. The only personal touch was a window-box of plants that Meg had added after weeks of grumbling that a conference room wasn't supposed to scare off clients by looking more sterile than an operating room. And while Meg's plants weren't nearly as magnificent as Clarissa's, Victoria had to admit that they did add some life to the place.

Her friend was nervously misting the plants right now. But she turned when Victoria walked in, her features tight with concern. "What's going on, Victoria? Why did you want us here so early and why couldn't I call you back about it last night?"

"Because I wasn't home until late. And because I wanted to talk to the two of you together."

"Well, we're together now," Paul announced without prelude. He shut the door, folded his arms across his chest, and waited only for Meg to put down the spray bottle before he addressed Victoria. "Now talk. Is this business or personal?"

"Both." Victoria stopped pacing and perched behind one of the chairs. "Paul, I'll bring you up to date with what Meg knows. Then I'll fill you both in on the rest."

She did just that, not stopping until after she described how hard she'd worked to find the Hope Institute, and what her suspicions had been after leaving.

Paul let out a low whistle. "Your father would go to those lengths to keep Audrey's whereabouts a secret?"

For a long moment, Victoria didn't answer. Then she spoke quietly and without emotion. "Under the right circumstances, yes. And these were the right circumstances."

"That sounds ominous. Victoria, what is it you think Audrey's suffering from?"

She'd expected the question. And she knew how to answer it. Candidly. Ensuring both Audrey's safety and the classified status of Zach's investigation took precedence over personal secrets.

This portion of the truth had to be told. Besides, these weren't strangers; they were Meg and Paul. Audrey would understand.

Victoria wet her lips with the tip of her tongue. "I've never spoken about this before. I'd appreciate your keeping it in confidence."

"Of course."

"You have our word," Meg assured her.

Another weighted pause. "Audrey has bulimia," Victoria admitted at last. "She'd had it since her teens. I'm sure you can guess who drove her to it. You've met my father. Anything that deviates from his idea of perfection is unacceptable. Audrey fell short. Not that she didn't try. She wanted to please him so much it made my insides churn. She never managed to do so. Finally, she gave up."

"Is that when she decided to travel abroad?" Meg asked gently.

"Um-hum. Her decision suited my father just fine. With Audrey gone, so was the risk of embarrassment if anyone found out about her illness. For him it was out of sight, out of mind. But not out of his control. Oh, no. He still wanted that. He arranged it so that Audrey was dependent on him financially and emotionally—no matter how coldly he treated her."

Paul looked thoughtful. "So you're saying that if she became ill enough to be hospitalized, it would be your father she'd call."

A sad nod. "He convinced her that he and he alone could control whatever happened in life. So, yes, she'd call him. She'd probably beg for his help. And he? He'd be horrified at the potential scandal. He'd do exactly what I feared if it meant keeping things quiet."

"Is this pure speculation? Because, from the way you're talking, it sounds like you know it for a fact."

"My father admitted it to me yesterday. Audrey left me a message the previous night on my answering machine. She tried to put my mind at ease by assuring me she was fine. She didn't sound fine. She sounded really out of it. So while I was relieved to hear from her, I didn't feel a whole lot better than I had before. Anyway, she said something about calling me because my father had told her I was worried."

"Which means he'd spoken with her."

"Spoken with her *and* seen her," Victoria corrected.

"He told you that?"

"When I confronted him, yes. He couldn't very well deny it. Although he did deny that Audrey was in any danger whatsoever. He said the Hope Institute was the best private medical clinic in Manhattan and that, thanks to their superior care, Audrey was improving every day. But they have strict confidentiality requirements. No one but my father is even supposed to know Audrey's there, much less try to see her. She's allowed no visitors, no phone calls, no outside contact except for him. I'm not even permitted to consult with her doctor. Institute policy."

Victoria paused. She'd laid the groundwork, explained the unusually severe policies of the Hope Institute. Now she had to drive home the extent of her anxiety over Audrey's well-being. After that, she'd lead into her commitment to their law firm. She had to create a believable enough scenario so that Meg and Paul didn't question why she'd feel compelled to take the drastic step she was about to take—one she'd never mentioned contemplating. They couldn't suspect anything dire. No criminal activities, no FBI investigation, no drug ring.

She *had* to pull this off—for everyone's sake.

Here goes, she braced herself silently.

"In my opinion, their rigid privacy policies are too extreme. They make me feel totally cut off, helpless, and filled with unanswered questions. Is Audrey sicker than my father realizes? Are the doctors at the Hope Institute as reputable as he believes? Is there some logical reason why I can't get special permission to see her?"

Victoria's voice choked and, with a sick sense of irony, she acknowledged to herself that the fears she was verbalizing were real.

"The bottom line is, I'm still worried sick," she concluded, recovering her composure. "In some ways, more so. My imagination is working overtime. I've got to get inside the Hope Institute and see for myself that Audrey is okay. I'm her sister. She needs me. My father might be able to remain unemotional about this, but I can't. Nor can I make him understand my position. So I'm going to keep my mouth shut and bypass him—just as I did to begin with." A swift glance at Meg. "Remember, I got the initial information about Audrey from my father's phone bills. I'll find whatever else I need the same way."

Meg's brows drew together in puzzlement. "You're going back to search your father's study?"

"No. I'm going to search his office. That's where I'll find out more about the Hope Institute and Audrey's admittance records. The office is where my father keeps his personal correspondence and documents." A hint of a smile. "Which brings me to an interesting twist. The way I manipulated things, I'll be spending a fair amount of time at Waters, Kensington, Tatem and Calder. In addition to getting access to information on Audrey, I'll be helping boost our firm's income."

"You lost me."

"Yeah, me, too," Paul concurred.

Very deliberately, Victoria met their gazes, intent on showing them how sincere she was—at least with regard to what she was saying. Guilt by omission rather than commission, she thought ruefully. "My father has his agenda, I have mine. I used his to accomplish mine. After he closed the subject of Audrey, I made a decision to carry out a plan I've been toying with for a while now. The timing was perfect. I simply took advantage of it."

"What timing?" Paul demanded. "What plan?"

"I bit the bullet and asked my father if Waters, Kensington, Tatem and Calder would refer corporate clients to you," she informed Paul. "He agreed—conditionally. In return for his cooperation, he said he'd expect me to serve as counsel to his firm. Two days a week, for three months. I accepted his offer. It's the perfect solution—one that gives me exactly the opportunity I need, to help our practice and Audrey."

"You accepted?" Meg asked incredulously. Victoria had always been adamant about not working with her father—in any capacity.

"Yes. It wouldn't have been my choice, had circumstances been different. But they're not. Audrey's being kept in that clinic, and London, Kensington and Stone needs a jump start. Speaking of which, my father and I worked out a retainer, just as I would with any new client. I negotiated a lot of money for us—forty percent of whatever I bill out for Waters, Kensington, Tatem and Calder plus whatever income is generated by the clients they steer our way. It's a win-win situation. Still, given the amount of time I'm committing and who I'm committing it to, I wanted to let you know right away." Victoria fell silent, gazed expectantly from one of her partners to the other, and held her breath as she awaited their reaction.

"Wow." Meg reacted first, sifting her fingers through her hair as she spoke. "This is quite a crusade you're taking on. I understand why you're doing it, but are you sure it's the right way to go about things? You'll have the pressure of ransacking your father's files without getting caught *and* the pressure of having him in your face, doing everything in his power to coerce you into staying on as a junior partner. Three months is a long time, Victoria."

"I realize that. So does my father. He's counting on that time working in his favor. But I know otherwise. And so should you. I'd never walk away from London, Kensington and Stone. I need you to believe that."

"We do," Paul said at once.

"Of course we do." Meg let out a slow breath. "This isn't about doubting you. I'm worried about you."

"Don't be. I've handled my father for twenty-eight years. I can handle him now." Victoria laced her fingers tightly together, summing up the situation in a few terse phrases. "My loyalties lie here. They always will. But I've got to find a way in to Audrey. I'm getting nowhere fast. I need your help. And your trust."

"You've got both." Paul adjusted his glasses on the bridge of his nose, his mind clearly racing. "Your father actually agreed to refer clients to me?"

"Yes. I'll get the process rolling next week."

"Is that when you're starting?" Meg asked.

Victoria glanced at her watch. "Officially, yes. But

I'm due over there at seven-thirty for a breakfast meeting. That's the other reason I was so adamant about wanting to talk with you guys now. I wanted to explain the situation to you before I walked through my father's doors to be paraded around like his prized thoroughbred." She sighed. "I'm not naive, Meg. What you said is true. My father sees this as his golden opportunity to mesmerize me with his world, to persuade me to stay. But *I* see this as a chance to get a handle on the Hope Institute, check for myself that Audrey is okay, and boost Paul's reputation and our firm's income. I'll do my snooping as expediently as I can. The sooner I get to Audrey, the better. As for my business association with Waters, Kensington, Tatem and Calder, in three months it will be over, no harm done." A rueful smile. "Who knows? After that, maybe my father will finally accept who I am and leave me alone."

"I wouldn't hold my breath," Meg muttered.

"Nor would I," Paul agreed. "But I've got to tell you, this opportunity is great. Finally, a chance to sink my teeth into some high-profile clients. This could make all the difference in the world." He shot Victoria a grateful look. "Thanks for thinking of me. You won't be sorry."

Meg's head jerked around, her startled gaze finding Paul. "You sound as if this course of action has occurred to you."

"It has." Paul dropped into a chair, draped an arm across its back, and looked Meg straight in the eye. "I'm not going to lie to you. I was getting nervous—really nervous. I don't need lots of money, but I need to eat. And, yes, I thought of asking Victoria to talk to her father. I held off, hoping business would pick up on its own. But it hasn't—not at my end. That doesn't mean I'm happy about what's going on with Victoria; I'm as worried about her sister as you are."

He angled his head toward Victoria. "I hope it doesn't

sound like I'm capitalizing on your sister's predicament. I'm not. I'm just relieved at the thought of some potential clients and income."

"I understand," Victoria responded. "And it never occurred to me. If you were so eager to cash in on my connections, you would have asked me to talk to my father a long time ago."

"I know how you feel about him," Paul acknowledged. "So I'll handle this magnanimous gesture of his with the utmost respect." A self-conscious clearing of the throat. "I'll call him today, and I'll set up a thank-you lunch—at his convenience."

"Great," Meg murmured in disgust. "Just what the man needs. To realize how indebted Victoria's partners are."

Paul scowled. "I'm not brownnosing; I'm just doing what's right. What's your problem with this, Meg? Kensington is just sending clients through our door. It's up to me to make them stay. And you know I've got the skill and the drive to do that."

"Stop, please." Victoria waved away the budding argument. She wasn't up for any more friction right now, no matter how benign. Besides, she knew both her friends. Meg thought with her heart, Paul with his head. But that didn't matter. When it came right down to it, they'd both be there for her in a heartbeat.

"I understand where you're both coming from," she declared, "and I appreciate each of your perspectives. Paul, do whatever you're comfortable with. But don't worry about sufficiently thanking my father. You're an amazing lawyer. When he hears his clients raving about your abilities, it's *he* who will be thanking *you*. Meg's only worried that you'll be feeding his ego and giving him more ammunition to sway my loyalties in his direction. You know—be part of the winning team? The truth is, nothing will alter his game plan. He already believes he's in the power seat. He always does."

"Yeah, I know." Paul gave Meg an apologetic grin. "Sorry, pal. I didn't mean to jump down your throat."

"No problem. I overreacted. Besides, I don't need to worry about your laying it on too thick. Humility's not in your nature." Meg's teasing retort was affectionate. But she still looked preoccupied, as if there was something bugging her.

Victoria soon found out what it was. And it had nothing to do with their firm's arrangement with Waters, Kensington, Tatem & Calder.

"You look exhausted," Meg stated bluntly. "You obviously didn't get a wink of sleep. And you weren't reachable last night. Why? Were you with your father, ironing out the details?"

"No. I wasn't with my father."

"I didn't think so. Need I ask who you *were* with?"

Trust Meg's dead-on emotional sonar.

"Obviously not." Victoria saw no point in lying. It was clear from the knowing glint in Meg's eyes that she'd already guessed—or at least she thought she'd guessed last night's scenario. Oh, she was right about whom Victoria had spent the night with, but wrong about what they'd done, why they were together. The worst part was, Victoria couldn't set her straight. "I was with Zach." She braced herself for the inevitable inquisition.

It never came.

Paul's surprised "Zach?" was cut off by Meg's purposeful shake of the head. He took her cue and fell silent.

"I'm glad," Meg told Victoria simply. "You two have some unresolved issues to clear up."

Meg was more right than she realized, Victoria mused, her insides tightening. They did have many unresolved issues. But the most dire of those issues weren't the intimate ones Meg was alluding to.

"Apparently we do." Victoria glanced at her watch, then stepped away from the chair. "I've got to run. Park Avenue awaits. Then it's on to court. And after that . . ." A slight pause. "If I don't get back here tonight, I'll fill you in tomorrow. Okay?"

"Why wouldn't you get back here—?" Paul took one look at Meg's disapproving expression and thought better of his question. "Fine. Good luck."

"Yeah, thanks," Victoria said dryly, smoothing the blazer of her tailored, toast-colored suit. "I'll need it."

16

Zach was right.

Some things never change.

Clearly, the offices of Waters, Kensington, Tatem & Calder fell into that category.

Victoria inched her way through the exquisite, endless walnut-paneled conference room alongside her father, thinking that—with the exception of state-of-the-art computers and a small number of new, young attorneys and newer, younger secretaries—the offices looked and felt much the same as they had when she was girl. Even the smells were the same: rich leather, expensive cologne, a hint of pipe tobacco, and fresh-brewed coffee.

Actually, today it was more than just coffee. It was a six-foot table filled with fresh-baked croissants and pastries, four kinds of juice, and three silver urns—two filled with coffee, regular and decaf, and a third with hot water for tea.

The room itself was packed, everyone of consequence having been informed that this was a command performance. Everyone of consequence included the some forty-plus attorneys who defined the ranks of Waters, Kensington, Tatem & Calder from new associate to senior partner, the paralegal and executive secretarial staff, and a few hourly employees. The latter, Victoria noted with disgust, were there only as waitresses—to serve breakfast to the senior partners and ensure everything ran smoothly. Not that there was any question things would run smoothly—not with Miss Hatterman patrolling the room and overseeing the breakfast buffet like an imperious maître d'.

No, nothing here had changed.

Except that now she was no longer just Walter Kensington's bright young daughter. Now she was a potential acquisition.

This was going to be quite an experience.

Moving from person to person, shaking hand after hand, Victoria felt like a bride on a receiving line.

A very reserved, very judgmental receiving line.

The senior partners were older, their faces craggier than they'd been the last time she had seen them, six or seven years ago.

Joseph Waters was a mere figurehead now, nearing eighty and semiretired, coming in when he chose to, usually to attend a grand-scale client meeting or a major convening of the partnership. Alfred Tatem was about her father's age, with a tight-lipped smile and cold blue eyes that delved with an icy intensity that was unnerving. Then again, that unnerving trait would be an asset in the courtroom. And since Mr. Tatem handled high-level corporate litigation as well as antitrust matters, the courtroom was his second home. So his intimidating veneer was as welcome to the firm as her father's.

Gregory Calder, who was in his mid-fifties, was bald and stocky, and daring enough to actually allow his teeth to show through his lips when he smiled—a rarity here indeed. Mr. Calder worked primarily with the newer Fortune 100 accounts he'd brought into the firm. To that end, he had a large number of the junior partners working under him, putting in eighteen-hour days to earn their next promotion.

There were four more senior partners—three of whom were in the image of the others.

Then there was Elizabeth Bonner.

Ms. Bonner had been with the firm for twenty years, the first female attorney to grace the halls of Waters, Kensington, Tatem & Calder. She was also the first and only woman in the practice who'd risen to the ranks of senior partner. Rumor had it that those factors, combined with the enormous amount of business she brought in, prompted her reputedly ongoing battle to have the firm name changed to Waters, Kensington, Tatem, Calder & Bonner.

So far, the battle was still raging.

In her early fifties, Ms. Bonner looked ten years younger. Slender and petite, subtly but expensively made up, she was impeccably dressed and poised, with short, elegantly styled auburn hair, steel-gray eyes, and a hard, no-nonsense demeanor that kept even Miss Hatterman in line. She was a crackerjack attorney whose versatility enabled her to handle everything from mergers and acquisitions to a select number of highly visible, extraordinarily lucrative matrimonial cases—all with the same level of brilliance and expertise.

Victoria didn't particularly like the woman, who possessed all the compassion of a power-hungry dictator, but she did hold a deep respect for her. She admired her keen legal mind, her versatility, and her sheer grit and determination. After all, fighting for recognition in a chauvinistic firm like this one—well, Victoria certainly didn't envy her.

Ms. Bonner shook Victoria's hand, assessing her thoroughly, not put off in the least by Walter Kensington's formidable presence at his daughter's side.

"Hello, Ms. Kensington. It's been quite some time," she said in a wintry tone.

"Yes, it has. Years, in fact. It's a pleasure to see you again, Ms. Bonner." Victoria grasped the older woman's fingers in a firm handshake, meeting her bold gaze with equally direct intensity.

"Let's see—Columbia Law, class of ninety-seven, graduated with honors and at the top of your class. Three years at Howell, Baker and Graves, primarily in the areas of matrimonial and corporate litigation. And now your own firm. Very impressive. I hear you'll be coming to work for us."

Victoria gave her a perfunctory smile. "I'll be *with* your firm two days a week for several months," she replied, wondering if Ms. Bonner had also memorized her college transcript. "I'm looking forward to it."

The use of "with" instead of "for" wasn't lost on Ms. Bonner.

Her reaction, however, was not what Victoria expected.

"I'm in the midst of outlining a summons and complaint in a very complex matrimonial case," she proclaimed, and Victoria could swear she saw a tiny glint of approval in those frosty eyes. "The CEO of a Fortune 50 company is being sued by his wife of forty years. I'd be interested in your input. Stop by my secretary's desk when you come in next week. She'll have a copy of the case for you to look over."

Victoria inclined her head. "Which of the parties do we represent?"

It wasn't her imagination. That glint was definitely there.

"His wife. She's run the house, the staff and, in my opinion, the more political aspects of her husband's career since the day they married. Not to mention raising four children and heading up several charitable organizations, all of which bettered her husband's standing in the corporation and the community. He's returned her devotion with a string of mistresses and the misuse of their joint bank accounts. His wife's had enough. She thinks she's entitled to more. I intend to get it for her—and then some. Given your propensity for such cases, I trust that's appealing?"

Maybe this woman wasn't so bad after all. "I'll see your secretary the first day I'm in," Victoria promised.

"Do that." Ms. Bonner nodded, then turned to accept a cup a coffee from one of the secretaries.

Victoria's father used the opportunity to steer her away, leading her deeper into the room. "You're doing well," he pronounced, the statement as close to praise as Walter Kensington ever offered. "There are a number of people I'd like you to meet before you leave for court."

"Of course." Victoria accepted the glass of orange juice she was offered by a young girl, smiling her thanks and knowing full well her father wouldn't think to introduce them. Secretaries and receptionists were invisible, as far as he was concerned.

He wasn't much better with the junior partners, particularly the female ones. A terse nod, a brief introduction, and it was on to the next person. Victoria had to keep herself from wincing at his openly condescending attitude toward women and subordinates. It reminded her of the way he treated Audrey.

Thinking of Audrey, Victoria's glance shifted in the direction of her father's office. No use in even considering trying to get down there this morning. It was at the other end of the floor entirely, with dozens of people blocking her path. It would have to wait until next week.

"Good morning, Mr. Kensington. At last—a chance to meet the daughter you speak so highly of."

Victoria's attention snapped back to the introductions at hand, and she turned, raising her chin to meet the approving gaze of a good-looking, dark-haired man in his mid-thirties. His features were lean and chiseled, his skin tanned, whether from a sunlamp or a week on the beach, Victoria wasn't sure. He was tall and broad-shouldered, his custom suit three times more expensive than the best off-the-rack designer suit. But his smile was genuine and welcoming, and his keen blue eyes inspected her with interest and a within-bounds hint of admiration.

"Ian. Good. I'm glad you're here," Walter Kensington greeted him, his approval obvious. "Victoria, I'd like you to meet Ian Block. He's been with us twelve years now, since he graduated from Harvard Law. He's one of our most promising junior partners."

Of course, Victoria thought dryly. *Harvard Law. Two points for Ian Block.*

"A pleasure, Mr. Block." She extended her hand.

"The pleasure is mine, Ms. Kensington." He shook her hand, his grip professional but friendly. "I've heard a great deal about you. I'm pleased you'll be working with us."

"As am I." Victoria smiled politely. Pausing, she took a sip of juice, ostensibly because she was thirsty, actually because she wanted a few seconds to size up Ian Block.

Magnetic, bright, sure of himself. A savvy politician *and* a Harvard grad.

He was a shoo-in for senior partner.

"Ian works closely with five of the eight senior partners," Walter confirmed her assessment by explaining. "Including myself. He's a fine corporate attorney, well on his way to a lucrative future."

Ah. Make that senior partner before he's forty, Victoria determined silently.

"You'll be working closely with Ian at the beginning—until you're up to date on the various corporate clients we're representing. He'll explain the assorted mergers and acquisitions we're negotiating, the litigations that are pending, et cetera." A meaningful pause. "He'll also decide which of our less time-consuming clients he can refer out to Paul London."

A clear message to be cooperative.

"That's fine." Victoria inclined her head, giving Ian Block a questioning look. "I'll be sure to see you when I get in next week. Which office is yours?"

"Halfway down on your left." He pointed. "My secretary, Miss Whiting, will buzz me as soon as you arrive. Which will be when, by the way?"

"I have to discuss those details with my father. I'm sure he'll advise you of my schedule."

"Miss Hatterman will be sending out a memo later today," her father assured Ian.

"Excellent." Ian's smile was like something out of a magazine. "Then, please, don't let me keep you. Your father mentioned you're due in court at nine."

"Yes, I am. I'll see you next week, then."

Victoria walked away, thinking there was something about Ian Block that bore further reflection: not his motives—those were glaringly obvious—but his subtle but perceptible attentions toward her.

She wasn't naive enough to believe he was taken with her, nor was she stupid enough to come on to her—at least not overtly. It had to be one of two things. Either he'd decided to earn extra brownie points with Walter Kensington by charming his daughter—a plan that was doomed to failure, since she wasn't susceptible to his charms and her father never gave a thought to her social life. Or, he was worried that she was his prime competitor, vying neck-and-neck for the next senior partner opening. If that was the case, he was sizing her up, deciding whether to disarm her or sabotage her.

Either way, he'd want to keep an eye on her, see what she hoped to gain out of this three-month affiliation with her father's firm.

His precious partnership was safe. She didn't want it. But his scrutiny—now that might present a problem, if it meant keeping close tabs on her whereabouts. She had no intention of letting Ian Block interfere with her search for information on Audrey and the Hope Institute.

Victoria went on to meet five or six more junior partners. Those introductions, like the one to Ian, were lengthy and eloquent, which meant that every one of those partners—all men, of course—were her father's personal favorites, destined for stellar careers. Each of them was cordial in a wary and patronizing way—wary because of the threat she represented, patronizing because of her gender.

Working here was going to be an exercise in self-control. If she didn't bite her tongue several times a day, she'd end up getting tossed out on her ear.

Shaking Ian Block loose and assisting Elizabeth Bonner with that matrimonial case were beginning to look like the highlights of her association with Waters, Kensington, Tatem & Calder.

Other than the information she was determined to uncover.

A half hour later, her father escorted her to the elevator, giving her a nod of approval as he dismissed her. "That went very smoothly. I'm pleased." He flourished an envelope, then pressed it into her hand.

"What's this?" Victoria's brows drew together as she tore open the seal and extracted what appeared to be a calligraphically addressed invitation.

"Your mother and I are hosting a dinner party Saturday night in honor of your affiliation with my firm. At the house. Nothing too elaborate. The partners and their wives will be there, as will our more prominent clients and their spouses."

Already? Miss Hatterman must have been penning her fingers to the bone till dawn.

"Father, Saturday night is two days away, and I—"

"Oh, and Jim and Clarissa will be there, as well. I spoke with Jim late last night. He was delighted with the news. He assured me he and Clarissa wouldn't miss the occasion."

Bribery, Victoria reflected, unsurprised by the maneuver. It was typical of her father. He knew damned well she wouldn't say no once she heard her uncle and aunt were coming. She'd realize they accepted the invitation specifically to offer her the moral support she needed.

She was half tempted to checkmate him.

Until the full extent of what he was unintentionally offering her sank in.

The firm's most prominent clients.

That included Benjamin Hopewell.

"Victoria? You're not going to disappoint me, are you? Your mother sat up half the night planning the menu."

Another twist of the knife used to persuade her. Her mother's emotional well-being.

"It's just that I have plans," she murmured, steering this head-to-head exactly where she intended it to go, at the same time supplying the specific information Zach had suggested—information she'd meant to supply earlier, but hadn't had the chance. Not that her father had noticed her fatigue enough to mention it, anyway. "An old friend of mine is in town. He and I are having dinner."

"He?" Her father's eyes narrowed. "Do I know him?"

Is he suitable? Victoria silently interpreted.

"Yes," she said aloud. "You've met him, although I'm not sure you'll remember. It was several years ago. Zachary Hamilton."

Damn, she wished her father wasn't such a master at maintaining his poker face. What was he thinking? How was he reacting to her mention of Zach's name? Was he aware of Zach's FBI affiliation?

"I remember Hamilton," was the undecipherable reply. "In fact, I believe we have some mutual clients. He's been in Europe these past years, as I recall."

"He's in New York to speak at a conference."

"Bring him with you."

Victoria chewed her lip, pretending to weigh her options. "I'm not sure—"

"The two of you can be alone another evening. Besides, whether it means renewing old business relationships or developing new ones, Hamilton will benefit nicely from face-to-face interactions with a roomful of CEOs."

"I don't doubt it."

Her father took that to mean consent. "I'll send a car to pick you up."

"We'll arrange our own transportation, Father."

"Very well," he said, magnanimous now that he'd gotten what he wanted. "I'll see you at eight."

9:03 A.M.

The maintenance attendant wheeled the cart to the door marked Private—his portal to the subterranean world in the Hope Institute's basement.

Unlocking the door, he flipped on the light switch, revealing a sizable room devoid of furnishings except for a clothing rack and an imposing stainless-steel chamber lined with dials and switches that occupied half the room.

He pulled the cart inside and shut the door behind him. The automatic lock clicked shut, guaranteeing no interruptions.

He walked over to the clothing rack and removed the items he needed, donning an aluminized apron, protective gloves, and a face shield. He returned to the cart, glancing at the words imprinted on the long cardboard box it contained: Fragile. Handle with Care. This End Up. A brilliant, if ironic, choice of words. But they did the trick, concealing the nature of the box's contents from curious staff members.

He wheeled the cart over to the stainless-steel chamber and threw the switch labeled Open. The chamber complied, its solid door gliding upward. He turned, slid his massive hands beneath the box, and pushed it effortlessly onto a cardboard roller and toward the intense heat that beckoned. The box moved respectfully into the chamber. He watched as it was swallowed up. Flicking the switch, he waited until the door had lowered silently. The Ready indicator glowed green. Satisfied, he pressed Start.

The machine roared to life.

Efficiently, it began its prescribed task.

17

5:34 P.M.

Zach propped his elbow on the bar counter, nursing his drink and glancing over his notes as he waited for Victoria to arrive.

Nothing new here. Same sketchy data the FBI had managed to put together after a fair amount of digging.

Basic stats. The Hope Institute: Opened its doors in the fall of 1991 as a private medical clinic. Part of Hopewell Industries. Sold in August 1997 to a Swiss holding company. Capacity to treat up to thirty patients. Employees: fourteen full-time nurses, eleven part-time nurses, and six technicians. Affiliated physicians: ten highly acclaimed medical specialists in the fields of oncology, neurology, psychiatry, and radiology—all with impeccable records. Groundbreaking treatments offered: advanced cancers, Alzheimer's disease, severe neurological and psychological disorders. Clientele: extraordinarily rich, renowned, privacy-conscious.

Well, their patients' privacy was certainly ensured. The Hope Institute was so low-profile it was practically invisible.

By the same token, invisibility would make it easy to transport drugs without being discovered.

So far, the electronic surveillance hadn't turned up anything suspicious.

Nor, for that matter, had Zach.

Today had been another seemingly uneventful day of fact-gathering outside the Institute. Same thin stream of employees coming and going at their usual times. One new patient arrived by limo and was admitted through the underground garage. One truck rumbled up to the building with a fuel oil delivery. Three more vehicles: two vans—one delivering linen, the other food—and a Hopewell Industries truck that unloaded several large pieces of medical equipment.

Nothing unusual for a hospital facility.

That didn't mean a thing. He'd only been compiling data for a week. And his instincts told him there were discrepancies just waiting to be found. All he needed was a little more time, a more comprehensive analysis, and one small inconsistency. After that, he'd be all over those bastards. He'd close in on them in a heartbeat. The FBI would have their syndicate and he'd have his retribution.

Zach scowled and rubbed the back of his neck. His muscles were so tight, they throbbed.

Not a surprise. He'd been on edge all day.

It wasn't hard to figure out why.

Talk about everything hitting at once. This particular investigation. Victoria landing smack in the middle of it. Seeing her again. Being unable to keep his hands off her. Mr. Cigar and how he factored into things. Walter Kensington and how *he* factored into things. How much danger Audrey might be in. How much danger extended to Victoria.

Shit.

Zach flexed his shoulders, trying to work out some of the strain, and the effects of a sleepless night.

All the raw, unresolved issues in his life were converging together and snowballing at once, and the resulting emotions were debilitating.

So while Victoria might feel she was off balance, so was he.

The hours he'd spent on that damned sofa had been hell.

Sleeping in her apartment, knowing how close she was, had driven him nearly insane. And not only because he wanted her to the point of obsession, but because he needed her, needed to reach out to her at a time when he felt so damned vulnerable.

The vulnerability had been with him all week, since he'd arrived in New York and reviewed the details of the investigation. It dredged up the worst memories of his life—memories he'd shared with no one but Victoria.

He wasn't a man who opened up easily. And with a loss as profound as this one, he didn't open up at all. But with Victoria, it had been a natural step, partly because of the way he felt about her and partly because of the circumstances.

She'd been in his hotel suite that first night the FBI called to request his help. Those amazing hazel eyes of hers had been filled with questions, but she hadn't asked them. At least not when he hung up. But a few hours later, when he'd jolted from sleep in a drenched sweat, shouting out his father's name, that's when the questions had come.

So had the answers.

She'd listened. She hadn't said a word. But she'd eased his pain simply by being there.

The truth was, he needed her to be there now.

Zach's scowl deepened. Last night had been rough, worse than he'd expected. He'd slept only in snatches. And those snatches had been plagued by the nightmares.

It had been some time since they'd resurfaced. When they first started, fifteen years ago, they'd been relentless, hammering at his brain night after night. Then time had done its job, and the frequency and severity eased, provoked only on those occasions when the government sought his help and the case struck too close to home.

Still, it had taken years for the painful void to begin healing. And the bitterness, the sense of flagrant injustice were still fiercely alive.

His father had been a longshoreman, the most honest, decent human being Zach had ever known. He'd been so proud of his son's sharp mind, his bright future. Zach was a junior at MIT—a year away from his degree in electrical engineering, geared up for graduate school in law and business. Nothing was going to stop Dave Hamilton from making sure his son had every advantage he'd missed out on.

The overtime had helped pay whatever Zach's scholarships and part-time jobs didn't cover. That's why his father had been at the docks that night. Just an innocent, hardworking man in the wrong place at the wrong time. A man who'd inadvertently walked onto the scene of a DEA stakeout, who'd gotten in the way of some filthy drug runner's bullet.

The government had personally delivered the news—along with its deep regrets—to Zach and his mother.

Their regrets hadn't helped. Neither had the token sum of money the union had provided.

Rose Hamilton, a frail woman by nature, had never been the same after her husband's murder. She'd lasted a year. Then she died quietly in her sleep, with the same dignity she'd displayed in life.

Zach had gone on to do exactly what his father would have wanted: he'd finished his education, started his own business, used his mind and resources to their fullest. That gave him a small semblance of peace—knowing that, somewhere up above, his father was proud.

Still, peace in itself wasn't enough. Zach needed a chance to *do* something, to actively stop scum like the one who'd killed his father and keep them from harming anyone else.

That chance had come four years ago.

It wasn't his personal history that brought the FBI to him. It was his expertise in competitive intelligence. But it was his personal history that made him agree to do their bidding.

That first case—involving a syndicate trafficking in

drugs and illegal weapons—had borne a strong resemblance to the one that had taken his father's life. But this case was the one he'd burned for. This case involved the same organization the feds had been busting their tails for over a decade to expose—the one that resulted in the stakeout that night at the docks. The syndicate had escaped detection by vanishing in its current form only to morph itself and reappear elsewhere in a slightly different form, like a dormant and mutating virus. A virus he meant to wipe out.

Talk about the ultimate retribution.

So Victoria wasn't the only one with a personal stake in this investigation.

He had one as well.

Zach finished off his drink, stared broodingly into the empty glass. He was hell-bent on blowing the Hope Institute wide open. But he knew better than to let his personal urgency interfere with his work. He'd been scrutinizing the place with his usual patient, comprehensive thoroughness. He'd successfully managed to keep his emotions on the back burner where they belonged.

Until Victoria walked back into his life.

Now he was slipping. He was losing his objectivity, his focus and, considering his feelings for Victoria, a whole lot more.

Sleeping on her sofa was crazy.

But crazy or not, he'd better get used to doing it. Because he wasn't leaving her alone in that apartment overnight until he was sure she was safe.

He realized he couldn't be with her every minute. Nor would she let him be.

She was so goddamned independent, so unwilling to let down those walls.

She'd let them down last night when he walked her home. Just thinking about that kiss made his body throb. Christ, everything was called a kiss. The frenzied way they'd come together, the feel and taste of her again . . .

Cut it out, Zach warned himself. This line of thinking wasn't going to help—not with the bottled-up pain and unresolved issues still looming between them. He had no idea where they were headed or if Victoria would allow herself to go there again.

Right now, her chief worry was Audrey.

On that thought, Zach set his glass on the counter, flipping shut his notebook and glancing at the clock behind the bartender. Twelve minutes past six. Victoria was late.

He swiveled about to peer out the window, reminding himself that this was Manhattan, that it was rush hour, and that Victoria was entirely self-sufficient.

Except that she was poking around in dangerous territory, and there was some professional creep tailing her.

As if on cue, the door opened, and Victoria stepped inside. She scanned the bar, her breathless state and wind-blown hair telling Zach she'd been running.

He waved, and she spotted him, combing her fingers through her hair as she made her way over.

"Hi," she greeted him as he came to his feet. "Sorry I'm late. I had to be back in court this afternoon and there was a stampede getting uptown."

"You took a cab, I hope."

She shot him a look. "No, Zach, I took the subway. If I'd taken a cab, I'd still be stuck in gridlock. Besides, haven't you ever heard the expression 'There's safety in numbers'?"

He couldn't argue that logic. "You weren't followed?"

"I don't think so." A tight smile. "Mr. Cigar was either afraid of being trampled to death or put off by the smoking ban in the subway."

Zach didn't smile back. "Hopefully, your father called him off after your Park Avenue visit this morning." He gripped her arm. "Come on, let's take a booth. I want to hear all about your breakfast." He led her to a corner table away from the general flow of traffic.

"Did you see anything at the Institute today?" Victoria

demanded the minute they were settled and two drinks had been ordered.

"Nothing that jumped out at me. That doesn't mean anything. I need some more data. Then I'll add up the pieces."

Her nod was restless but resigned. She knew his work, how much time and patience it required.

"You look beat," Zach observed gently, noting her drawn face, the dark circles under her eyes. She hadn't slept any better than he. And her day had to have been tough. "How did your talk with Meg and Paul go?"

An ambivalent shrug. "Pretty well. Paul was psyched about the idea of getting some corporate clients—the kind that pay. That made it easier. Meg was more protective, but she understood."

"And your breakfast? How was that?"

"An experience." Victoria fiddled with the top button of her blazer. "That place is the ultimate fossil. It's the only place on earth still filled with dinosaurs."

A corner of Zach's mouth lifted. "How many of them are gentle brontosauruses, and how many are bloodthirsty Tyrannosaurus rexes?"

Her smile was strained but genuine. "That remains to be seen. But there were more than enough of the latter at breakfast to keep me from doing any snooping today. I would've been caught."

"I agree. You'll start next week."

"No, I'll start Saturday night." She dug around in her purse, extracted an envelope, and handed it to Zach.

His brows drew together as he took it. "What's this?"

"An invitation. To a formal gathering at my parents' house."

Glancing at it, Zach made a disgusted sound. "Your official debut. And you didn't decline?"

"On the contrary, I accepted. And when I mentioned to my father that you were in town, he suggested you be my escort. According to him, you can use this time to woo a roomful of prominent CEOs, some of whom are your clients, while the remainder should be."

"How thoughtful of him," Zach returned dryly. He gave Victoria a measured look. "I know your father's motives. He's trying to reel you in. What are yours? And don't tell me you plan to rummage through his study during the party. You'll never get away with it."

"I'm not that reckless. Besides, I've already found everything I'm going to at the house. No, I have something entirely different in mind. All my father's most notable clients will be at that party, including, I'd wager, Benjamin Hopewell." She watched as a glint of anticipation sparked in Zach's eyes. "I thought you'd be pleased. A firsthand opportunity to get a handle on the chairman of Hopewell Industries. Tell me, do I get a referral fee?"

Zach studied her while the waitress delivered their drinks and a bowl of nuts.

"You're back to being flippant," he pronounced. "That means one of two things. Either you're really unnerved about Mr. Cigar or you're really unnerved about us. Which is it, Victoria?"

A weighted pause, during which she lowered her lashes, played with the ice in her drink. "There is no 'us,' Zach. I'm just tired. It's been a really long day, and an unbearable week."

"So we're going to pretend it never happened?"

"No. We're just not going to let it happen again." She laced her fingers together and leaned forward to meet his gaze. Zach had the feeling she was about to deliver a well-rehearsed closing argument—one she didn't want to give but felt compelled to.

He watched as she steeled herself, masking her emotions behind a wall of facts.

"Last night you asked me how many men there had been since you left. The answer is none. That shouldn't surprise you. It's no secret I'm not the type for a casual affair, or I wouldn't have been a virgin when we met. Sharing myself—physically and emotionally—came hard enough before. Since you and I split up, it's damned near impossible. I can't and won't endure that kind of pain again. So when I said I can't have an affair with you, I meant it. Can we please leave it at that?"

Zach knew what he should be feeling. Guilty for pushing her, admiring of her candor, receptive to the plea he knew hovered beneath that stoic veneer. Instead, all he could feel was a jolt of exhilarated relief. There hadn't been anyone else. No one. Not in her bed, and more important, not in her heart. He had no right to feel this rush of possessiveness, this damned chauvinistic elation.

But he did.

Because it told him far more than Victoria would even admit—not just to him, but to herself.

"Zach?" she pressed.

"I appreciate your honesty," he replied, holding her gaze. "I'll give you the same." His fingers brushed hers lightly. Then his hand covered hers, enveloping it with the heavy weight of his palm. "I don't plan to seduce you. Nor would I play on your weakness for me—or mine for you. On the other hand, I can't promise to ignore the unresolved feelings between us. Or the chemistry. So if we end up in bed, it will be because we both want to be there. Fair enough?"

She swallowed, nodded tersely as the heat of his touch seeped through her. "I suppose it'll have to be." She took a quick gulp of her drink—for fortification rather than to quench her thirst. Zach could see her wheels turning, see her grappling with whatever it was she was about to say. Whatever it was, she didn't want to give in to the words. But they were going to burst free nonetheless.

"So now that you know how uneventful my life's been since you took off for Europe, it's your turn," she informed him in as casual a tone as she could muster. "You haven't told me a thing about these past four years—other than the fact that you've been swamped with work. Did you settle anywhere in particular? Was there one special place, more so than the others, that left its mark? Are you eager to get back there so—"

"Victoria." He silenced her quietly, putting an end to her qualms and to the hint of susceptibility they implied—a susceptibility she'd view as intolerable. It felt damned good to know she cared, but he wouldn't do this to her. Not when there was no basis for what she was really asking. "There's no one in my life. Not in any city, any country, or any continent. I've lived practically like a monk." His grip on her hand intensified, along with his gaze. "I was as shattered as you."

She cleared her throat, struggled for a lighter note. "A monk, huh? I guess that made it easy, when the FBI called, to jump right on a plane for New York."

"It *was* easy—for several reasons. My solitary lifestyle was just one of them. As for jumping on a plane for New York, I didn't. I flew into Logan. I visited my parents' graves, then drove down from Boston that night."

Reflexively, her fingers curled closer in his. "I know how difficult those visits are for you. I'm sorry."

"Actually, it was less painful this time. Probably because of the circumstances."

She gave him a questioning look. "Circumstances? You mean because more time has passed?"

"No. Because I intend to bring closure to things."

"What—?"

"Victoria, let's get into this later," he said abruptly. This was one topic that would have to wait. If he was going to take this step, to open up to her again and confide just how close to home this case was, he wasn't going to do it in a bar. He needed to be alone with her.

Besides, one emotional hurdle at a time. Victoria had finally allowed herself to talk about her life after their breakup. He hadn't expected that, not so soon. But her fatigue and the past week's stress had won out, not to mention that last night's kiss had thrown her. She'd just admitted to him that she'd lived a celibate existence these past four years. She needed to know how he'd lived, what he'd done and felt . . . or hadn't.

He intended to tell her.

"You wanted to know about my life in Europe," he reminded her. "It was a lot like yours here, except more transient. I lived in seven countries—no, eight. Honestly, I lost track. Sometimes I stayed a few weeks, other times a few months. I worked. I spent as little time inside my head as possible. And I tried like hell to forget you. I failed miserably."

She was staring at the table again. "What about the FBI? Did they contact you while you were abroad?"

"A few times, yes. Most of the government work I did was for the CIA. I developed intelligence on various organizations they suspected of fronting for illegal activities. I also trained some of their agents in competitive intelligence."

"But when you left for Europe, it was at the FBI's request," she reminded him.

"Yes and no. Initially, it was their assignment. They wanted me to develop intelligence on an exporter of machine tools they believed was dealing in drugs and firearms. It turned out to be an international operation. I flew to Europe to check out the players at the receiving end. After that, Interpol took over. They got their men."

"But you continued taking FBI assignments, too."

"They contacted me when they needed U.S. intelligence. Mostly I analyzed written data they provided. Nothing I couldn't handle long-distance."

"Until now."

"Yes. Until now."

She ran her tongue over her lower lip. "And the SCIP conference you're speaking at?"

"What about it? I'm giving the keynote next Thursday. The timing worked out well."

Victoria's lashes lifted, and she eyed him speculatively. "Conferences are planned months in advance. How did you manage to work out the details?"

He wasn't going to lie to her—not even if it meant scaring her off. "SCIP contacted me on several previous occasions, inviting me to speak. I declined. I ran into one of their board members in London last February. He told me this year's conference was in New York. As you're aware, so are many of my U.S. clients. He asked if I'd reconsider. I didn't say yes. But I didn't say no, either. When the FBI's investigation into the Hope Institute started heating up, I gave SCIP a call. They were kind enough to squeeze me in, even at that late date."

"Squeeze you in? They probably cheered loud enough for you to hear across the Atlantic. You're one of the foremost experts in your field."

Zach shrugged. "The point is, I set things up in advance, left the door open to come back."

"So you could touch base with your clients?"

"Hardly. I wouldn't need an excuse for that. Nor was it necessary. I'd meet them when they traveled to Europe. And my staff here was handling things just fine." He leaned forward. "Maybe there was a part of me that knew it was time to come back, if only to figure out why I was so hell-bent on staying away—and if that reason still existed. I'm not good at living in limbo, Victoria—or at leaving loose ends. Especially not in matters that strike close to home."

Shutters descended. "*That* trait I've experienced firsthand."

"Victoria." He tugged at her fingers, forced her to raise those shutters, to face him candidly. "I know you blamed me for the decision I made. Do you still?"

Her sigh was sad, as if she felt very old. "It wasn't the decision I blamed you for, Zach. At least not the one you made for *you*. It was the decision you made for *me*. I understood you had ghosts to face—ghosts you needed to put to rest. God knows, I could relate. But I had my own ghosts, my own plans. I was stunned and hurt that you couldn't see where I was coming from, what I needed. You expected me to blindly follow you. To leave my family, law school, a career I desperately wanted and was only a year away from starting. To marry you and rush off to Europe so you could purge your demons, help break up every drug cartel the government sniffed out. I couldn't."

"I didn't expect that." He made a rough sound, a humorless laugh as he realized what he was saying. "Who am I kidding? It might not have been what I expected, but in essence it was exactly what I asked you to do. My only excuse is that I didn't think of it that way. I assumed we'd go to Europe, I'd quickly stop those animals, and—"

"And you'd move on to the next investigation that hinted at a chance for retribution," she finished quietly.

He couldn't argue. She was right. She'd seen the handwriting on the wall. He hadn't. He'd been a single-minded fool. Oh, he'd realized that some time ago, after his irrational fury had cooled—but the damage had been done, the profound ties severed. The problem was, he'd been consumed with his own need to rectify the past. And Victoria? She'd had a foresight he hadn't, an ability to see the future his actions were dictating.

"You were a lot more astute than I," he stated flatly, not even trying to minimize his part in their breakup. "But I'm asking you to believe that my self-centeredness was based on stupidity, not a lack of sensitivity. I would never expect you to abandon your career and your family. Europe wasn't meant to be permanent. We were. I should have realized the direction I was heading in. I didn't. All I realized was that I had to take that assignment, and that I wanted you with me. As for your unwillingness to go, I understood it. I just couldn't accept it."

Victoria swallowed, her voice nearly drowned out by the clinking of glasses and arriving customers. "I believe you. I wasn't blameless, either. I could have negotiated a compromise. Instead, I walked away. Some of what you said back then was true. I *was* obsessed with protecting my mother and sister. Maybe I still am—although I think I've finally started accepting what Uncle Jim's maintained all along. The strength I project for Mother and Audrey has to come from within each of them, not from me." Her smile was sad. "Let's sum it up by saying we were both pigheaded and shortsighted, and leave it at that."

"What if I don't want to leave it at all?"

Zach's question hung in the air, a palpable entity that loomed larger than life.

Tension rippled through Victoria, and when she answered her voice was oddly choked. "We have to."

"Why?"

"Because—" She broke off, fiddling with the edge of her napkin, and Zach could sense her emotional turmoil. "Do you know what the ironic part was?" she managed at last. "I actually considered going with you. Briefly. But briefly was enough to scare me to death. Realizing I cared about you enough to walk away from my responsibilities, my future, was the most terrifying feeling I've ever known. Except for the pain I went through after you left. That was even more terrifying. To be that vulnerable to someone . . ." She gave a fierce shake of her head, her features set in hard lines of determination. "Never again. Never, ever again."

"Victoria—"

"I'd better get going." She tugged her hand away, blinking back the hint of moisture in her eyes. "I've got a dinner meeting with a client."

"Cancel it." He wasn't going to let this drop. Not now. Not when they were so close.

"No." She slid out of the booth. "I made a commitment."

"Then call and say you'll be late."

"There's no point. This conversation is over."

Zach was on his feet. "No. It's not." Even as he countered her words, he knew he was fighting a losing battle. He recognized that stubborn lift of her chin. She was going to keep that damned appointment—for a lot of reasons. Fine. He'd shelve this for later. But they were going to see it through. And then they were going to see where it led.

"I'll walk you to your meeting," he informed her. "We'll continue this discussion later."

"I'm going a block away, Zach." Victoria took a step backward, putting some physical distance between them. "Besides, if you start acting like my bodyguard, Mr. Cigar will get suspicious—*if* he's still out there."

Reality intruded, and Zach bit back his frustration. "Fine. But I'll be at your apartment tonight—*with* an overnight bag. A very conspicuous one, so Mr. Cigar will assume I'm there for more than a nightcap. When?"

She hesitated, then, seeing the unyielding expression on his face, relented. "Ten. I'll be home by then. I'll also be tired. Too tired to talk."

"Fair enough—for tonight." He'd promised not to prey on her vulnerability. He intended to honor that promise.

He also intended to break down those goddamned walls and have her back.

"With regard to Saturday night's party," he reminded her, conscious that she was backing away, equally conscious that his voice would soon be swallowed up by the enthusiastic customers swarming the bar. "Consider me your escort. We wouldn't want to disappoint your father."

"Or slow down your investigation," she added, giving him a pointed look. "As we've both noted, some things never change."

"No," Zach muttered under his breath as Victoria wound her way through the crowd and out of the bar. "They sure as hell don't."

6:30 P.M.

She was still in that bar on Sixtieth Street with her boyfriend. Hamilton, that was his name. Then she was going over to Sixty-first Street to meet a client. That left plenty of time for him to finish what he was doing and catch up with her.

He nipped off the end of his cigar, simultaneously glancing around to make sure no one was nearby. Ms. Kensington's apartment building was quiet. But then, it always was at this time of day. Everyone who lived here worked long hours. That's why he chose six-thirty to drop by.

He placed the unlit cigar between his lips and leaned against the lobby wall, quickly skimming through her mail.

The usual. Same all week long—bills, solicitations for a free credit card, and an invitation to some legal seminar in Seattle. Nothing personal. And definitely nothing mailed from her sister before she'd left Italy.

He shoved the mail back in its cubbyhole and slammed the aluminum door. Time to head out and see what Ms. Kensington was up to—*without* letting her see him. His instructions were clear. She was supposed to think he'd stopped keeping an eye on her.

He brushed by a workman with a telephone handset dangling from his belt, not even making eye contact as he passed.

"Her office is done," the man mumbled, focused on getting downstairs to the basement and locating the telephone interface box. "I'll be finished here in ten minutes."

The man with the cigar nodded, continuing on his way.

He stepped outside and lit his cigar, casually walking down the steps and into the flow of pedestrians hurrying up and down East Eighty-second Street.

They'd soon find out if this Hamilton guy was really just an old boyfriend looking to get laid.

Or if he was really something more.

18

"Father, please . . . I'm frightened." Audrey fidgeted into an upright position in her hospital bed, that motion alone taking a good portion of her strength. She was weak—so weak. But she was even more afraid. The walls were closing in on her. She had to get out. "I can't . . . take it anymore. Please, help me."

"I *am* helping you, Audrey," Walter Kensington replied firmly. He sounded detached. The truth was, he was annoyed. This entire conversation was a nuisance. It was also, however, necessary.

He glanced at his watch for the third time in the last few minutes. It was after eight. He had to get Audrey under control and bring this all-too-familiar session to a close so he could get to his appointment.

"We've been over this a dozen times. You're sick," he said tightly. "Look at you. You can barely sit up. You've been fully conscious only since yesterday, and you're about to eat your first real meal. I don't have to tell you how much damage you've done to your body." *Or to me.* His unspoken words hung in the air. "This particular setback was bad. Very bad. You've got to stop carrying on and let the doctors do their job. It's the only way you'll regain your strength."

Audrey drew an unsteady breath, struggling to control her emotions, to not disappoint her father again. Her eyes widened with panic as he made a move toward the door. "You're leaving again?"

He stopped, standing stiffly and regarding her as one would an annoying child. "I'm late for a meeting."

Sweat broke out on her brow, and she could feel that dangerous pounding in her chest begin again. "Don't . . . leave me," she whispered, despite her best intentions.

His expression hardened. "Stop it. I won't tolerate another bout of hysterics. You've already embarrassed me enough. Pull yourself together."

Her fingers knotted in the sheet, that horrible dread erupting inside her. She began to shake. "I'm trying." Another unsteady breath. "Can't you please . . . make arrangements . . . for Victoria to visit?" she tried. "I know it's against the clinic's rules, but—"

"No, I can't." Now Walter was becoming angry. Audrey was making him late for a meeting he'd anticipated all week, and she was going around in senseless circles. "I've bent the rules as far as I can for you. Any more, and the hospital board will ask you to leave. I won't compromise your status as a patient here. There's no other facility where you'll receive this expert level of care. Look at it this way: the sooner you get better, the sooner you'll be free to see your sister. How's that for an incentive?"

"An incentive . . . yes," Audrey repeated, visibly trying to contain her mounting fear.

Recognizing the symptoms—the rapidness of his daughter's breathing, the faraway look in her eyes, the high, trembling quality of her voice—Walter scowled. The last thing he needed was another of her irrational bouts. Each time she lapsed into one, her condition deteriorated. "I'm going to have the nurse bring you a sedative."

All the color drained from Audrey's face. "I don't want . . . to be doped up again. Not like before."

"You won't be." Walter was already opening the door, signaling the nurse in the hall. "I'm not suggesting anything extreme. Just a mild sedative. It will quiet you. There's no need for heavy medication—*if* you get better on your own."

A meaningful silence, during which father and daughter exchanged looks.

Audrey knew just what that look meant.

"Do we understand each other?" Walter inquired.

A resigned nod.

"Good. Now take the tranquilizer I'm requesting. Eat your breakfast. Follow the doctor's orders. And don't embarrass me again."

Audrey lowered her lashes. "I won't."

Satisfied that he had things under control, Walter issued a few terse orders to the nurse and headed off.

He was already fifteen minutes late.

8:15 A.M.

Sipping a cup of coffee in her kitchen, Victoria made a final scan of the guest list her mother had faxed her. She was relieved that Benjamin Hopewell's name was on it with the words "will attend" after it. She was equally relieved to see the same notation after Uncle Jim and Aunt Clarissa's names. Having their comforting presence at this pretense of a party would make the night-long ordeal easier. Not that she intended to tell them she was checking into her father's ties to the Hope Institute. No, she'd already made that mistake once. She wouldn't repeat it. But they *would* know she was on display, courtesy of her father. They'd also put two and two together and realize that, after four painful years apart, she and Zach had somehow reconnected, that he was back in her life. So they'd expect her to be tense. And they'd do their best to put her at ease.

The very thought of the upcoming evening had her stomach in knots.

And walking into that party on Zach's arm, acting out a part that came far too naturally, wasn't making it any easier.

Determined not to dwell on this subject, Victoria rose, walked down to the second bedroom, the one that served as her home office. She'd work. That would keep her mind off tonight.

She flipped on the computer and sat down behind it, waiting for it to boot up. She'd dial into her office system. That way she could access their legal software to do some research. She needed precedents to substantiate the case she was putting together for Doris Webster, her recently acquired client who'd been emotionally and financially exploited by her husband. In seizing all their assets and taking off with his pert little assistant, the high-powered corporate exec had not only cheated and abandoned his wife, but destroyed her self-image. Mrs. Webster had been a basket case when she came to Victoria's office last week. And all because of the self-serving snake she'd given thirty-five years to.

His offenses smacked of the ones committed by the defendant in Elizabeth Bonner's matrimonial case.

Victoria had made that mental connection the minute Ms. Bonner brought up her client. She'd stored away the parallel for later. Well, later was now. Maybe she could find some data that would help Mrs. Webster and Ms. Bonner's client at the same time.

She logged in with her password, drumming her fingers impatiently on the desk as she waited for the connection to be made. She was grateful for the information computers provided once you were on them, but she hated how much time it took to get where you needed to be.

Her hands were poised on the keyboard when the message popped up: *Access denied. User already logged on.*

She rolled her eyes.

Just what she was in the mood for. A computer glitch.

She tried again and got the same message.

Great. What was wrong with the network now?

Disgusted, she left her desk, fully aware that just sitting there would do nothing but aggravate her. Instead, she'd divert herself for a few minutes, give the system a chance to straighten itself out.

She went to the kitchen, refilled her coffee cup, and toasted half an English muffin.

Twenty minutes later, she returned to her desk.

This time she got in without a problem. She noticed she had an unread e-mail from the system administrator. Maybe that would explain what had happened.

She opened the e-mail and scanned it. Evidently, there was some wiring problem on her local network. The problem was being dealt with and should be cleared up soon. In the meantime, she should excuse any faulty messages she received that prevented her from logging on, and please try again in a few minutes.

Well, what do you know, she thought. *I actually did something right pertaining to a computer, without being spoon-fed beforehand.*

Leaning forward, she began her work.

9:35 A.M.

The private office at the Hope Institute was a shambles.

Then again, it usually was when they were through.

The man picked up a cushion from the carpet and tossed it back on the sofa, followed by another. In a matter of minutes, no one would be able to tell that the room had doubled as a love nest the past hour.

The woman concentrated on zipping up her slacks, rearranging the collar of her silk blouse until it lay just right. "We've been in here too long."

"Probably." Her lover abandoned his task and turned to face her. "But I really don't care. Besides, the door is locked, so there's no chance of discovery."

She nodded. "Still, I'd better go. I have to get to work."

"You're going in today?"

Her delicate brows arched. "You sound surprised. I put in just as many weekends as you."

He made an impatient sound. "I realize that. But I

assumed you had things to do. Tonight is the party. Or have you forgotten?"

"You know better than that. I'll be there."

"Not on my arm, unfortunately." He walked over, pulled her against him, and kissed her with a pent-up frustration that belied the languid sexual satisfaction he'd displayed just moments ago.

She kissed him back, responding for one long, hot minute before she pulled away, smoothing her hair into place. "I wish I were going on your arm, too," she murmured. "But we both know that's impossible." She walked over to the mirror, quickly reapplying her lipstick and makeup. Regardless of how wild and hot she became when they were together, she had a knack for making herself look elegant and poised at the drop of a hat.

She snapped her compact shut and turned to face him. "We'll have our time together."

"It's too infrequent to suit me."

"I agree." Her lips curved slightly. "We could indulge ourselves at the office."

"Very amusing. That's far too risky—even for us."

"Let's not rule out anything. Who knows? We might just get desperate enough to take that risk." She scooped up her purse and walked by him, pausing to brush her palm across his jaw. "In the meantime, I'll see you tonight."

She unlocked the door and shut it quietly behind her.

He waited a full three minutes. Then he left.

It was a half hour later when the nurse walked by that same spot on her way to check on a patient. She saw the rectangular scrap of gray plastic glistening outside the office door. Pausing, she bent to pluck it off the threshold. A key card, she noted, but an unfamiliar one. Certainly not one of the pale yellow cards used at the Institute.

She turned it over in her hand and saw 280 Park Avenue printed on its flip side. Ah, that explained who it belonged to.

She'd have to return it next time.

7:05 P.M.

Victoria applied a touch of mascara and stepped back to inspect her reflection in the full-length mirror.

The mauve cocktail dress was perfect for the occasion. Its crushed velvet material was soft and lovely, its lines flattering in their simplicity. Spaghetti straps and a low, square neckline exposed her neck and shoulders, and the Empire waist cut just beneath her breasts, then fell into a straight skirt that fit her closely from bodice to a few inches above her knee. A simple pair of pearl studs at her ears and a matching pearl choker and bracelet, and the outfit was complete. Even her hair she wore simply—brushed loose and grazing her bare shoulders.

Just the way Zach liked it.

She hated that she cared so much, that she, who lectured Paige regularly that good looks were secondary, was preening and fussing like a high school senior on her way to the prom.

Okay, so she wanted to look good for him. So she wanted to see that flicker of admiration in his eyes. Was that so terrible? She hadn't indulged herself like this in four years. Meg was always telling her how unhealthy that was. Well, now she was behaving in a healthier manner. No need to blow the whole matter out of proportion. She was a normal twenty-eight-year-old woman who felt good when an attractive man—a man she'd once been in love with—appreciated her appearance. Period.

She slipped on her off-white high heels, scooped up her matching evening bag, and glanced at the clock on her dresser. He'd be here any minute.

As if on cue, the phone rang.

Victoria crossed over and picked it up. "Hello?"

"It's me." The echoing quality to Zach's voice told her he was on his cell phone. "I'm running a little late. I stopped to get the results on that cigar."

"And?"

"And they dusted for prints. There weren't any—at least none that were clear enough to lift."

She wasn't surprised. But she was uneasy about the ramifications of Zach's actions. "What did you tell them?"

"That I was doing a favor for a friend—which I am." Zach paused for a moment. "There's nothing else to tell them. We don't have an ounce of proof that someone's following you, other than our eyes and our instincts. And we certainly can't tie this guy to the Hope Institute. Don't worry. I said nothing further about Audrey *or* your father."

"Thank you," Victoria replied softly. She cast another quick look at the clock. "Where are you? Should I call Robert and say we'll be late?"

"If we are, it won't be by much. I'm already in the car. The hotel manager arranged to have it delivered to the door. I'll be at your place in ten minutes. Barring any unforeseen traffic, we'll be in Greenwich by eight-thirty. You decide whether or not that warrants a call."

"Fair enough." Victoria nodded, mentally reviewing the situation and determining her best course of action. "I'll give Robert a quick buzz. Since my father's designated me guest of honor, it will calm him down to know I'm on my way and not backing out of his party. That will make things easier on my mother."

"Sounds like a sensible approach."

"Thanks for calling. I'll see you soon." Victoria disconnected the call, then dialed her parents' number.

Outside, parked a few buildings down on East Eighty-second, the technician leaned forward in his van. He adjusted the dials on his audio equipment, although he paid little attention to Ms. Kensington's thirty-second chat with the family butler.

So Hamilton had been checking out cigar prints. That brought a number of questions to mind. Who'd done the fingerprint analysis? Why would they do it with no real explanation provided—*and* at seven o'clock on a Saturday night? It had to be a personal favor.

Okay, let's assume a high-powered guy like Hamilton had friends in all kinds of places.

Still, why would he call on those friends for a trivial matter like this? Just to score brownie points with Victoria Kensington?

Maybe. If so, he was certainly going to great lengths just to get her in bed.

Well, he was about to get some help in that department. Because after tonight, the lovely Ms. Kensington would have plenty of time to concentrate on her lover. She'd no longer be preoccupied with the man with the cigar.

Tonight, she'd get some help rearranging her priorities.

19

The Kensington house was ablaze with lights, humming with the arrival of guests, when Zach drove through the estate's iron gates and down the winding drive.

"Now this brings back memories," he muttered, glancing around. "Although there never was this much activity when I brought you home."

"Yes, well, when my father hosts a party, he hosts a party," Victoria returned dryly, watching the parking attendants rushing around like mice, one getting behind the wheel of a Jaguar, the next driving off to park a Mercedes 500 SE. "It's amazing how my parents can make this happen with three days' notice." Her brow furrowed. "I hope Mother's all right. She sounded keyed up when I talked to her yesterday. Then again, she thrives on stuff like this. It's one of the perks to being married to my father—at least in her mind."

Zach shot her a sideways look. "Are you okay? I can feel your tension all the way over here."

Victoria nodded, staring at the dashboard. "I'm fine about being paraded around like a prize thoroughbred. I don't like it, but I can stomach it. What I'm not fine about is poking around for dirt on my father. I'm half hoping we'll resolve it all in one conversation with Mr. Hopewell—that he'll say something to clarify things in a way we haven't considered, and eliminate any chance that my father's guilty of anything criminal."

"I know." Zach reached over and gave her fingers a gentle squeeze. "I'd like it to go that way, too."

"But you doubt it will."

"Yes, I doubt it will."

She threw him a dark look. "The ever candid Zachary Hamilton."

"Would you rather I lied?"

"No."

"Good. Because I'm lousy at it, especially when it comes to you." His gaze swept her, just as it had when she greeted him at the door. "You look unbelievably beautiful."

There was no squelching the hard lurch her heart gave, or the warmth that spread through her. "Thank you." She forced a smile. "You look pretty incredible yourself."

And he did. Zach was charismatic enough in his regular clothes. In a tux, he was devastating.

"I'm glad you feel that way." Zach steered into the circular drive, then waited for the car in front of them to be ushered away. "Party time," he observed, as one of the attendants darted toward them. "Ready?"

"I think so."

"Very well, guest of honor, let's see what we can find out."

He put the car in park, got out, and walked around to assist Victoria. Tossing the keys to the parking attendant, he wrapped an arm around Victoria's waist and led her up the stairs and through the front door.

The house was brimming with people, all dressed in classic evening clothes, all chatting with dignified reserve as they moved from one spacious room to another. The women's heels clicked on the oak floors, mingling with the sound of clinking crystal and polite laughter.

The party was a success.

It took Victoria exactly thirty seconds to determine that. But then, she had years of experience. She'd been witness to countless affairs like this one since she was little—too little to see over the second-floor railing. She and Audrey had gotten past that obstacle by squatting down and peeking through the banister slats, watching the hallway fill up with wealthy and debonair guests.

Being an uninvited observer sure beat being the star attraction.

"Miss Victoria." Robert was right there to greet them, giving Victoria a genuine smile. "You look lovely."

"Thank you, Robert." Victoria indicated her escort. "I don't know if you remember Zachary Hamilton. It's been a while."

Robert inclined his head in Zach's direction. "Mr. Hamilton. Yes, I do recall. It's been several years. Good evening, sir."

"Robert," Zach acknowledged politely.

"Are most of the guests here?" Victoria asked in a low voice.

Robert nodded. "All but a few. Your aunt and uncle were among the first to arrive."

Relief flooded Victoria's face at Robert's underlying message. Reinforcements were on hand. "Good." She glanced about the glittering hallway. "Is Mother in the living room or the salon?"

"The salon. Most of the guests are there, as well. The bar is set up in the dining room, as are the main dinner courses, which will be served at nine. Hors d'oeuvres are circulating now. You'll find attendants with trays in both the salon and the living room."

"Thanks. First I'll check in with Mother, then I'll find Uncle—"

"Ah, Victoria." Walter Kensington strode over, distinguished and handsome in his black tux, white dress shirt, and gleaming gold cuff links. "I was just talking about you." He waited stiffly for his daughter's perfunctory kiss on the cheek, his sharp gaze fixed on Zach. "Welcome back to the States, Mr. Hamilton. I'm glad you could join us."

"I'm pleased to be here." Zach extended his hand and shook Walter Kensington's in a firm but impersonal grip.

"You know a good portion of the guests here tonight," Walter said, with a wave of his arm. "Feel free to mingle. Introduce yourself to some prospective clients. Get a drink. Get something to eat. Enjoy yourself."

Victoria clenched her teeth. Her father's words were as good as a dismissal. He was showing Zach the lay of the land, instructing him to find his own way—warning him that any interference into what was intended to be his daughter's debut would not be appreciated.

"Father, it's not necessary for—"

"I'll do that," Zach interrupted her. "I'll keep Victoria just long enough to get her a drink. After that, I'll deliver her back into your hands. I realize there are a number of guests you want her to meet. I have a similar agenda for myself. So I'll leave you to your business, while I conduct mine."

A flicker of respect registered on Walter's face. "I'm glad you understand."

"I do—completely." Zach pressed his palm to the small of Victoria's back, propelling her gently toward the dining room. "Give us five minutes."

"I'll be in the salon."

Victoria was fighting to control her anger as Zach escorted her to the bar and ordered two glasses of cabernet.

"I feel like a damned Barbie doll," she muttered under her breath. "Just dress me up and pass me around in my very own decked-out dreamhouse."

Zach's lips twitched. "At least you're in demand. I'm the superfluous Ken doll, just here for show." He handed her a glass of wine. "Take it in stride. Your father has your evening mapped out. Use it to our advantage. Any one of the people you'll be chatting with might end up giving us what we need."

She sipped her wine, arching a pointed brow at him. "Yeah, right. Meanwhile, you'll find Mr. Hopewell—the person we *really* want to talk to—and pump him for information."

He flashed her that crooked grin. "I'll share. You have my word."

Victoria felt her lips curve. "I'll hold you to that."

They made their way across the hall to the salon. Walter Kensington saw them immediately and excused himself from his circle of guests.

"Good luck," Zach murmured, his breath ruffling Victoria's hair.

"You, too." She watched as her father made his way to her side.

"Your daughter, as promised," Zach informed him. He lifted his glass of wine ever so slightly in Victoria's direction. "Have fun. I'll catch up with you later." He strolled deeper into the room, greeting a few of the guests with as much ease as if he were the host.

"Zachary," she heard a plump man with thinning hair say. "I had no idea you were in from Europe."

"I just got in last week," Zach supplied.

"How long will you be here?"

A noncommittal shrug. "I'm not sure. I've got business to finish up and a conference to attend. Both are in New York."

"So you'll be here a while. Excellent."

A while, Victoria found herself thinking. *How long will that be?*

"Let's start by greeting the partners in my firm," Walter was instructing her. "Reinforce the fine impression you made on Thursday. Then we'll move on to my prominent clients, most of whom are here, and some of whom you might remember."

"First I want to say hello to Mother," Victoria replied in a firm tone. She'd only allow herself to be manipulated so far. "Then I'd like to do the same to Uncle Jim and Aunt Clarissa. After that, I'm at your disposal."

Her father's jaw tightened, then relaxed as he scanned the room and found what he was looking for. "Your mother's with Alfred and his wife," he proclaimed, speaking of Mr. Tatem. "We'll go over there first. As for Jim and Clarissa, they're milling around the living room. You can find them later."

That was as close to a compromise as her father ever came.

"Fine." Victoria clutched her glass in her left hand, freeing up her right for handshakes. Holding her head high, she maneuvered her way over to the grand piano, where a professional pianist had just begun playing and where her mother stood, chatting with Mr. and Mrs. Tatem.

"Victoria." Barbara Kensington smiled, her pale green eyes lighting a bit—eyes that, beneath their perfectly applied makeup, were far too sad and tired. "When did you arrive?"

"Just now." Victoria leaned forward and gave her mother a warm hug.

"You look lovely."

"So do you."

Barbara Kensington was dressed exquisitely, as always. She was wearing a stunning black satin designer suit, and her light brown hair was arranged in an elegant chignon. Victoria only wished her mother's life was half as enviable as her appearance.

Repressing that thought, she turned her attention to the couple poised next to her. "Mr. Tatem." Her first handshake of the evening. "It's a pleasure to see you again. This must be your wife." A shift in handshakes. "I'm Victoria Kensington."

"Carla Tatem," the blond woman with the keen blue eyes responded with a cordial smile. "I've heard a great deal about you, Victoria. Congratulations on being the newest addition to Waters, Kensington, Tatem and Calder."

Victoria glanced at her father, hoping he would clarify

her role at his firm, but he made no effort to do so, nor did he look bothered by Mrs. Tatem's assumption.

"Victoria is an outstanding attorney," her mother jumped in to praise. "We're extremely proud of her. Walter is delighted that she's taking this step. She'll be a valuable member of the firm."

God, this was worse than she'd expected. Now even her mother was alluding to her affiliation with Waters, Kensington, Tatem & Calder as if it were permanent. Then again, she shouldn't be surprised. No doubt her father had issued clipped instructions to his wife before the party.

"Speaking of which, I want Victoria to circulate," Walter inserted, furthering his cause. "It's important that our clients get to know her."

"Of course." Alfred Tatem waved them away. "Go ahead. Mingle. I'm off to refill my drink. Ladies?" he asked his wife and Barbara Kensington. "May I refresh yours, as well?"

"You go ahead," Barbara said brightly. "I'm going to make sure our other guests are comfortable." With a practiced smile that came from years of experience, she went to do just that.

"Father," Victoria said quietly as her father steered her in whatever direction he had in mind. "I'm of counsel to your firm, remember? *Temporarily* of counsel. I haven't joined you in any real or permanent sense. So I don't appreciate your misleading—"

"Not now, Victoria," her father cut her off. "I see George Placard, the founder of Placard, Knotts, and Riley. His advertising company's worth about two billion, and growing. He's a long-standing client of ours. Let's go."

Victoria didn't do much breathing over the next hour.

She moved from client to client, attorney to attorney, wishing the damned introductions were over so she could work the room on her own. She certainly couldn't ask any probing questions with her father glued to her side.

Ironic, isn't it? she thought dryly. *He hasn't spent this much time with me in all my twenty-eight years combined.*

Every chance she got, she scanned the room for Benjamin Hopewell. Twice she caught sight of him. Once he was in heated discussion with Elizabeth Bonner, the second time he was in equally heated discussion with Zach.

She'd give anything to hear the details of that conversation.

Finally, when her father decided he'd made enough inroads for the time being—a decision that coincided with having almost no one left to introduce her to but a few of his junior partners, coincidentally the four female ones he'd blatantly ignored during Thursday's introductions—he excused himself and went off to join two of his colleagues.

The first thing Victoria did, before even beginning to poke around, was to seek out the junior partners her father had slighted and to introduce herself.

Karen Hollerman and Joy Carlson were both in their mid-thirties, attractive, intelligent, and more than a little wary of her. Lillian Pershing, in her later thirties and intent on following in Elizabeth Bonner's shoes to someday become a senior partner, was more than wary. It took all her efforts to mask her open resentment of Victoria. Only Marsha Blythe, who was about forty and stunning in an elegant, cosmopolitan way, was friendly and pleasant. Even so, Victoria could sense a certain amount of tension emanating from her. Like the others, she viewed Walter Kensington's daughter not only as a competitor, but as an unfair and unwelcome intruder.

The truth was, Victoria couldn't blame them. These women had sacrificed a great deal to get where they were. They'd relinquished their social lives, killed themselves working for affluent clients they didn't necessarily believe in, and, on a daily basis, fought a tough, uphill political battle. They'd made a choice that Victoria had no desire to make.

She did her best to put them at ease, but short of changing her mind and not working at their firm, there was little she could do to appease them. There was no way they'd believe she didn't have her eye on a partnership. Not if she explained her priorities from today until next year. Their thought processes were just too different from hers.

Having mended fences to the best of her ability, Victoria began making her own rounds. She went into the dining room, waited while the attendant carved two slices of filet mignon and placed it on her plate along with some fresh asparagus spears, and surveyed the room. Miss Hatterman, who was included in all business affairs, was moving about, checking out the efficiency of the dining attendants and the quality of the waiters. Nothing unusual there. Victoria often thought that Miss Hatterman acted more like a wife—without the physical intimacy—than a secretary. Then again, after all these years, maybe she was entitled to regard herself as Walter Kensington's other half. She doubtless knew him better than anyone, including his family.

Victoria's fork paused halfway to her mouth. Miss Hatterman. What an excellent place to start.

She strolled over to the older woman. "Miss Hatterman. As usual, you've arranged a lovely party."

The unsmiling, sharp-featured woman inclined her head. "Your mother did most of the work. I merely assisted her. But I'm pleased you're enjoying yourself. The party is, after all, in your honor."

"I appreciate that. Everyone has been very welcoming. Although I feel as if I've met hundreds of clients tonight. I hope you'll help me keep them all straight."

"Of course. But it won't be necessary. You're your father's daughter. And no one retains more information or has sharper instincts than he. You'll be just fine."

"Thank you for your vote of confidence," Victoria replied. Sharp instincts, huh? Well, hers were telling her she was heading down the wrong path. She wasn't going to get a thing out of the tight-lipped Miss Hatterman, willingly or otherwise. If pushed, the executive secretary would clam up, become suspicious, and end Victoria's attempts before they began.

Time to get out of this dead end.

"I'm going to find my aunt and uncle," she told Miss Hatterman. "I've scarcely waved hello, and I've been here over two hours. Will you excuse me?"

"Of course."

Victoria put down her plate and left the dining room, trying to figure out her next move. She'd chatted with enough of her father's clients to realize there was no visible link between any of them and the Hope Institute. Except, of course, Benjamin Hopewell, who her father had somehow managed to bypass when he'd paraded her around the house. True, she'd met Mr. Hopewell several times over the years. Still, she would have thought her father would want to make her highly visible to such a major, long-standing client, to drive home the fact that she was now on board at Waters, Kensington, Tatem & Calder.

It was high time to find Benjamin Hopewell.

She found him without a problem. Making her way over to him was another matter entirely. He was surrounded by a group of people, three of whom were Elizabeth Bonner, Ian Block, and Zach.

As it was, Ian spotted her first and disengaged himself from the group, flashing her a charming smile as he walked over. "Ms. Kensington. I was wondering where you'd disappeared to. I half thought you'd collapsed from exhaustion."

Half thought? Victoria wondered. *Or half hoped?*

"I'm not that fragile, Mr. Block," she returned with an equally charming smile. "But I appreciate your concern."

He took the cool retort in stride. "Of course not. Are you enjoying yourself?"

"Enjoying myself and learning a lot. Matching names to faces will ease my way when I get started at Waters, Kensington, Tatem and Calder."

"Which is Monday, as I understand it."

She nodded, wondering if he'd already formed a strategy where she was concerned. "Monday afternoon. I have two client meetings at my own firm that morning."

He ran a hand over his clean-shaven jaw, studying her thoughtfully. "I'd imagine the transition would be difficult, going from a small firm that's just getting off the ground to a large, prominent one that's been thriving for decades."

She met his gaze head-on. "In some ways, yes; in others, no. Each type of firm has its benefits. Obviously, the monetary compensations are much greater at a prestigious firm, as is the notoriety. But there's something very fulfilling about providing legal counsel on a more personal basis. Then again, money has never been my prime motivator. Neither has a desire for power." She shrugged. "I'm not saying I'd toss either of them away—if I could have them on my terms. But if not, not. Life's a trade-off, Mr. Block. I'm sure you know that."

"All too well." His tone was casual, but his blue eyes were intense. "Do your partners share your altruism?"

A warning bell sounded in Victoria's head, telling her that Ian Block was going somewhere very specific with this. "I wouldn't call it altruism. But our goals are similar, yes. Why do you ask?"

"Because your father made it clear that Mr. London is avidly seeking referrals. I was wondering why, if wealth isn't an incentive."

Ah. Paul. So that's what this was about. Now the question was, why? Was Ian Block trying to needle her about her firm's underdog status, or was he reminding her that he controlled Paul's advancement opportunities?

Either way, it smacked of a power trip.

"Paul's interest in solid referrals stems from a couple of things," she stated flatly. "First, as you pointed out, ours is a fledgling firm. We need a few lucky breaks to gather momentum. And second, Paul is a superb corporate attorney who's eager for a challenge."

"Gather momentum," Ian repeated. "Is your firm struggling financially?"

"We're holding our own. We're not rolling in money, but we're not losing any sleep over keeping our doors open, either. And we're certainly not planning to compromise our objectives or our integrity to do so."

"A direct enough answer."

"An honest one. I prefer it that way. It saves my having to extricate myself from a lie. Which is what I'd be doing right about now, I suspect."

"And why is that?"

Her brows arched ever so slightly. "Because you know exactly how my firm is doing. Otherwise, you never would have asked the question. Which means you've now determined whatever it is about me you were trying to determine—be it how frank, how self-assured, or how loyal I am, or any combination of the three. Let me make it easy for you." She counted out on her fingers. "I don't lie. I don't squirm. And I don't hedge about the status of London, Kensington and Stone."

"So I see." Ian gave her an approving, if condescending, nod. "I also see that you're as formidable an opponent as your father."

"The same must apply to you, or you wouldn't be on a fast track to the top." She was pushing it, and she knew it. It was one thing playing who-can-out-psych-whom, keeping things cryptic and indirect. Now she was getting personal. She should probably stop. But her adrenaline didn't agree. Nor did her logic. If she saw this angle through, she just might clear the air and make it tolerable to work with this man.

Either that, or make working with him a nightmare.

"The fast track—is that how you perceive me?" Ian inquired in an offhand tone. "I'm flattered."

"It's not how *I* perceive you that matters. It's how my father perceives you. And I think we both know where things stand on that score."

"Your point?"

Victoria went for the gold. "Your agenda is to make senior partner before you hit forty. I say, go for it. But here's some advice. It's going to take every drop of your mental energy to go the distance. So don't waste any of that energy on me. I'm no threat to you. I'm not interested in becoming a partner at Waters, Kensington—senior or otherwise. The sooner you believe that, the easier it will be on us both. After that, who knows? We might find we actually work well together. The alternative is to spend the next three months playing cat and mouse. And, let me warn you, I'm very good at that game. I'm never the mouse."

Her final claim evoked a flicker of amusement. "Why does that sound like a warning rather than a reassurance?"

"It's neither. It's a fact."

"I'll have to take you at your word, won't I?"

Victoria inclined her head, gave him a cool, appraising look. "My word is good, Mr. Block. Ask around."

"I will." That charming smile was back in place. "I feel as if I've just been blindsided by a surprisingly compelling closing argument."

"I have that effect on other attorneys."

He chuckled. "I can imagine."

"Can you also imagine working with me without unnecessary tension?"

"Tension's good for us. It keeps us on our toes." He didn't answer her question—or maybe his next statement did. "By the way, call me Ian. Mr. Block sounds too old—even more so when someone in her twenties says it. I'm only thirty-seven. Don't age me."

"Ian," she agreed, wondering if she'd truly convinced him she wasn't the enemy or if this were some new tactic he'd decided to employ. Only time would tell. "And feel free to call me Victoria. I'm used to a more informal environment. Besides, it'll avoid confusion, since my father and I have the same last name."

"True." He glanced down at his goblet, saw it was empty. "Well then, Victoria, may I get you a drink?"

"Already done." Zach appeared out of nowhere, a glass of wine in each hand. "Here you are." He handed Victoria her cabernet.

She blinked, trying to read his expression. He looked as if he wanted to tell her something. Whatever it was, he obviously couldn't say it in front of Ian.

It had to pertain to Mr. Hopewell.

"Thank you." She took the wine. "Have you two met?"

Ian eyed Zach, clearly trying to assess his relationship to Victoria. "We were introduced earlier this evening, although I've read about Zachary's accomplishments in our alumni newsletter."

"Alumni newsletter? Oh, Harvard." As she spoke, Victoria realized that Zach's years and Ian's years at Harvard Law had probably overlapped.

"Um-hum. I graduated a year after Zachary arrived, so we didn't really cross paths. But his rise in the world of competitive intelligence is written up in glowing terms. And you—how do you two know each other?"

"Zach is my date tonight," Victoria supplied. "We're old friends. We met when I was in law school and he was a guest lecturer."

Ian gave Zach a questioning look. "You lectured at Columbia?"

"For a semester or two, yes. I wanted the students to understand how competitive intelligence is practiced within legal bounds."

"Ah." Ian nodded. "That makes sense. It teaches a respect for both our professions. And in the process, it hopefully breeds a generation of attorneys with a conscience."

"That's what I had in mind. A little idealism can't hurt in this high-pressure, blind-ambition world of ours." Zach glanced at Victoria. "Speaking of professionals with a conscience, in addition to present company, of course, I haven't even seen your aunt and uncle. Are they here tonight?"

She took his cue. "Yes. I waved at them twice. I still haven't managed to talk to them."

"Is now a good time, or are you and Ian in the middle of something?"

"No, now is fine." She turned to Ian. "Would you excuse us? The truth is, I feel very rude overlooking my family."

"Please, go ahead." Ian pointed toward the dining room. "I'll get that drink I was alluding to, and rejoin the group I was with."

Victoria's gaze flickered to Benjamin Hopewell. He was smiling and gesticulating to Elizabeth Bonner and Lillian Pershing, who'd also wandered over. "They seem to be enjoying themselves. What's the conversation about?"

"When I left?" Ian shrugged. "The usual—whose golf game is the most impressive."

"Now they're on to health care in the new millennium," Zach updated him. "Poor Hopewell's got his hands full defending the system."

"I'll give him some help." Ian moved off to do so.

"*That* was counterproductive," Victoria muttered. "Mr. Hopewell is one of my father's biggest clients. Ian will plant himself by his side and field negative questions like a White House press secretary. It'll be another hour before I manage to get Mr. Hopewell alone. And I've already spent two hours trying to find a way to do that."

"There's no need. Let it be."

Victoria's eyes narrowed. "What does that mean?"

"It means the topic we're interested in has already been probed. To do so again would be like waving a red flag in front of the wrong people's faces."

"Already been probed—by you. Without me there. How convenient."

"Not convenient. Necessary. You were in the middle of your two-hour royal procession. I had to grab the chance when I had it." Zach's tone took on an intimate note. "Believe me," he murmured, "I was no happier about your inaccessibility tonight than you. And not just for the reason we're discussing."

"Zach . . ."

He reached out, and his fingers traced the stem of her wineglass, lightly brushed hers. "Drink. After the past few hours of being center stage, you need it. Then, let's go find your uncle and aunt."

She stared up at him, thrown off balance by his sudden change in behavior. Struggling to keep a clear head, she brought her glass to her lips, thereby severing the contact of their fingers. "You're not going to elaborate on whatever you and Mr. Hopewell talked about?"

"Oh, I'll elaborate—later. For now, let's just get through this party and get out of here." He watched her sip her wine, and his gaze darkened, lingering on her mouth as it surrounded the rim of the crystal. "My concentration and tolerance are fading—fast."

Victoria abandoned the sip and opted for a gulp. Zach was pulling out a few more of the stops. She could feel it. And half of her wanted to bolt. But the other half, the brutally honest one, reminded her why she'd lingered over her appearance tonight, cared so damned much about his reaction.

Well, she was certainly getting the reaction she'd hoped for. The question was, what was she going to do about it?

"Stop agonizing," he suggested huskily. "There's nothing to decide now. We're in public. Save the decisions for later."

He wanted her. It wasn't only his pointed innuendos, or even his body language. It was the expression on his face, that intense, heated expression she remembered too well.

A few days ago she would have sworn this would never happen. She'd never walk this path again. And she was terrified to walk it now. Having an affair with Zach—it was unthinkable given what they'd once meant to each other. She knew that. The problem was, her feelings for him were so complicated. And mixed in with the rest was a powerful sexual attraction that made her insides burn and her limbs turn watery. If she let herself . . .

But she couldn't.

He was her Achilles' heel—the embodiment of all her pain and weakness. He was the one who'd carved that emotional hollow inside her, a hollow that, even now, only he could reach. She had to protect herself, no matter how great the temptation to let go.

She squared her shoulders. "My aunt and uncle are probably in the living room. Let's go."

Zach nodded, wordlessly accepting the temporary barrier she'd erected. He took her arm and led her through the stream of guests.

She spied Clarissa and Jim standing near the living room's bay window with a small group of people. She caught her uncle's eye, and whatever he saw there must have communicated some of her emotional turmoil, because he touched Clarissa's shoulder and politely excused the two of them, escorting his wife over to Victoria and Zach.

"I was wondering if you'd been devoured by the crowd," he teased, returning her fond hug.

"Almost." She turned to Clarissa, who looked stunning in an ice-blue cocktail dress. "You look exquisite." She pressed her cheek to her aunt's. "Thank you for coming," she whispered.

Clarissa smiled, understanding Victoria's meaning, but not letting it show. "I return the compliment. You're a beautiful guest of honor." Her gaze drifted to Zach, and her smile became more reserved. It was clear where her loyalties lay. "Nice to see you again, Zachary. It's been quite some time."

"Too long. And the pleasure is mine." If Zach noticed the cool reception, he didn't show it. He clasped Clarissa's hand, then Jim's. "Looking at the two of you, it's hard to believe four years have passed. Neither of you has changed a bit."

"It's our nonstop work schedules," Jim qualified in a

lighthearted tone. "They keep us young. Clarissa and I are never idle long enough for age to notice us, much less to catch up."

Zach chuckled. "In that case, there's hope for me, too." He shot Clarissa a questioning look. "You're still at Mount Sinai, I presume?"

"Yes," she acknowledged. "I'm about to finish my tenth year there."

"What research are you currently involved in?"

"Interestingly, we just touched on it. I'm in the middle of a study on the aging process. We're making great strides in isolating the factors that control it. If we can zero in on what causes it to accelerate or slow, we might be able to eventually add years to the human life span."

Zach's brows raised. "That's fascinating. Are you researching mental as well as physical aging?"

"Oh yes." Clarissa nodded. "Seeing a keen mind deteriorate is almost worse than seeing a healthy body do the same. And as for physiological preservation, I'm referring to sustaining the internal organs, keeping the muscles and tissues alive and vital. In other words, health and well-being, not vanity and youthful appearance. This is about quality of life, and longevity itself. Who knows? With enough time and resources, we could actually arrest the aging process entirely." A reproachful pause. "Did I just get on my soapbox?"

"Not at all," Zach assured her. "I spend too much time listening to people whose only passion is money. Hearing someone whose passion is her work is a breath of fresh air."

"Now you know how Aunt Clarissa stays young," Victoria added with more than a touch of pride. "She and Uncle Jim. They both devote their lives to enhancing life for others. Mind, body, and spirit."

"Speaking of which, how are you holding up?" Jim asked quietly. "It's been a long evening, this debut of yours."

Victoria wondered if her uncle had any idea just how hard the evening had been. "I'm in one piece," she replied lightly. "Although I'm afraid that everyone here thinks I've come on board at Waters, Kensington, Tatem and Calder as a permanent fixture—including my parents."

Her uncle's smile was sympathetic. "They're proud. Think of it that way."

"I'm trying."

"Good. Because your father is on his way over."

Scarcely were Jim's words out when Walter Kensington appeared at their sides. "Victoria. Here you are. The guests are starting to leave. Your mother's at the door, getting ready to see them off. She's waiting for you."

Victoria's brows rose. Apparently, she was part of tonight's good-bye crew. And judging from her father's unyielding tone and authoritative stance, she had no choice in the matter.

She hated being manipulated. She hated misrepresenting herself, which she'd been doing all evening by saying nothing to contradict her father's implications that her employment at his firm was permanent. After all these hours, she wanted nothing more than to refuse her father's request, stay right where she was, where she preferred to be, rather than joining him to act out the final scene in this sham.

On the other hand, she'd been trained since birth that public confrontation was akin to manslaughter. And frankly, in this case, it wasn't worth the fallout. Nor was it worth the anguish she'd cause her mother. Not for a few good-byes.

Fine, she decided, feeling her uncle's soothing gaze, her aunt's supportive smile. She'd complete the role she'd been assigned. At least then this party would end and she could go home.

"Would you excuse me?" she asked, glancing from her aunt and uncle to Zach.

"Of course." Jim spoke for them all. "See the guests off. Clarissa and I will have a nightcap with Zachary. After that,

I think he should take you home. You look exhausted. I know tonight marks an exciting step in your career, but that's no excuse for neglecting your health. Nothing's more important than that."

Walter's jaw tightened as his brother's message came through loud and clear. He didn't comment on it, instead gesturing for Victoria to accompany him. "Come. Let's make sure you say good night to the appropriate people."

The "appropriate people" were the same endless line of guests she'd been introduced to three or four hours ago. Except this time the list included Benjamin Hopewell.

"Victoria." Tall and fit for a man in his sixties, Mr. Hopewell clasped her hand, the tan on his rugged features accentuated by a thick head of snow-white hair. "I didn't get a chance to see you, much less to congratulate you, all night. I'm delighted you've signed on with your father's firm and, as a result, that you'll be working with me."

"It's good to see you, Mr. Hopewell," she acknowledged, sidestepping his reference to her supposed position at Waters, Kensington, Tatem & Calder, simultaneously fighting the impulse to blurt out her questions about the Hope Institute. She had to trust Zach. If she didn't, she could wind up hurting Audrey rather than helping her. "You're looking well."

"Am I?" He smiled ruefully. "I'm suddenly feeling quite old. I remember when you came up to my knee. Now you're a grown woman, not to mention a formidable attorney. Where did the years go?"

"If we knew that, we'd stop them from going there," Elizabeth Bonner declared, joining them as she slipped into her evening jacket. "Are you leaving, Benjamin?" she asked him. "I have some agreements with me I was hoping to turn over to you for review. They're in my car, which is being brought around. Can you wait?"

"Of course," he agreed politely. "Good night, Victoria," he turned back to say. "It's always a pleasure to see you."

"Thank you. I hope our professional paths will cross soon." Victoria spoke automatically, her mind veering off in another direction entirely. Elizabeth Bonner's appearance had certainly been timely. Was that coincidental? It didn't seem that way. In fact, it seemed as if she'd intentionally whisked Mr. Hopewell off. But why—to avoid Victoria? Had she been asked to do it? For that matter, why had she spent so much of the evening at Mr. Hopewell's side?

This bore some reflection.

"Good night, Victoria," Ms. Bonner was saying crisply. "I'll see you Monday afternoon. That file we discussed will be ready. We'll talk before the end of the day."

"Yes," Victoria agreed slowly, studying the attractive older woman. "We will."

20

It was after midnight when Zach drove the car through the gates and turned onto the road.

Victoria emitted a huge sigh, sinking into the seat and shutting her eyes. "Thank God. Freedom."

He chuckled. "That bad?"

"Worse." She cracked open an eye. "What did you find out from Mr. Hopewell?"

"Hmmm." Zach glanced at his Rolex. "A minute and a half. That's a record, even for you."

"Are you going to answer me?"

"Of course." Zach stopped teasing her and steered the car toward the parkway. "You're going to be disappointed, though. What I got wasn't a confession. Just the opposite, in fact. I'm pretty sure the guy doesn't know the first thing about what's going on in that place."

"Give me specifics."

"Okay, specifics. We discussed Hopewell Industries and the entire health-care business. I mentioned the Hope Institute, said I knew someone who'd placed a relative there. He didn't tense up or try to steer clear of the subject. I pursued it, from a business standpoint, asking if he'd regretted selling the Institute, since it was obviously a big moneymaker. His reaction was straightforward and logical. He said no, that even though his company was now strong and on its feet again, he didn't think it was prudent to invest so much capital in a medical facility. I asked if he still did business with the Institute, and he confirmed what we already knew—that his corporation sells medical supplies to them. I even went so far as to ask if he'd kept a seat on the Institute's board, and he said no, that he'd sold the business outright. The details he provided were exactly those the FBI gave me. I don't think he was lying."

"Great." Victoria frowned. "That only adds new questions. Such as, if Mr. Hopewell's out of the picture, why did my father keep me as far away from him as possible? He never even brought me over to speak with the man, and he's one of Waters, Kensington's biggest clients. And when I finally did speak with him for the first time, why did Elizabeth Bonner appear out of nowhere and usher him off?"

Zach shot Victoria a sidelong glance. "Elizabeth Bonner? You think she's involved?"

"I don't know. Maybe I'm being paranoid. Or maybe I've watched too many detective movies. But it sure seemed like she was anxious to get Mr. Hopewell out of that house, and at the exact moment—the first moment—I happened to be speaking to him. Not to mention the amount of time she spent stationed by his side tonight." Victoria ran her fingers through her hair, angled her head to face Zach. "Does that sound crazy?"

"Nothing sounds crazy. You made some good observations. What you saw could be coincidence. Or it could be part of Ms. Bonner's efforts to get her name added to the firm's by doing the bidding of a senior partner with the power to put it there—someone who directed her to keep Hopewell busy and away from you."

"And by that someone, you mean my father."

A nod. "Unless, of course, she herself is involved. She could be working with your father on the Hope Institute account. The problem with that theory is that my gut tells me Hopewell's not a player here. So why would your father want to keep you away from him?"

Victoria's fingertip traced the leather grain of the seat cushion. She knew her father's mind, knew what he valued. If his connection to Benjamin Hopewell was strictly honest, there was just one explanation for his behavior.

"He wouldn't want a scene."

"What?"

Victoria didn't realize she'd spoken her thoughts aloud until Zach responded.

"I said, he wouldn't want a scene." She sighed. "In my father's mind, a scene is defined as anything that might arise out of an inappropriate question or remark. He knows I'm worried about Audrey and that I've doubted his candor with regard to her situation. He also knows I do my homework. So he realizes I'd know about Mr. Hopewell's onetime ownership of the Hope Institute. Bringing up that subject would be right in character for me. For my father, well, not only would he view that as a major indiscretion, but one that might incite an unpleasant display. You get my drift."

"Yeah, I get it." Zach rubbed the back of his neck. "More rules by Walter Kensington." A pensive pause. "Maybe."

Victoria turned her head away and stared rigidly out the window. The night was dark and drizzly, and the Merritt Parkway was quiet, with only an occasional pair of headlights slicing the darkness. The trees lining the side of the road whizzed by, the whirring of the tires the only sound in the car.

"You're angry," Zach said at last.

"I'm not angry. I'm frustrated, and defensive, and . . . yes, maybe a little angry." She kept her face averted. "You're a logical man by nature. And when it comes to your work, you're objective; you go by the facts. So, I tell myself you're not intentionally trying to implicate my father. Yet you seem to want to believe the worst of him. Why?"

"I don't want to believe the worst of him, Victoria. I want to get at the truth," Zach stated bluntly. "But as for being objective, I'm not. Not in this case. Because if your father is guilty—and I do mean *if*—you're going to be hurt. And when it comes to you, I'm anything but objective."

Tension filled the car.

Swallowing, Victoria tried to keep her voice steady when she replied. "I understand that. I do. But I don't think *you* understand how personal my stake is in all this. It's my family we're talking about, Zach. My sister, whose health is a mess. My mother, who's so fragile I shudder to think what she'd do if she found out about all this, much less if it became public. And my father who, with or without his knowledge, might be linked to a drug syndicate." She had to force out that last part. Even now, the idea made her sick. "So forgive me if I can't be as stoic as you. I don't doubt your concern for me, but for you this is just another FBI case—"

"No," Zach interrupted. "It's not."

Something about his tone made her whip her head around. He sounded strained, his voice rough, taut.

His appearance confirmed it. His gaze was fixed on the road, but his grip on the steering wheel was rigid, his jaw clenched so tight she could see the muscle working in it.

"Zach?" she asked tentatively.

"The other night in the bar, you asked what kind of closure I was looking for," he said in a controlled monotone. "The most basic kind. I want to wipe out the bastards who were responsible for my father's death. I never had the chance. Now I do."

Everything inside Victoria went very cold. "Are you telling me that this drug syndicate is the same one who shot—?"

"That's what I'm telling you."

"Oh, God." Reflexively, she reached out and laid her hand on his sleeve. She could feel how stiff his forearm muscles were, even through the layers of his tux and shirt. And that was nothing compared to what was going on inside him. She could only imagine what this was doing to him. "Zach, I'm so sorry. I had no idea."

"Why would you? You're used to my going after close facsimiles. Why would you assume this was the real thing?"

She swallowed, watching his profile, remembering how hard it was for him to talk about his father's death. "Have you discussed this with anyone? Do they know how close to home this case strikes?"

"The FBI, you mean?" A slight shrug. "They're not stupid. They have my entire history on file. I'm sure they figured out I'd have the incentive to help them before they even contacted me. They probably viewed it as an added bonus to my competitive intelligence skills. But, no, I haven't discussed it with anyone. No one but you."

He glanced down at his sleeve and studied her fingers there before turning his gaze back to the road. "So, believe me, Victoria, I don't want the wrong people punished. This is not about bringing down your father. It's about bringing down anyone affiliated with that drug syndicate, peeling away the layers until we put every last one of them behind bars. Then my parents will be at peace. And so will I."

Her hand slid up to the steering wheel and covered his as she tried somehow to absorb his pain. No one knew better than she how much this tragedy had dominated his life. And here she was, accusing him of being detached when, in fact, he was as deeply and personally involved in this investigation as she. "I'm so sorry," she repeated softly, her fingers intertwining with his, rubbing against them in slow, gentle caresses. "If you need to talk, I'm here."

It was meant as comfort.

It turned into more.

Electric charges sizzled between their joined hands, charges heightened by the emotions underlying Zach's revelation and the intimacy of knowing he'd shared it only with her. Zach captured her fingers and brought them to his lips. He brushed soft kisses across her knuckles, uncurling her fingers to kiss each one. He pressed her open palm to his mouth, savored her warm skin, his fingers sliding between hers, holding them apart. His tongue glided forward, traced the tender recesses he'd exposed, licking her sensitive flesh in slow, suggestive motions that were blatantly carnal.

Victoria began to tremble, desire slamming to life inside her. She didn't have the strength or the will to fight it. Not this time. Maybe it was the kaleidoscope of events that had erupted in one week's time. Maybe it was just emotional meltdown. Regardless, all she wanted was this, Zach, and the joy of losing herself in the magic they'd once made with their bodies.

Later, she wondered if they would even have made it home, or if they would have stopped at the closest motel, scrambled frantically into the room and made love before ever reaching the bed.

She'd never know.

The unmarked black sedan roared out of nowhere. It tore up the left lane, rounded the curve until it was directly beside them, then began forcing them over to the side.

"Christ." Zach grabbed the wheel with both hands, struggling to maintain control of the car. Sparks flew from the passenger side as the guardrail tore off paint and metal. Quickly, he jammed his foot on the brake, trying to put some distance between them and the other car.

The other car would have none of it. It slowed down to match Zach's pace, continuing to crowd him.

"Is he drunk?" White faced, Victoria tried to peer into the other vehicle. But the windows were as dark as the night, and she couldn't make out anything about the driver.

"No. He's stone sober," Zach replied, scrutinizing the roadside in the hope of finding a means of escape. "And trying like hell to—"

There was a break in the divider. Even as Zach jerked the wheel in that direction, the unmarked sedan surged over, striking Zach's side of the car once, twice, shoving him off the parkway.

Zach gave the wheel a sharp turn. Their car swerved onto

the grass and bounced down a shallow decline. Unable to make out anything now that the street lamps were gone, Zach operated on instinct. He slammed his foot on the brake, sending the car weaving from side to side toward what he hoped was the thicket of bushes he'd spotted just before veering off the road.

He'd remembered right.

They rammed into the bushes. Twigs snapped, scratched their windshield, and yielded, the thick brush slowing their motion as they advanced.

Finally the car came to a halt.

Back up on the road, their assailant slammed down on his gas pedal and, with a loud roar, drove his car into the night.

Silence.

Zach jerked into motion, releasing his seat belt and reaching for her. "Victoria. Are you all right?"

She stared at him in dazed bewilderment, then looked down at herself, assessing her slightly battered but uninjured state. A shaky nod. "I think so." Actually, she felt numb. "Whoever was in that car just tried to kill us."

"No," Zach corrected. "Not to kill us. Just to scare us." He cupped Victoria's face between his hands and studied her features. "You're sure you're not hurt?"

"Positive. Unless you count a few bruises and a bad case of shattered nerves." She drew an unsteady breath. "What do you mean, just to scare us?"

"He had ample chance to kill us. He didn't. Instead, he picked an open area to shove us off the road. He obviously chose it on purpose. That was a scare, not a murder attempt."

Victoria squeezed her eyes closed. "This is about the Hope Institute. We're being warned. *I'm* being warned. They want me to stop poking around." She swallowed. "Which means they suspect I'm still doing that. How, I don't know. And who would they send? Mr. Cigar? I was hoping he'd stopped watching me. If it was him, how did he know where I was going tonight? Did he follow us all the way to Greenwich? Or . . ." Her voice quavered. "Did my father tip him off?"

"Don't." Zach caressed her cheeks with his thumbs. "Don't start thinking like that. For what it's worth, I don't believe your father would hurt you. This wasn't his idea. I don't buy it. You're his legacy, his chance to carry on the Kensington name. He respects the hell out of you. And you're his daughter. Let's remember that."

"*We* do. Does *he?*"

Tenderly, Zach kissed the top of her head, then reached for his cell phone. "Let's get out of here."

The car was in decent shape, considering what it had been through. The entire passenger side was a mass of shredded metal and paint, but the driver's side had just a few dents, and mechanically the car was fine. The police wrote up the report, chalked it up as the act of a drunk driver, and sent them on their way.

The ride home was silent.

"I'm going to return the car at the hotel and explain what happened," Zach said quietly as they rounded Sixty-fourth Street. "Then we'll catch a cab to your place."

Victoria nodded.

"You go inside," Zach instructed as they pulled up in front of the familiar red awnings that heralded the entrance to the Plaza Athénée and a doorman came around to assist Victoria from the car. "Wait for me in the lounge or the lobby. I won't be long."

She settled herself in the hotel's posh, gleaming tiled lobby, resting her head against the back of the French antique chair and thinking that it felt like six months rather than six hours since she'd left the city that night.

"Ms. Kensington?" A uniformed attendant with a distinctly European accent appeared by her side.

"Yes?"

He handed her a glass of sparkling water. "Mr. Hamilton asked me to give you this, and to say he'll be with you shortly."

"Thank you," Victoria said gratefully, taking the glass. "It's been a rather harrowing evening."

"So I heard. I'm terribly sorry. If there's anything you need, don't hesitate to ask."

"The water is perfect. Thank you."

With a half bow, the attendant hurried off.

The Plaza Athénée, Victoria thought, sipping her water and taking in the classic ambience of the elegant muraled lobby with a private inner glow. It had been four years since she'd walked through those doors. And nothing had changed. It was still the most exquisite, dignified hotel imaginable, a step into a world that was a continent and a lifetime away.

At the front desk, late-night clerks shuffled papers as efficiently as if it were midday rather than one-thirty in the morning. In the rich mahogany alcove that housed the managerial station, the concierge spoke with a few hotel guests who were night owls looking for the best local hot spots. And in the elevators, staff members wheeling food carts rode up to deliver room service to waiting guests.

A soft smile touched Victoria's lips. How many nights had Zach taken advantage of the hotel's twenty-four-hour room service to have wine and cheese sent up at 2 or 3 A.M. because they'd been too absorbed in each other to eat? How many nights had they skipped dinner altogether?

She glanced down and studied her palm, touched the soft places Zach's lips had grazed a few hours earlier. They'd be in bed right now if that maniac hadn't pushed them off the road. They'd be together in a way she'd tried desperately to forget and couldn't. Maybe she was being a fool. Maybe those snatches of happiness she'd talked about really were all they had. Maybe tomorrow's pain didn't matter. Maybe . . .

"Victoria?"

Her head snapped up and she blinked, still lost in her reflections.

Zach was standing beside her chair. He extended his hand, helped her to her feet, placing her empty glass on a nearby table. "We're all set." He frowned when he saw how disoriented she looked. "Victoria," he said carefully, sounding as if he'd struggled with a decision, then made it. "It's been a long night. You're at the breaking point. Why don't we stay here? I've got a bottle of cabernet in my room. You can have a glass and go to bed. I'll stay in the living room. My suite's almost as big as your apartment."

For more reasons than she cared to contemplate, that sounded like heaven. "If you throw in a long soak in that incredible bathtub, you've got yourself a deal," she heard herself say.

"Done."

They rode up in the elevator without speaking, and Victoria stepped out on the tenth floor, automatically heading for Suite 1010. It always had been Zach's favorite. Actually, it reminded her a lot of him—worldly, magnificent, and understated. She remembered the suite in vivid detail. Plush blue carpet, blue floral drapes, a full living room, a dining room that led out to the solarium and balcony, and a bathroom she could lose herself in.

And, right off the bathroom, a bedroom brimming with memories.

It looked exactly the same, right down to the antique furnishings. But then, a hotel was supposed to be consistent. It was what brought guests back time after time, to stay in the same comfortable surroundings, enjoy the same amenities.

Conjure up the same memories.

"I'll pour the wine," Zach said, locking the door and heading across to the dining room's mahogany end table. "You run your bath."

Victoria complied, going into the bathroom and shutting

the door. This room was sheer opulence, all marble, with every amenity you could ask for. She turned on the bath taps and wriggled out of her clothes, shrugging into the thick terry robe that hung on the back of the door.

Zach had been wearing it. The robe had his scent, together with the scent of his cologne.

She padded out to the living room where he was standing, having poured two glasses of wine. His gaze drifted over her, but he said nothing, just handed her a glass. She took it with her.

Five minutes later, she was immersed in heaven, hot water lapping around her, a glass of good cabernet on the ledge. She sank down in the tub, closed her eyes, and let the heat envelop her. She didn't want to think about anything, not the party, not the Hope Institute, and definitely not the person who'd run them off the road. Mentally, she was drained, too tired to do much of anything. But not physically. Physically, she felt warm and languid, yet revitalized by the bath, relaxed enough to rest but too awake to sleep.

It was with great reluctance that she left the tub twenty minutes later, and then only because the water had turned cool and her skin had started to pucker. The ends of her hair were damp, but she felt no compulsion to dry them. She just left them to air dry, slipped back into the robe, and went out.

She'd thought perhaps Zach was dozing, because the suite was silent. But he was standing on the balcony, staring at the lights of the city. He looked up when she emerged and, seeing her, came back inside.

"Are you okay? You were in there a long time."

"Um-hum." She ran her fingers through her damp strands of hair. "Just unwinding."

His lids were hooded, hiding his gaze, and droplets of rain clung to his hair. "Unwinding sounds good. I think I'll do the same."

"A shower?" Victoria asked. Zach didn't like baths.

"A shower," he confirmed.

She glanced down ruefully at herself. "I stole your robe."

A corner of his mouth lifted. "I'll get a lawyer. In the meantime, I'll suffer with a towel." He walked past her, paused, then continued to the bathroom. "Help yourself to the bed."

"Thanks. I will." She went to the bedroom doorway, then turned. "Good night."

"Good night."

Wrapped in the terrycloth robe, Victoria curled up on the bed, willing sleep to come.

It didn't.

She lay awake for almost an hour, first listening to the shower water run, then hearing Zach move around as he got ready for bed.

The clock told her it was two-fifty. She'd had a disaster of a night. She should be out for the count.

But she wasn't. And she knew exactly why.

She looked around the room, felt its bittersweet familiarity, and gave up the battle, letting the tidal wave of memories wash through her. How many hours had she and Zach spent in this bed? Countless. They'd wanted each other with a hunger that was bottomless, endless, insatiable. She'd never imagined being so wildly uninhibited, never knew such intense passion existed. Then again, she'd never believed Zach existed.

But he did.

She'd wanted him urgently, incessantly.

She still did.

With a shiver, she rolled onto her side. Her skin felt hot, the roughness of the terrycloth making it tingle. Her heart was beating rapidly, and she couldn't stay still.

Zach was awake. She could hear him tossing and turning, probably battling the same deluge of memories she was. Finally, she heard him get up as he abandoned sleep altogether. She squeezed her eyes shut, willing herself not to care that she could put an end to their torment with one simple act.

Indifference wasn't in the cards.

Neither was abstinence.

He came to her doorway, hovered there as he looked in to check on her. She felt his presence, reminded herself that she could ignore him, wait for his shadow to vanish, and, until it did, pretend to be asleep.

She didn't.

She opened her eyes, propped herself up on one elbow. "Hi."

"Hi." His voice was rough. Even in the dim glow cast by the light he'd left on in the living room, she could see he was wearing only a pair of jeans. "I thought you were sleeping."

"I wasn't. I'm not." With a sense of inevitability, she stood, walked toward him.

"Victoria." There was a fierce expression on his face, a look of almost pained restraint. "I . . ." Whatever he was going to say was never uttered. Their gazes met and locked, and Victoria reached out, lay her palm on his bare chest. He caught her wrist, brought her palm to his mouth, and kissed it as he had earlier, this time with an urgency that burned through them both.

"I want to," Victoria whispered to his unspoken question. Then she was in his arms, crushed against him, tugging his mouth down to hers even as his hand crumpled in her hair, dragging her mouth up to his. Their lips met in a frenzy of need, parting instantly so their tongues could meld, so they could deepen the kiss before it began.

Zach lifted her off the carpet, devouring her mouth again and again as he carried her to the bed. He unbelted her robe, and she shrugged out of it, then yanked at the button on his jeans.

She was naked before they reached the bed. He was naked a heartbeat later. He pushed her backward onto the sheets, the weight of his body covering her, anchoring her there.

There was nowhere else Victoria wanted to be.

She couldn't touch him fast enough, completely enough. She wanted to rediscover every inch of him at once. The powerful breadth of his shoulders, the muscled planes of his back, the hair-roughened wall of his chest. It was all so achingly familiar, so unbearably erotic. Her entire body was on fire, burning with need, pulsing with four years of pent-up longing. She arched, rubbed herself against him, the throbbing between her legs so acute it bordered on pain.

Zach caught her wrists, pinned them to the bed, and began devouring her. His mouth was rough, hungry, his teeth lightly scraping her skin as he tasted her neck, her shoulders, the scented hollow at her throat. His hands shook as they shaped and caressed her breasts, defined the curves of her waist, her hips, her thighs. He bent her knees, pulled them up and around him, needing to feel himself between her legs. Then he lowered his head, his lips closing around her nipple, tugging it into his mouth with a suction that made tiny explosions of pleasure erupt inside her so that she cried out. He shifted to her other breast, his lips surrounding her nipple, pulling and tugging until she was frantic.

His fingers slid between her thighs, slipped inside her, discovering the wetness that shattered his control.

"I can't wait." His voice was guttural, his motions jerky as he kneed her legs farther apart.

She helped him, wrapping her legs around his flanks and, reaching down, closing her fingers around his erection.

Zach's breath hissed out between his teeth, and he probed at the entrance to her body, then pushed inside. Bracing his arms on either side of her, he thrust all the way in, cursing as he felt her body's resistance, the tender skin fighting to accommodate him after four years of abstinence.

"Tory." The endearment brought back a flood of memories as poignant as the feeling of his body penetrating hers.

Tory. No one but Zach called her that. And he only called her that in bed, when he was deep inside her and there was no world outside the one she had in his arms. "God, sweetheart, I'm sorry." His voice was harsh with worry and regret, even as he continued to thrust back and forth, moving deeper and deeper inside her, withdrawing only to push all the way back in. "Dammit. Goddammit. I'm hurting you."

Victoria's breath was suspended in her throat. Yes, she felt raw, stretched, her flesh unused to this intrusion. But she was caught up in a maelstrom of sensation so acute, so magnificent, she couldn't bear it. Her nails dug into Zach's shoulders, her hips lifted greedily, her thighs clenching around him even as her internal muscles coiled tighter and tighter around his rigid penis. The pleasure intensified with each thrust, and she arched to meet him again and again and again, a harsh cry of frustration and need escaping her lips. She wanted this to last, needed to make it do so. But she couldn't. Her body wouldn't wait. Not after four years without.

"Zach." Her hands slid down his back, gripped the base of his spine, and she urged him into her, faster, harder.

He needed no encouragement. He was battering her with his thrusts, unable to slow down, to think, or even to breathe. He was pounding toward his own climax, his entire body screaming to pour itself into her.

Victoria arched, a low sob wrenching from her throat, her body shuddering as the spasms boiled up inside her. She pulsed around him, gripping his entire length, drawing him high into her at the exact moment he needed to be there.

He climaxed like a wild man, grabbing the headboard's mahogany posts, his knuckles turning white as his hips pumped convulsively. He spurted into her, hot bursts of completion, and Victoria clung to him, let the pleasure spin itself out, helpless in the throes of her own orgasm, shaken by the magnitude of his.

Recovery took longer than the act itself.

Victoria sank into the bed, blanketed by Zach's body, too spent to move. Her mind was blissfully empty, her body still quivering with aftershocks. She felt Zach shudder, felt his breath release on a sigh. Then he relaxed, his weight pressing hers into the mattress. He was still inside her, and neither of them made any move to change that.

Long minutes ticked by.

Finally, Zach stirred, turning his head so his lips were just above Victoria's ear. "Did I hurt you?" he asked in a rough, gravelly voice.

"No." Her own voice was barely audible. She was shaking, she realized. Then again, so was he.

Zach released the headboard, his hands moving down to cradle her head, his weight shifting to his elbows. "Victoria."

She opened her eyes with the greatest of efforts, met his stunned gaze in the darkness of the room. Rather than lazy with sexual satisfaction, his features were set in stark lines of amazement. His breathing was still ragged, his face sheened in perspiration, and strands of dark hair clung to his forehead.

"Victoria." He said her name again, his probing gaze searching her face.

"Hmm?" It was all she could muster.

"I wanted to slow down. I couldn't."

"I know. Neither could I." She reached up, brushed the damp wisps of hair off his forehead.

"Sweetheart, I—"

"Shhh." Victoria silenced him, pressed her fingers to his lips. "I don't want to talk. I don't want to think. I just want to feel." She caressed his jaw, slid her hand around to stroke the nape of his neck, run her fingers through the wet silk of his hair. "Can we do that?"

He moved his head from side to side, savoring her touch. Then he reached down, capturing her other arm and bringing it around his neck. "We can do anything and everything you want," he muttered thickly, bending to take her mouth under his.

Borrowed time. That was the phrase that drifted through Victoria's head. It was what they were on. A dazzling respite before the insurmountable issues slammed back to the forefront, before the painful aftermath of what was really happening in this bed intervened and the sober reality of their investigation redominated their lives.

All that would occur soon enough.

But not tonight.

Zach must have felt the same sense of urgency, the same yearning as she to grab these stolen moments while they lasted, because he drew back abruptly, a look of almost fierce determination on his face. "Tonight is ours," he declared, his thumbs caressing her cheekbones. "God knows we deserve it. Nothing exists but us. No regrets. No outside world. No walls."

"Just what I had in mind," she murmured.

He lowered his mouth to kiss her again, savoring her lips in a slow, sensual exploration. "We're going to live every fantasy I've had these past four years, and then some. You're going to lose yourself in my arms. I'm going to drown in your body. And nothing, *nothing,* is going to intrude."

Blindly, Victoria nodded, streamers of wet heat unfurling inside her at the images Zach's words conveyed. It had been so long, so long and, despite the magnitude of her first climax, she wanted him again.

Zach felt her response. He went very still, his eyes darkening to near black, his body hardening inside hers. "God, how I want you," he ground out, his hands gliding down the length of her arms, sliding underneath her so he could grip her bottom, lift her into him. "You have no idea how much. But you will. Because I'm going to have you, again and again. And you're going to have me. All night. Every damned second."

Her hips arched in response, her legs wrapped around

his. The night was too short, she thought, drunk on sensation. Mere hours from ending. She shoved aside that realization, hurled herself into the moment.

Sharp pleasure exploded through them both.

Zach sucked in his breath, reading the expression on her face as if she had spoken. Teeth gritted, he thrust forward, pushed all the way inside her. "The hell with tonight. Plan to spend all day Sunday in bed."

21

Sunday, April 23
2:30 P.M.

The Hope Institute was quiet.

Lunch had been served. The trays had been collected. Nurses wrote up reports at their stations, preparing for the afternoon shift to take over. Patients slept, watched TV, or dozed. Doctors, having completed their rounds, exited the building through the underground garage.

The disinfection team assembled in Conference Room A.

The Institute's attorney of record walked over to the door to detain Frank Harper, the head of security, before he entered. They spoke in a quiet undertone. "It's done?"

"Yup."

"You're sure they weren't hurt?"

"Positive. They were scared shitless, but fine. I made sure. Leaman followed them home. He just called in. He's hanging around Hamilton's hotel. They're in there, safe and sound. Also, I got a report from our hacker. Victoria Kensington's computers are clean, at work and at home."

"Good." A satisfied nod. "Do we know how Zachary Hamilton fits into all this yet?"

"Not yet. Soon. My guess is, he's just helping her out so he can get laid."

"Don't guess. Know." A restraining hand on Harper's arm as, behind them, the team leader called for the meeting to begin. "Remember, no one is to find out about last night's fender bender."

"Gotcha."

They entered the room.

Harper locked the door, and the group convened around the oval table.

"This meeting is covered under attorney-client privilege," the team leader pronounced. "Now, let's start with a status report on existing patients." A purposeful look at Gloria Rivers, the RN at the table. "Where do things stand?"

Ms. Rivers folded her hands in front of her. "Mr. Kenwood's bad. I don't think he'll last the week."

"We expected this. He's already outlived the time set forth in his original prognosis by six months."

"I know. He's responded beautifully. No complaints—from him or his family." Ms. Rivers frowned. "Speaking of families, we have a more immediate concern. Mrs. Housley's and Mr. Pratt's next of kin are calling daily. They're upset that their visits have been suspended for so long. The taped messages aren't appeasing them anymore."

"Not surprising. It's been a good couple of months." A contemplative pause. "Very well. Call both families. Stagger the calls—one today, one early tomorrow. Express our condolences. Arrange for two separate counseling sessions at the Institute. When the families arrive, make sure to review with them all the papers they signed. If all goes smoothly, they can pick out the urns on the spot." A glance at the attorney. "All that's in order, I assume?"

"Perfectly."

"Good."

"I'll take care of it." The nurse scribbled down a reminder. "Also, we have two patients who were discharged last month coming in for follow-ups. Shall I go through the customary procedure?"

"Yes. Give them the injection here, the pills to take with them."

"Okay." More scribbling. Uneasily, Ms. Rivers pushed aside her pad, rolling her pen between her fingers. "I have one more priority matter to discuss. Audrey Kensington. She's becoming increasingly agitated. You instructed me to keep her off heavy doses of medication, but I'm not sure that's possible. Not if you want to keep her from upsetting the other patients."

The team leader turned to glare at the attorney. "I thought she'd been handled."

"She was."

"Not effectively enough, it seems. Fine. I'll handle her myself. Her presence is compromising the Institute. She's got to go." A dismissive wave, and a quick glance at the meeting agenda. "On to new arrivals. We're expecting two tomorrow. Mrs. Housley's room is already filled, but Mr. Pratt's is still available, as is the one directly across from it. Prepare those two rooms for new patients."

2:55 P.M.

They were in one of those meetings.

Now was her chance.

Audrey wriggled off the bed, leaned against the night table to gather her strength. She had to do this. And it had to be now. The nurses were changing shifts and wouldn't be in to check on her for at least fifteen minutes. The powers that be were occupied in the conference room. It was the only time she could pull it off.

She dragged shallow breaths into her lungs, trying to ease the dizziness she was already beginning to experience. She wasn't ready to be off the bed. But she couldn't let that stop her.

She brushed damp strands of hair off her face, ignoring the weakness that enveloped her like a heavy blanket. She gathered her hospital gown around her. Slowly, knees wobbling, she made her way to the door. She peeked through the glass, scanning the hall.

The area was deserted.

The phone was just around the bend.

She had to get there.

Arms quivering, she pushed at the door.

3:30 P.M.

Zach knew their time was almost up.

Propped on one elbow, he watched Victoria sleep, drinking her in with a wonder he'd known only once before and never believed he'd know again.

He reached out to trace the silky curve of her shoulder, the delicate column of her spine. She was curled on her side, her back to him, her hair a disheveled black cloud on the pillow, her exquisite features utterly peaceful.

Her breathing was deep, even. She was exhausted. So, for that matter, was he. They'd made love for hours, until long after dawn had become day. Then they'd slept, but only in snatches, awakening every hour or so to reach for each other, to drown in the pleasure their bodies made together. Sometimes their coupling was slow and seductive, a building of sensual tension, as varied and creative as his fantasies. More often it was swift, frantic, a desperate need to be fused as deeply and completely as possible.

The bed was a shambles. There was only one pillow remaining on it, and that was the one under Victoria's head. The bedding was a tangle on the floor, and even the sheet Victoria had pulled over herself when she'd dozed off a short while ago had slipped down and was now twisted around her hips.

God, she was beautiful.

Of its own volition, Zach's palm shifted, whispered over her breast. Yes, he'd had her—again and again. But the wanting hadn't lessened. It never would.

He leaned forward, cupped her breast more fully, pressed his lips to the side of her neck. He nuzzled her, inhaled the fragrance of her skin, the heavy scent of their lovemaking.

That alone made him hard.

He continued stroking her, felt her nipple pucker beneath his touch. He rolled her to her back, drew her hardened nipple between his lips, circled it with his tongue. She made a soft sound of pleasure, her eyelids fluttering slightly before sliding shut again. Her lashes swept her cheeks, telling Zach she was still asleep.

He shifted his weight, easing her legs apart and rising to his knees between them. He caressed her calves, her thighs, combing his fingers through the soft triangle of hair between them. His fingertips slipped inside her, stroked erotic circles on her flesh. She was already wet from their lovemaking, and the wetness intensified, her body responding even in slumber. With another broken murmur, she began squirming, her head tossing on the pillow as the cobwebs of sleep faded. He waited only until she was fully awake, until her lashes lifted and her stunned, aroused gaze found his.

Then he opened her with his fingers and lowered his head.

Victoria cried out, her hands groping for Zach at the first stroke of his tongue. He shuddered, losing himself in loving her. Her taste, her scent, her softness—it all made him crazy. And her sharp whimpers of pleasure nearly pushed him over the edge. Desire slammed through him like gunfire, and he deepened his caresses, draping her thighs over his shoulders and sinking his tongue deep inside her. He cupped her bottom, lifted her closer to him, his lips devouring her, his tongue swirling over her swollen flesh until she arched wildly, dug her fingers into his hair, crying out his name and convulsing in his arms.

He didn't wait.

Crawling over her, he thrust all the way inside before her spasms had lessened. He withdrew, pushed deep again, fighting back his orgasm as he watched her face. She was perfect, her features flushed and damp, her eyes glazed with sensation, her breath coming in pants. She realized how close he was. He saw it in her eyes, knew it the instant she reached up, pulled him into her, and wrapped herself around him inside and out. Her climax gripped him, pulsing around his erection, squeezing him until all restraint shattered. Zach groaned, his fingers biting into her hips as he matched her wildness with his own.

He came violently, hard spasms that slammed through him, jetted into her. His entire body jerked with the impact, and when it was over, he just sank onto her, into her, not even trying to move.

Victoria's limbs unclenched and relaxed, her fingers trailing lightly up and down his spine. "Thanks for waking me," she murmured in a lazy voice.

Zach smiled against her hair. "Sorry I did?"

"What do you think?"

"I think you might forgive me."

"I think you're right." She stirred, turning her head toward the clock. "What time is it?"

"Does it matter?"

She swallowed, his question dragging reality back to the forefront. "Yes. It matters."

"It doesn't have to."

"Zach, please." She kept her gaze averted. "We agreed not to talk."

"That was when we had a whole night ahead of us. Now . . ." His hands, balled into fists, made deep depressions in the pillow beneath her head. "I can already feel you pulling away. Ironic, isn't it, considering how tightly joined our bodies are?"

She wet her lips with the tip of her tongue. "Our bodies aren't the problem. They never were." Her gaze shifted back, finding his. "Can't we just call this an incredible night in bed and stop trying to make it more?"

"No. We can't. *I* can't. What's more, neither can you."

"I can try." She pressed at his shoulders until he eased off her. Then she climbed out of bed, groped on the floor for the robe, and headed for the bathroom. "I'm taking a shower. Then I'm going home. A lot's happened since yesterday. I need some time to think."

"To think. You mean to put up those damned walls of yours."

"Call them what you want. They're my only means of protection."

Protection. That was an interesting topic—one that had occurred to him some hours ago.

"Victoria, are you still on the pill?" he asked bluntly.

She froze in place, her rigid stance confirming his suspicions. She'd gone on the pill four years ago, when they first started sleeping together. The other day she'd told him there had been no one since him. And knowing Victoria's dislike for taking medication of any kind, even Tylenol, why would she have continued taking the pill?

"Well?" he pressed.

She was already racking her brain as she turned to face him, and the color flooded back to her cheeks as she remembered. "We should be okay. I just finished my period Wednesday." Never one to shirk responsibility, she raised her chin and added, "This was my fault. I'm the one who knows my birth control status. I should have realized and said something. I'm just not used to thinking about protection. When we were together, I was on the pill, so condoms were never an issue. And since I haven't been with anyone else, my only experience has been—" She cleared her throat. "That's no excuse. I was careless."

"Don't apologize. I'm more at fault than you. This possibility occurred to me sometime around dawn. I could have brought it up. I didn't. Because it didn't matter. No, that's a lie. It *did* matter. I was half hoping I'd get you pregnant." Zach watched her eyes widen, but he didn't retract his words. He couldn't. They were the absolute truth.

He swung his legs over the side of the bed and advanced toward her. "Think back. This wasn't the first time we lost our minds. First, there was the beginning, before we knew we'd end up in bed. Then, there were those times before your prescription could be counted on by itself. Times we couldn't keep our hands off each other, couldn't wait long enough to open the condom packet, much less use it. Times when all we could think about was falling into that bed, when all I wanted was to get inside you, when all you wanted was to have me there." He gripped her shoulders in his hands. "Have you forgotten?"

Victoria went very still. "No," she said with quiet dignity. "I haven't forgotten. That's the problem. I haven't forgotten anything. And I don't have the strength to go through it again. I told you the other night, I can't have an affair with you."

"Is that what you call these past twelve hours—an affair?"

"I call them too much for me to handle." She backed away. "I'm very vulnerable right now, Zach. I'm also very confused. Your pressuring me isn't going to help. You tried that once. We both know how it ended."

He swore, bit back what he'd been about to say. Talk about being caught between the proverbial rock and a hard place. She'd opened an emotional door to him last night, a door that would only stay unlocked for a brief time. If he waited outside too long, the door would shut again, this time forever. If he pushed his way in, he'd destroy the precarious feelings that had compelled her to open it in the first place.

It was a no-win situation.

One he intended to win.

"You made your point," he replied, making no move to reach for her again. "I won't push you. Take your shower. Go home and think. But before you come to any decisions, we're going to talk. That's the least you can give me, Victoria. Especially since whatever you decide will affect us both."

"Okay." She ran a hand through her disheveled hair, looking even more dazed and disoriented than she had after last night's car accident. "Later, we'll talk."

He didn't press her for a definition of when later would be.

She didn't offer one.

Victoria didn't let herself think while she showered. She was too out of it, and Zach was too close by. When she got home, she'd let down her defenses and analyze her thoughts. For now, she just needed to get herself together and get home.

She went through the motions, washing away all the tangible evidence of last night's passion, letting her mind remain blissfully numb.

A short while later, she emerged from the bathroom to find a multicolored running suit laid out on the bed and a pair of Nikes placed on the floor beside it. On the chair nearby were a thick pair of sweat socks.

She swallowed, hard. It was just like Zach to be so thoughtful, to consider her comfort no matter how complicated things were between them.

Pushing aside the emotions that threatened to resurge, she yanked on the clothes, slung her cocktail dress over her arm, and left the bedroom.

Zach stood near the dining room table, shirtless, his hands shoved in the pockets of his jeans. He watched her with a brooding expression. "All set?"

"Yes." She indicated the running suit jacket as she zipped it up. "Need I ask where this came from?"

He shrugged. "We're on the Upper East Side. Clothing stores are plentiful. And the hotel staff's accommodating. I thought it would be more comfortable than your dress."

"It is. Thanks."

"I'll have the concierge get us a cab."

"I'll do it. And it won't be *us* that needs the cab. It'll just be *me*." She crossed over to the phone, purposefully averting her gaze. She was in no mood for Zach's inevitable reaction. He'd be adamantly opposed to her going home unescorted—for emotional and safety reasons. But none of those reasons was going to stop her. Not this time. She needed space.

"Actually . . ." she continued, readying herself for an even more severe reaction—one that wasn't entirely without merit. What she had in mind was probably stupid, considering last night's car episode. But, she reminded herself defensively, she couldn't become a prisoner to her fears.

Besides, if she had to be honest, she was more unsettled by what was happening between her and Zach than she was by the prospect of their road-rager attacking her in the middle of a crowded Manhattan street. He'd accomplished what he set out to do. Now, he was presumably in wait-and-see mode.

"Actually?" Zach prompted in a deceptively quiet tone.

"First, I'll check my answering machine. If no one's looking for me, I think I'll walk. It'll do me some good. And now that I'm dressed for the occasion—"

"You're not walking."

She lifted the receiver, meeting Zach's angry protest with an unyielding stare. "Zach, whoever's out there is not going to do a repeat performance on Sixty-fourth Street in broad daylight."

"You've got a mile hike. I don't like it."

"I'll take whichever streets have the most sidewalk traffic. There's safety in numbers. And I'm not asking for your permission." She punched up her number, waited, then entered her code to retrieve messages. "One message," she murmured aloud. "Probably some solicitor trying to sell—" She stopped in mid-sentence as Audrey's voice reached her ears.

"Victoria?" Audrey sounded very nervous, her voice sounded thin and faraway. "I wish you were home." There was a lot of interfering background noise, and the message was so faint, Victoria could hardly hear it. She strained her ears, listening. "I need to talk to you. I don't know where to turn. I'm so weak." A long pause, after which the speech became more indistinct. "They give me . . . lots of medication. It's like they want me to get well . . . but till I do . . . they're keeping me too drugged up to get off the bed. Thought it was for my own protection . . . now I'm not so sure. Something's not right. I don't know what it is. But I think Father . . ." A muffled sound, followed by a whimper, a few scuffling noises, and a click.

Dial tone.

22

"Oh, God." Quickly, Victoria replayed the message. Still unable to hear it clearly, she saved it and slammed down the receiver.

"What is it?" Zach was beside her.

"That was Audrey. Something's wrong—very wrong. I've got to get to her." She was already heading for the door.

"Wait." Zach caught her arm. "You can't charge into the Hope Institute. You'll never get past that pit-bull receptionist. And if something really is wrong with Audrey, you'll only make things worse. Now, slow down and tell me what the message said."

Victoria nodded, forcing her legal training to eclipse her fear. Details. She had to calm down and remember details. "It was hard to hear her. The connection was bad and her voice was slurred. It sounded like she was calling from somewhere public, like a corridor. She said they were keeping her heavily medicated and that she thought something was going on. She didn't say what. She was interrupted. I think someone must have found her using the phone. I don't know. Like I said, the message was disoriented and faint. I want to listen to it firsthand."

"Okay, then let's get to your apartment." Zach crossed over to the bedroom, grabbed a sweater, and shot her a look before yanking the sweater over his head. "And, yes, I'm going with you, so don't argue. This isn't about us anymore.

This is evidence. If there's something incriminating on that tape, I'll contact the FBI. They'll be thrilled to have a reason to march in and search the Hope Institute."

Victoria hesitated, besieged by that all-too-familiar emotional tearing, although not for the reasons Zach assumed.

His features hardened. "Do you honestly believe I'm using this as an excuse to take you home?"

"Of course not." She fiddled with the zipper of her running suit jacket. "There's something I didn't mention. At the end of her message, Audrey said something about my father."

Zach's expression didn't change. "What did she say?"

"Nothing specific. She was interrupted before she could finish. If I remember right, her exact words were 'I think Father . . .' and then she was cut off."

"That's hardly an incriminating reference."

"I know. But I assumed—"

"That I'd jump all over it and have your father arrested." Zach shook his head. "Didn't you hear anything I said in the car last night?"

Victoria felt a stab of guilt. "Yes. I'm sorry. I know you're not after my father unless he's guilty. I'm just so used to shielding my family."

"Well, don't worry about your father. He's the one member of your family who takes excellent care of himself."

"Maybe I'm afraid." The words were out before she even realized she'd uttered them.

Zach paused. "Afraid of what?"

"That he *is* guilty." She found herself expressing aloud the very fear she'd harbored all week. "I feel horribly disloyal for even thinking it, much less saying it, but what if it's true? Zach, what will that do to my mother?"

This time he went to her, gripping her shoulders in his hands. "She'll get through it. You'll help her. Your aunt and uncle will help her. You have a supportive family, Victoria. Your mother's not alone."

She nodded, battling the urge to cry in Zach's arms. "I've got to get home. I want to listen to that message." She saw the depth of compassion in his eyes. "And, you're right. You should hear the message, too." A heartbeat of a pause. "I want you to hear it."

In the garage beneath the Hope Institute, the audio technician headed for his van. He hadn't checked the tape yet today. There had been no need. A few hours ago he'd called Leaman, who'd reported that Victoria Kensington was still at her boyfriend's hotel, where she'd spent the night. Knowing that, he didn't expect the bug he'd planted at the telephone interface box to have picked up much in the way of calls. Not since that unsettling message from Hamilton last night, which he'd reported right away.

Still, he had a few free minutes. And it paid to be careful.

He climbed into the van, put on his headphones, and pressed the playback button. Two hang-ups. One incomplete call. And one message, picked up by the machine at 2:59—a little over an hour ago. Lounging back in his seat, he listened.

Thirty seconds later, he jerked upright. Shit. That was Audrey Kensington calling her sister. How the hell had she gotten to a phone?

He'd investigate that screwup later. Obviously, from the sounds of struggle, the nurses had found her and brought her back to her room. But no one on the disinfection team knew about this. If they did, he'd have been notified so he could take care of it.

He had to erase that tape before Victoria Kensington heard it.

He was about to press Stop and get on that, when another recorded call began playing. The dialing of the number, two rings, the answering machine . . . and the tones of someone accessing it from outside. Then Victoria Kensington's horrified "Oh God . . ." and a hang-up.

Shit.

She'd already heard it.

Sweat broke out on his brow and he wiped it away, forcing himself to think calmly. Fine. So she'd heard it. He couldn't change that.

But he had to make sure no one else heard it. That message had to vanish, now, before she got her hands on it. Or worse, before she played it for the authorities.

He grabbed his cell phone and punched in Leaman's number as he set up his frequency analyzer.

"Yeah?" Mr. Cigar picked up.

"Are they still at the Plaza Athénée?"

"They haven't budged. They're probably still rolling around in the—"

"No, they're not." He got ready to decipher the tones she'd pressed so he'd have her access code. "They're probably about to make a dash for her apartment. Stall them."

"Stall them? Why?"

"Her sister left her a message a little while ago. She's already accessed it. I gotta get into that machine and erase it. Buy me fifteen minutes."

"How am I supposed to—?"

"I don't care. Throw yourself in front of their fucking cab if you have to. Just do it." He slammed down the phone and got busy.

His first hunch proved to be right. 4-9-7-2. It figured.

She was as predictable as everyone else. April 9, 1972. Her birthday.

He remembered that detail from the file he'd been given.

Good thing he had such a knowledgeable source.

Victoria and Zach were going nowhere fast.

Traffic outside the hotel was at a standstill.

Today, of all days, some jerk had decided to flag down a cab, climb in, and then, half a block down and directly beside a parked moving truck, throw open the door and start a huge argument with the driver. With one leg in and one leg out of the cab, the guy had effectively stopped traffic from passing.

The argument was still going on when they jumped out of their cab and took off on foot.

Leaman bent down low in the back seat of the taxi, hiding all but his one exposed trouser leg from view. He had to make sure he wasn't recognized. With that in mind, he kept his head down until his driver told him the coast was clear. Then he straightened, grinning as he imagined the poisonous looks they'd thrown his way when they blew by. He stayed still, watching and waiting as they made their mad dash uptown.

When they were out of sight, he hopped out of his cab.

A mile would take a long time to walk, he thought with a satisfied smile, handing his driver the promised hundred-dollar bill. He ambled off and lit a cigar. There would be more than enough time for Fenton to deal with the answering machine and erase Audrey Kensington's message.

Another disaster averted.

Victoria burst into her apartment, going straight to the answering machine. She was frowning by the time Zach locked the front door and joined her.

"What's wrong?" he asked.

"The LCD display. It should say 'one,' for one saved message. It doesn't. It's just showing the time, like there's nothing recorded." She pressed the play button.

"No messages," the electronic voice announced.

Blinking, Victoria raised her head and stared at Zach. "I don't understand. I *know* I didn't erase it."

Now it was Zach who was frowning. "The only way you could have wiped out what Audrey said is by inadvertently pressing the machine's erase sequence after retrieving your messages. But you didn't press *any* buttons—not after the second time you played back her message. You just hung up. That should save whatever calls were there." He picked up the answering machine, checked all its connections, then put it down. He pressed play, and was greeted with the same: *"No messages."*

"I don't like this," Zach muttered.

Victoria was feeling more frustrated by the minute. "That message was there a half hour ago. Now it's gone. My machine didn't suddenly start malfunctioning. Someone erased Audrey's plea for help." She pivoted, scanning the apartment suspiciously. "Maybe someone broke in."

"I didn't notice any signs of a break-in." Zach went to the front door, opened it, and studied the top and bottom locks intently. "Nothing looks as if it was tampered with. Check the rest of the apartment, see if anything was disturbed."

Rapidly, Victoria moved from room to room, checking everything she could think of, from her jewelry to her files. Nothing had been touched.

Not that she expected it would be. This wasn't about robbery.

"Everything's intact," she told Zach, returning to the hall. "And, no, my father doesn't have the keys. There's only one spare set, and I keep those in my office desk."

"I wasn't going to suggest your father broke into your apartment," Zach replied tersely. "That's hardly his forte. Actually, my guess is no one broke in. I think your answering machine was accessed from outside." Pausing, Zach rubbed a hand over his unshaven jaw. "The logical order of events would be that whoever found Audrey making that call to you overheard enough to know her message was a cry for help and had to be erased. That would explain the abrupt hang-up." He cleared his throat. "Does anyone but you know your access code?"

"No. Not my partners. Not my family. And *not* my father," she added vehemently.

"Is the code easy to figure out?"

A shrug. "That depends on how clever the figurer is—and how close to me. It's the numerical digits of my birthday." Victoria's mouth snapped shut as she realized she was, once again, pointing an involuntary finger at her father.

Dammit. Why did every avenue lead to him?

She eyed Zach, assuming he'd be thinking along the same lines.

He wasn't.

Rather than looking like a tiger closing in on its prey, Zach look troubled, as if all the pieces didn't fit. "Do you remember what time Audrey's call came in?"

"Just before three."

"And you didn't pick it up until over an hour later." A hard shake of his head. "If your father found Audrey calling you, or if he was frantically paged by whoever did, why wouldn't he erase the message the instant he figured out your access code—which, for a man as brilliant as your father, would probably take ten minutes tops. Why wait an hour?"

"I don't know."

"It doesn't make sense. He'd want that tape wiped out ASAP."

"*If* he's involved. Maybe my father isn't the one who did this."

"Maybe not." Zach's scowl deepened. "Let's try a different approach. We're assuming a criminal discovered Audrey making her phone call. It could just as easily have been some innocuous nurse doing her job. That nurse would have no interest in the content of Audrey's message or in knowing who she'd called—only that she should be confined to bed. That would explain why there was no rush to investigate."

"But if that's the case, the nurse would have no reason to *ever* pursue it any further. She'd simply mention it to my father or Audrey's doctor the next time they were in. Which I highly doubt was at four o'clock on a Sunday afternoon. Prominent doctors don't make their rounds then. And I *know* my father wouldn't visit then. He'd have too much to explain to Mother. So why was my answering machine broken into? It doesn't make sense."

"I agree."

Something about Zach's tone brought her up short. She stopped speculating and gave him a hard look. "You know something."

"I *think* I know something," he corrected. He glanced at the answering machine, then began counting off on his fingers. "Two seemingly unrelated incidents since yesterday. First a maniac pushes us off the road. Then your answering machine is violated. Both without provocation."

"Okay," Victoria agreed, tucking her hair behind her ear. "You're right. How did that lunatic on the parkway know I was still poking into the Hope Institute? And how did someone know that Audrey's call was incriminating enough to need to be erased? And, finally, how did he know exactly when to erase it? It's almost as if these people know what I'm thinking and what I'm doing."

An odd light glittered in Zach's eyes. "I'd be willing to bet they do."

"How?"

"By bugging your phone."

"What?" She froze. "You just got finished saying you didn't think anyone had broken into my apartment."

"They didn't need to. The bug's probably at the interface box in the basement of your building. It's less risky and equally effective. Think about it, Victoria. You yourself just said it's as if they know what you're doing before you do it. A bug would explain everything: how they knew the nature of Audrey's call, how they knew you were still checking into the Institute, even how they got your access code."

Victoria turned slowly, staring at her telephone as if it were a foreign object. "You're saying they're taping all my calls?"

"Yes. And listening at regular intervals to whatever their

tape picks up. When you're home, my guess is they're more on top of their monitoring, just in case any of your calls pertain to them and you're there to take immediate action. When you're out, they're less worried. And last night and today, they knew you were out. Mr. Cigar must have reported that you were at my hotel. So, they weren't in any rush to play back today's tape. Which accounts for the lapse in time between Audrey's leaving her message and their erasing it."

Abruptly, Victoria's chin shot up as Zach's theory hurled another piece into place. "They were listening last night before I went out. They heard your call to me. They heard you say you took the cigar butt and had it dusted for fingerprints. That's how they realized we're still checking into the Institute. And that's why they came after us last night."

"I tipped them off," Zach said in disgust. "That's why that son of a bitch nearly killed us."

"If you're blaming yourself, don't. You had no idea they were listening." Victoria rubbed her palms together. "What about breaking into my answering machine? How did they manage that?"

Zach's mouth set in a grim line. "Their bug would have picked up the call you made from the hotel, checking your answering machine. An access code is nothing more than a series of touch tones. Anyone good with audio equipment can analyze and reproduce those."

"I see." She considered that. "They realized I'd heard Audrey's message, so they made it disappear as quickly as possible."

"Right."

Victoria drew a slow breath, nodding as she accepted the explanation. "What do we do from here?"

"We wait till morning. We *don't* use the phone, except to order takeout. First thing tomorrow, I'll walk you to work. That won't look suspicious, not even to Mr. Cigar, who'll be watching you like a hawk. He knows about our little incident on the Merritt Parkway the other night. He'll expect you to be unnerved. He'll follow us, see me escort you upstairs to your office. He *won't* see me pick up your spare set of keys and take them with me when I head out for the FBI field office."

"What if they've now assigned someone to follow you? He'll see you go to Federal Plaza and guess you're meeting with the FBI."

Zach shrugged. "They already know I have law enforcement contacts, thanks to last night's call. If they're smart enough to figure out who, so be it. Let them sweat. It might make them careless. In the meantime, I'll have the feds send an agent here to sweep your phones while you're out—someone who's an average-looking Joe. He'll probably find what he's looking for at the interface box. But, just to be on the safe side, he'll let himself into your apartment and check each telephone and the whole place for bugs. Now that I think about it, we'd better have him sweep your office, too. Late tomorrow night should be good, after everyone's gone home. Especially you. That way Mr. Cigar won't be there. He'll be outside your apartment, like a good watchdog."

Victoria's mind was going a mile a minute. She forced herself to organize her thoughts, the same way she did in the courtroom.

First things first.

"You're so damned cavalier. If whoever's guilty figures out you're helping the FBI with their investigation—and me with mine—they're going to feel cornered. That would put you in danger."

A corner of Zach's mouth lifted. "Worried about me?"

She didn't bother pretending. "Yes."

"Thank you," he said tenderly. "But don't be. I learned how to watch my back a long time ago." His gaze was frank, without reservation or apology. "I intend to watch yours, too. With or without your permission."

Victoria wasn't sure how to answer that, so she didn't. "How do you know where their audio guy's stationed? What if he's right outside and he sees the FBI agent go into my apartment?"

An amused chuckle. "That would be any agent's dream. He'd pick the guy out in a minute, and our phone tapper would be history. Unfortunately, I doubt he's that dumb. He's probably parked a block or two away or in a basement or garage somewhere between here and the Hope Institute. As for the agent being spotted, give the FBI some credit. They're pros. They know just how to blend in and look harmless. No matter where this guy's parked, he won't notice them."

"But he *will* notice when his equipment stops picking up a signal, and his tape starts coming out blank," Victoria pointed out. "Once the feds remove the bugs, whoever planted them will realize we're on to him."

"Yup." Zach's eyes narrowed. "So we're going to leave those bugs right where they are. Otherwise, not only will their electronics guy know we're on to him, he'll find a way to install new bugs. No, we'll pretend it's business as usual. Period. That way, he'll continue taping your calls, exactly as he's been taping them all week. Except that the information he gets will be only what you want him to have."

Another long-range plan, Victoria thought fitfully, impatience mingling with worry and frustration.

"I hate this," she declared, her hand slicing the air. "Always reactive, never proactive. Dammit, Zach, my sister's in trouble. How long can I go on playing this passive cat-and-mouse game?"

"As long as it takes to get Audrey out in a way that won't endanger her safety or worsen her condition." Zach wasn't pulling punches. He was in his tell-it-like-it-is mode, purposely offering a response based in logic, not emotion. "You don't know how far these people will go, what they're capable of. Neither do I. If you do something reckless, Audrey might pay the price. On the other hand, you're not sure how sick she really is. If she's as bad as your father said, she needs the help she's getting. You can't assume she's being harmed. You can't even assume she was rational on that tape. You can't assume anything. Think like a lawyer, Victoria, not like a devoted family member."

"I'm trying."

"So am I." Zach's tone took on an edge. "Don't you think I want to storm in there, drag out whoever's involved in this syndicate, and choke them with my bare hands?"

Victoria gave a weary nod. "I'm sure you do. Okay, okay. We'll do it your way—at least as far as this electronic surveillance goes. I'll have my own chance to be proactive, starting tomorrow. I'll be inside Waters, Kensington, Tatem and Calder. And I'm going to bust my tail until I find some concrete evidence." She massaged her temples, the events of the last twenty-four hours resurging to drag her under now that her adrenaline was starting to drop. "I'm going to lie down for a while. My brain is about to explode."

"Right. You never did get that space you needed." Zach's tone was nondescript. He scooped up the gym bag he'd thrown together—some toiletries and a change of clothes—so he could leave directly for the field office tomorrow without stopping off at his hotel. "Get some rest. If it's okay with you, I'll take that shower you already had. Then I'll crash, too."

"Help yourself."

Victoria wished she'd chosen a different phrase than that. The shower was fine. So was the crashing. But *where* he crashed—that was another story. The bedroom was out. She might be emotionally raw and desperately in need of some time to collect her thoughts, but she wasn't stupid. No matter how confused she was, how bone weary and overwhelmed, she was dead sure of one thing. If Zach got into her bed, all hopes of thinking would vanish. "Zach . . ." she began.

"I know what space means, Victoria," he interrupted

quietly. "I'll be using the living room sofa, just as I have all week." He leveled that penetrating stare at her. "Do your soul-searching. Take whatever time you need. Face whatever fears you have. But do it with your eyes open. And, for both our sakes, don't choose now to become a coward."

23

Monday, April 24
12:30 P.M.

If being a coward meant being afraid, then Victoria was guilty as charged.

She stared out her office window, watching the Madison Avenue crowd thicken as the lunch hour progressed. Swarms of purposeful professionals, all with places to go, appointments to keep, agendas to meet.

Usually she was among them.

Not today.

Today she was using the only half-hour block of unscheduled time she had to think.

How ironic that thinking would take precedence over doing. Especially today, when she had a monumental task to accomplish—and that was on top of having to straddle major commitments at two different but equally bustling law firms. She had to make strides in finding some evidence on the Hope Institute—and whoever was at its helm.

Yet, despite all that, her turmoil today was more internal than external.

Dear God, she was so afraid.

First and foremost, she was afraid for Audrey, afraid that she herself would make a wrong move and worsen an already terrifying situation for her sister. She was damned either way. If she continued to dig, she ran the risk of provoking the wrong people. That could endanger Audrey. On the other hand, doing nothing could endanger her more. It all depended on whether Audrey's fears were simply the result of her own condition or whether they were based on something she'd found out, something that implicated the Institute.

Or that implicated its legal counsel.

Shutting her eyes, Victoria pressed her forehead against the windowpane, wondering for the hundredth time how her father factored into the drug syndicate Zach was investigating. Was he merely the Hope Institute's attorney of record? Was he aware of what was going on there? And how far would he be willing to let things go?

He'd never sacrifice Audrey. That much Victoria had to believe. No matter what else he was, her father wouldn't hurt his own child.

Which brought to mind the frightening incident on the Merritt Parkway the other night. She couldn't accept that it was her father who'd sent that bastard to shove her car off the road.

No, he would never actively hurt his daughters.

But would he turn his back while someone else did?

A shiver rippled up her spine.

Her father claimed Audrey was sick. Very sick. Maybe he was telling the truth. Maybe whatever medication Audrey was on was making her delusional. Maybe her fear stemmed from that. Victoria couldn't rule out that possibility. She couldn't storm into the Institute and demand to see her sister. She couldn't even call and demand to speak to her.

But she could broach the subject with her father.

She'd made that decision in the wee hours of morning, after another sleepless night and more tossing and turning than she cared to remember.

She couldn't just ignore that phone call from Audrey. She had to do something, however tentative, to ensure her sister's well-being. And this was the only solution that made sense. It wasn't intrusive enough to make things worse for Audrey, nor was it so passive that it allowed her sister's cry for help to go entirely unheeded.

She'd approach her father, cautiously, tell him only what he'd be advised of anyway, if he hadn't been already. The nurses were sure to mention Audrey's attempt to call her, whenever he next visited the Institute. Victoria would bring it up first, with concern, not accusation, and hopefully elicit his help in ensuring Audrey's well-being.

If he was innocent.

If he was guilty, her discussion would appease any qualms he had that Audrey's call had left her suspicious.

Either way, Audrey would be protected.

She'd take care of this the minute she got to her father's Park Avenue office—two hours from now.

After that, she had another avenue to probe. And that avenue was Elizabeth Bonner.

What did that woman know, and why had she whisked Benjamin Hopewell away from the party at the very moment he'd been chatting with Victoria? Where did she factor into all this?

Victoria had her work cut out for her.

She turned back to her desk, picking up the cup of now-cold coffee. She sipped at it, not even noticing its temperature.

As for the rest of her fear, it all stemmed from Zach—Zach and the tangle of emotions she'd been grappling with since yesterday.

The facts were the facts. She fallen into that bed with her eyes wide open. It had been every bit her decision to make love with him, not once, not twice, but all night and half the next day. She didn't regret her decision. Not even now, when the inevitable confusion and pain were twisting her insides into knots. It had been worth it. The sheer, exquisite physical pleasure, the blind spontaneity of action and reaction—and, yes, the mindless capitulation to feelings and emotions, even vulnerabilities, all were too magnificent to describe.

But the inescapable What now? loomed larger than life,

pounding at her skull and making unresolved circles in her mind.

The passion between them had grown even more over-powering than it was four years ago. So, God help her, had the feelings. But the issues still remained. His, and hers. His, only he could address—something he obviously intended to do, since he'd insisted that they talk before she came to any decisions on her own. Although, what could he say to counter the obvious? The single-minded resolve with which he was approaching this FBI investigation spoke volumes. He was still driven. She didn't blame him. She just couldn't live with it—not when it meant compromising her own priorities in order to satisfy his.

He'd never actually ask her to do that. He hadn't then. He wouldn't now. But it would happen nonetheless. The very nature of his work, his commitment to honoring his father's memory, would ensure that.

And what would that mean for her—following him around the world? Where would that leave her family, her career, her clients? Not to mention her own fundamental need to control her own life, to be independent?

That brought her to the heart of her own issues—issues that had been magnified by so many things: the pain of their breakup, the lengthening list of broken women she'd come into contact with in her professional life, the ongoing worry over her mother and sister. She'd become harder—no, more determined. She clung to her independence like a suit of armor.

Like the protective walls Zach kept referring to.

In essence, they were back where they'd left off four years ago, only with more time and scars between them. Scars deep enough to make them hold back those three magical words—words they'd once murmured over and over but that now seemed too painful to say.

But they were there. She couldn't escape that. The words were there, definitely for her and, knowing Zach as she did—seeing the look in his eyes, feeling the fervor of his lovemaking—for him, as well.

He wanted to face this head-on, to tear away the self-protection that was her second skin and confront their feelings. She wasn't sure she could give him that.

No, that wasn't the truth. She *could* give him that. But at what cost? And was she willing to take the risk?

Maybe Zach was right. Maybe when it came to this, she was a coward.

Which left her . . . where?

A light knock on her door brought her head up. "Yes?" she asked in an unsteady voice.

"It's me." Meg stepped into the office, a concerned expression on her face. "Are you okay?"

Victoria averted her gaze, lifting her shoulders in a half shrug. "I guess. Why? Do I look unglued?"

"You look tired. This plan to dig around at your father's office must be taking its toll."

"It is. In fact, I'm headed over there in a little while to get started." Victoria busied herself perusing some files, keeping her head down so Meg couldn't see her face. Her emotions were too close to the surface right now, and she wasn't about to have them read by her all-too-astute friend. In fact, she'd deliberately avoided mentioning the near collision on the parkway Saturday night for just that reason. Meg was already worried about her. If she learned about the car incident, she was bound to react with that natural heartfelt compassion of hers. At which point, Victoria would burst into tears—something she just didn't do. Plus, she'd have to dodge Meg's questions about the accident and invent explanations she herself didn't believe.

It was simply too much.

"I have one more appointment—Doris Webster," she supplied instead, keeping her tone as conversational as possible. "Then it's pack up the old briefcase and march over to Waters, Kensington, Tatem and Calder. I'm tense about it,

I'll admit. I'm also tired—I didn't sleep very well last night. And I had a rough morning. Faye Larimore was here. Do you know that poor woman just became the latest casualty in her company's downsizing? She now has no job and no health coverage. And her son really needs those twice-a-week counseling sessions. Of course, her husband refused to contribute a dime. He'd rather watch her suffer. And until I get her a decent settlement, there's not a damned thing she can do."

Abruptly, Victoria stopped babbling, her fingers gripping the Larimore file. "Meg, why do women constantly put themselves in the position of being victims?"

"Not all women do. And not all men let them." Meg shut the door and leaned back against it. "Do you want to talk about it? And I don't mean the Larimore case. I mean what's eating you up inside."

"The Hope Institute. How sick Audrey is." Victoria was clutching at straws and she knew it. But she hadn't cried on Meg's shoulder the first time. She wasn't going to start now. "There's not much to say. Obviously, I haven't gotten into the files at Waters, Kensington, Tatem and Calder yet. But I will. I'm just hoping Audrey's getting better, and that this place my father's chosen for her is as reputable as—"

"Victoria, I'm talking about Zach. And you know it."

There it was, spoken loud and clear by her friend. Oh, she could sidestep the question, the same way she was sidestepping the crux of the whole Hope Institute corruption. But what was the point? Meg knew. She'd always known. To deny it would be both futile and childish.

Victoria forced herself to meet Meg's gaze. "Yes, I know you're talking about Zach," she admitted, with as much composure as she could muster. "The problem is, I'm not sure what to say about him. About us. About what's happening between us." She turned up her palms in a helpless gesture. "I spent four years forgetting him. *Trying* to forget him," she amended. "Then he walked back into my life a week ago, and I'm drowning. I'm fighting like hell to break the surface, but it's not working. I'm going under—fast. I've told myself it's memories, it's attraction, it's passion. But I'm lying. I know it, and so does Zach."

Meg tucked a strand of hair behind her ear, quietly digesting her friend's revelation. "Have you slept with him?"

Meg's choice of words were bitterly ironic. "We didn't do much sleeping. But, yes." Victoria massaged her temples. "What's the matter with me? Why can't I just have a wild fling like the rest of the world and chalk it up as great sex?"

"You know the answer to that." A glimmer of realization sparked in Meg's eyes, and she folded her arms across her breasts. "But you need me to say it anyway, don't you? Of course you do. Because you don't want to be the one to say it yourself. Okay, here it is. There are two reasons why you can't write this off as a wild fling. Number one, because you're a one-man woman. You might be hard as nails in the courtroom, and eyes-wide-open about life, but face it— somewhere inside you lives a die-hard romantic. Which leads me to number two. You're in love with Zach. You've been in love with him for four years, and you'll be in love with him for the rest of your life. Does that answer your question?"

"Brutally."

"Good. Now here's mine: What are you going to do about those feelings? Are you going to deal with them, or continue pretending they don't exist?"

"I know they exist, Meg. But that doesn't mean I can—"

"Can what?" Meg demanded, marching forward until she could press her frustrated fists against the desk. "Give in to them? Victoria, this is love, not a prison sentence. It's something to fight for, not against. Yes, getting it right is going to mean hard work, but since when has that stopped you?"

Pausing, Meg eyed her friend speculatively. "You never

told me what made things end between you and Zach the first time. My hunch is you did. At least in part. You're scared to death of being dependent. Well, you're not. You wouldn't be dependent even if you ran off to Europe, married Zach, and had twelve kids. You'd be a partner, an equal, someone who was not only needed, but who needed in return. Instead, do you know what you are? A victim. The very thing you're fighting so hard *not* to be. Not a victim to a man, but a victim to your own self-imposed barriers. Is that what you want?"

The cold truth of Meg's words punched Victoria in the gut. "I never thought of it that way," she acknowledged. "But even if I did, there's so much more to get past than my emotional baggage. There are some real obstacles here."

"Fine. Then confront them," Meg chided gently. "Overcome them. Stop being a coward. It doesn't become you."

A shaky smile tugged at Victoria's lips. "You're the second person to call me a coward since yesterday."

"I'll bet I can guess who the first person was." Meg shook her head in exasperation. "Victoria, being independent and being alone are two different things. The first is already in your nature. You couldn't change it if you tried. The second is your choice. And if you opt for it, you're an idiot. You have an amazing man who's so in love with you he can hardly see straight. If you let him go, I think I'll have to kill you."

Victoria couldn't help but laugh. "That would make an interesting scenario. Poor Paul would be stuck defending you."

"Not likely. He'd farm me out in favor of his corporate clients. Besides, I'd be guilty, even if it was justifiable homicide."

"Pretty harsh words." Victoria chuckled.

"Maybe. But am I getting through?"

Abandoning the lighthearted banter, Victoria nodded.

"Loud and clear. Thanks, Meg. You're a great friend. You've given me a lot to think about."

"Good. Think quickly. That keynote speech of Zach's is Thursday. After that . . ." A shrug. "It's up to you whether or not he has a reason to stay."

Not entirely, Victoria mused, her insides twisting as she once again pondered the big picture. *It also depends on how things unfold at the Hope Institute, and when this whole ugly investigation comes to an end.*

"Victoria?" Meg prompted.

"Hmm? Yes, I promise to think fast. Right now, that's *all* I can promise. When I come up with answers, you'll be the first to know."

Meg's eyes twinkled knowingly. "Or maybe the second."

2:30 P.M.

Victoria made her way through the posh offices of Waters, Kensington, Tatem & Calder and went straight to Miss Hatterman's cubicle.

The stony-featured woman looked up from her keyboard as Victoria approached. Approval glinted in her eyes as she took in Victoria's tailored wool suit, which was a deep hunter green—suitably muted in hue. "Ms. Kensington. Welcome to your first day. Has someone shown you to your office?"

"Not yet." Victoria gripped the handle of her briefcase with rigid purpose. "I wanted to check in with my father first. If he's free, that is."

Not a flicker of reaction. "I'll see." She ignored the telephone on her desk and its intercom feature. Instead, she pushed back her chair and rose, walking the short distance to his private domain. A brief knock at the tightly closed door. She waited a few seconds, then opened the door and entered, closing it with a firm click behind her.

Victoria wasn't surprised. She knew the drill. Miss

Hatterman was trying to avoid a potentially sticky situation. Whether he was in or out, Walter Kensington kept his office door shut. As a result, he could declare himself "out" whenever he chose to. And if he chose to now—well, his secretary was letting him do so, an impossibility if he answered his intercom page.

Not much chance of him going that route. Not when his daughter was finally obeying his wishes by showing up, on command, for her first day of work at his law firm.

Sure enough, Miss Hatterman returned, gesturing as she went to her desk. "Go right in."

"Thank you."

Victoria approached her father's office with a mixture of curiosity and uneasiness. How would he react when he saw her? Would he be relieved or unsurprised that she was unharmed? Was he already aware that someone had driven her off the road Saturday night, or would it come as a shock? And what about Audrey? Did he know she'd tried to call Victoria again?

Time to find out.

Gazing fixedly at the gold nameplate on the door, Victoria readied herself and knocked.

"Come in."

"Hello, Father." She crossed the threshold of his imposing domain, watching him turn away from the windows to face her.

"Victoria." No visible reaction, and a greeting that was customarily terse. "Your start at Waters, Kensington, Tatem and Calder is finally here. I'm pleased. I've awaited this day for a long time."

Damn that poker face of his. Not a flicker of anything other than approval at her presence.

"I'm pleased to be here, too." She walked over, hesitated as she reached him, then found her way over to one of the plush chairs across from his desk and sank into it. A kiss, even a perfunctory one on the cheek, would be bad form in her father's eyes. This was, after all, his law firm, not their living room.

"Before I find my office and settle in, I wanted to stop by and thank you for Saturday night's party. I meant to call you and Mother yesterday, but things have been hectic since I left Greenwich the other night."

A mildly questioning lift of the brows. "Hectic? How?"

"To begin with, some lunatic tried to run Zach and me off the road on our way back to the city. It was pretty terrifying."

Her father's stare bored through her. "What do you mean he tried to run you off the road? Was he drunk?"

"It would seem so, yes," she answered carefully. "The whole thing happened so fast. It was on the curvy section of the Merritt Parkway. He crowded us until we had to veer off into the trees. Fortunately, we weren't hurt. The car, on the other hand . . ." She gave an offhand shrug. "Anyway, we spent the wee hours of Sunday morning filing a police report. I was pretty shaken."

"I would imagine." He was scowling now. "But neither of you was hurt."

"No."

"Good." Obvious relief.

"And then, as if that weren't enough, Audrey tried calling me yesterday while I was out."

"So I heard." Walter's mask was back in place. He now sounded more irritated than anything else. "Apparently, nothing I said to her got through."

Victoria's ears perked up. "What do you mean? What did you say to her?"

"I visited your sister at the Institute early Saturday morning. She was starting to show some improvement, at least from a health standpoint. I wish I could say the same with regard to her maturity level. Instead of appreciating the progress she's making, she was upset because she wants you to visit her. I told her that was out of the question until she was better. She seemed to accept my decision. At least I thought she had. Evidently, I was wrong."

"I see." Victoria leaned forward, reacting with precisely the straightforward protectiveness her father would expect. "Maybe she doesn't understand the Institute's policies with regard to visitors. I know I don't."

A glower. "We're not starting this again, are we?"

"No. I'm simply pointing out that Audrey's not as pragmatic as you. She's emotional. She probably needs you to explain things to her in a way she can accept. Gently. Sympathetically. So she'll realize that the Institute's limitations are there for her own good. She's fragile right now. You know that."

"Only too well." Walter crossed over, seated himself behind the massive cherry desk, and made a steeple with his fingers. "I took care of things this morning. I was there when Audrey woke up. I repeated the reasons for her confinement. She knows she can see you as soon as she's released. That calmed her."

Victoria's insides clenched, but she forced herself to show only her customary amount of concern. She had to walk this tightrope. Audrey's safety was on the line. "Is she really all right? Because she sounded so disoriented on the phone. I could hardly make out her words."

"She is disoriented. Some of that's the medication. She's also frightened by her body's ups and downs. But her doctor has assured me she's improving. She's eating, sitting up, responding well to her therapy. Saturday was a setback. Things are back on track now."

"You're sure?"

"Very."

She had to stop now. Any more pushing and her father would start to get suspicious. She'd verified all she could. Her father had seen Audrey, which meant her sister was safe. As for ensuring the continuation of that safety, well, if the worst were true and her father was actively involved with the drug syndicate, her response just now must have reassured him that Audrey's call hadn't done any permanent damage. According to the way she'd presented things, hearing her sister's voice had made her anxious, but it hadn't pushed any panic buttons. Hopefully, the result of that would be, at worst, that Audrey would be more heavily guarded, but not punished.

Even that thought made her ill.

Her father was sitting in taut silence, watching her and waiting to see whether or not she meant to drop the issue.

She looked him squarely in the eye and drove home her point. "All right, Father. You know I'm not comfortable with the Hope Institute's policies. But I trust your judgment. You want the same thing I do—the best care for Audrey. I feel better knowing you saw her today, and that she wasn't as upset as she sounded in her message. Just, please, send her my love. And tell her that the day she's released, she and I have a date. Will you do that for me?"

Walter emitted a sigh. "Yes, Victoria, I will." He reached for a file. "Now, I've got a client meeting to prepare for. Shall I ask Miss Hatterman to show you to your office?"

"That won't be necessary." She took the hint and rose. "I'll find it. And I won't be in it for long. I have two people to see before I get settled—Ms. Bonner and Ian Block."

"Ian is expecting you," her father replied, not even giving lip service to his fellow senior partner. Was that because he didn't acknowledge Elizabeth Bonner as such, or because he was hoping to divert Victoria from touching base with her for some other, uglier reason?

"As I told you last week," he continued, "you'll be working closely with Ian. There's no one better equipped to familiarize you with the various corporate clients we represent. He's on top of the mergers and acquisitions we're negotiating, our pending litigations—everything I want you involved with. For that reason, I arranged to have your office near his. Just ask his secretary to show you in the minute you get down there. Let's see, her name is Miss White or Miss Whiting—something like that. She'll take you to Ian, no questions asked."

Victoria winced. This time it wasn't her father's lack of respect for his subordinates that got to her. It was the realization that he'd obviously instructed Ian Block to drop everything when she arrived. That would do wonders for their working relationship. She'd just broken the ice with the very ambitious Mr. Block. Now she was afraid they'd be back to square one.

If so, she'd deal with it. She wasn't here to make friends. She was here to get information.

Still, it would be easier if her road wasn't paved with enemies. So, she'd stop at Ian Block's office first, do some damage control.

But after that she was going to find Elizabeth Bonner.

24

As it turned out, Ms. Bonner found her.

Victoria had just stepped into her new office—a room much too large to be temporary, just two doors down from Ian Block—when the older woman walked in.

"I heard you'd arrived." Ms. Bonner carried herself with the presence of a savvy politician—one who was far too aloof to be up for reelection. Then again, it wasn't Victoria's vote she'd be campaigning for.

She looked stunning, the essence of a wealthy professional woman, her navy silk suit exquisitely cut, her makeup flawless. "I'm on my way to a client meeting. I wanted to tell you that the file we discussed is on my secretary's desk. Pick it up when you have a moment."

"I will. Before you go—" Victoria added quickly, determined to learn something before her subject disappeared—to a client meeting, she'd said. Funny. Her father was also on his way to one of those.

"Yes?" Ms. Bonner was halfway to the door.

"I did some research for a matrimonial client I'm currently representing. There are quite a few parallels between that case and the one you're bringing me in on. I brought some notes to go over with you. I was hoping to do that this afternoon."

"That won't be possible. I'll be tied up for the rest of the day. Later this week, perhaps." She glanced at her watch.

Why is she in such a hurry? Victoria wondered. *Is it to get to her client or away from me?*

She braced herself and took a dangerous stab at finding out. "I don't mean to be presumptuous, Ms. Bonner," she said in a puzzled tone, "but when we spoke last week you seemed very eager for my input on this case. Enough to bring it up before I'd even started working here. Has something changed since last Thursday's breakfast?"

An icy stare. "Nothing's changed, Ms. Kensington. I simply have a meeting to get to. As I'm sure you realize, I have a great many clients to divide my time among."

"And I'm just a new, young attorney, one who's not even a permanent member of your firm," Victoria returned, acting on instinct. "I understand that. I'm not arrogant enough to expect you to rearrange your schedule to suit me. I just want to be sure that's what this is about. I'd hate to think you were avoiding me."

A flicker of surprise—and something Victoria could swear was discomfort—flashed across Ms. Bonner's face and, just as quickly, was gone. "Why would I be avoiding you?"

You tell me, Victoria wanted to blurt. "Forgive me for overstepping my bounds, Ms. Bonner. But I'm a very direct person—much like you, I suspect. I want my time at Waters, Kensington, Tatem and Calder to be productive. I'm aware that in order to make that happen, I have a great deal of resentment to overcome, since everyone assumes I'm here as a result of nepotism. I'm willing to take on that challenge. But I didn't expect it to extend to you. Nevertheless, I'll ask you outright: Do you have some problem with my being of counsel to the firm?"

Elizabeth Bonner shut the door with a firm click. "Let me get this straight," she said, her brows raised in haughty astonishment. "Are you asking if I'm threatened by you?"

"No, I'm asking if you're bothered by my last name. We both know my relationship with my father doesn't make me popular. Do you feel I'm undeserving of the opportunity he's given me?"

"If I did, you wouldn't be here. I speak up loud and clear, Ms. Kensington, especially when it comes to employees I don't believe are worthy candidates. Your credentials are outstanding. So is your reputation. That's why you're in this office. Not because your last name happens to be Kensington. As for my personal feelings on the subject, frankly, I'd welcome another woman who's strong enough to battle her way to the top—*if* your performance matches your résumé. Does that answer your question?"

"Yes," Victoria replied, everything inside her screaming *No!* Impressive as Ms. Bonner's reply had been, it hadn't addressed the real issue.

Time to be more direct.

"I appreciate your candor, Ms. Bonner. And again, I apologize for being presumptuous. I was just concerned. First you rushed off Saturday night, then again now. I wanted to make sure I hadn't offended you in some way."

"Saturday night?" Again that odd expression.

"At the party," Victoria prodded. "When I was speaking with Mr. Hopewell. You left rather abruptly. Actually, so did he. But that didn't concern me. I've known Mr. Hopewell since I was a child. Besides, I'm not working for him— except as a representative of this firm, of course."

Ms. Bonner cleared her throat. "I had some papers to give Mr. Hopewell. I assure you, my departure had nothing to do with you."

A knock sounded at the door, and Victoria wanted to choke whoever was out there.

Ms. Bonner opened it.

Ian Block stood on the threshold, the embodiment of handsome corporate charm.

He looked surprised to see the older woman, and his gaze flickered from her to Victoria and back. "Excuse me. I didn't realize you were—"

"I was just leaving." Ms. Bonner turned to Victoria, her frosty veneer back in place. "Pick up that file and look it over. Oh, and make an appointment with my secretary for later this week." Her nod was crisp. "Ian." She left the office.

Ian looked after her, then stepped into Victoria's office. "Did I come at a bad time?"

"No, of course not." Frustration churned at Victoria's stomach. What was that woman hiding? "We were just discussing a matrimonial case Ms. Bonner wants me to work on."

"I see." Ian shut the door. "I was wondering why I hadn't seen you yet. According to the wisps of gossip that have drifted my way, you've been here almost an hour."

Ian's dry tone found its mark, and Victoria's head came up. She searched his face, trying to determine how much of the original resentment was back. "I hope you didn't revise your schedule because of me. I'm perfectly able to get started on my own—no matter what instructions to the contrary you've been given."

One brow rose. "Is that your way of saying you don't want my help? Or that you won't report me if I don't offer it?"

"It's my way of saying I'm open to your help—*if* you have the time and inclination to offer it. If not, I won't be writing up a complaint and turning it in to my father."

"Thanks for letting me know." Ian's chiseled lips curved into a tight smile. "So, I see you're settling in nicely. It's unusual for Ms. Bonner to pay a visit to a junior associate."

"I'm sure it was a courtesy. Just like your offer to help."

Ian's expression didn't change. "Except she has nothing to gain—or to lose."

"Neither do you. Or have you already forgotten our conversation Saturday night?"

"I remember it. But, like any good attorney, I require proof."

"Fine. Then keep a close eye on me and you'll get some."

"I did—Saturday night, in fact. I noticed you charming Benjamin Hopewell at the front door. A shrewd move. He's one of our biggest clients."

"Charming him?" Victoria almost burst out laughing at the irony of Ian's assumption—on many levels. "That's hardly what I was doing. Actually, Mr. Hopewell was remarking about how tall I've gotten since the last time he saw me, and I was assuring him he looked well even though so many years had passed. Not exactly a dazzling win-over attempt on my part. No, Ian, you're safe. I wasn't snuggling up to one of your clients. I was simply saying hello. Or good-bye, as the case may be. He ran off to get some papers after that."

"Papers. Right."

The sarcasm in Ian's voice was beginning to rankle her. "You say that as if you doubt it. Do you honestly think I'd try to woo away one of your clients right in front of you?"

"Actually, no."

"Then why the sarcasm?"

"Because Hopewell wasn't picking up any papers."

"Then why would he say he was?"

Silence.

"Ian?" Victoria's heart started pounding. Could she be on the verge of learning something? "If Mr. Hopewell wasn't getting papers, what was he doing?"

Another brief hesitation. Then Ian shrugged offhandedly. "You might as well hear your first bit of office gossip. Not that it's a secret, just a quiet reality you got a glimpse of Saturday night as they rushed off together. Oh, I know they're both consenting adults. But there's been some disapproval among the senior partners. Conflict of interest and all that. Even though they're both far too intelligent and level-headed to let their personal relationship interfere with their professional one."

Victoria blinked as the meaning of Ian's explanation sank in. "You're saying that Ms. Bonner and Mr. Hopewell are involved?"

"For years now."

"You know this for a fact?"

"The whole office does, Victoria. Ms. Bonner wouldn't deny it if you asked her. She's a firm believer that her personal life is her own and she should be free to see whomever she pleases. She just chooses not to take out newspaper ads about it. Especially now, when she's so eager to have her name added to the firm's."

"I see." Victoria wanted to scream. Here she was, zooming in on odd behavior she'd convinced herself was tied to the dealings at the Hope Institute, when all she'd really picked up on the other night was the impatience of two lovers who wanted to be together.

So much for Elizabeth Bonner.

Strange, though, that Ian Block would be the one to so blithely mention this. It was totally out of character. He, who was the essence of protocol, determined not to make a ripple as he sliced the waters leading to his coveted senior partnership. Why would he divulge word of Elizabeth Bonner's affair with Benjamin Hopewell?

She shot him a sidelong glance.

What he'd told her had to be true. The affair was too easy to confirm, and Ian was too smart to get caught in an outright lie.

No, he was playing mind games with her. He'd told her this intentionally—*and* made sure to add that the senior partners disapproved of the affair. By "senior partners," he was clearly alluding to her father. Well, he needn't have bothered. She knew her father's values only too well. In his book of rules, an attorney-client love affair would be appalling. In fact, this little tidbit more than explained his dismissive attitude toward Elizabeth Bonner.

Did Ian hope Victoria would be similarly offended? Was he hoping to drive a rift between her and Ms. Bonner? Doubtful. He'd done his homework on her. He knew from her caseloads alone that she was liberal in her acceptance of people's life choices.

He also knew from experience that her father wasn't.

Was that what this was about? Was Ian trying to pit her against her father?

Now *that* possibility made all the sense in the world.

A falling out between her and her father would clear the decks for Ian's promotion. And what better way to accomplish that than by baiting her—*and* by baiting her at no risk to himself, using a piece of throw-away gossip everyone already knew about?

So this whole Elizabeth Bonner conversation was part of Ian's agenda. It had no bearing on the information she'd come here to dig up.

Dammit.

She ran a hand through her hair in frustration.

Instead of solutions, all she was finding were more complications. And in the process, she was running into one dead end after another.

"Victoria? Have I shocked you?" Ian interrupted her thoughts to ask.

She looked up, found him studying her pensively.

She'd be damned if she gave him any food for thought. Let him wonder if his bait had been snatched.

"I don't shock that easily," she replied, her impassive tone and expression neither confirming nor countering that statement. "Actually, I'm relieved to hear you people take time out for recreation." She inclined her head, intentionally dismissing the subject before Ian could pursue it further. "Shall we go down to your office and get started familiarizing me with your clients?"

"Absolutely." Still scrutinizing her, he opened the door, gestured for her to precede him. "After you."

Outwardly composed, Victoria walked down to Ian's office, her thoughts in a tangle.

If Elizabeth Bonner wasn't the link here, then she'd have to find another connection to the Hope Institute.

More and more, it seemed as if that connection could be no one but her father.

4:00 P.M.

Zach shut the door to his hotel suite, tearing open the package the FBI had just sent over by special messenger. He pulled out a videotape, which had a Post-it stuck on marked "Urgent. Start at 2:35. Profiles being run." He recognized Meyer's handwriting.

Whatever activity had been recorded taking place at the 2:35 spot on the tape, it was pretty critical. Critical enough for Meyer to be running profiles on whoever appeared there, and for him to want Zach to review it right away.

Curious as hell, Zach popped the tape into the VCR, pressed Play and then Fast Forward, so he could advance the tape to the right spot without missing anything along the way.

The images were flashing rapidly across the screen as he settled himself on the living room sofa. Keeping a careful eye on the VCR's time indicator, he glanced through the rest of the package contents. Included were copies of the Hope Institute's monthly bills and a pair of cell phones—the secure ones he'd requested when he visited the field office that morning. Good. Now Victoria could call him, or anyone else for that matter, without fear that someone was listening in. And he didn't have to waste time figuring out whether his hotel and cell phones were bugged as well.

He scanned the bills, which consisted primarily of the Hope Institute's last few utility statements: water, oil, gas and electric, phone. Meyer had finished doing his own check on these and, having found nothing out of the ordinary, was turning them over to Zach for closer inspection.

Actually, when Zach had stopped in earlier, Meyer had been almost through with that task. But he'd abandoned it in order to hear Zach's update. The feds were far more interested in the Merritt Parkway attack and Audrey's message than they were in a review of routine bills. Not to mention how intrigued they'd been by Zach's theory that Victoria's phones were bugged—a theory they immediately jumped on. They'd sent one of their men right out to Victoria's apartment to check out the place.

As expected, he'd found the bug in the basement at the interface box.

As requested, he'd left it there.

They were closing in on these bastards. Zach could feel it.

He examined the most recent telephone bill. Calls to Waters, Kensington, Tatem & Calder appeared five or six times. That would be explained away as updates to Walter Kensington on his daughter's condition. Zach skimmed the other calls. Even though they'd all been verified by the FBI as legitimate, he quickly compared them to the last few telephone statements to see if there were any changes.

Nothing out of the ordinary.

Next came the electric bill. No change there.

Same with the fuel bills—oil and gas.

The tape was nearing the 2:35 mark, so Zach pressed Stop. He was about to refold the bills and put them away when something odd struck him about the fuel bill.

The costs for gas were high—very high, considering the Hope Institute had oil heat. He'd read that spec in the general description the FBI had first provided him. He'd also seen the oil truck arrive. True, the Institute's gas consumption was consistent from month to month, but that didn't explain why it was so high. According to his fact sheet, only their hot water was heated by gas.

He whipped out his pad and made a note to himself to double-check that detail and to see what, if any, additional cooking facilities or medical equipment the Institute had and if they operated on gas. Something here didn't ring true.

He shoved aside his notebook and hit Play, hunkering down on the sofa and staring intently at the TV.

First the usual stream of traffic.

Then a slow-moving maroon Lincoln Town Car turned

into the Institute's private drive and descended into the underground garage. Interesting. That car didn't look familiar. He backed up the tape until he had a clear view of the rear license plate. Hitting Pause, he checked the numbers. Nope. He'd never seen it before. He rewound the tape a bit more, then squinted at the car windows.

A frail, elderly man was seated in the back. A new patient, Zach surmised. Either that, or a returning one, here for outpatient treatment. No matter. The man's image was too faint to run a profile on. And his arrival hardly warranted the kind of reaction Meyer's note suggested.

There had to be more.

Zach released the pause function and let the tape continue playing.

A few more minutes of passing traffic.

Abruptly, the doorman opened the front door of the Hope Institute, and five staff members—two men and three women—emerged, walked down to the curb, and stood there, gazing uneasily around.

Now, *this* was unprecedented. No Institute employees ever lingered outside the building for long periods of time. And certainly not five of them at once.

Zach peered closely. The two men were security guards, judging from their uniforms. Two of the women were nurses. He recognized them, not only from their attire, but from their strides and general appearance. He'd seen them dash in and out of the Institute before, but he'd never gotten a clear view of their faces. He did now. The third woman was that militant receptionist Miss Evans.

What were they doing out there?

The question had barely formed when the answer presented itself.

A gray Rolls Royce glided down Seventy-eighth Street and up to the sidewalk in front of the Hope Institute, where it stopped.

This front-door activity was definitely a first.

Zach abandoned the sofa altogether, dragging a chair over so he could sit right in front of the TV.

The tape continued rolling.

The driver of the Rolls hopped out on the right side and opened the back door. A balding man emerged, then walked around and tugged open the opposite door, after which he reached in to help a stooped woman get out on the curb side. The driver unlocked the trunk and pulled out a walker, which he hastily placed on the pavement beside the car. Glaring at him, the woman waved him away.

"I can walk on my own."

"Please, Mrs. Flanders." It was Miss Evans who spoke, her soothing voice clearly intercepted by the infrared bug and only slightly out of sync with the movement of her lips. "Why don't you have your driver take you in through our underground garage? There's a ramp there that leads to a lovely corridor, with no steps for you to climb. It would be so much more comfortable for you. Miss Rivers and Miss Groves"—a swift gesture at each of the two nurses in turn—"can meet you down there. I'm sure you'll find it far easier—"

"I'm not going under any building. I don't go through basement doors. I go through front doors. Do you know who I am? How rich I am?" Mrs. Flanders barked in a gravelly tone. "Janitors go through basements. I go through foyers."

"Yes, ma'am." Miss Evans sounded resigned. She darted another quick glance up and down the street, then scooted around to take Mrs. Flanders's elbow.

The balding man hastened to her other side, holding her arm in the loving manner of a son.

Behind them, the two nurses gathered up her belongings.

"Beatrice, take her coat and her walker. She'll need the walker once she gets inside." This time it was Miss Rivers who spoke. Younger by at least fifteen years than the gray-haired Beatrice Groves, she was attractive and trim, with honey-blond hair and an authoritative manner. She was obviously superior in rank—the Institute's head nurse would be Zach's guess.

"I'll have someone from maintenance get the luggage," she continued. "I need to get back inside and administer medication to two outpatients." She picked up a vanity case that, opened and on closer inspection, looked more like a traveling drugstore. She glanced through it, studying the vials of medication. "I'll take these. They're old prescriptions. Mrs. Flanders's new medication is ready. As is her room. It's been made up since yesterday."

"Of course." Beatrice Groves's brow furrowed, and she shot an odd, probing look at her supervisor. Then she lowered her gaze, tucking a strand of gray hair back in her bun. "I'll take her coat and overnight case to her room."

Something about the older woman's tone must have alerted Miss Rivers, because she inclined her head and eyed her thoughtfully. "What's wrong? You haven't been yourself all day."

A brief hesitation. "I keep thinking about poor Mr. Pratt, whose room Mrs. Flanders is taking," Beatrice replied quietly. "I had such hopes that he'd improve . . ." She sighed, gave a sad lift of her shoulders. "We've lost four patients these past few months. I guess it's getting to me."

"I know." Miss Rivers patted her arm. "But think about all the patients we've saved, those who respond well and leave here cured. Hopefully, Mrs. Flanders will be one of the lucky ones."

"You're right."

"Of course I am. Now let's go inside. The last thing our patients need is for us to cause a spectacle on Seventy-eighth Street." She turned, including the two security guards in her instructions.

With a terse nod, they all complied. Beatrice followed Miss Rivers up the stairs and into the Institute, where Miss Evans, along with their new patient and her son, had already disappeared. The security guards did a final scrutiny of the area, then did the same.

Zach watched until he was sure the scene had played itself out. Then he whipped out his fact sheets and began poring over them. Four deaths, Beatrice had said. That was news to him.

There it was. No wonder the FBI was so eager for his take on things.

According to their reports, no death certificates had been filed by the Hope Institute in the past six months. Talk about a major discrepancy. And there was something else bothering Zach—something he needed to verify.

He continued leafing through the pages.

There.

According to the required documents filed by the Hope Institute, the clinic had only a thirty-bed capacity. On top of that, there was a four-month waiting list to get into this elite clinic. The natural assumption, therefore, was that all those beds were filled.

Clearly, they weren't. At least one new patient had been admitted today. And four others had died, without a shred of paperwork being filed.

What the hell was going on in this place?

Zach picked up one of the secure cell phones and punched in a number.

"Meyer," the harried voice at the other end answered.

"I see no record of any death certificates," Zach stated without preamble.

"Yeah, well, neither do we."

"Then where are they putting Mrs. Flanders—are there additional rooms we don't know about?"

"None on file with the city."

"I've got a bad feeling about this. When will the profiles be ready?"

"A day, maybe two. Because once we have the basic specs on each employee, we want to poke around, get any personal slants we can."

"Call me the minute you've got something to work with. Pay special attention to that Beatrice Groves. My instincts tell me she's on edge about something. We might be able to use it to get her to help us."

"You read my mind."

Zach paused, still bothered by the fuel bill amounts—amounts that seemed so out of whack. "Meyer, do me a favor and check out something else."

"Name it."

"See if any of the cooking facilities or medical equipment at the Institute run on gas. Because if they don't . . ." Zach frowned. "There's something going on at this clinic. Something beyond drug drop-offs. I'm beginning to think we've just uncovered the tip of the iceberg."

25

Dinner was a pizza and two glasses of wine, eaten in taut silence at Victoria's kitchen table. Zach delivered the food himself, showing up at Victoria's door at eight o'clock, overnight bag in hand, ready to hash over the day's events.

She'd let him in, looking utterly worn out, her nerves frayed and much closer to the surface than usual. Despite the lateness of the hour, she'd only just arrived home from her first grueling afternoon at Waters, Kensington, Tatem & Calder. She was still dressed in her business suit and pumps, her hazel eyes tired and troubled, her frustration palpable—and understandable, given the entire day of dead ends she began describing to Zach.

Hearing Zach's update left her even more on edge.

She stared grimly at the secure cell phone he gave her, listened as he explained he had its mate. Then, with a nod of thanks, she went and slipped the phone into her purse, returning to set the table, open a bottle of wine, and serve the pizza.

Afterward, they sat there nibbling as the clock ticked its way to eight-thirty. Victoria stared down at her food, her lashes veiling her expression.

Zach sipped his cabernet, studying Victoria's strained posture and trying to figure out how much of that strain was based on what he'd told her, how much on what she'd told him, and how much on the agonizing she was doing over what had happened in his bed at the Plaza Athénée this weekend.

Not what they'd done. What they'd felt.

Pensively, Zach chewed, weighing the risks of trying to draw her out. He might get results. Or he might widen the gap between them.

A sudden, totally unrelated thought struck—one that troubled him too much to leave alone. He shoved aside his plate, not mincing any words in pursuing the idea. "You're upset. Is it because I told the FBI details about your involvement in all this?" he demanded. "Nothing I relayed was a breach of trust, Victoria. I never mentioned Audrey's bulimia. And I purposely avoided exploring any avenues that might get sticky—namely, ones that would directly implicate your father. I just told the feds what they needed to know in order to protect you—and what I'm ethically obligated to tell them as my client. The truth is, I had no choice at this point. Not after the near miss on the Merritt, the bugging of your phones—"

"Zach—stop." Victoria waved away his explanation. She raised her head, and Zach felt a tug at his heart when he saw the combined fatigue and confusion in her eyes. "I *am* upset. But it's certainly not because you talked to the FBI. I knew you'd have to give them details. We're beyond the point where amateur sleuthing is enough to fix things. Something serious is going on at the Hope Institute. After what you told me you saw on that videotape"—she sucked in her breath— "I'm more worried about Audrey than I am about discretion. As for my father, I'll protect him to the best of my ability. More than that . . ." She gave a helpless shrug. "What I can't stand anymore is the waiting. Tomorrow I'm doing something."

"What?" Zach asked warily.

"Nothing drastic, just definitive. My father's got a lunch meeting. I heard him tell Ian that. He'll be gone from noon until two-fifteen. Miss Hatterman takes her lunch from twelve-thirty to one-thirty every day like clockwork. While they're both gone, I'm going into his office and poking around."

Zach frowned. "If anyone finds you there—"

"I'll come up with a backup plan, just in case. But don't worry. No one will find me. Father keeps his door shut at all times. No one can see who's in the office. And it's pretty isolated. I'll have enough time to access his computer files. If there's any evidence there, I'm going to find it. I've exhausted every other avenue. And I have a gut feeling we need to act fast."

"Yeah." Zach sighed, rubbing the back of his neck. "I have the same feeling."

"Speaking of acting fast . . ." Abruptly, Victoria shoved back her chair and rose, her tension so acute, Zach could feel it. "That brings me to the other thing I'm agonizing over—us." She gripped the edge of the table. "I've done a lot of thinking today. In fact, that's all I did, whenever I got a break from being indoctrinated in the superior ways of Waters, Kensington, Tatem and Calder. I'm ready for that talk of ours—as ready as I'll ever be."

She drew a slow breath, clearly steeling herself. "I was going to make some coffee and take it into the living room but, frankly, I'm afraid I'll lose my nerve by the time it's finished brewing. Besides, right now I need wine more than you need coffee. Is that okay?"

Soberly, Zach nodded, coming to his feet. He knew this was the moment of truth, although he didn't let that awareness show. This was Victoria's time to talk, to voice her fears and reservations.

After which, he'd have his say.

But one thing was for sure. He had no intention of letting things end up any way but one.

Saying nothing, Zach picked up the two half-filled glasses and followed Victoria into the living room.

She took her glass from him, wandered over to the window, and stared out.

"I'm not sure where to begin," she murmured, keeping her back to him. "I may be reluctant, but I'm also realistic. I know what happened in that bed was a lot more than a weekend of incredible sex. And, yes, I'm scared to death. You call it cowardice. I call it self-protection. It doesn't matter. The end result is the same—you and I are both paying the price." She paused, taking a sip of wine. "You keep telling me that some things don't change. Well, I agree—you're right. But what if those things include us? What if we are who we are and nothing can change that?" She swallowed hard. "Because if that's true, I don't think we have much to talk about, feelings or not."

"We have everything to talk about." Zach came up behind her, forcing himself not to touch her, although he was close enough so his breath ruffled her hair. "And the answer is, some things *do* change. People change, thanks to time and experience. Or, maybe 'change' is the wrong word. They grow, get more insightful, more aware. They see things differently than they used to. More clearly. Their priorities shift. And suddenly everything just clicks. They realize exactly what they need to make them whole. Even if they were blind enough to lose sight of it the first time."

Victoria's fingers trembled on the stem of her glass. "Our past shapes who we are."

"But it doesn't dictate what we do. Not if we're smart enough to intervene. And one thing we both are, is smart. Too smart not to have learned from the last four years. Too smart not to see how rare and precious what we have together is." He couldn't help himself—his palms curved around her shoulders, slid down her arms and back up again, shimmying over the soft wool of her blazer. "Victoria, tell me to stay in New York," he commanded huskily. "Tell me not to go back to Europe. Say you're ready to build a life with me—the kind of life we both stupidly threw away before."

He drew her back against him, took the glass out of her

unresisting hand, and placed it on an end table. "Lower those walls for me—just for me." He bent, pressed his lips to the pulse at her neck and felt the hard shudder that ran through her. "Meet me halfway. I won't hurt you again. Trust me. And trust me when I say I'll never try to change you or destroy the role you play in the lives of those you love."

"I can't sever ties and spend my life chasing down—"

"You won't. *I* won't," Zach interrupted, his breath warm against her ear. "I can't swear the nightmares won't ever surface. Now and then they still jar me out of sleep. But I'm finished chasing ghosts. Because the only thing worse than the nightmares is not having you next to me when I wake up." His grip tightened. "Yes, I came back here to silence some demons. I'm doing that by helping the FBI crack open the Hope Institute. But when I said I came back to find closure, I wasn't only talking about my father. I was talking about us."

He turned her around, tugged back her head so their gazes locked and he could see the naked emotion in her eyes. "Finding us again—that's a miracle I thought I'd lost forever. But I haven't, have I?"

Victoria squeezed her eyes shut. "I'm not sure I can bear the intensity of these feelings again. They're overwhelming, consuming. When you left—"

"I'll never leave again." His thumbs caressed her cheeks. "I promise. All you have to do is ask me to stay."

"Zach—"

"Ask."

Her lashes lifted, and a low sob escaped her throat as the wall crumbled to dust. "Stay," she choked out. "Please. I need you. I don't want to, but I do—"

His mouth swooped down to cover hers, and he drank in her words with fierce, utter possession. "And I need you," he muttered, crushing her in his arms, dragging her against him. "You have no idea how much . . ."

He was even more frantic than he'd been the other night.

Right now, at this moment, the need to be inside her was wild, urgent, bordering on compulsion. He didn't even try to fight it. He just kept kissing her, taking her mouth in deep, hungry caresses, his tongue melding with hers as he unbuttoned her blazer, shoved it down her arms and to the floor. Her blouse followed, although Victoria hindered the process, her hands gliding under his turtleneck sweater, moving over the warm, hair-roughened wall of his chest. She leaned forward, pressing her lips to his skin, lapping lightly at his nipples. Zach felt a red haze explode in his head, and he broke away, yanked the sweater over his head, and flung it down. Victoria continued kissing him, reaching for the button on his slacks and starting to sink down onto the rug.

"No." Zach caught her elbows, swept her up and into his arms. He felt a primal male need, one that far exceeded the physical. It was a need to have her in her most intimate domain, the place she'd lain awake nights and dreamed of him—dreams he hadn't been able to share.

He was about to share them now.

"I want you in your bed." Crossing the living room in long purposeful strides, he continued to devour her mouth, reaching around with one hand to unhook the front clasp of her bra. The lacy scrap of lingerie vanished somewhere between the living room and the hall. Then Zach's mouth was on her breasts, drawing her nipples into hard, wet points as he made his way down the hall.

Victoria's back arched on a cry, and she barely managed to point in the direction of her bedroom. "There."

She kicked off her shoes as he crossed the threshold, and she pulled him onto the bed with her as he worked down her skirt, stripping off her pantyhose and panties with it. She whispered his name, unzipping his pants, then slipping her fingers inside his briefs and caressing him until he lost control, nearly tearing the material as he yanked off the remainder of his clothes.

He pressed her back against the pillows, framing her face between his palms and kissing her deeply as his naked body blanketed hers. His thighs wedged between hers at the same instant that hers parted for him, anchoring his hips in the cradle between.

He had to be inside her.

Bracing his arms on either side of her head, he stared down at her, his gaze burning into hers. He raised up, found her damp passage, and thrust all the way inside.

Victoria's breath suspended as her flesh yielded to his. She enveloped him, her muscles softening and clamping down all at once. Her back arched, and she took him even deeper.

Zach groaned, buried his face in her neck, fighting for control. But it was a losing battle, and he knew it. Everything inside him was already tightening, converging, his emotions acting as fuel for his body's fire.

He couldn't wait.

He began thrusting, fast and deep, and Victoria moaned softly, her nails digging into his back as she wrapped her arms and legs around him, lifted herself into each thrust. Her body responded to his penetration with reckless haste, the pleasure coiling, spiraling upward. He could feel how close she was, her muscles clenching tighter and tighter around him, her head tossing on the pillow.

Close, but not close enough. He was unraveling—fast.

"Tory," he ground out, a hard shudder racking his body as he forced himself to go still. Gritting his teeth against the reflexive motion of his hips, he made a last-ditch effort to delay the all-too-fast culmination roaring down on them.

"Don't," Victoria commanded, her fists shoving at his back, trying to make him start moving again. She was frantic, her limbs trembling, her muscles quivering on the brink. "Don't stop now . . . Zach, I'm dying."

He gave up, gave in to the inevitable. Hooking his arms beneath her knees, he opened her fully, holding her that way as he drove into her—again and again—and catapulted them both over the edge.

She went taut . . . and shattered, climaxing in a rush, crying out his name. Her spasms gripped him, milked him—and that was all it took.

He lunged forward, pouring into her even as he did, his entire body jolting under the impact, emptying his very soul into hers.

Then, peace. God, after four years. Peace.

He collapsed on top of her, too weak to form a coherent thought, much less to move. Never in all his life had he felt so drained and so full all at once.

The room was silent, the only audible sound the rasping of their breath.

Time passed, although how much, Zach hadn't a clue.

Then Victoria shifted ever so slightly beneath him, her lips brushing his sweat-drenched shoulder. "I love you," she whispered. "I've never stopped."

The spontaneity of her words meant almost as much as the declaration itself, and a hard knot of emotion tightened Zach's chest.

"Tory." His hands clenched in her hair. "God, I love you so much." His voice was raw, shattered, the sound of a man who'd found his life again. "More than you can ever imagine."

She shivered, a tiny quivering motion. "Is this really happening?"

"Definitely." Zach raised himself up and stared into her eyes—eyes that were filled with tears. He should wait, should make sure she was ready for this, that this was the right time. He should do a lot of things. But he didn't.

"Marry me." His thumbs captured her tears. "The minute Audrey's safe and the Hope Institute's exposed. We'll live here in New York, close to your family and your law firm. Or we'll buy a house in the suburbs, keep this apartment for the nights we work late. Whatever you want. Just say you'll be my wife."

Last time she'd panicked, backed away like a frightened rabbit.

Not this time. This time she didn't miss a beat.

"Yes," she stated simply. "Yes, I'll marry you. I want that very, very much. More than even I realized." She sniffed, gave him a watery smile. "A house, huh? That sounds wonderful. Does a real-life Jackson come with it? Because my little pal and I"—She waved her arm in the direction of the stuffed dog perched on her rocking chair—"have waited a long time for an actual canine friend."

Zach angled his head and gazed solemnly at the stuffed toy. "You kept him."

"I kept everything. Including the memories. I couldn't let go."

"Thank God for that." He kissed her. "A real Jackson it is. Several, if you want. We'll fill the house with puppies."

"And children?" she asked softly, watching his face.

A hard swallow. "You know how much I want that. I'm just trying not to rush you."

Victoria's brows arched, and she glanced pointedly down at their still-joined bodies. "You could have fooled me."

He followed her gaze, gave her a crooked grin. "For the record, I brought condoms with me tonight. They're in the living room, packed in my bag."

"Ah, a useful place." Victoria laughed, looping her arms around his neck. "I'm relieved to know you're so responsible."

Zach's smile faded, and his eyes narrowed intently on her face. "Are you sorry?"

"If I was, I wouldn't have let this happen. You know that as well as I do."

Yes, he did. And his body leaped at the implications. "Does that mean what I think it means?"

Victoria rubbed her leg against his. "That depends on what you think it means."

He rolled onto his back, taking her with him, his body rigid, imbedded deeply in hers. "Come here," he muttered thickly, drawing her mouth down to his. "I'll show you."

26

Tuesday, April 25
12:45 P.M.

Miss Hatterman was at lunch.

Walter Kensington was at his meeting.

And Victoria was on her way to his office.

Thumbing through an acquisition file, she walked casually in that direction, passing by the handful of secretaries and clerical staff who were working this part of the lunch hour. Leaning over their computer terminals, they were absorbed in their work, not paying the slightest attention to Victoria or where she was going.

She reached the private hallway down which her father's office and Miss Hatterman's cubicle were located. She went as far as the secretary's quiet alcove, then paused, glanced quickly behind her.

Nothing.

She scooted by, heading for the thick cherry door that heralded her father's inner sanctum. She'd seen him leave the office and head for the elevators almost an hour ago. But, just to be on the safe side, she knocked.

Silence.

In she went.

Leaning back against the shut door, she scanned the room, assuring herself it was empty.

It was.

She didn't turn on a light. It would just be something else

to remember reversing on her way out. Besides, there was plenty of sunlight thanks to the huge expanse of windows.

She went straight to the desk and pressed the power button on the computer.

The machine whirred to life, making the customary sequence of humming sounds as it booted up.

Then an unfamiliar screen appeared with a picture of what looked like an IBM credit card. She began typing, but the keyboard was dead.

She frowned, staring at the screen. She'd been prepared to try out passwords in order to log on. She'd even made a mental list of possibilities. But the damned machine wasn't even letting her get that far.

What the hell did she do now?

She inspected the tower and keyboard, wishing she had a better technical understanding of hardware. To her, a computer was a computer. That was as far as her expertise ran.

Zach's ran a whole lot farther.

She whipped out her secure cell phone and punched up his number.

"Hello." He answered on the first ring. He sounded as tight as a drum. Worrying about her, no doubt. He knew what time it was, what she was doing.

"It's me."

"I guessed. Are you okay? I'm wearing out the rug."

"I'm fine. I'm in his office. But I can't get the computer to respond. It's as if the keyboard is locked or dead. I turned on the power. The machine booted up. Then it flashed a strange screen with a picture of some credit card. No request for a password, nothing. And I can't enter a thing."

Zach's wheels were turning. "He must be taking more extreme security measures. Not a surprise, if he's got something to hide. What brand of computer is he using?"

"It's an IBM with an LCD display."

"Okay." Zach paused again to think. "Take a look near the keyboard," he instructed. "Do you see a small, dark gray plastic device with an IBM logo? It's not big enough to fit a floppy disk. More like a credit card with electrical connections."

"Yes." Victoria's gaze riveted to a dark gray gadget with a rectangular slot that matched Zach's description. "I see it."

"Damn," he muttered. "That means the computer needs a Smart Card to gain access to the computer, and a personal identification code in order to get in. God knows where your father hides the card or what his PIN code is. Get out of there, Victoria."

"No." Her gaze was already darting around the office. It wouldn't be in the floor-to-ceiling bookshelves. Nor would it be in the furniture. It wouldn't be anywhere out of reach. Her father required control. He'd want his Smart Card at his fingertips. Somewhere personal, where only he would look.

Her eyes fell on the model cars.

She picked up the Rolls Royce first. It was the crowning jewel of his collection, Rolls's newly introduced Silver Seraph. He'd commissioned one for himself, crafted in the same deep blue as this model. Both had arrived at his home the same day—the original for his garage, the ready-to-be-assembled model for his desk.

He'd completed it that weekend and brought it here on Monday for display. It was an exquisite replica, flawlessly assembled, right down to the Spirit of Ecstasy mascot.

She ran her fingers over the hood, the roof, the doors, the trunk. Then she opened the passenger door and groped along the inside surfaces.

"Victoria?" Zach said in her ear. "What are you doing?"

"Looking for the Smart Card." She flipped the car upside down.

There, Velcroed to the underside, was a card with an IBM logo on the front and the name Walter Kensington written in ink on the back. "I've got it."

Zach released a reluctant breath. "Fine. Now slide it into the reader, connector side first."

She did. A few seconds passed. Then a small box appeared on the screen, prompting for a PIN code. "Yes," she hissed. "Thank you, Zach. You're wonderful."

"Don't hang up," he commanded.

"I can't break into a computer and talk to you at the same time."

"Put the phone on the desk. At least I can hear you that way. I need to know you're all right."

Victoria nodded. "Okay."

"And, Victoria? You only have three shots at getting in. If you don't guess the right PIN code by then, you'll be locked out until the administrator resets your father's password—*and* investigates the attempted break-in."

"Got it. Wish me luck."

She set down the cell phone and began trying her list of potential codes.

First, the name of her father's favorite wine. No. Next, the date of his hole-in-one. Dammit. Again, no luck.

One more strike and she was out.

She racked her brain, trying to think with her father's mind.

What would he choose? What meant something to him that no one else would think of?

The model cars.

She looked down at the Rolls Royce, lying upside down on the sweeping curve of the semicircular desk. Of course. Cars were his passion. Not only that, but he had so many of them that he could update his password any time he felt a change would be prudent.

Well, this little baby was the cream of his crop, his favorite by a landslide. It was also rare as hell, not in most people's vocabularies, much less their garages. If he'd thought to hide his card here, why wouldn't he use it as his PIN code?

Taking a deep breath, she typed in SILVERSERAPH and hit the enter key.

Her heart slammed against her ribs for what seemed like an eternity as she waited for the computer to respond—or to lock her out for good.

She was in.

She had to bite her lip to stifle a cry of exultation. Whooping aloud wouldn't be smart. The last thing she wanted was to be heard. Besides, there was no time for self-congratulation. It was already one-fifteen. She had to hurry.

"Zach," she murmured quietly, leaning close to the phone. "I did it. It's a normal log-on from here." She pressed the control-alt-delete keys to log on to Windows NT.

The screen changed, flashing the domain and user name—and the password space. The cursor flashed meaningfully alongside the word "password," instructing her to enter the appropriate keys in order to gain entry.

She paused, fingers hovering above the keyboard.

Her father didn't like complications. He'd go the least cluttered route possible, arrogantly believing no one could get this far.

Again, she typed SILVERSERAPH and hit the enter key.

Whirring sounds told her she'd spanned the last hurdle.

A few deft mouse clicks, and a listing of directories appeared.

Rapidly, she scrolled down. There was no Hope Institute. But there was a Hopewell Industries. She clicked on it, and nearly groaned aloud when she saw the number of files listed beneath it.

On a hunch, she snatched up the cell phone. "Zach?"

"I'm here."

"What dates do you have on the Hope Institute?"

"Dates . . ." The rustle of papers. "It opened in the fall of 1991—September thirtieth, to be exact. It was sold by Hopewell Industries on August twenty-second, 1997."

"Thanks." She clicked on the date column header and began skimming the list for those dates. She found the 09/30/1991 entry and opened it. Nothing unusual, just papers documenting the clinic's opening. She moved to 1997. There it was—08/22/1997.

She opened the file.

The word "confidential" was written in bold block type across the top of the page—and every successive page she scrolled through.

Each time, she ignored it.

It was a whole group of legal documents, beginning with a contract of sale transferring the Institute to a Swiss holding company. No names of specific buyers were listed. Not a surprise.

After that, the documents were marked "Institute contracts." Intently, she scanned them, one by one.

It took her two minutes to realize what she was looking at, and ten seconds to decide what to do.

She opened her purse, whipped out the floppy disk she'd brought, and shoved it into the drive. Then she furiously clicked the mouse to copy the files to the floppy.

"Zach, I've got something," she said tersely into the phone. "I can't read through all these legal documents now—there are too many of them. It would take me an hour."

"You don't have an hour, Victoria," he bit out. "It's one-twenty-five. Miss Hatterman will be back any minute. I want you out of there."

"I'm copying the files onto a floppy. I'll be gone right after that." She cocked her head, listening for sounds from outside the office. But the walls were too thick to hear anything.

So as not to waste time, she picked up the model Rolls Royce and shut its doors, making sure it looked untouched. Hovering over the computer, she waited, car in hand, ready for the copying function to finish so she could yank out her father's Smart Card and Velcro it back into place.

The disk drive whirred as it did its job.

Damn, these things were slow.

"Victoria." Zach sounded livid. "Get the hell out of there. Now."

The whirring stopped.

"I'm done." She ejected the disk, shoved it in her purse, and began the shut-down process.

Three minutes later, she turned off the computer. She pressed the Smart Card back in its spot beneath the model Rolls Royce and set the car in its original spot on the desk.

Finished.

She scanned the office once, making sure she'd forgotten nothing.

Reassured, she snatched up her file and the cell phone, then headed for the door.

"I'm going to hang up now," she told Zach. "I've got an acquisition file with me that I was reviewing with Ian for my father. I'll pretend I'm looking it over as I walk back to my office—just in case Miss Hatterman's back at her desk. I'll call you later."

"Be careful."

"I will." She clicked off the phone, stuffed it back in her purse.

When she emerged from the office a minute later, she was engrossed in the contents of the file, her brow creased in thought.

Head bent, she walked by Miss Hatterman's desk.

It was still empty.

She'd reached the open area near the secretaries and receptionist and was about to turn down the corridor that led to her office when Miss Hatterman hurried by. "Ms. Kensington," she acknowledged with a nod.

"Hello, Miss Hatterman." A cordial smile, an unruffled demeanor.

After which, Victoria headed straight for her office. She crossed the threshold, shut the door, and collapsed behind her desk.

A minute longer and she would have been caught.

She pressed her fingers to her temples. Well, she hadn't been caught. But that was little cause for celebration. Because if what she had seen in her brief glimpse of the documents was anything close to what she thought it was, her father had more invested in the Hope Institute than even Zach realized.

6:30 P.M.

"Hi." Zach was waiting right outside 280 Park Avenue when Victoria stepped out of the building that evening.

Without the slightest hesitation or regard for the streams of commuters pounding the sidewalk on their way to Grand Central Station, he drew her against him and kissed her—a slow, lingering kiss that left her breathless.

"What was that?" she managed, when he finally lifted his head.

A corner of Zach's mouth lifted. "That was a loud-and-clear message to Mr. Cigar about your plans for the evening," he murmured. "It was also an I-missed-you kiss from the man you're going to marry and who worried himself sick about you all day." His smile faded when he saw the strained look on her face. "Are you all right?"

"Ask me that after you've seen what's on the disk."

He didn't ask any more questions, just nodded, steering her toward the curb. "The traffic's let up. We'll catch a cab. We can send out for something to eat."

"Instead of my apartment, can we go to your hotel?" Victoria surprised him by asking. "It's closer. We can have dinner there—in your suite." She glanced around, checking out the swarms of people and wondering how far away Mr. Cigar was and whether he was within hearing range. "Room service will send up food whenever we're ready."

Zach understood she was speaking cryptically, although he was clearly puzzled by her choice of destinations—puzzled, but not the least bit unhappy. "Sounds great."

He signaled for the next taxi.

They limited their choice of topics while they rode—which, fortunately, wasn't too long. Traffic had eased as the rush hour wound down, and their driver was a cowboy who weaved past every car and pedestrian on the street.

Fifteen minutes later they were in Zach's suite.

Victoria went straight over and poured herself a glass of wine.

"That bad?" Zach asked.

"I hope not. But I think so."

"Okay, pour one for me. I'm ordering you some dinner."

"I'm not hungry."

He paused halfway to the phone, eyes narrowed. "Victoria, you look like hell. You're eating, if I have to force-feed you."

Despite her tension, Victoria couldn't help but smile. "You're still as overbearing as ever. You're lucky I love you."

An intimate look that singed her to her toes. "Yes, I know I am. And later I plan to show you how grateful I am, until I have you convinced."

"Grateful?" Victoria's brows arched in amused disbelief. "You're not the grateful type. That kind of convincing might take hours."

"I'm selfless. I'll suffer."

Unexpected laughter rippled through Victoria, and she gave a hard, amazed shake of her head. "Only you could make me laugh right now." She broke off, regarding him soberly. "Thank you."

"My pleasure."

Zach turned, went to the phone to order their food, and Victoria poured his wine, bringing both glasses into the living room and placing them on the table near where Zach had set up his IBM ThinkPad laptop. She settled herself on the sofa. Opening her purse, she pulled out the disk and stared broodingly down at it.

"Dinner will be up in a half hour," Zach announced, coming over to join her. He lowered himself to the cushion, twisting around so he could face her. "Why didn't you want to go to your apartment?"

Victoria's gaze lifted to meet his. "Originally I planned to. Then I started thinking. The FBI verified that someone's tapped into my phones. Maybe that someone's done the same thing to my computer."

Zach's forehead creased in a scowl. He, better than anyone, knew Victoria wasn't one to jump to conclusions—not without a basis. "It's possible. Why? Did something happen to make you suspicious?"

She shrugged. "I didn't think so at the time. Now, I'm not sure." She told Zach about the couple of occasions when her computer had denied her access, insisting that the user was already logged on. "And when I did finally manage to log on, I had an e-mail from the system administrator. It said something about there being a wiring problem on my local network—a problem that might be causing me to get faulty messages that prevented me from logging on."

"It probably also said the problem was in the process of being cleared up, and advised you to try again in a few minutes." Zach's scowl deepened. "That's a classic hacker technique. He'd post that e-mail before breaking into your system just in case you tried getting in when he was already logged on. My guess is he was checking to see if you'd saved anything on your hard drive that related to the Hope Institute, or if you'd really let the matter drop."

"Whoever 'he' is," Victoria muttered.

"Probably a well-paid hacker hired by whoever hired Mr. Cigar."

Walter Kensington's name hung between them—an ugly but irrefutable possibility.

"Victoria," Zach emphasized quietly. "Don't jump to conclusions."

"I'm trying not to. In any case, my home computer is tied

in to my office system, so our hacker managed to check both. Not that there was anything to find." Her gaze returned to the disk, which she turned over in her hands. "Now's another story."

"Bringing that disk here was a smart move," Zach concurred. "There's no point in taking chances."

"No, there isn't. And while I might not be up on hackers and their methods, that bug on my telephone got my wheels turning. Anyway, here." She handed the disk to Zach.

He stared at it for a moment, and Victoria sensed he had something else to tell her, something she wasn't going to like. "I spoke to Meyer earlier," he said, jumping in with both feet. "He sent a man to your office late last night. There's a bug on the phones there, too."

That fact didn't surprise her—not at this point. But she had a sneaky suspicion why Zach didn't want to get into this. "How did the FBI handle things?"

"They left the phone tap where it was." Without missing a beat, he continued, addressing her anticipated objections before she could raise them. "I know you're going to have issues with that, because you'll feel it violates Paul and Meg's privacy. You're right. It does. But it'll only be for a few days. If the feds remove the bug, it'll undo everything we've worked for, not to mention putting you and Audrey in danger. Your partners will understand when you explain— after the investigation's over. Besides, whoever's bugging the phones isn't interested in anyone's conversations but yours. They're probably not even listening during the hours you spend at your father's firm. So don't fight me on this."

Zach's logic was indisputable, and Victoria gave a weary sigh. "Fine. I'm not sure I have the strength to fight anymore. I'm numb."

"No, you're not. You're just on overdrive." Tenderly, Zach caressed her cheek. "As for having the strength to fight, you'll *never* lose that. It's too deeply ingrained. And you're too good at it."

She smiled at his gentle teasing. "You're right. I don't know what I was thinking."

He brought her fingers to his lips. "It'll be over soon, sweetheart. I feel it in my gut." He gestured toward his laptop. "Ready to check out this disk?"

"As ready as I'll ever be."

He fired up the ThinkPad and, when the Windows desktop icons appeared, he inserted the disk.

A few minutes later he was looking at the same documents she'd skimmed earlier that day.

There were several of them. A will, a living will, a power-of-attorney, a medical services agreement, and a trust and estate agreement. They all had one thing in common: they gave full control to the Hope Institute and full authority—and every drop of related legal business—to Waters, Kensington, Tatem & Calder.

Zach scanned the documents in silence. Then he stopped, selecting all the documents and clicking on the print icon. He turned to Victoria, who'd been reading over his shoulder, her expression grim. "I get the picture," he said. "I assume you didn't have enough time to analyze the specifics."

"No."

"Okay. We'll do it together now." He reached over, plucked the pages out of the printer, and moved closer to Victoria, settling himself directly beside her so she could see.

She half wished she couldn't.

The power-of-attorney form was straightforward, its purpose clear as day. Walter Kensington was given unconditional power of attorney for each of the Hope Institute's patients. No exceptions.

The trust and estate agreement was similarly binding, naming Waters, Kensington, Tatem & Calder as sole legal administrators of the estates of all Hope Institute patients.

After that, the documents got more disturbing.

The medical services agreement included a confidentiality section that legally required each patient to maintain complete secrecy with respect to all his dealings with the Hope Institute—including everything from doctors' names to the reason for the patient's admission. Next, there was an indemnification section that "saved and held harmless" both the Hope Institute and Waters, Kensington, Tatem & Calder, protecting them from "any and all claims" that might arise as a result of the patient's dealings with or treatment by the Hope Institute. Finally, there was an exclusivity section outlining mandatory outpatient visits for those patients well enough to leave the clinic—visits naming the Hope Institute as sole provider.

The living will provided that all decisions regarding life-support systems, medications to prolong life, and so on, would be determined and administered solely by the Hope Institute, who would be "indemnified and held harmless" with respect to such determinations, as would its legal counsel.

Last and most sobering, both the will and the living will specified that the patient, his or her family, and the estate irrevocably agreed, upon the patient's death, to immediate cremation, with all arrangements made by the Hope Institute.

A painful silence filled the room as Zach turned the last page, then placed the documents on the table.

Victoria broke the silence first, making a harsh sound and dropping back against the sofa. "My God, Zach. What are they doing in that clinic?"

"I don't know." He raked a hand through his hair. "But whatever it is, they've built a goddamned fortress around the place—both legally and physically." He made a steeple with his fingers and rested his chin on it. "Waters, Kensington, Tatem and Calder is making a fortune off this arrangement. That much is clear."

"Yes, but what's *not* clear is why the Hope Institute patients would agree to sign these documents. It makes no sense. These are affluent, intelligent, worldly people. Yet they're agreeing to sign away their most basic rights, and the rights of their families. Why? What's at stake here isn't just money—it's control over their lives."

"Maybe that's exactly why they're willing to do it. Maybe they're desperate, and they believe this is the only place that can cure them."

"And what's the Hope Institute promising? What is it they're doing that convinces these patients to relinquish every ounce of control for a chance at a normal life? And why such extreme measures—including mandatory cremation, for God's sake?"

"Cremation would certainly explain the high gas bills," Zach deduced tersely.

In a flash, Victoria bolted upright. "You think they're cremating the patients right there at the Institute?"

"It makes sense, doesn't it?" Zach angled his head toward her. "It's the only way to protect themselves and whatever it is they're hiding. No bodies. No autopsies. No death certificates—at least not until they're ready to issue them." A grim look. "Meyer called me a few hours ago. He has no explanation for the size of the Institute's gas bills. According to the permits on file with New York City, they have only limited cooking facilities and no medical equipment that uses gas."

"But you think they have a crematorium. One nobody knows about." Victoria squeezed her eyes shut. "I think I'm going to be sick." She wet her lips. "Zach, I've tried to think like a lawyer. I've managed till now. After this—I can't. My sister's in that . . . place. I've got to get her out."

This time Zach didn't argue. Instead, he fell silent again—although Victoria knew this silence meant he was thinking. "There's only one way to get Audrey out of there," he said at length. "Also to find out what's really going on—*and* to get our hands on whoever's running things. I've got to get inside the Hope Institute."

27

"Zach, what are you talking about?"

He pivoted until their eyes met. "I'm involved in a criminal investigation. Well, that investigation's broadened. The illegal activities taking place at the Hope Institute clearly extend far beyond drug dealing. I don't know what the connection is, but whoever's running this sick show does. I'm going in there. And I'm not coming out until I've made sure Audrey's safe and I've got the evidence needed to convict everyone involved."

"How do you propose to do that?"

"With some help." Zach leaned over, picked up his cell phone, and punched in Meyer's number. "It's me," he said in greeting. "Did you get that profile on Beatrice Groves?" A long pause, during which Zach nodded a few times, his jaw clenched, but a purposeful gleam forming in his eyes. "That's exactly what we need. Get it done tonight. I want Miss Groves at the field office tomorrow before her shift at the Institute starts. I'm sure you got her schedule for the next week. Is she on morning or afternoon tomorrow?" Another pause. "Good. That gives us all morning to talk to her. I'll be there early. Yeah, I've got new information. A lot more than we bargained for."

"Zach," Victoria interrupted in a firm voice. "Tell Mr. Meyer I'll be at that meeting, too." Anticipating the agent's refusal, she leaned past Zach to his computer. She ejected the disk and gathered up the printed pages. "Tell him the new information you mentioned is actually not yours, but mine. If he wants to see it, he should expect to include me at your meeting."

Zach's lips twitched. "Meyer?" he said into the phone. "I won't be alone. The person who got the information for me will be there, too. Victoria Kensington." He grinned at whatever expletive Meyer used, the force of which Victoria could hear from the sofa. "Yeah, she's here with me. And I'd suggest you concede to her demand. I told you, she's as stubborn as they come. And since the information's in her possession, you don't have much choice."

Another pause.

Then: "That's a smart move. Oh, and Meyer? Tomorrow morning, send a car to the service entrance of the Plaza Athénée to pick us up. As you know, Victoria's got that guy with the cigar following her. He thinks she and I are . . . occupied in my suite. Let's not give him cause for doubt. Which we won't if we leave and come back through the service entrance. He'll think we're up here the whole time. Yeah, eight-thirty is fine. We'll be ready."

With a crooked grin, Zach pressed End and placed the cell phone on the table. "He agreed."

"I'd hardly say he agreed. You backed him into a corner."

"No, you did." He chuckled.

"You've told him I'm stubborn?"

"Um-hum. And loyal. Both of which you are. As I've said, I wouldn't want to face you in a courtroom." Zach's smile faded, and he inclined his head, studying her intently. "Are you okay?"

"About what—Audrey? Or my father?"

"Both."

"No," she replied honestly. "What did the FBI find out about Beatrice Groves?"

"She lives in a seniors' complex. Meyer's initial check shows that she's been supplying some of her needier and frailer neighbors with free medication. I guess we can all figure out where she's getting it. Meyer's double- and triple-checking his facts now."

Victoria's heart gave an involuntary twist. "Most of Meg's clients are elderly. They can scarcely pay for their groceries, much less their medication. And the government doesn't do enough to help. Zach, if this Beatrice Groves is stealing medication for her neighbors, she's probably doing it as a last resort. I realize it's illegal. But to use something like that against her—"

"I don't plan to use it against her," Zach interrupted. "But she won't know that. It's leverage. It will keep Miss Groves from telling anyone she's helping us. And she will help us—out of that same compassion that makes her help her neighbors. She knows something, Victoria, something that's making her uneasy about the Hope Institute. I sense it. And whatever it is, it'll help me get Audrey out of there."

Renewed fear knotted Victoria's gut. "I'm praying she can tell me Audrey's all right."

"She can and she will. In the meantime, I won't insult you by saying don't worry. But I will ask you to try to think rationally. You know Audrey was fine as of Sunday, when she left you that message. You also reassured your father by buying into his explanation and leaving the matter in his hands. So, there's no reason to believe Audrey's in any immediate danger. And I repeat what I said to you in the car Saturday night—whatever your father's failings, I don't believe he'd physically harm his daughters. That's even if the worst is true, and he's running the show there. Which we're still not sure is the case."

"I hope to God you're right." Victoria tunneled her fingers through her hair. "His name is on every single document, in a confidential file we found on his computer." She pressed her lips together, fighting an internal battle that was tearing her apart. "Even so, I've got to believe his involvement is only on paper. If I don't, I'm not sure I can hold it together."

"Reserve judgment. Wait till all the evidence is in." Zach stood, held out his arms. "Come here."

Victoria went straight to him. "Thank you," she breathed, her face pressed to his shirt. "I can't tell you what your support means to me."

"Then don't. Tell me you love me instead."

She pressed closer. "I love you."

He kissed the top of her head. "There's nothing else we can do tonight. Let's have dinner. Then I'll start showing you that gratitude I was talking about."

FBI Field Office, 26 Federal Plaza
Wednesday, April 26
9:20 A.M.

Beatrice Groves was wringing her handkerchief when Victoria and Zach accompanied Meyer into his office to talk to her. Beforehand, they'd spent twenty minutes alone in a secluded room, reviewing the facts and discussing their strategy. The evidence Meyer had compiled against Miss Groves was irrefutable. His men had talked to a dozen senior citizens in her apartment complex, all of whom spoke appreciatively about how she'd supplied them with their medication.

Meyer had no more desire to prosecute her than Zach did. But he was ready to pretend otherwise, if need be.

The other questionable piece of information the FBI had uncovered pertained to Gloria Rivers. It seemed that Miss Rivers, who was indeed the Institute's head nurse, lived in a lavish two-bedroom apartment on the Upper East Side—an apartment whose monthly rent was three times the amount that Miss Rivers brought home as her salary from the Hope Institute. Further digging revealed she had no other sources of income, no recent inheritances, and no affluent friends or relatives. But she did have a substantial retirement fund, an extravagant lifestyle, and no outstanding charge card bills.

All the more reason to see what Beatrice Groves had to say, and how much of what was troubling her related to the head nurse.

Victoria took one look at the elderly woman, and her heart went out to her. Miss Groves was clearly terrified, her lined face ashen, her eyes wide, blinking furiously as she watched them enter the office.

"Good morning, Miss Groves," Zach said cordially, pulling up two chairs so he and Victoria could sit near her, as arranged, rather than across the more formidable desk where Meyer perched himself. "I'm Zachary Hamilton. You've already met Special Agent Meyer." For the moment, he intentionally avoided mentioning Victoria's name.

The older woman's lips trembled as she looked from one man to the other. "Why was I brought here?" she asked. "Am I under arrest?"

Meyer shrugged. "That hasn't been decided yet. It depends."

"On what?"

Zach leaned forward, interlacing his fingers and eyeing her intently. "The FBI has proof you've been illegally distributing prescription drugs. We could press formal charges. But the truth is, we have bigger fish to fry. We need your help. Give us that help, and we'll settle for pulling the plug on your pharmaceutical Santa Claus routine rather than criminal prosecution."

She wilted in her seat. "They're just poor people who need medicine."

"We realize that. Which is why we'd opt for leniency—if you cooperate."

"I don't understand. How can I possibly help you?"

"By telling us about the Hope Institute. We're far more interested in what's going on where you work than where you live."

A surprised, slightly wary expression. "Why are you investigating the Hope Institute?"

"I can't divulge that now. Suffice it to say, we have good reasons." Zach paused. "Somehow I think you already know that."

That panicked expression returned. "I don't *know* anything. I just . . ." Her voice trailed off.

"We're the good guys, Miss Groves," Meyer stated bluntly. "We're trying to help your patients, not hurt them."

"They're receiving the finest care," she said defensively. "That much I can tell you." More twisting of her handkerchief. "I can't discuss the Institute. I signed a confidentiality agreement when I took my job."

"Is stealing medication part of that agreement?" Meyer shot back. "I doubt it. In fact, I'm sure the Institute would be very unhappy to learn you've been helping yourself to their inventory—regardless of how charitable your cause. Don't make us test that theory."

Beatrice Groves looked close to tears.

"Listen to me, Miss Groves." Zach's voice was gentle, his manner soothing—and Victoria suspected it wasn't entirely for effect. He felt bad about having to browbeat the elderly nurse. "The matter we're investigating is serious. Lives are at stake. Saving lives is why you became a nurse, isn't it? It must be why you chose to work at a place like the Hope Institute, where the illnesses you're fighting are so critical."

Mutely, she nodded.

"Then, please, help us. Not only to protect yourself. To protect those in your care."

Zach's sincerity wasn't lost on Miss Groves. She pressed her lips together, loyalty to her employer already battling moral conscience and fear of prosecution. Zach's plea added compassion to the balance.

It was enough to tip the scales in their favor.

"What exactly is it you want to know?" she asked, her voice a bit steadier.

"For starters, how many of the Institute's hospital rooms are empty?"

"None." Beatrice was visibly relieved by the noninflammatory question. "We have a long waiting list. We had two empty rooms. Both were filled Monday."

"I see." Swiftly, Zach brought the conversation around to where he wanted it to be. "Speaking of Monday, you were very upset when you went out to get Mrs. Flanders. Why? Is it because of the four patients the clinic recently lost?"

Beatrice startled. "You were watching me?"

"Not only you. Everyone who was outside."

"I see." Her handkerchief was beginning to fray at the edges. "Yes, I was upset about that. Losing patients is never easy." She paused, her hesitation palpable.

"But?" Zach prompted. "Please, Miss Groves, if something else is bothering you, we must know what it is."

"Or you'll put me in jail," she replied bleakly.

"Miss Groves, no one wants to put you in jail." It was Victoria who interceded, right on cue. It was up to her to finish what Zach started, to gain Miss Groves's trust and secure her cooperation.

"Prosecuting you is not the goal here," she repeated. "Protecting innocent people is. If you care about your job and your patients, you'll help us. In that way, the only people who will get hurt are those who deserve to. Otherwise, innocent patients might be victimized. Patients like my sister."

"Your sister?" In the process of nodding bleakly at Victoria's reasoning, Beatrice shot her a quizzical look, making a baffled gesture with her hands. "I don't understand. Who are you?"

"My name is Victoria Kensington. Audrey Kensington is my sister."

"Oh . . . Audrey." Genuine concern crossed the elderly nurse's face. "So you're the sister she's so eager to see."

"Yes." Victoria's insides tensed, and she gave in to the very real, very personal worry that had been eating her alive these past days. "Is she all right, Miss Groves? I have to know. Is Audrey safe? Is she well? Because the last time I saw her, she wasn't. She collapsed at my feet."

"Oh, dear." Beatrice wet her lips. "That must have been the day she had that bad reaction to her medication and ran away. We were all so worried. It was a relief to get her back. She's doing much better now, although she's still weak."

A bad reaction to her medication. Yes, that's what their father had said. "What type of medication was Audrey receiving?"

"Specifically? I'm not certain. But rest assured, our treatments are groundbreaking."

"I see. In other words, you'd have to consult her chart to know exactly what she's being given."

"No. I don't have access to those details."

Victoria's brows knit in puzzlement. "Because you're not the nurse assigned to Audrey?"

"Because only Miss Rivers knows exactly what medication each patient receives."

Silence.

"Please explain," Zach instructed her.

"It's another of the Institute's rules. As I said, our treatments are revolutionary. I was told from day one that most of the medicines we administer are proprietary combinations of drugs the Hope Institute intends to patent. To avoid the possibility of industrial espionage, Miss Rivers is the only nurse permitted to handle or dispense them. That, of course, doesn't apply to the more common prescriptions. Any of us is authorized to dispense those."

It was obvious Miss Groves was proud of the Institute's progressiveness.

Unfortunately, to the others in the room, that progressiveness smacked of something else.

"These proprietary combinations," Zach pressed, "surely you've caught a glimpse of what the vials read?"

"They're in unmarked containers, with only the patient's name printed on the label. Again, for security purposes."

Victoria felt bile rise in her throat. "And Audrey reacted badly to one of these innovative drug combinations?"

"Yes. But her medication was changed immediately after that. She's much better now, honestly, Miss Kensington." A gentle smile touched Beatrice's lips. "Except that she misses you."

"But my father visits her often, right?"

Another guarded look. "Yes. Every few days."

Victoria didn't need ESP to know what that look and tone meant. She knew from experience. "But he upsets her. His visits make things worse."

"He does seem to agitate her a little," the nurse admitted.

"What about before Audrey was admitted," Victoria asked, forcing out the words. "Did my father visit the Institute on his own?"

"You mean to check out the facilities?" Beatrice frowned, trying to remember. "It's possible. He did look familiar, now that I think about it. It would certainly be understandable for him to want to get a firsthand look at the clinic that would be treating his daughter. Although it seems to me his visit was some time ago."

"How long?"

A shrug. "A year. Maybe longer."

"Miss Groves," Zach said, taking over the reins and steering the conversation in a different direction. "You're an intelligent woman. Didn't the level of secrecy at the Institute ever strike you as odd?"

"Until recently—no. The patients are well cared for, the staff is superb. Oh, of course I noticed the rules are strict. But our patients are very well-to-do. Some of them are public figures. They're adamant about protecting their privacy—including the fact that they're sick, much less *how* sick. The Hope Institute is sensitive to their needs. We allow them to keep their dignity, at the same time that we provide them with the most extraordinary health care money can buy. The truth is, most of our patients are looking for a last chance. And we're the only ones who can give them that chance—often successfully. The restrictions, the secrecy, it's all insignificant next to that. It also becomes second nature after a while."

"But something changed that for you. What was it?"

An apprehensive expression crossed Beatrice's face. "Monday morning. You asked what was troubling me when I went out to receive Mrs. Flanders. Well, it was more than the loss of our four patients. I'd just seen the families of two of those patients being ushered into the counseling rooms. Mr. Pratt's son and Mrs. Housley's children."

"Mr. Pratt—that's the patient whose room Mrs. Flanders was taking."

"Yes."

"And the counseling rooms—what are those used for?"

"That's where the families are advised of their loved ones' passing. Our psychiatric staff meets with them, helps them come to terms with their loss."

A puzzled frown formed between Zach's brows. "Why did this trouble you?"

"Because both Mr. Pratt and Mrs. Housley died over two months ago. I don't understand why their families are only being notified now."

"Did you ask Miss Rivers?"

"Yes, as we walked by the counseling rooms. She became very flustered. She practically dragged me out of the building to collect Mrs. Flanders. She never answered my question."

Zach's jaw set. "Has she ever behaved that way before?"

"No." Beatrice shook her head. "She's always composed. I've never seen her lose that composure."

"Not with anyone? Not even with whomever she's closest to at the Institute?"

"Miss Rivers isn't close to anyone—at least not at work. She's an aloof woman. She keeps her distance, probably because of her position as head nurse. Everyone respects her, period. But she's one of the most diligent nurses I've ever seen. She's never missed a day of work. She's always there for at least two shifts a day. And she never lets any of us take over for her—not even so she can grab a bite to eat."

"What about when she goes home? Who administers the patients then?"

"Their individual doctors. Miss Rivers coordinates everyone's schedule to make that possible. And she's on call twenty-four hours a day."

"A regular Florence Nightingale," Zach muttered. He rubbed the back of his neck, leaning back in his seat and glancing at Meyer.

"We have enough," Meyer replied.

"Enough for what?" Beatrice looked distressed again, and resumed twisting her handkerchief. "What is this about?"

Meyer cleared his throat. "There are illegal activities going on at the Hope Institute, Miss Groves. Only a few people are involved—we think. With your help, we'll find out who those people are and arrest them."

"Illegal activities?" Beatrice sounded more overwrought than stunned. "What kind of illegal activities?"

"For one thing, some of those unmarked containers aren't proprietary medications. At least not the legal kind."

"You think someone at the Institute is dealing in narcotics."

"I don't think it. I know it."

"No." Beatrice wet her lips. "Those medications you're referring to go to our patients. If you're implying that anyone, including Miss Rivers, would give illegal narcotics to our patients, you're wrong. Everyone at the Hope Institute values human life. It's unthinkable."

"I agree, but not because whoever's doing this values human life. They value cash. They don't lose any sleep over the fate of their users. But, no, I don't think they're dispensing their stuff to your patients. Narcotics dealers don't hand out drugs. They sell them. What I *do* think is they're probably camouflaging the stuff by storing it with the unmarked containers of medication the Institute wants to patent—at least until they can turn it over to their contacts and get paid."

"Do you think Miss Rivers is guilty?"

A shrug. "Someone is. Our job's to find out who."

"And once you do, what will happen to the Institute?"

"I honestly don't know," Meyer said frankly. "That depends on who's involved. Hopefully, your clinic will survive the scandal and go on providing the top-notch health care you described. But the point's moot. Because right now, those services are being used to cover up a felony. It's our job to catch whoever's committing that felony."

Sad realization crossed Beatrice's face. "This isn't just speculation on your part," she murmured, more to herself than to Meyer. "You're sure."

"Yes," Zach told her quietly. "We're sure. Someone's making a lot of money doing ugly, illegal things. And it's obviously not just drug money we're talking about. Think of what you saw on Monday. Why would families be told their loved ones had just died, when they'd actually passed on months ago? Because the fees paid to keep those loved ones on at the Institute would stop coming the minute news of their deaths arrived. So why not keep everyone believing they're alive as long as possible?"

"I thought of that horrifying possibility. But if it's true, where are the bodies being kept?" Beatrice's face was chalk white, a sure indication that she had no idea cremations were taking place on the premises.

"Miss Groves . . . Beatrice, listen to me," Zach said, ending the conversation by gesturing for Meyer to hand him a glass of water. "The less you know, the better. We want to keep you safe. But we need your help. *I* need your help."

"All right. But what can I do?" Her hands were shaking as she took the cup Zach pressed into them.

"You can be my nurse. My exclusive nurse."

Meyer's "Huh?" mingled with Beatrice's "I don't understand."

Victoria understood, only too well. She and Zach had conceived and reviewed this plan during the wee hours of the morning.

Now they had to convince Meyer to act on it.

Clearly, Zach wasn't giving him a choice. He shot the agent an unyielding look. "Give me a few minutes with Special Agent Meyer," he told Beatrice. "Then I'll explain. Suffice it to say, I'm about to become the newest patient at the Hope Institute."

28

"Forget it." Meyer folded his hands behind his head, leaning back in his chair and scowling. "I knew we'd have to get someone on the inside. But it's not going to be you."

"Yes, it is." Zach stood, his back against the door, staring Meyer down. Victoria remained seated, hands folded neatly in her lap—for now. Beatrice had been escorted out for a cup of coffee.

"I know more about the ins and outs of what's going on at the Hope Institute than any of your agents," Zach reminded Meyer. "I've also got the business, the legal, and the technical background to pull this off. That's everything the job requires."

"Except agent training."

"You'll provide that. I'm a quick study. I'm intelligent and I'm motivated. I can master whatever skills you think I'll need for the short period of time I'll be in there."

"Yeah? So, tell me, Hamilton, how's your acting ability?"

A corner of Zach's mouth lifted. "I've convinced you I like you, haven't I?"

"Cute." Meyer pursed his lips, eyeing Zach speculatively as he considered the validity of his arguments. "Let's say I agree to send you in. What kind of identity am I creating?"

"Identi*ties*," Victoria corrected, pouncing like a cat, speaking up for the first time since Beatrice left the room. "Two of them. One, a filthy rich, neurotic computer software genius who's CEO of his own company; the other, a high-powered corporate attorney who represents him and shows up to sign his admittance papers."

Meyer's head snapped around, and his scowl returned. "Forget it, Ms. Kensington. You're not getting involved."

"I'm already involved, Mr. Meyer. I have been since the day Audrey fell at my feet in Central Park and I started investigating the Hope Institute. I'm being followed and wiretapped. Someone drove me off the road Saturday night, erased my answering machine, and God knows what else. He's now hot on my heels, waiting to see what I'll do next. My father is your key suspect, not to mention being legal counsel for the Hope Institute. My life's in danger, my sister's life's in danger, and now, thanks to his association with me, Zach's life's in danger. Could I be any more involved? Besides, we're racing the clock. You need a real attorney to pull this off—a sharp one who's familiar with the case, not a field agent you'd have to bring up to speed."

Pausing, Victoria pulled out some notes and passed them calmly across the desk to Meyer, one page at a time. "Here are some details on our chosen identities. We're from California—Silicon Valley, to be exact, given Zach's occupation. He's a technology wiz who designs computer chips for military satellites. He did his job, then went off the deep end. All the pressure the government laid on him—you know how pushy those feds can be—and the poor guy cracked up. The Hope Institute was referred to him by a source he won't divulge. He also won't go anywhere else. His security clearance will restrict the information I can provide, which gives me a great fall-back position."

She passed that page to Meyer, skimmed the next. "That brings us to me. As I said, I'm going to be the one to admit our gone-over-the-edge CEO. I'll be present to protect his interests, which are immense. He's a billionaire. And with that knowledge, and a fat check, the Hope Institute is bound to welcome him, vacant rooms or not. They'll give up one of their offices if they have to. Convincing them of that is my job. Your job is to bring this guy to life, right down to his bank and brokerage accounts."

She glanced over the final page, then handed it to Meyer. "I'll be easier, since I won't be staying. I just need the usual driver's license, social security number, passport, birth certificate—nothing too elaborate. Except a name that's listed in the Martindale-Hubbell Law Directory and that can be verified by the California Bar Association. I'll be newly admitted in New York, so they won't expect my credentials here to be listed yet. But give the New York Bar a call and get their cooperation, just in case the Institute should run a phone check. Oh, as for Zach, he'll need psychiatric coaching, although I can give him some pointers on nervous breakdown symptoms. I'm familiar with a variety of mental illnesses; my uncle's a psychiatrist. Still, your experts will do a better job."

She leaned back, refolded her hands in her lap, and gave Meyer a professional nod. "I think that's enough of a start."

The agent's jaw was practically touching his desk. He blinked, looked down at her copious notes, then turned to Zach. "Stubborn? Loyal? Try a bulldozer."

Zach's lips twitched. "Effective, isn't she?"

"If you want to call it that." Meyer shot Victoria a look. "Tell me, Ms. Kensington, did you leave any of the details to us?"

"Of course. I only wrote the profiles, with Zach's input, of course. The hard part—making us real people—I'll leave to you. Oh, and our names can be chosen at your discretion, as well, depending on what's unused—or, in my case, used but borrowable." She paused, reconsidered. "Actually, make Zach's first name David. I think it's a fitting tribute, don't you?" She angled her head in Zach's direction.

"Yes," he agreed quietly, a profound current of communication running between them. "Very fitting."

"David. That was your father's name," Meyer muttered.

"That much I get. Fine. That's doable. Any other instructions, Ms. Kensington?"

"Not right now," she returned dryly. "But if I think of anything, I'll call you. I've got a secure cell phone, and your private number."

"Great." Meyer rubbed his forehead. "I'll need a day or two to make this happen. But we can't afford to wait. Especially now that Miss Groves is aware of our investigation. She might be on our side, but she's also scared. That's bound to show. I doubt it would be long before someone at the Hope Institute became suspicious. We've got to have this whole thing wrapped up before that happens."

"Fine," Zach agreed. "How about getting me admitted on Friday? The only commitment I have between now and then is the keynote speech I'm delivering tomorrow at the SCIP conference. That leaves me plenty of time to be briefed on who I am and how I should behave, and Victoria time to make preliminary phone calls setting things up with the Hope Institute."

"Friday." Meyer folded his hands in front of him, stared Zach down. "Hamilton, let me explain something. Being briefed is just part of what you've got ahead of you. If we decide to shoot for Friday, you're going to need every minute between now and then to learn the skills you lack—from breaking into locked rooms to making it look like you haven't. This isn't James Bond. It's for real. And it's dangerous."

"I'm aware of that," Zach replied soberly. "I'm not taking the challenge lightly. I'm neither cocky nor a fool. I realize I've got a lot to absorb. I'll spend day and night at the field office, if I have to. But, Meyer, if I didn't think I was the best person for this job, I'd say so. I want these bastards caught as badly as you do. Maybe more."

Meyer nodded slowly. "Yeah. I know you do." He studied his folded hands. "I'll call our Los Angeles field office to get a Hollywood makeover expert and arrange to fly him in from LAX on the red-eye. Touch-ups aren't going to cut it. You'll need to be unrecognizable. New faces, new builds." Meyer arched a brow at Victoria. "What if your father's there when you bring Zach in to be admitted?"

"*If* my father's there, it won't be a problem. He scarcely sees the people he looks at, unless they're of benefit to him. He'll walk right by me." She brought her voice down to a slightly huskier pitch, punctuated it with a Californian accent. "I'll be a total stranger."

"Speaking of that, let's ask Miss Groves for a photograph of herself," Zach put in. "We'll let one of the FBI artists have at it."

"Why?" Meyer demanded.

"To make her look like someone else—someone who strongly resembles Beatrice but isn't." Amusement curved Zach's lips. "You want to see acting ability? I'll show it to you. That picture is going to become David Whoever's deceased mother. And when he sees Beatrice Friday morning at the Institute, it'll be like having her back again."

Again, Meyer nodded. "Make enough of a fuss and Ms. Kensington can insist that Beatrice Groves is assigned to you."

"As my sole caretaker. That'll eliminate the problem of anyone guessing I'm in disguise. It'll also make it easier for me to get around the Institute. I'll be in such pathetic shape, no one will guess I'm capable of causing problems. Beatrice can just wheel me around, supposedly for mental stimulation, a change of scene, an hour in front of the TV. Hell, I'll be practically invisible."

"Yeah, well, you'd better be. For everyone's sake. Especially yours."

Thursday, April 27
10:30 A.M.

It was almost time.
Victoria sat in the living room of Zach's hotel suite, star-

ing at her secure cell phone. Zach was at the SCIP conference. She wasn't due at Waters, Kensington, Tatem & Calder until noon. She'd intentionally scheduled herself that way: a few hours today, a few tomorrow. It would fulfill her two-day-per-week commitment while leaving this morning free for phone and FedEx arrangements and tomorrow morning free for getting Zach admitted to the Hope Institute.

Meyer had called an hour ago to advise her that their profiles were complete and had been installed in the necessary computer databases. Full identities had been established, including, in Zach's case, tax returns, bank accounts, and brokerage accounts, the gross dollar value of which would make heads spin. His medical records, photo and bio, and signed power of attorney were being messengered to the Hope Institute as they spoke, along with a check for $250,000.

Everything was a go.

Victoria eyed the clock: 10:32. She'd give the powers that be at the Hope Institute another five minutes to read through the material, look at the check, and pick themselves up off the floor. Then she'd call.

She and Zach had memorized their identities, knew them through and through. Zach was David Karr—president and CEO of Karr Technology, Silicon Valley, California. A brilliant electrical engineer and innovator, Karr had exclusive government contracts, the most recent of which was designing specialized computer chips for the U.S. military. The details of the contracts and the designs were classified. Four months ago, after completing a particularly high-pressure segment of the assignment, Karr became ill and took a leave of absence.

That's where the psychiatric files kicked in.

The confidential medical records that had been delivered to the Hope Institute that morning diagnosed Karr as suffering from chronic adjustment disorder brought on by an overabundance of stress. His specific symptoms were work inhibition and withdrawal from reality, and were complicated by a neurotic fear of unknown and unfamiliar people. The medical section of the records began with a long list of Karr's allergies, including an acute intolerance and/or severe negative physiological reactions to most tranquilizers and sedatives. In bold, black letters, the records stated that, as a result of that intolerance and/or reactions, Karr should not receive medication of any kind.

That was the safety net the FBI had thrown in to make sure Gloria Rivers didn't try out any drug cocktails on Zach.

The records concluded by stating that psychotherapy had been employed, with a modicum of success, although the patient was still highly symptomatic. He was nonviolent, however, and harmless to himself and to others. A temporary change of scene, complete with R and R, was recommended.

It was the ideal depiction, given what Zach needed to accomplish.

As for Victoria, she was Catherine Hughes, rising partner at Brandes & Steede, a prominent corporate law firm in Silicon Valley. That identity switch had been easier than expected. Not only did Brandes & Steede actually exist, the FBI had contacts there—contacts who'd assured the feds of their cooperation. To add to that, Ms. Hughes was real, too—or rather, she *had* been real. She was a fine attorney who, unfortunately, had died of an aneurism just last week. Using her identity made everything much cleaner and easier to pull off. All her colleagues had to do was stick to the truth, other than the pretense that Ms. Hughes was still alive and that she represented the interests of David Karr.

Besides, Victoria only had to play her role once or, at worst, twice if for some reason she had to make a return trip to the Hope Institute. Zach had to live his role for several days—or for as long as it took him to find the evidence they needed.

Victoria massaged her temples. She was beat. She'd

spent six hours at the FBI field office last night for the initial part of her training, and she had another six to go tonight, when the makeup artist finished his work. How Zach was holding up was beyond her. The amount of time he'd spent at the field office was double hers—all day and night yesterday, with another twelve hours scheduled there today. The only reason he'd left at all was to return to the Plaza Athénée each night.

Part of that was to catch some sleep. Part of that was to be with her. And part of that was to convince Mr. Cigar that nothing suspicious was going on, that they were falling into bed each night like good little lovers should. It was the only way to keep his focus where they wanted it. As for staying at the hotel, that was also for Mr. Cigar's benefit. From there, they could slip in and out of the service entrance and into the FBI's unmarked car without being spotted—something they could never pull off if they stayed at Victoria's apartment, especially not as David Karr and Catherine Hughes. The instant an unfamiliar face walked out of 170 East Eighty-second Street, Mr. Cigar's warning bells would go off.

So the Plaza Athénée it was.

Victoria shot a last purposeful look at the clock: 10:38. Time for her to call the Hope Institute and start the ball rolling.

Correction. Time for Catherine Hughes to call the Hope Institute and start the ball rolling.

Taking a slow, calming breath, she punched up the number.

"Hope Institute. How may I help you?"

It was that pit bull, Miss Evans.

"Good morning." Victoria made sure to use her huskier voice, and the more pronounced, drawn-out West Coast syllables. "This is Catherine Hughes. I'm David Karr's attorney. I trust you've received the documents and cover letter I messengered over?"

"They arrived a little while ago, yes." Miss Evans sounded wary, curious, and flabbergasted, all at once.

"Excellent. Then I trust your physicians have had time to review the records. I'm tied up with meetings all this afternoon, but Mr. Karr would like to begin his stay with you first thing tomorrow morning. Shall we say . . . nine-thirty?"

Miss Evans cleared her throat. "Ms. . . . Hughes, did you say?"

"Yes. Catherine Hughes. Just as it says on the power of attorney."

"I . . . we . . . appreciate that Mr. Karr chose the Hope Institute for his convalescence. However, I have a few questions I must ask. First, who referred Mr. Karr to us? We do require references. And second, while we're pleased with Mr. Karr's faith in us, we must ask what made him select the Hope Institute. We're thousands of miles from Silicon Valley, and Mr. Karr's illness doesn't require the degree of critical care we provide."

Victoria allowed a brief stony silence before she replied, "Frankly, Ms. . . . ?"

"Miss Evans."

"Miss Evans. Let me begin by telling you that we researched your facility quite thoroughly. Mr. Karr doesn't make imprecise or uninformed decisions. So, why did he choose you? I should think that's obvious. Reputation and privacy. Mr. Karr requires both. As for the length of our commute, I'm sure your patient roster has included prominent individuals who have traveled a lot farther than cross-country to get here. In Mr. Karr's case, he specifically chose New York, since he's adamant about getting as far away from home as possible. He may not be terminally ill, but he needs a total separation from his familiar environment. And, as to the nature of his illness, our research didn't indicate that you've revised your admission standards to include only those who are terminally ill. Is our information incorrect?"

"No, no, of course not." The pit bull sounded flustered. "It's just that—"

"Is it lack of space? Our background check did turn up the fact that you have a rather extensive waiting list. I presume we can bypass that—under the circumstances," Victoria added pointedly.

She let the last sink in. Miss Evans would understand. "The circumstances" meant a quarter of a million dollars.

She could almost see the pit pull staring greedily at the check, gripping it tightly between her fingers.

Miss Evans cleared her throat again, this time nervously. "Before we discuss the availability issue, there is the matter of references. I need the name of whoever referred Mr. Karr to us, as well as the dates that person was a patient here."

"Do you have security clearance?" Victoria inquired coolly.

Silence.

"I assume that means no. In which case, I must decline your request on my client's behalf, due to national security interests. Mr. Karr's personal and medical history, both of which I forwarded to you, will have to suffice. That, and the substantial check I included. As I understand it, that should cover a stay of several months. Mr. Karr is willing to pay that amount on a monthly basis, as compensation for the special provisions you're making on his behalf."

"I see." Miss Evans paused. "May I ask you to hold a moment?"

"Certainly." Victoria waited for the elevator music that proclaimed she was on hold. Then she covered the mouthpiece with her hand and grinned. She could taste impending victory. The pit bull was on her way to a decision maker for an official okay. Once they heard the astronomical sum of money that was involved, and the fact that they had an entire day to run security checks on David Karr and Catherine Hughes, they'd decide this was a no-lose situation.

And Zach would be in.

"Ms. Hughes?"

That hadn't taken long.

"Yes?"

"I appreciate your patience. Tomorrow morning at nine-thirty would be fine. We look forward to meeting Mr. Karr. Do you need directions to the Institute?"

"No. Mr. Karr's driver is familiar with Manhattan."

"Fine. We have a private entrance for your convenience. Just have your driver pull into the parking lot that leads under our building. We'll meet Mr. Karr at the foot of the ramp." Miss Evans gave an uneasy cough. "You *will*, of course, need to sign the necessary paperwork."

"That's one of the reasons I've accompanied Mr. Karr to New York," Victoria affirmed in a crisp tone. "Have we covered everything? Because I'm already late for a meeting. I presume the remaining details can wait until tomorrow."

A brief pause. "Certainly. We'll finalize everything then."

"Good. If necessary, I can be reached at 555-4972." Victoria recited the number the FBI had given her—an untraceable number that rang in their office and, as of yesterday, was answered by Catherine Hughes's voice mail. "Good-bye, Miss Evans."

Victoria pressed End and let out her breath. Done.

She punched up Meyer's private line.

29

Friday, April 28
1:31 A.M.

Eight hours to go.

Victoria lay quietly in the circle of Zach's arms, staring out the bedroom window, wide awake and thinking about what lay ahead. She was a bundle of raw nerves and emotions. It wasn't worry over whether she and Zach could pull off their deception. She knew they could. They were so convincing in their roles, she half believed they really were David Karr and Catherine Hughes.

No, it was the enormity of what they were taking on, the dread of finding out who was involved—and, most of all, the sheer terror of what Zach might be walking into.

If she had any doubts about how much she loved him, they were blasted to bits by the overwhelming fear that shook her at the thought of anything happening to him. She'd finally found him again. She couldn't lose him.

Pressing her lips together, she forced herself to face up fully to the risk Zach was taking—and why he was taking it.

Yes, it was for his father, for the FBI, for the resolution of a nightmare.

But it was also for her.

Her, and their future together.

A horn blared in the street below, but the sounds of Manhattan didn't offer Victoria their usual comfort tonight. Neither would finding a legal loophole for one of her clients, or drinking a good glass of cabernet. Not this time. This time all that would comfort her was ending this ordeal, getting Audrey out of that place, and seeing Zach walk out of the Hope Institute safe and sound.

Because if anything happened to him . . .

Victoria's throat tightened, and her eyes burned from a combination of fatigue and unshed tears. She accepted the significance of her reaction, just as she accepted the twisting pain in her gut, the overwhelming sense of emotion.

They all stemmed from her feelings for Zach.

Feelings she now embraced without question, and labeled precisely what they were.

They were love.

For better or worse.

Please let it be for better.

As if reading her thoughts, Zach tightened his embrace. "I thought you'd drifted off."

"I can't."

"I know." He kissed her hair. Turning her in his arms, he tipped up her chin so he could study her expression. "I'll be fine," he whispered, his knuckles caressing her cheek. "After four years, nothing is going to keep me away from you. Nothing."

Victoria was unprepared for her own reaction. She burst into tears, hard sobs racking her body. "I—I'm sorry," she choked out, covering her face with her hands. "I can't believe I'm falling apart like this."

"Shhh." Zach pulled her close, molded her body to his. "It's okay."

"What's okay?" she asked in a quavery voice, her face pressed to his bare chest. "Our investigation? Or my hysteria?"

"Both. And you're not hysterical." His hands smoothed up and down her back, the motions becoming slower, more intimate. "You're human." He swallowed, his body hardening against hers. "For that matter, so am I."

Abruptly, he tugged back her head, and Victoria could

see the intensity burning in his gaze. It was a reflection of
her own profound emotion, channeled into something tangible and desperate, a fundamental need to be one. "How am I
going to survive without you the next few nights?" he muttered thickly. "I can't last without being inside you."

"Zach . . ."

"Shh. Come here." He pulled her over him, dragged her
mouth down to his. "This is how it will be. Now. Forever.
Believe that."

Victoria nodded, responding with a fervor that matched
his. She scrambled into a sitting position, straddling Zach's
hips. Then she rose up, her fingers surrounding his erection,
guiding him inside her. She lowered herself onto him, taking
him as deep as she could. With a soft shudder, she began
moving—up, down, up, down—her hands splaying across
Zach's chest for balance as his hips bucked in response,
arched to meet each of her downward motions.

Their lovemaking was frantic, awareness of the danger
Zach was about to face making their joining sharp, urgent, a
frenzied reaffirmation of their feelings. His hands clamped
down on her waist, his body lunging powerfully into hers,
nearly lifting her off the bed with the force of his thrusts.
Victoria cried out, her inner muscles clamping down around
him, tightening until the pleasure became unbearable, her
body taut as a rubber band ready to snap.

Zach snapped first. He reached his limit, one hand pressing into the small of Victoria's back, the other working its
way between their tightly joined bodies. His fingers found
and caressed her, his mouth eating at hers as he anchored
her in place, drove all the way inside her.

They came together, violent spasms that erupted like
fireworks, crashing through them again and again until they
tapered off, first to dizzying ripples of sensation, then to
peace.

Victoria collapsed onto Zach, her limbs too weak to support her. Zach's arms locked around her like steel bands,

holding her close, his body trembling with aftershocks. Their breath came in harsh rasps, and they stayed wrapped in each other's arms, her head pillowed on his chest, his hand tangled in her hair.

"Tory." It was a love word, uttered reverently and with an immeasurable sense of awe.

"I love you," she whispered fiercely. "Zach, please, be careful."

He nodded, his lips in her hair. "With an incentive like this, do you doubt I will?"

She smiled against his hot skin. "No."

"There are distinct advantages to being in love with a bulldozer."

His attempt to make her laugh worked. "Really? Such as?"

"Such as the incredible job you just did demolishing me. I'm impressed. See for yourself—I'm a total wreck. Not that I'm complaining."

"You liked that, did you?" She raised her head, shot him a teasing look. "Hurry home and I promise you an encore."

"A lifetime of encores," he corrected, sifting his fingers through her hair. His expression became solemn. "It's almost over, sweetheart. Hang in there a few more days."

Her smile vanished. "Only if you do."

"Deal," he vowed. His fingers continued untangling her shoulder-length strands. "I'll call you the minute I see Audrey," he murmured. "I'll make sure she's all right—and that she stays that way."

Victoria propped her chin on his chest. "Thank you."

"I'll tell her who I really am. That'll ease her panic."

His announcement elicited a worried frown. "Zach, I'm not sure that's a smart idea. I don't know what kind of state Audrey's in. What if she inadvertently says something to one of the nurses—something that gives you away?"

"She won't. Not once I tell her your safety's on the line. Audrey adores you. She'd never put you in danger."

"But if she's drugged up . . ."

Zach shrugged. "She sounded coherent in her message. Besides, it's a chance I have to take. First, because she's your sister. And second, because she probably knows, or suspects, something's going on in that place. It's the only explanation for the tone of her second call to you. She was scared. Even if she really did run away because of a bad reaction to whatever they're giving her, it doesn't explain why she's frightened now. According to Beatrice, they changed her medication. So what's she afraid of? And why did they cut off her call to you? I need to know."

"Zach, stop. You're scaring me."

"Don't be scared," he soothed. "Even if I'm right, Audrey's nervous, but she's safe. Maybe because of your father. Maybe in spite of him. Either way, she's fine. Beatrice told us so. The question is, are they keeping her sedated because she knows something? Or is she really as sick as your father says? I intend to find out."

Breaking off suddenly, Zach squirmed over to the edge of the bed, keeping a secure arm wrapped around Victoria, holding her squarely on top of him, his body imbedded in hers. His other arm groped on the floor, fumbling through his hastily discarded clothes. He found what he was searching for and pulled it out of his jacket pocket. "In the meantime, I have something just as important I intend to do—right now."

"What?" Startled by the sudden change in subject, Victoria wriggled a little, trying to peek over Zach's shoulder and figure out what he was up to.

He resettled himself, a small square box in his hand. "You know how traditional my values are." He eyed their joined bodies, a corner of his mouth lifting. "Okay, maybe not *entirely* traditional. But for the most part, they are. I can't get away from it; it's how I was raised. So humor me." He caught her left hand in his, brought her palm to his lips. "Monday night I asked you to marry me. You said yes."

"I remember," she said softly, her heart giving a tug of anticipation.

"Say it again."

Victoria's lips curved. "Ask me again."

He flashed her that crooked smile that made her bones melt. "Victoria Kensington, will you marry me?"

"Yes. Definitely and emphatically, yes."

Zach snapped open the box, revealing the glittering facets of a single diamond set in a simple platinum setting. The emerald-cut stone sent little kaleidoscopes of moonlight shimmering through the darkness of the room.

Victoria swallowed as Zach slipped the ring on her finger. "It's beautiful."

"So are you." He covered her mouth with his, kissed her tenderly.

"When did you do this?" she whispered.

"I made a stop at Tiffany's on Tuesday. The minute I saw this ring, I knew it was right." A poignant pause. "Just like when I saw you."

"It's perfect." Victoria held up her hand, moving it so she could watch the diamond glisten.

"They're holding a set of wedding bands for us. Those are perfect, too, but I wanted you to decide with me." Zach shot her a questioning, hopeful look. "Too overbearing?"

"No." She shook her head, tears shining in her eyes. "Not too overbearing. Not this time."

"Then I'll press my luck. Would it be too overbearing to insist on a May wedding?"

"Nope."

"Really? Then how about if I dragged you down the aisle? Too overbearing?"

Victoria laughed, brushing her lips to his. "Maybe. But it's a moot question. Because you can't drag someone who's already racing to get there."

"That's a relief." He caressed the nape of her neck. "Seriously, if you want a bigger wedding, I'll wait. But no later than June. That's my absolute limit."

Soberly, Victoria shook her head. "I've never wanted a

big wedding. To me, they always seemed to be more for the guests than the bride and groom. I want this day to belong to us. And, under the circumstances . . ." She paused, met Zach's gaze. They both knew what the circumstances meant. They meant that her father might not be free to attend a wedding, or anything else for that matter. "Under the circumstances," she continued, struggling to keep her voice steady, "I think it would be for the best if we made the occasion quiet and private. Just immediate family and close friends. Is that all right?"

"Um-hum." Zach kissed each corner of her mouth. "You know it is. As long as the ceremony ends with us being pronounced husband and wife, I don't care who else is there."

"I'll wait till you're back from the Hope Institute to share the announcement with my family—for lots of reasons. Who knows? Maybe Audrey will be well enough to attend, and my father will be there to give me away. As for Meg and Paul, I'll tell them right away. They'd kill me if I didn't spill the news of our engagement. Especially Meg, who practically beat me into confronting my feelings. Oh, and Paige, my secretary, who thrives on passion and romance. She'll be gushing over this one for a month. Stories of us and our amorous reunion will outlast Maurice and probably her next five boyfriends. And wait till she sees my ring . . ." Victoria rolled her eyes.

Zach's lips curved, but he looked more thoughtful than amused. "Tell them today," he urged quietly. "Take the three of them out to dinner. It'll do you some good."

"No." The word was out before Victoria realized she'd said it. "I can't. Not while you're in that place. There'll be plenty of time to celebrate. But tonight, I'm coming back here, supposedly to spend the night with you. Remember, Mr. Cigar will never see you leave the hotel today. The limo's driving around to the service entrance to pick up David Karr and Catherine Hughes. After Karr's admitted, it'll bring Ms. Hughes back to the same spot. I'll scoot upstairs, change my clothes, and walk out of the hotel as myself, on my way to Waters, Kensington,

Tatem and Calder. Mr. Cigar will see me leave. He'll assume you're still up here working in your suite. I'll reinforce that assumption by racing back here at the end of the work day." She pressed her lips together. "Besides, I'm not going to be much fun to be around until you're out of the Hope Institute and this whole nightmare is behind us."

Zach framed her face between his palms. "At least promise me you'll stop by your office and tell Meg and Paul our news. Maybe go out for a drink. If they ask where I am, tell them I'm tied up in business meetings all weekend."

"Zach . . ."

"Sweetheart, I can take care of myself," he interrupted softly. "If I get in a bind, Meyer's standing by. He's reachable by cell phone all weekend. So are you, for that matter." Zach's thumbs stroked her cheekbones. "Didn't I give you my word? I'll be fine. I'll be back before you know it. Use this weekend to get some rest. Because you're going to need lots of stamina for my homecoming."

Her nod was shaky. "Speaking of getting some rest, you should do that now. It's almost three A.M, which means six and a half hours till show time. And I doubt David Karr will be doing much relaxing during his stay at the Institute."

"You've got that right." Zach tucked her head beneath his chin, pulled the blankets around them. "We should both sleep. Close your eyes for a few hours."

"Okay."

A minute of silence ticked by, during which time Victoria forced her eyelids shut.

"By the way," Zach murmured, "I'm glad you didn't find my plans for our future overbearing. Because I forgot to mention that I contacted a top-notch Realtor and the best breeder of Jack Russell terriers in the tristate area. We're meeting with both of them next weekend."

"Ah. Well then, I'll enter the appointments in my Day-Timer as soon as we get up," Victoria assured him wryly, her chest tightening with emotion.

They both knew that, normally, she would have shot back an impassioned objection, just as she always did when Zach tried to run the show on his own. Not this time. Because this time his reasons for taking such definitive steps had nothing to do with his penchant for taking charge. This time he was deliberately planning their future in order to make it feel real, close at hand.

She only prayed that it was.

30

Friday, April 28
9:33 A.M.

The limo rolled down East Seventy-eighth Street.

"You two all set?" Special Agent Atkins inquired from beneath the rim of his chauffeur's cap.

"All set," Zach assured him.

"As set as we'll ever be," Victoria qualified dryly.

"Yeah, well, that's as good as it gets," Atkins retorted. He gave them a once-over in his rearview mirror, his terse nod telling them he believed they were ready. "We're on." He veered the limo into the driveway that led below the Hope Institute, easing around the underground curves.

Zach squeezed Victoria's fingers, then released them, dropping his hands into his lap and adopting a dazed expression as he stared off into space.

The moment of truth had arrived.

Victoria stole a quick glance at Zach and, despite her apprehension, had to suppress a smile at how un-Zach-like he looked. David Karr's suit and tie screamed "pocket-protector," as did the well-worn briefcase he kept appended to his leg. His hair was cut short, black tinged with gray, and slicked close to his head. His coloring was sallow, the area around his eyes puffy, and his nose was pencil-thin, as were his eyebrows. Every so often he'd sniff, glance around like a scared rabbit, then rub his palms over his trouser legs and resume staring off into space.

With a deep breath, Victoria assumed the role of

Catherine Hughes. She tugged her navy blazer over her buxom figure and adjusted her stylish wire-rimmed glasses on her nose. She'd memorized her alter ego's features, and she knew without looking that she appeared to be a forty-year-old woman, complete with a few telltale lines attesting to that fact—lines that had been added by the FBI makeup artist and that were deliberately visible through Catherine Hughes's smooth layer of powder and foundation. Her fine blond hair was worn in a blunt-cut chin-length style meant to flatter a woman nearing middle age. Her lips were set in a forceful line, and her jaw was tight, assertive, as if she were ready to deliver a killer closing argument. Poised, self-assured, Ms. Hughes was every inch the corporate attorney, a veritable force to be reckoned with.

The limo slowed, and Victoria snapped into action. She collected her Coach leather briefcase, waiting only until Atkins came to a stop before she threw open the door and climbed out. She was already on her feet and in motion by the time the FBI agent scrambled out of the limo. She strode around the back of the car, coming to a halt when she reached the right rear door through which Zach would soon exit.

The double doors of the Institute flew open, and Miss Evans hurried out, accompanied by Gloria Rivers, who pushed an empty wheelchair down the ramp.

"Ms. Hughes?" the pit pull inquired, displaying a smile Victoria would have sworn she couldn't crack. "Welcome to the Hope Institute."

"Thank you." Victoria's tone and expression were cordial, but impersonal. "I assume you're Miss Evans."

"Yes. And this is Miss Rivers, our head nurse." The receptionist gestured in her direction, and Victoria gave the head nurse a curt nod.

"A pleasure," Gloria Rivers responded.

Miss Evans shot an inquisitive glance at the limo. "Shall we assist Mr. Karr?"

"He'd prefer that his driver and I do that. Martin?" Victoria signaled to Atkins, who hurried around and opened the back door.

Zach sat perfectly still, giving no indication he was aware anyone was watching him or that his door was ajar. He continued staring straight ahead.

"Mr. Karr," Victoria said calmly. "We're here." She walked over, gripped the wheelchair, and maneuvered it over to the limo. "Martin and I will help you." A purposeful nod at the burly FBI agent.

Atkins leaned into the car. "It's me, Mr. Karr. Martin. I'll get you settled."

Zach inclined his head just enough to eye his driver speculatively. "Martin . . ." An anxious sniff. "Okay, it is you. That's all right then." He allowed Atkins to assist him out of the car and into the wheelchair—but not before snatching up his briefcase first. He clutched the case tightly to his chest with both hands, staring ahead with that same dazed expression.

Victoria took over behind the wheelchair, gesturing for Martin to get the bags while she wheeled her client in. "Miss Rivers, would you mind taking my briefcase?" she asked, handing Gloria the Coach attaché as she spoke. "I'll need it inside. Don't bother with Mr. Karr's. He keeps it with him at all times."

"Certainly." Gloria Rivers cleared her throat. "Wouldn't you rather I pushed the—"

"No. Until he feels comfortable, Mr. Karr would prefer that I be the one to assist him."

"I understand. With regard to the luggage, though, your driver needn't go to any trouble. Our attendants will take Mr. Karr's bags to his room."

"Martin will do that."

This time Gloria balked. "But—"

"Mr. Karr doesn't like strangers handling his possessions. Martin will see to the bags."

"Very well." Gloria gave a nervous cough. "But someone from security will have to accompany him. No unauthorized outsiders are allowed in the Institute. I hope you understand. We're very protective of our patients and their privacy."

"That's the very reason we selected your clinic for Mr. Karr's recovery. Martin," Victoria instructed, pivoting to face Atkins, "a staff member will escort you to Mr. Karr's room. Please deliver his luggage, then wait for me in the limo."

"No problem, Ms. Hughes."

That having been dealt with, Victoria pushed Zach up the ramp, Miss Rivers at her heels.

Miss Evans zipped on ahead. Waiting only until Martin had joined the group, bags in hand, she whipped out a pale yellow key card—the same color as the hospital gown Audrey had been wearing when she collapsed at Victoria's feet—and slipped it into a slot beside the double doors.

The doors swung open.

They made their way down a short corridor to a carpeted elevator that was waiting for them. Miss Evans gestured for everyone to precede her. Then she punched the button marked 1, and the door slid closed, sending the elevator gliding noiselessly up to the main floor.

With a muted *ding*, the elevator stopped and opened.

At last, Victoria thought, wheeling Zach out with a wave of relief. They were inside the Hope Institute.

Directly in front of them was a partition wall, with specially operated glass doors on either side. Beyond those doors, Victoria could see the reception area she remembered only too well. Obviously, the underground elevator bypassed the only section of the Institute that was even remotely accessible to outsiders and deposited them directly in the main hallway that led to the Hope Institute's private sanctuary.

"I'll leave you in Miss Rivers's capable hands," Miss Evans announced. "I must get back to my desk. But first . . ." She walked over to the wall and pressed a buzzer. "I'll wait here with Mr. Karr's chauffeur. Someone from security will be here in a minute to show him to Mr. Karr's room."

Atkins nodded, standing aside with the bags.

"This way," Miss Rivers instructed Victoria, turning on her heel and heading away from the elevator.

Victoria swerved Zach's wheelchair around and followed.

The clinic was immaculate, its walls papered in a soothing peach and yellow print, its white floor tiles so shiny you could see your own reflection in them. After walking down a brief center hallway, Victoria spotted on their left a cluster of rooms that appeared to be offices and conference suites. Farther down, and set a respectable distance apart, were a half-dozen impressive oak-rimmed doors—three on either side of the hall. Patients' rooms, Victoria surmised. She could see a few uniformed staff members clustered outside one of them, reviewing a file.

Zach didn't react at all. Slouched in the wheelchair, he continued to stare ahead, vacant and glassy-eyed, as if totally detached from his surroundings.

"Right in here." Miss Rivers unlocked the door to the second conference suite and held it so Victoria could wheel Zach in.

The head nurse was just about to shut the door behind them when Beatrice Groves stepped into the room, an apologetic look on her face. "Excuse me, Miss Rivers, but may I see you when you're finished here? We only received Mr. Karr's preliminary file, and I want to make sure the nurses have all the information necessary to make his stay a happy—"

"Mother?" Zach interrupted, jerking upright. "Mother!" His voice echoed with incredulous wonder. He bolted from the chair, making his way over to Beatrice. He circled her, his eyes wide, his breathing shallow and uneven. "It *is* you . . . Mother . . ." Dropping his case, he embraced her.

Victoria acted instantly, ignoring Gloria Rivers's startled expression and Beatrice Groves's sharp intake of breath to hurry over to her client. "It's all right, Mr. Karr," she reassured him, easing him away from Beatrice. She took time to study the woman, though, and a hint of amazement dawned in her eyes. "Astonishing. What's your name?"

"Beatrice Groves." The elderly nurse still looked taken aback. But she exercised great self-control, years of training having prepared her to remain composed when confronted with incidents such as this. Which was, of course, exactly the way she'd been instructed to act by Meyer. "I'm a senior member of the Institute's nursing staff."

Zach shook his head emphatically. "No. You're—"

"I know," Victoria soothed him.

Beatrice blinked, schooling her features and giving Zach a friendly smile. "Hello," she said, making sure not to agitate Mr. Karr further by denying his claim.

"Her resemblance to Mr. Karr's mother is truly remarkable," Victoria murmured, still inspecting Beatrice.

"It's not a resemblance. My mother's here," Zach announced, clearly agitated by the contradiction. "This is just what I need to get well. She'll take care of me. She always has. Ms. Hughes, you can go."

"That's fine, Mr. Karr," Victoria agreed. "I'll sign the necessary papers. Then I'll go."

"Papers are a good idea. Draft one that says only my mother can take care of me. I don't want doctors or any of these other people at the Institute involved. I don't know them, and I don't want them near me."

"I'll see what I can do. Why don't you sit down and let me talk to her."

"That nurse who brought us in here doesn't believe me," Zach declared angrily, bending over to grab his briefcase. "She thinks I'm crazy. Well, I'm not. Just exhausted. And edgy. But I'm not crazy." He stalked over to a chair, flung down his briefcase. Flipping open the top, he rummaged through the contents. "I'll find the picture of my mother. I still carry it. You'll show it to the nurse."

"I will, Mr. Karr. If you'd make yourself comfortable—"

"What's Mr. Karr's first name?" Beatrice asked Victoria in a subdued tone.

"David."

"David?" Beatrice called, looking directly at Zach. "Why don't you give me the picture and then have a seat at the table. Ms. Hughes and I will work things out."

That seemed to curb his rapidly escalating distress. "I knew you would." He walked over and handed Beatrice a photo, hovering there for a moment.

"Sit down, David, and relax," she instructed gently.

He obeyed, leaving her side with great reluctance, inching his way to the conference table, but never taking his gaze off the woman he thought to be his mother. He pulled back a chair, lowered himself into it, facing Beatrice as if he feared she might vanish in an instant. Fidgeting anxiously, he took out a pen and began fiddling with it, watching the three women talk and waiting for a signal that everyone believed him and that his mother would be allowed to assume her maternal role in his life.

Victoria angled herself toward Beatrice so that her face was averted from David Karr's. "Thank you, Miss Groves," she murmured, her appreciation entirely genuine. Let the truth be known, she was relieved as hell by the elderly nurse's convincing performance. These first few moments between Zach and Beatrice had been among the FBI's biggest worries. Could she or could she not play her part without giving them away? Clearly, she could. Whether it was professional pride or relief that reinforcements had arrived, Victoria didn't care. It eliminated one big chunk of her worry.

"If you look at that photo, you'll see why Mr. Karr is so vehement in his belief," she continued, pointing at the touched-up snapshot of Beatrice. "The resemblance is uncanny."

Beatrice's eyes flickered to the photograph, then widened in surprise. "Oh, my."

Peering over the older nurse's shoulder, Gloria Rivers sucked in her breath. "My goodness. It could be Beatrice's sister. That's Mr. Karr's mother?"

Victoria nodded. "She passed away years ago," she added in an undertone. "Mr. Karr was very devoted to her. Since he became ill, he insists on carrying her picture around at all times. He seems to believe she's still among us. The doctors say it's a defense mechanism. It gives him a sense of security to have his mother close by during this trying time." A thoughtful glance at Beatrice. "If he actually thinks you're she"—Victoria pursed her lips—"it might ease his transition to the Institute."

She mulled that over for a minute, then abruptly came to a decision. "Miss Rivers, I'd like Miss Groves to assume sole responsibility for Mr. Karr's care. I'll agree on Mr. Karr's behalf to compensate the Institute handsomely for the inconvenience, of course, as well as giving a personal check to Miss Groves for her extra efforts."

Gloria Rivers frowned. "Our nurses aren't allowed to accept personal payments of any kind. As for the Institute, this request is highly irregular. What level of compensation did you have in mind?"

"I realize that you'll have to hire a temporary nurse to take care of Miss Groves's current patients. How about twenty-five thousand dollars for your out-of-pocket expenses and ten thousand dollars per week to cover the additional payroll costs? And that's on top of the quarter of a million dollar monthly fee Mr. Karr is already paying."

Victoria could swear Gloria Rivers was going to jump up and down. "That's very generous," she replied calmly, and Victoria gave her high marks for self-restraint. "I'm sure something can be worked out—*if* Miss Groves is amenable." She shot a questioning look at Beatrice, and

Victoria almost laughed aloud at the pretense. If Beatrice said no, she'd probably be fired on the spot.

"I'd be delighted to help Mr. Karr," Beatrice assured her. "And I'd never think of accepting payment, with or without Institute policy. I'm a nurse. Helping patients is my job."

"Then it's settled," Victoria pronounced. She slanted a sideways look at the conference table, where Zach was becoming increasingly more agitated, rubbing his sweaty palms against his trousers, his breathing quick, erratic. "I'll tell Mr. Karr. It will calm him down."

"There will, of course, have to be certain stipulations . . ." Miss Rivers added swiftly.

"No stipulations." Victoria shot that down at once. Seeing the head nurse's displeasure, she faced her, her own eyes narrowed determinedly. "Miss Rivers, I'll be blunt. Mr. Karr doesn't require anywhere near the degree of care the Hope Institute can provide. He chose your clinic for its location, its reputation, and its privacy. He's paying an exorbitant amount to stay here. What stipulations could there be? He's not allowed medication, he's had more than enough hours of psychotherapy, and he's seen the finest doctors in the country, all of whom diagnosed his condition the same way: chronic adjustment disorder brought on by stress. The cure? A change of scene, some R and R. Surely an experienced nurse like Miss Groves can provide that."

"Of course she can." Gloria Rivers gave an uneasy nod. "It's just that, as I said, this is highly irregular. In fact, it's never been done."

"Mother?" Zach called out, loosening his tie and rubbing the back of his neck. "I'm dizzy. And I'm hot."

"I'll get you a cool cloth," Beatrice replied.

He looked panicked. "You'll come right back?"

"Absolutely." Beatrice glanced at Miss Rivers. "I'll just be a minute. In the meantime, you and Ms. Hughes can work out the details."

Gloria nodded, watched Beatrice leave. Clearly, she was torn by indecision.

"I think we're finished working things out," Victoria stated. "Am I right, Miss Rivers?"

A peevish stare. "I'm in an uncomfortable position, Ms. Hughes," she said in a quiet undertone. "I don't set administrative policy. And, as I said, this is a first."

"There are always firsts." Victoria lowered her voice as well, but her adamant tone and rigid stance were clear indications that there would be no compromise in her demands. "So why don't you give me whatever admission papers I need to sign. I'll look them over and review them with Mr. Karr. Miss Groves can stay here with us to keep Mr. Karr calm. Go find your decision makers. Tell them that, if they want Mr. Karr's money—including the additional amounts we just discussed—they'd best sign an agreement assuring us that Miss Groves will be Mr. Karr's sole caretaker. Rearrange her shifts, do whatever you have to do. Let her sleep on a cot outside his room, if need be—at least for the first couple of weeks, until he's comfortable with the rest of the staff. After that, we'll revisit the situation and talk about who's suitable to relieve Miss Groves. But up to that point, she's it. Is that acceptable? Or do you want a hysterical patient on your hands—one who'll walk right out that door if he's refused?"

"Walk out?" Miss Rivers gasped. "But I understood Mr. Karr specifically chose our Institute—"

"He did. But that was before he believed his mother was here and you were keeping him from her. He's in a very unsettled state, Miss Rivers. Strangers upset him. Look how anxious he's become just from the few he's encountered today. I'm no doctor, but it seems to me he's found the perfect life preserver to cling to—his mother. If you deny him that, or worse, tell him Miss Groves isn't who he thinks she is, I think he'd walk out of here in one of your New York minutes."

The head nurse looked like a cornered rat. She pressed her lips together, weighing whatever resistance she might receive from her superiors against the obscene amount of money involved.

The scales weren't even close to being balanced.

She gave a terse nod. "Very well, I'll do my best." An unyielding glare. "Just understand that you're forfeiting Mr. Karr's right to medication. None can be administered without my supervision."

"I'll do one better than understanding it. Put it in writing."

"Excuse me?"

"I said, add that to the document you prepare. It's more than fine with me. In fact, I insist. Because, as I specified, Mr. Karr is to receive no, I repeat, *no* medication. Not only is he highly allergic, as his records indicate, but he becomes extremely agitated when he even sees pills, needles, or intravenous equipment. He's had terrible experiences with all of them. So include that in your document. It will protect Mr. Karr, and it will protect you against a crushing malpractice suit."

"I suppose that can be done." Miss Rivers seemed to perk up at that suggestion, probably because Victoria had just given her a great way to stifle the flack she was about to receive. Malpractice protection—it was the perfect out.

"So that eliminates our final obstacle," Victoria concluded.

"Yes, apparently it does." Gloria Rivers regarded Mr. Karr's counsel with more than a touch of admiration, silently recognizing that Catherine Hughes had her over a barrel. The woman was a pro, just as her background check had revealed. "Why don't you have a seat with your client, Ms. Hughes? I'll leave the paperwork for you two to review. Beatrice will stay; I'm sure Mr. Karr will find her presence reassuring. I won't be long."

Nodding, Victoria went over to the conference table to

give her client the welcome news, while Miss Rivers hovered near the doorway, tapping her foot and awaiting Beatrice's return.

"Where's Mother?" Zach demanded instantly, jumping to his feet. "Why isn't she . . ." He broke off as Beatrice hurried back into the room, a dampened washcloth in her hand.

"Here we go." She sat down next to Zach, gesturing for him to take his seat, and angling her chair so she could face him. Once he'd complied, she mopped his brow with the washcloth. Simultaneously, her trained fingers found the pulse at his wrist, checking to see just how agitated he was. "Is your heart racing a little?" she murmured.

"It was. It's slowing now."

"Good. Just sit and relax. I'll stay with you." Her glance flickered quickly from Victoria to Miss Rivers. The head nurse issued a terse nod to Beatrice's unspoken question.

Satisfied that everything had been settled, Beatrice continued speaking to Zach in a soothing tone. "Ms. Hughes has some papers to go over with you. After that, I'll take you to your room. Is that all right?"

His entire body seemed to sag with relief. "Yes. That's great." An enormous sigh. "I'm so glad you're here."

That seemed to clinch it for Miss Rivers. She snapped into action, crossing over to the table and producing a manila file folder, which she handed to Victoria. "I'll see to that new document. I won't be long."

She shut the door behind her.

As agreed, Zach, Victoria, and Beatrice stayed in character. They had no idea whether or not they could be seen or heard. And they didn't intend to find out the hard way.

Victoria settled herself on Zach's opposite side. She opened her briefcase, taking out a copy of the power of attorney she'd forwarded to the Institute, along with evaluations by two of the fictitious doctors the FBI had conjured up for Karr's medical records—evaluations stating that, in their opinion, David Karr was harmless to himself and to others, and required only several months in a stress-free environment to facilitate his recovery. Listening with half an ear as Beatrice spoke quietly and gently to her patient, Victoria set aside her papers and began methodically sifting through the Hope Institute's legal documents.

None of them was a surprise. They were replicas of the boilerplates she'd copied from her father's computer. With one difference.

Rather than a blank line at the end of each document, her father's signature was penned neatly in the spaces provided.

Swallowing her nausea, she handed the papers to Zach one at a time while briefly explaining the terms and conditions. He gave an occasional absent nod and scanned a page here and there. Mostly, his gaze kept darting to Beatrice to ensure she hadn't left.

Finally, having finished reviewing the documents, Victoria folded each one over to its respective last page—the page with the signature lines. She then laid out the documents in a row, waiting for Miss Rivers's return so they could be properly executed and witnessed.

She'd just completed arranging her lineup when Miss Rivers reentered the room, a single-sheet document in her hand.

"The agreement you requested has been drawn up," she said, looking flustered, as if she'd been through the mill. "It's ready for your perusal."

"Good," Victoria replied. She extended her hand, took the sheet of paper, and pored over it.

The terms of the agreement, as per her instructions, provided that, for a period of two weeks' time and barring any unforeseen circumstances beyond the Institute's reasonable control, Beatrice Groves would be David Karr's sole medical attendant, and that for the duration of that time, Mr. Karr would not be permitted to receive medication of any kind and in any form, including intravenous. Any extension of the agreement had to be in writing, signed by Walter

Kensington for the Hope Institute, and Catherine Hughes for David Karr, as per his power of attorney. Compensation for the specified considerations was an initial payment of $25,000, plus $10,000 per week for each week that Beatrice Groves acted as exclusive caretaker for David Karr, the entire amount of which was in addition to the agreed-upon monthly sum of $250,000.

Everything appeared to be in order except that, in this case, the bold line at the bottom designated "Walter Kensington, Esq., Attorney of Record, Hope Institute," was lacking a signature.

"Your attorney will be executing this?" Victoria inquired in a tight, crisp voice.

"Of course. His office faxed us this copy for your approval. As soon as you've given it to us, a duplicate set of originals, signed by Mr. Kensington, will be prepared and messengered to the Institute. You'll have them before leaving Mr. Karr in our care."

"Very well." Another quick glance at the page. "Everything appears to be in order. Have Mr. Kensington deliver the executed originals." Victoria nearly choked on her father's name. "I'll sign your standard papers, in the interim."

"I'll act as your witness. Give me a minute to call Mr. Kensington's office." Gloria Rivers left the room, returning a minute later to join them at the conference table. "Everything's been arranged."

"Then I'll sign these and let Miss Groves get Mr. Karr settled in."

Zach began rubbing his trouser legs again, sniffing uneasily as he did. "Did you arrange for my mother to be the only one taking care of me?" he asked Victoria. "Otherwise, I'm not staying."

"I did, Mr. Karr. She'll be your sole caretaker," Victoria told him reassuringly. "I'll sign the papers and you can go to your room—with your mother."

He looked quickly at Beatrice for corroboration. She gave it, giving his arm a gentle pat. His sniffing stopped, and he stopped rubbing his trousers, sitting quietly while Victoria completed her business.

Gritting her teeth, Victoria signed each document with the new handwriting she'd mastered, and passed it to Miss Rivers for witnessing. Each time she wrote "Catherine Hughes," she stared at her father's signature beside it and felt a knot of betrayal twist inside her.

Dear God, Father, what have you done? How deeply involved are you? How much have you thrown away—and for what?

None of her inner turmoil showed on her face as she passed the final document to Miss Rivers. "That's everything but the new agreement."

The head nurse examined the forms. "They're all in order."

Beside Victoria, Zach began fidgeting again. "Do I need to wait for all the legal details to be ironed out? I'm tired. I didn't sleep well last night. And as long as my mother's taking care of me, the rest doesn't matter." That slightly frantic look returned to his eyes. "I really need to be away from all this commotion, all these people. I need to lie down, to be in my room."

Gloria Rivers assessed him with a practiced eye. Victoria could almost read her thoughts: too much stimuli. Patient is showing symptoms of stress.

"There's no reason for you to wait," the head nurse replied. A quick, consenting signal to Beatrice. "Why don't you take Mr. Karr to his room? Ms. Hughes can wait here until the agreement arrives. She'll sign it and be on her way."

Beatrice rose. "Good idea." She helped Zach to his feet and led him over to the wheelchair. "Come, Mr. . . . David," she corrected, remembering who she was supposed to be. "I'll take you upstairs. You've got a lovely, sunny room on the second floor. It's nice and big; there's more than enough room for a cot. I'll have one sent up for me immediately."

"Good." He sank into the wheelchair, looking utterly drained. "Then you'll stay with me while I nap."

"I'll be right there. And when you wake up, we'll have lunch."

"In my room," he qualified. "No more people."

"In your room. Just the two of us." She maneuvered the wheelchair toward the door.

"Get well soon, Mr. Karr," Victoria called. "I'll be back next week for a visit."

"Hmm? Okay. But I'll be fine. My mother's here . . ." Zach's head was already drooping when Beatrice wheeled him out of the room.

31

Victoria tossed and turned all night.

The bed was unbearably empty without Zach in it. And the knot in her stomach was even more unbearable.

She was up before dawn, sitting in the hotel suite's cozy dining area, drinking coffee.

The rest of the admission process had gone like clockwork. Miss Rivers had acted as her sentry for the half hour until the agreement arrived. The originals, complete with her father's signature, had been delivered to the conference room, where they'd been signed by Catherine Hughes, witnessed by Gloria Rivers, and added to the stack of papers Victoria packed in her briefcase when she left.

Atkins had asked a few questions, then delivered her back to the service entrance of the Plaza Athénée, where she'd transformed herself back into Victoria Kensington— minus her engagement ring, which she slipped into her purse for later—and dashed off to Waters, Kensington, Tatem & Calder.

Walking into her father's firm that day had been one of the hardest things she'd ever done. Facing him would have been even harder.

Thankfully, she hadn't had to. He'd been at lunch when she arrived, then tied up in meetings all afternoon. She'd spent most of the afternoon with Ian Block, helping him research a corporate litigation case he was handling. Ian was his usual charming, sharp-edged self, challenging her legal knowledge at every turn—whether to instruct her or test her abilities, she wasn't sure.

He *had* thrown her off balance once. And it hadn't been in their legal discussions. It had been when he'd asked her about Zach.

"We haven't had much occasion to talk since Saturday night's party," he'd said lightly, leaning back in his desk chair. "So tell me, are you and Zachary Hamilton an item?"

Victoria had been perched at the edge of Ian's desk, her pen gripped between her teeth as she skimmed some pages that had just come off the printer. She lowered the pages, removed the pen from her teeth, and arched her brows. "An item?"

Ian's smile was rueful. "Am I overstepping?"

"That depends. Why do you want to know? Idle curiosity, friendly interest, or harmful intent?"

His smile vanished, and a cool sort of wariness came over him. "Meaning?"

"Meaning, don't bother keeping track of my social life to score points with my father. I'm an adult. I go out with whomever I choose to. My father never interferes. Nor does he worry that my work will suffer. He knows better. Besides, he's already aware I'm seeing Zach. So there's no mileage there."

The wariness disappeared as quickly as it had come, and a spark of dry humor flickered in Ian's eyes. "Interesting," he murmured, hunching forward to prop his elbows on the desk. "Now *that* particular course of action never occurred to me. Although I suppose it should have. Your father is extremely proud of you. He thinks you're a brilliant attorney. That was obvious Saturday night. I imagine he'd view very few men as being worthy of you. If I brought to his attention that you were seeing one of those unworthy men, then helped him do away with the cad, I'm sure it would earn me high marks."

Normally, Victoria would have been amused by Ian's caustic wit. Today she hadn't been.

"I'm beat, Ian," she'd said, coming to her feet. "I don't mean to be abrupt, but it's been a long week and I'm not in the mood to spar. Can we please get back to work?"

"As you wish." He'd eyed her speculatively. "Any answer to my question?"

"Why are you interested in Zach? From what I gathered, you two don't even know each other."

"We don't. Other than through reputation and other Harvard alumni."

"Then why the questions?" Victoria had shot him a taunting look of her own. "Unless, of course, *you* were thinking of asking me out?"

"And if I was?"

That *had* elicited a smile. "You're too smart for that. Fraternizing with Walter Kensington's daughter? Too risky. If we broke up and things got messy, it could ruin your chances at that big office down the hall."

Ian had chuckled. "I suppose you're right." A shrug. "My loss."

"More likely, your gain. At least that's what you're hoping—career-wise, that is." Victoria finished glancing through the printed pages, marking the pertinent points. "Good luck in your quest. After a week here, I can still confirm I don't want that partnership. It's all yours." She'd handed him the highlighted pages. "Look at the bright side. I'd be terrible for you, anyway. I'm not the lady-on-the-arm-of-a-successful-megabucks-attorney type. I'm independent. I have my own ideas *and* my own legal practice. Our schedules would clash. So would our priorities. Oh, and I'm a lousy cook."

Laughter had rumbled in Ian's chest. "I'm relieved. Now I won't feel so deprived on my lonely trek to the top."

"I doubt it'll be lonely." She headed for the door, to return to her own office and to continue the on-line research she'd been conducting. "You'll just be smart enough to choose the right companion along the way."

He would, too. One thing about Ian, he had his life plan in order. Whatever woman he eventually selected as his mate would fit right into it. His professional future would come first—always. And his partner would love that idea. She'd be beautiful, poised and elegant, and happy to spend Ian's money, appear on his arm, and bask in his limelight. The perfect trophy wife.

Well, that description sure as hell didn't fit her.

So much for the prospect of Ian being interested in her. And hopefully, so much for his questions about her and Zach, whatever his reasons were for asking them. He'd know the status of their relationship soon enough—*after* she told her father. Which she wasn't ready to do at this tenuous time. In fact, she wasn't ready to speak with him at all.

To that end, she'd spent the rest of her hours at Waters, Kensington, Tatem & Calder closeted in her office so she wouldn't run into him. At four-thirty, she'd shot out of there like a bat out of hell, after explaining to Ian that she had a late-afternoon meeting at her own firm.

That hadn't been a lie.

Victoria took another sip of coffee, smiling a little as she remembered the scene she'd created when she'd burst into London, Kensington & Stone, thrilled to find that both her partners, as well as Paige, were still there.

She'd paused outside the door just long enough to slip her engagement ring back on before marching in to deliver her announcement.

It didn't take a prophet to figure out who'd notice the ring first.

"Oh my God." Paige had slammed down the phone on whoever she'd been talking to, and practically lunged across the front desk to grab Victoria's hand. "It's gorgeous! And it's huge! It must be two carats. I bet he got it at Tiffany's. It screams Tiffany's. Am I right?" She didn't wait for an answer. "I knew this was coming. I could tell by the way he looked at you, and the way you've been mooning around. I knew it!" She twisted around to shout, "Paul! Meg! It's urgent! Get out here right away!"

They'd exploded out of their offices simultaneously, practically colliding in the secretarial area.

"Jesus, Paige, it's just Victoria," Paul had said in exasperation. "What if I'd be in there with a client, and you—"

"It's not *just* Victoria," Paige had interrupted, holding Victoria's hand high in the air, displaying it as if it were the Heisman trophy. "It's Victoria and *this*." She whirled back to Victoria, her blue eyes wide. "Did you know this was coming? How did he propose? Did he get down on one knee? That would be *so* cool, and *so* romantic. But Zach's the romantic type. I could tell by the way he demanded to see you when he first walked in, then ignored my protests and marched right down to your office. Meg says you two have been in love forever. She didn't want to tell me, but I dragged it out of her. Wow, Victoria, that's like something out of a movie. When's the wedding? And what about your honeymoon? Are you going to an island, or—"

"Paige!" Paul bellowed. But he was grinning as he silenced her, rolling his eyes good-naturedly as he walked by her desk to inspect Victoria's ring for himself. "This is for real then," he said, giving Victoria a questioning look.

"Very for real." It was the first time Victoria had spoken since Hurricane Paige had descended. "And you guys are the first to know." She'd accepted Paul's hug, then gazed past him, watching as Meg walked over, a huge smile on her face. "Go ahead," Victoria had invited, "say 'I told you so.'"

"No way. I'd rather say I'm so happy for you." Meg hugged her. "But I am glad you came to your senses," she'd muttered for Victoria's ears alone. "Where's Zach?" she asked, drawing back and speaking in a normal tone. "I want to tell him how lucky he is."

"Unfortunately, he's tied up on work-related stuff for

most of the weekend," Victoria had replied, not having to feign her regret. "Which, according to him, is his loss and your gain. He insisted I take you guys out for a drink to celebrate—on him."

The four of them had shared a warm, lighthearted hour at a local bar, toasting Victoria's engagement, with Meg and Paul making good-natured I-told-you-so jokes, and Paige examining Victoria's ring at different angles and in different types of light.

Zach was right. The time with her friends *had* been good for her, if for no other reason than to distract her for a while.

But once she was alone in Zach's hotel suite, with only a long, dark night and indefinite hours of uncertainty looming ahead, the apprehension had returned big-time.

It was now daybreak. And the apprehension hadn't faded.

What was happening inside the Hope Institute? What had Zach found out? Had he seen Audrey? And, most important, had he managed to keep his identity a secret? Because, if not . . .

Her secure cell phone rang, breaking into her thoughts and causing her to spill the entire contents of her coffee cup as she lunged to answer it.

"Hello?" she snapped out, her fingers biting into the receiver.

"It's me." Zach voice was terse, hushed.

"Thank God. Are you all right?"

"Fine. But I've got to talk fast. Beatrice is guarding my door, making sure no one's coming. If I hang up suddenly, you'll understand. I saw Audrey. She's okay, just kind of drugged up. From the way she's acting, I'd say they were giving her sedatives to keep her under control, not some miracle drug to treat her bulimia. But I'm not sure. The important thing is, she's not in any danger. I couldn't tell her who I was—not yet. There wasn't time, and she wasn't really lucid. But I'll find a way."

"Don't, Zach. If they figure out who you are—"

"They won't," he interrupted, continuing to speak in that same urgent whisper. "I'm giving all the information I've got so far to you, since I don't know when I'll have the chance to call Meyer."

"I'll call him."

"Not yet. I need more time. I have to find proof tying the Hope Institute to the drug syndicate. I also need to find out who their damned CEO is. I'll have to get into their computer system for that, because whoever this CEO is, he's practically invisible. Not a surprise, given what he's mixed up in. There's a hell of a lot more going on here than just drug money and fraud."

"Like what?"

"I'll get to that in a minute. In the meantime, I was busy last night. I found the crematorium; it's in the basement, along with a steel storage cabinet I'm willing to bet holds urns filled with ashes—the remains of patients whose relatives have yet to be told of their parting. I also found the audio engineer's room. He's got to be our wiretapper. He has a cabinet loaded with audio tapes of the patients' therapy sessions. *And* he's got lots of equipment, including digital editing gear. My guess is that's how the Institute keeps relatives paying—by making them think their loved ones are alive. They cut and paste the patients' words, then use them to leave phone messages saying all is well. Voilà—life after death. The bodies are cremated, no death certificates are filed—at least not for a while—and no one's the wiser, so the money keeps pouring in. If I'm right, that's the technique they used to leave Audrey's first telephone message. They spliced her words together to say what they wanted. You thought her voice sounded stilted? It was."

Victoria sank into a chair, her mind reeling. "That's enough to arrest them on, Zach. I'll call Meyer and he'll send in his men, so you can get out of there—"

"No. Not yet. Not until I have proof. Right now, there's

too much speculation, and too much wiggle room that would allow them to explain their way out of the charges—especially with your father representing them. Besides, I'm onto something more. That's what I was alluding to before. I found a room with some cryogenic medical containers, the kind used to transport body organs or medical samples. They get through customs with a letter of authorization or a permit. The procedure's highly regulated by the Centers for Disease Control, so the containers don't usually get opened by customs."

"You think that's how the drugs got into the country?"

"Yes and no. Not the kind of drugs you mean, but, yes, that's how I think the drugs got here." Zach paused, probably glancing over at Beatrice to make sure he wasn't risking discovery. "I think the FBI's barking up the wrong tree. That's why they're coming up empty, and why their dogs aren't sniffing out any narcotics. That room with the medical receptacles—I saw Gloria Rivers go in there empty-handed. When she came out, she had containers of medicine, marked with patients' names. You know, the ones Beatrice said are proprietary drug combinations developed by the Institute?"

Reality punched Victoria in the gut. "You think she took them from those receptacles. You think the Hope Institute is importing illegal drugs and using them on their patients."

"It would explain a lot. But I need evidence. I can't even get a warrant to search the place without it. And I need the name of the Institute's CEO. Hopefully, I'll find it in their computer files. I don't want him slipping through our fingers. Gloria Rivers is nothing but a pawn. She might not even know what she's handling—although I suspect otherwise."

"Zach—"

"Sweetheart, I've got to hang up. The morning shift is starting to arrive. I can't risk anyone seeing me with my cell phone. I'll call the next chance I get. Remember, Atkins is keeping an eye on you in case Mr. Cigar tries anything. But he won't. Not if you spend the weekend in my hotel suite. And when you do go out, only go to places you'd normally go. That'll keep him satisfied. We're nearing the home stretch. I love you."

With a soft click, the call disconnected.

Victoria was shaking as she punched End and lowered the phone to the chair. Yes, everything Zach suspected made sense. Too much sense. Illegal drugs, smuggled from outside the country, but not to sell. To use on patients as guinea pigs, making obscene profits in the process. It would explain the secrecy, the restrictions placed on outsiders, the demand for cremation. The Institute kept the evidence inside their private walls, then destroyed it afterward, so no one would know.

That prospect shed new light on the elaborate posthumous arrangements delineated in the Institute's legal documents.

Documents prepared by her father.

Sickness welled up in Victoria's throat. Did her father actually know all this was going on? Was he really so hungry for wealth and power that he'd stooped to this?

She couldn't—wouldn't—believe it. He was many things, but not a sacrificer of lives.

Maybe his guilt was limited, but to what extent? And even if it was, did it matter? To her, yes. To the courts, no. As legal counsel, he signed every contract. And he'd go down with the CEO.

Legal ethics warred with the fine bonds of family loyalty. He was her father, for God's sake. When she'd committed herself to this investigation, she'd done it to uncover his part in all this so she could bargain for leniency. She'd believed there was a limit to his unscrupulousness, even if that limit was only a respect for human life.

She believed it still.

On that realization, she raked both hands through her

hair. She had to give her father one chance, one chance to prove himself before this entire thing broke wide open and the FBI brought down the Hope Institute, together with everyone involved, including him.

But how? How could she go to him and tell him what she knew without jeopardizing Zach in the process?

Zach needed the name of the Institute's CEO. There was no guarantee their computer files could give him that. But there was every guarantee Walter Kensington could. He was an officer of the corporation. He'd have to be to sign all their contracts, including the original contract of sale he'd drawn up between Benjamin Hopewell and the buyer of the Hope Institute. He knew who was behind the smoke screen of that Swiss holding company. He'd known who he was dealing with then, and he knew it now. He'd never agree to represent an anonymous client—not only would it be like walking a minefield blindfolded, it would mean relinquishing control.

Unthinkable.

So her father knew this CEO's name. It was up to her to get it—and hopefully throw her father a life preserver in the process.

There was only one way to go about this. That was to leave Zach out of it. No one knew he was David Karr. No one knew he was in the Institute right now, digging for evidence. So if she handled this right, his involvement would never come up.

She'd have to play her hand carefully, make sure her father stayed the mouse and she the cat, whichever direction he veered in. And she'd have to go about it in such a way that it gave Mr. Cigar nothing out of the ordinary to report. But she had to try. Not only to spare her father, but to help Zach. He needed proof. She could get it. Besides, she couldn't just sit tight, doing nothing but waiting and worrying.

Her gaze fell on the clock. Almost 7 A.M. She'd have to hurry.

She rose and headed for the shower.

Waters, Kensington, Tatem & Calder
8:15 A.M.

It was raining again, just like the Saturday morning two weeks ago when Audrey had collapsed at her feet in Central Park.

Her father wasn't at the club. Victoria had called to make sure, and the golf pro told her that he'd been there at six, canceled his game, and said something about heading to the office if anyone asked.

Good. This conversation would be easier there. And Mr. Cigar would assume she was going to her desk.

She slipped her key card into the slot beside the door and walked in.

The office was quiet, only a few junior partners and their secretaries in, busting their tails on a corporate merger agreement that had been dropped on them late yesterday. Otherwise, the activity level was nil, the outer office quiet, the inner sanctuaries dark.

She made her way directly to her father's office and knocked.

"Yes?" His voice sounded mildly surprised, and none too pleased. When he went in on weekends, it was to catch up. He liked peace and quiet.

Well, he wasn't getting any this morning.

Victoria went in, shutting the door in her wake. "Father, I need to see you. It's urgent."

Walter Kensington looked up from behind his formidable cherry desk. His brows snapped together, more in annoyance than concern. "Victoria, you're not dressed for the office."

She glanced down at herself and realized that, compared to her father's crisp suit and tie, her cable-knit sweater, khakis, and blazer made her look as if she were going slumming. Ironic that was all he cared about. He didn't ask *why* she was underdressed in his precious corporate domain or, for that matter, what she was doing in the office at all at eight o'clock on a Saturday morning, in an obviously agitated state. All he commented on was the fact that she hadn't abided by the dress code.

"I realize that," she replied. "I'm not here to work. I'm here to see you—privately."

Something about her tone must have conveyed the gravity of what was on her mind. Her father studied her for a moment, then lowered the pages he'd been reading, leaning forward to prop his elbows on his desk and steeple his fingers. "What is this about?"

She advanced toward him, flattened her palms on the desk's gleaming cherry veneer, and stared him down. "It's about me trying to save your skin."

Ice glittered in his eyes. "I don't know what you're talking about. What's more, I don't care for your tone."

"And I don't care for your actions. But you're my father. So I'm intervening—before it's too late. Either listen to me, or I guarantee you'll end up in prison."

"Prison," he repeated, his lips thinning into a tight, angry line. "What kind of threat is that?"

"It's no threat. It's a reality based on your involvement with the Hope Institute. And I don't mean as it pertains to Audrey. I mean your serving as the Institute's corporate counsel, drafting agreements that call for all patients to relinquish their control—over their lives, their deaths, their estates." She swallowed, determined to keep her emotions totally in check. "I need to know—how deep is your involvement, Father? How much are you aware of, based on firsthand experience, and how much has transpired while you conveniently looked the other way? I need to know if I'm going to effectively represent you—or even be able to look you in the eye."

Walter Kensington's color had deepened, and his features were taut with fury. "Where did you get this alleged information?"

"It's not alleged. It's factual." She picked up the Silver Seraph, turned it upside down, pointing at the Smart Card. "I saw the forms firsthand on your computer files. All of them, right down to the cremation clauses. It's a neat little arrangement. The bodies are destroyed, the Hope Institute is protected, and Waters, Kensington, Tatem and Calder gets all the trust and estate business. I'm sure you make a fortune."

For the first time in her life, Victoria saw her father's control snap. He rose slowly, like a cobra ready to strike. *"You broke into my computer?"* he fired out, gritting his teeth to keep the sound from echoing outside his walls. *"How dare you!"*

"How dare *I?*" Victoria stood her ground. "You're using people as human guinea pigs, and you're questioning my methods of gathering information?" Her heart was thundering in her chest. "Did Audrey find out, Father? Is that why she ran away and tried to find me? Or did she already know firsthand? Is she one of your human guinea pigs, too?"

Her father slapped her across the face, hard, something he'd never done. "Don't you ever say such a thing to me," he spat, a vein throbbing at his forehead. "Your sister might be a self-destructive, pitiful excuse for a Kensington, but she's my daughter. I would never harm her. As for what you call human guinea pigs, I call them desperate people looking for a second chance at life. And as for the proprietary medications, the patents should be . . ." He stopped himself before he could say anything incriminating. "You came here to tell me you're going to the police with this?"

Despite the stinging pain in her cheek, Victoria felt her first surge of hope. "Proprietary medications," she repeated. "Is that what you believe they are?"

"I don't *believe* it; I *know* it." He was still furious—furious enough to have abandoned his poker face. His certainty was genuine.

"You're wrong," Victoria informed him. "They're illegal

drugs, smuggled into the country. And I don't need to tell the police. The FBI already knows."

Her father was silent for a minute. "Your facts are incorrect."

"No. Yours are." Victoria pressed her palms together. "Here are the accurate facts. You're representing a clinic that's receiving the medications it administers from an international drug syndicate. The Institute is also cremating its patients right there on the premises. And do you know why? To rake in extra cash by pretending the deceased patients are still alive and collecting a few more months' worth of payments from their families."

For the first time, Victoria saw doubt flash behind her father's anger.

She took full advantage, continuing with her itemized revelation. "Why do you think they were so upset when I started poking around? They sent someone out to follow me. I'm sure you know that. And last Saturday night, I doubt that was a drunk who drove me off the road. It was someone who was worried about my persistence. Maybe they knew I'd talked to Benjamin Hopewell at the party. Because I did. Is he still involved in the Hope Institute? Is he the CEO? I don't think so. But you drew up the contract of sale, and the articles of incorporation. So you *do* know. Tell me who it is, Father. Tell me and let me help you. Or do you want to take the fall for someone who'd be thrilled to let you?"

Walter pursed his lips. "You say the FBI knows all this. Why haven't they made arrests, then?"

"They're gathering the final pieces so they can grab everyone, including the CEO. Whether or not they do, arrests will be made in a day or two. I'm trying to get a jump on that by coming to you now, when you still have something to bargain with—the CEO's name. Right now, you can still give yourself up, give them a name, in exchange for leniency. Once you've been arrested, that opportunity vanishes."

"You've obviously been in contact with them. Did they send you here?"

"No." This, Victoria could answer honestly. "They'd be furious if they knew I'd taken this risk. Don't you think I realize I'm exposing my hand? I'm as clever as you about keeping my cards close to the vest. But this time the stakes are very high, and very personal. You're my father. I didn't believe you could go that far. Evidently, I was right." She swallowed. "Tell me his name, Father."

"I can't. Not until I've spoken with my client. At this point, I have only your word to go on. As you know, that's not enough."

Yes, she did know. What she *didn't* know was how he'd respond to her next question.

"Fine," she acknowledged quietly. "Go to your client. Confirm what I've said. I'll give you twenty-four hours. Just tell me this: When he asks where you got your information, will you tell him?"

An odd expression crossed her father's face. "In other words, will I hand you over to this corrupt individual you're describing? No more than you handed me over to the FBI. I'll do what I need to do, and then you'll do what you need to do. All I ask is that you hold off until I've fulfilled my legal obligation and conferred with my client. You're my daughter. My reputation is on the line—a reputation I've spent a lifetime building. Respect that fact. Respect me and the position I'm in. I deserve that much."

Wordlessly, she nodded.

Her father cleared his throat, as if he'd come too close to an emotional display. "Tell me, Victoria, where does Zachary Hamilton fit into all this?"

Victoria had been prepared to field questions about Zach. She'd intended to answer only what the powers that be at the Hope Institute already knew or could surmise: that he'd helped her out by taking the cigar butt and having it dusted for fingerprints. That whoever had done the dusting had referred her to her FBI contacts. After that, it was imperative they all believed she'd run on her own.

She hadn't planned to do what she did next. It just happened.

She fumbled in her purse and pulled out her engagement ring, slipped it on her finger. "Zach's going to be my husband. That's how he fits into all this. He knows I'm worried about Audrey, and that I suspect I'm being followed. He wants to protect me. He has no idea things have gone this far. He certainly doesn't know I'm here with you." She held out her hand to display the ring, more for impact than approval. She neither expected nor needed her father's blessing. Still, on some fundamental level, she wished he could be happy for her. "I was waiting to tell you about our engagement. I wanted Audrey to be fine and out of the Hope Institute. And I wanted my instincts about you to be right so you could walk me down the aisle."

"I see." Her father pursed his lips, eyeing her rather than the diamond. His forehead creased in thought, as if he were deciding which stock option to exercise. "Hamilton is intelligent, respected, extremely affluent, and well connected," he announced.

Victoria didn't know whether to laugh or cry. Even now, with his own future hanging in the balance, Walter Kensington's priorities didn't change. The list of Zach's virtues he'd chosen to enumerate was thoroughly typical.

"Yes, Father, he's all those things. He's also the finest man I've ever known."

To her surprise, her father nodded. He studied her ring, that odd expression flickering across his face. "You're happy with him, then."

"Very."

Another nod. "Then I'm pleased for you." A frown. "Hamilton's based in Europe. Your legal career—"

"Won't be affected, Father. Zach's going to relocate. He and I plan to settle within commuting distance of Manhattan."

Victoria gave her father a tight smile. "I still won't accept your partnership offer. But I'll be nearby enough for you to continue pressuring." She turned and walked toward the door. "Call me after you've conferred with your client. If I haven't heard from you by tomorrow morning, *you'll* hear from *me*."

"Victoria?"

She glanced back questioningly.

"I accept your offer to walk you down the aisle."

32

Victoria retreated as far as Miss Hatterman's cubicle, then ducked inside.

She wouldn't let herself feel guilty for what she had in mind. She'd given her father every chance to tell her the name of the Hope Institute's CEO. Not surprisingly, he hadn't. She couldn't blame him. He had a responsibility to his client, corrupt or not. She'd been prepared for his reaction. As a result, she'd made plans to get what she needed in a more creative way—and help her father in spite of himself, just in case his conscience didn't prevail over his commitment to attorney-client privilege even after he'd confirmed the truth. She was more determined than ever to save him from himself now that she knew for certain his culpability was limited.

Miss Hatterman's area was dark, piles of work neatly stacked up on her desk to be tackled first thing Monday morning. But darkness was fine for what Victoria had in mind.

An instant later, she saw what she was waiting for.

One light on the secretary's phone lit up. It was her father's private line. He was making a call.

And Victoria knew just who he was calling.

She was half tempted to eavesdrop. But she couldn't take the chance. If her father's keen ears heard the telltale click of another extension being picked up, she'd blow her one and only opportunity. She had to have patience—for everyone's sake.

The light vanished, then flashed back on. Her father was obviously searching for his client. The second time the light stayed on long enough to indicate the elusive CEO had been reached. Two minutes, three. Then, the light went off, this time for good. Not a shock that the call was brief. Walter Kensington always conducted important business meetings in person. And Lord knew, this meeting was important. Her father's entire career and future were on the line.

Quietly, Victoria left the office and took the elevator downstairs.

She lingered in the lobby, knowing that the minute she stepped outside, Mr. Cigar would be on her trail. She had to time this just right, so she could do what she had to without alerting him.

A whirring sound told her the elevator had been summoned. Her head snapped up, and she watched the ascending floor numbers. When the elevator stopped on fourteen, she knew who was getting in.

She paused until it began making its descent. Then she turned on her heel and left the building.

Outside, she began walking briskly, as if she were headed somewhere important. She glanced at her watch and frowned, seemingly troubled by the time. Mr. Cigar should have a clear view of her. It was Saturday, and there weren't many commuters dashing about.

She timed reaching the corner just as the light changed and traffic resumed moving up Park Avenue. Abruptly, she pivoted, as if waiting to cross over to the other side of Park.

From the corner of her eye, she saw her father hail a cab in front of his building. She didn't spare a glance in that direction. The last thing she wanted to do was to alert Mr. Cigar to her father's presence. Hopefully, he had his eye on her, not her father. At the same time, she didn't want her father to spot her. So, to play it safe, she stepped behind a heavyset woman whose arms were loaded with bundles and who was also waiting for the light to change.

The minute her father's taxi sailed by, she stepped out from behind the woman and her bundles and marched over to the edge of the curb. Perfect. Another couple of unoccupied taxis were cruising up the street. With a quick, dark scowl at her watch, she raised her arm to flag one down.

Please, she prayed silently. *Don't let this be one of those days they decide not to stop.*

It wasn't.

The first cab eased toward her, its sleepy-eyed driver eyeing her as if trying to decide whether or not this fare was worth the trouble of stopping. Victoria gave him a bright smile. He pulled over. She scrambled in, slammed the door, and said, "At the risk of sounding like a bad movie, follow that cab." She pointed.

The cabby twisted around and blinked. "What?"

She had to talk fast. Her father was already a block ahead. "I'm a lawyer. I work with that man. He forgot some important papers. I've got to give them to him."

"Yeah?" The cabby searched the empty seat beside her. "So where are the papers?"

Great. She had to get a nosy driver.

"Okay," she amended. "You got me. The truth is, he and I are lovers. His wife just found out about us. I've got to warn him before he sees her."

The cabby's approving gaze swept Victoria. "The man's got good taste." He turned, scowling at the road. "He's almost two blocks ahead of us."

"But it's Saturday and there's not a lot of traffic. Please. We're going to lose him." Victoria whipped out a twenty-dollar bill. "He's not going far." She hoped that was true. "Just a mile or two. I'll double whatever the fare is, and add this twenty as a tip."

"You got it, lady."

In true New York cabby style, the driver floored the gas and zoomed through the red light.

They narrowed the gap between the two cabs pretty quickly, weaving in and around other cars to keep their quarry in sight.

"You're lucky it's Saturday, lady. Otherwise you'd be in deep shit."

"I know." Victoria was forcing herself not to lean forward and look agitated. If Mr. Cigar had found a way to follow her—which she doubted he'd been able to pull off, given how fast she'd acted—she didn't want him to suspect she was in hot pursuit of another vehicle.

With dollar signs in his eyes, her cabby dodged red lights and poky drivers, fairly flying up Park Avenue. Twenty blocks. Thirty. Where the hell was her father going?

The other cab turned west on Eighty-fifth Street and shot up to Fifth Avenue. There it turned south and continued at a much slower pace. Victoria watched it, a horrible sense of dread forming in the pit of her stomach.

"Slow down," she instructed her driver in a taut voice.

"Why? I thought you wanted to catch up to—"

"Slow down!" she ordered, seeing the other cab veer over to the curb and stop.

Oh, God, no.

Her father bolted out, tossed in a few bills, then strode over to the adjacent building: 1029 Fifth Avenue.

Jim and Clarissa's address.

Victoria could taste her morning coffee rising from her stomach, feel it burning in her throat. "Pull over."

She watched her father say a few quick words to Leonard, who responded with a rueful shake of his head and a negative reply. Walter Kensington then tensed with anger, delivering a biting retaliation, which made Leonard flinch. The doorman tried again to dissuade him, saying something tentative—but Victoria's father cut him off immediately. He barked out a command, slicing the air with his palm and pointing vehemently at the apartment. Leonard relented, calling upstairs with the expression of a condemned prisoner. He hung up, gave Walter a terse nod, and stepped aside as Victoria's father blew by him and disappeared into the apartment.

"Lady? Are you getting out or not?"

Dazed, Victoria looked at the cabby. "What?"

"Are you getting out?"

"Oh. Yes." She glanced at the meter, pulled some more bills out of her wallet and handed them to him, along with the twenty. "Thanks."

"Any time." Grinning, the driver stuffed the cash in his pocket. "And listen. If you don't mind my saying so, you're a knockout. Find yourself someone else. That guy's old enough to be your father."

"Yeah. Right." Victoria climbed out, feeling like a condemned prisoner herself. Her uncle? Oh, God, please don't let this be happening. Please let there be some other reason why her father was here.

But what? What could possibly take precedence in her father's mind over saving his neck? Why would he go anywhere other than straight to the Hope Institute's CEO?

Even if that's why he's here, lots of people live in this building, she reminded herself. She shouldn't, *wouldn't*, jump to conclusions.

She walked slowly up the sidewalk, too shaken to think straight. One thing was for sure—if her worst fears were confirmed, she was in no condition to take any on-the-spot action. Not until she pulled herself together.

First things first. She had to get the facts.

"Miss Kensington." Leonard stared when he saw her. Normally, he welcomed her like a close friend, beaming and teasing. Not this time. This time he looked positively green. He was already a wreck from his altercation with her father, and now this. "What can I do for you?"

Victoria swallowed. "Is Dr. Kensington at home?"

"Well, yes, but—"

"Is that who my father just went up to see?"

Leonard began twisting at the rim of his cap. "Miss Kensington—"

"I need an answer, Leonard. Did my father ask to see Dr. Kensington and did you send him up to the penthouse? Yes or no?"

Reluctantly, the doorman nodded, dousing Victoria's last flicker of hope. "Yes. I tried to stop him, but he was insistent. He said it was urgent. Something about a business matter they were both involved in that was about to blow apart."

Her uncle. Her only constant. Everything she'd counted on and believed in. It couldn't be.

Is that why he'd been so adamant about defending his brother? Is that why he'd encouraged her to walk away from her investigation of the Hope Institute? Had he been trying to shake her loose before things got out of hand?

No. Not her Uncle Jim.

"Why would you try to stop my father from going up?" she asked Leonard woodenly, needing the answer, praying not to hear it. "Did Dr. Kensington ask you to?"

Leonard averted his gaze. "My instructions were to allow no one up. Dr. Kensington isn't alone. Please, Miss Kensington, I can't say any more. And I can't let you go up there."

"Don't worry, Leonard. I'm not interested in going up—not right now." *Dr. Kensington isn't alone? Who else could possible by up there with him? Mr. Cigar? The lunatic who'd run her off the road? The Institute's audio engineer and computer hacker? All of the above?*

Her emotions were out of control. She had to regain perspective before she could do anything. She had to consider the facts rationally, work out a strategy.

She tried to swallow, and failed. "Thank you, Leonard. I'll take a walk and come back later. Don't even mention I was here."

* * *

Walter struck the penthouse door with his fist. "Open it," he commanded.

The door swung open, and Walter stalked inside.

"I just learned some very disturbing facts," he began. "I sincerely hope you can deny them."

"What facts are those?" Clarissa Kensington belted her silk dressing robe more tightly around her waist, smoothing a hand over her pale hair. "And why are you barging in here at nine-thirty on a Saturday morning? I'm not even dressed."

"Because our careers are at stake," he snapped. "Not to mention our reputations and our freedom. I'm not interested in your attire. I'm interested in your explanation."

Clarissa went to the dining room and poured herself a cup of coffee. "Coming here was stupid, Walter. What if Jim had been home?"

"My brother's in his office. I verified that right after I called Mount Sinai and found out you were here."

Walter followed her into the dining room, glints of anger flaring in his eyes. The last thing he cared about was Clarissa's annoyance at having been disturbed. He had only one objective—verifying Victoria's accusations. He knew Clarissa better than anyone, even Jim. Not in an intimate way, but in a real one. He knew her mind, her convictions, the lengths she'd go to to realize them. She was single-minded in purpose, an astute, unfaltering businesswoman. The Hope Institute was her baby, and it had been since she'd discovered it was on the selling block, approached him with an offer, and anonymously acquired it from Benjamin Hopewell. Had the subsequent provisions she'd made to achieve her ends pushed the limits of the law? Without a doubt. He knew that better than anyone, having advised her, prepared the documents, and walked that legal tightrope. He knew all the ethical, moral, and yes, legal issues involved. But the criminal offenses Victoria had hurled at him? *Those* he knew nothing about.

He cut right to the chase. "Is it true the medications you're administering to your Hope Institute patients are really illegal drugs smuggled in by an international syndicate?"

She frowned, taking a sip of coffee. "That's an ugly spin to put on things. I've saved a dozen or more lives and lengthened the life spans of more terminally ill patients than I can count. I've given them hope, relieved unspeakable pain, and afforded them a quality of life they could only dream of. So stop making it sound like I'm a common drug dealer who peddles crack on the streets."

Walter's exhalation of breath smacked of ire and disbelief. "Clarissa, do you understand the significance of what you're doing? Legally, not medically. You're not bending the law, you're breaking it. You're a criminal."

"I'm a doctor," she corrected icily, her normally serene tone sharp with indignation. "I save lives—something the medical community has forgotten about while being paralyzed by red tape and afraid of lawsuits."

"There's more. What about when those lives can't be saved? Deceased patients were supposed to be cremated, and their ashes turned over to their families *immediately*. We inserted that provision to protect what I believed to be your intellectual property while filing for patents. Now I'm told there are no patents, and the conveyance of the cremated ashes are delayed so the patients' families will continue to make payments under the false assumption their loved ones are alive. Is this true?"

That particular allegation seemed to upset her. Her pale brows drew together, and a pained expression tightened her features. "I really dislike doing that. I resort to it as seldom as possible. But, Walter, the Institute's overhead is high. As it is, I pour thousands of dollars of my personal funds in to help pay for our research. Then there's our staff. We have brilliant doctors who must be compensated for their services—and I don't mean at the measly rates they're paid by managed health care.

I mean *real* compensation. We also have the finest nurses in Manhattan. They, too, get salaries—generous ones. Not to mention that the medicines we import take a huge chunk of our profits. Running an extraordinary, one-of-a-kind clinic like the Hope Institute costs money. So, yes, occasionally we have to be a little creative to get it. I console myself with the fact that the people we get it from are so rich these payments are like pocket change to them."

"Creative. We're talking about smuggling, prescribing and administering illegal drugs, and perpetrating fraud." Walter's mind was racing, searching for answers, for outs.

Clarissa sidestepped his accusations to incline her head quizzically. "Where did all this information come from? Or do I really need to ask? Victoria. I thought we'd convinced her to back off. I see I was wrong."

Walter went very still. "*We? I* spoke to her. What exactly did *you* do to convince her?"

His menacing tone elicited a genuinely puzzled look. "I told you I'd hired someone to keep an eye on her."

"From a distance. Just to make sure she wasn't planning any more surprise visits to the Institute. Not to harass her. And certainly not to harm her."

"*Harm* her? Where did that come from? Leaman follows people. He doesn't hurt them."

"Someone ran Victoria off the road last weekend when she left Greenwich. The police think it was a drunk driver. Was it?"

Twin spots of red appeared in Clarissa's cheeks. "Are you suggesting I'd hire someone to *kill* Victoria?"

"Or just put her out of commission or scare the hell out of her. Did you?"

Clearly, Clarissa was furious. "No. I don't intimidate, incapacitate, or murder people. I cure them—or at least I try. That's what this entire veil of secrecy around the Institute has been for. Further, on a personal note, I've been more of a parent to Victoria than you have."

"Which brings us to Audrey," he bit out, too unnerved to digest, much less address, that personal dig. His eyes narrowed on Clarissa's face. "What really caused Audrey's heart palpitations to become so severe and her breathing so erratic? One of your illegal drugs? Have you been pumping them into my daughter?"

Clarissa slammed down her coffee cup. "Stop making them sound like narcotics, Walter. They're not. They're medications, just like the ones currently used in our country, only better. These just don't happen to be accepted yet by the tediously slow FDA. As for Audrey, you know what happened. She reacted badly to one type of drug, so we switched her to another. She's doing much better now. For her own protection, we're keeping her mildly sedated—just enough so she won't try running off again. And need I remind you that you were the one who begged me to admit her as a patient? That's the only reason she's in the Institute to begin with. You wanted to keep her illness under wraps, while my clinic got her well."

Walter raked a hand through his hair. He couldn't argue that point. It was true.

"You never answered my question," Clarissa reminded him. "Was it Victoria who uncovered all these facts?"

"No," Walter replied, lying as skillfully as he did in court. "Victoria had nothing to do with this, other than to make me uneasy with the questions she raised. You and I both know it's been several years since I personally handled day-to-day legal work for the Institute. So I asked a discreet, reliable source to check into things for me. I just got my answers this morning. They alarmed me—with good reason, I now see."

"Really." She shot him a steely glare, her tone as close to threatening as Clarissa used. "Then I suggest you deal with your alarm *and* your misplaced sense of guilt. Yank Audrey out of the Institute, if that makes you feel better. Believe me, you'd be doing me a favor. She's a constant disruption. As for firsthand, day-to-day dealings with us, you yourself just said it's been some time since you took part in those. Feel free to distance yourself entirely, if it makes your hands feel cleaner. Keep delegating all our work the way you have been. I have no complaints about my current legal counsel. But don't do anything stupid. Any purging of your conscience would be a breach of ethics. You're my attorney. I'm your client. Anything we discuss stays between us."

"It's a little late to invoke attorney-client privilege. I've been advised that the FBI already knows about the drug smuggling."

Clarissa went very still. "What?"

"My source tells me the FBI is about to make arrests." Walter's jaw squared. "I'm not going to prison for you, Clarissa. Not for actions I knew nothing about. I've got to protect myself—and my law firm. I'll do whatever I can to extricate Waters, Kensington, Tatem and Calder from the firestorm that's about to descend. I've worked my whole life to build what I have—I won't lose it by protecting you and your criminal acts." Staunch determination glittered in his eyes. "It's true I represented you in purchasing the Hope Institute. I drafted your legal papers—*all* of them. I built the best damned legal fortress around your precious clinic. I even looked the other way about your patent-pending drugs. But that's all I did."

"Other than making yourself and your firm a fortune in the process," Clarissa threw back at him. "The trust and estate work alone earned you millions."

"Fine. I'll readily admit that, too. But nothing more." He turned, retraced his steps to the door. "As for the attorney I assigned to handle things for you, I intend to speak to him today. In the meantime, I suggest you find yourself a good criminal defense attorney."

Clarissa stared after him, listening as the door slammed and the elevator began its descent.

Behind her, the bedroom door swung open and a bare-chested man stepped out. "That was pretty intense."

"He's on his way to speak with you." She whirled around. "How did the FBI find out—"

"They didn't." He held up his cell phone. "I just heard from Leaman. He's across the street, just outside the park. You'll never guess who's there, pacing up and down Fifth Avenue and casting furtive glances at the apartment."

"Victoria?"

"None other. Leaman lost her for a while, right outside Waters, Kensington, Tatem and Calder, where it seems she made an early-morning stop. When she zipped out of there and jumped into a cab, he had a hunch she might be on her way here. He was right. So you tell me, where did Walter Kensington get his information? From his daughter. A daughter he's protecting. And a daughter whom we've had followed and whose phones we've had tapped for the past two weeks. Had Victoria visited or spoken with the FBI, we'd be the first to know. It's a bluff. Regardless, we can't leave things as they are. The Institute will have to be cleaned up—at least until this potential fiasco dies down."

"Cleaned up?" Clarissa repeated in appalled disbelief. "You mean, destroy the medications?"

"Just the current supply," he clarified swiftly. "We only have to look squeaky clean for a while, in case Victoria does go to the authorities. It's just a precaution—but a necessary one, in light of the previous visit the feds paid to the Hope Institute. We'll dispose of the drugs, the urns, the tapes—everything that might incriminate the Institute. Then Victoria can make as much noise as she wants to. There'll be no evidence. She and the authorities will be forced to let it go. After which, it's business as usual."

Clarissa gave a reluctant nod. "I suppose that's our only option. But I'll want a new shipment as soon as possible."

"You'll have it." Preoccupied with the current situation, he frowned. "No matter how fast our maintenance staff works, it will take a couple of days to clean up the whole Institute. In the meantime, Victoria can't be trusted to leave things alone. And obviously, neither can her father." He walked over to the window, shifted the curtain, and peered out. "Leaman's going to keep me posted. I'll wait till he tells me Victoria's left. Then I'll get her alone and put out the fire."

Clarissa leveled a wary stare at her lover. "Put out the fire—how?"

He smiled, walking over and putting his arms around her. "Nothing dramatic. I'm hardly the Clint Eastwood type. I'll just find an effective way to sidetrack Victoria until our cleanup is over. As for her father, he trusts me. I'll win him over. Relax, darling. I'm *very* convincing when I want to be." He lowered his head and nuzzled the side of her neck. "You, of all people, should know that."

"I do." She held herself back. She still wasn't certain, and she intended to be, before she let herself sink into his sexual spell. "That accident Walter was talking about—I'm assuming it was a drunk driver who ran Victoria off the road."

"Um-hum." His fingers slipped inside her robe, cupped her breasts.

"I'm not being coy. I'm asking you a question."

"And I'm answering it." He unbelted the robe and let it slip to the floor, walking her backward until she was pressed up against the wall. He pinned her there as he unzipped his pants and wedged his thighs between hers. "I had nothing to do with Victoria's accident. I was still at the party, watching you, and wishing I could do this."

In one fierce, uncompromising motion, he entered her.

33

Victoria had made her decision.

She was going to confront her uncle, and he was going to explain this nightmare away. To hell with being rational. She refused to believe that Jim Kensington, the wonderful, honorable man who dedicated his life to helping others and who'd been the closest thing to a confidante she ever had, was the CEO of the Hope Institute. There had to be another explanation.

She waited until her father had jumped into a taxi and sped away. Then she marched across the street and up to Leonard.

"Your father left, Miss Kensington."

"I saw. I want to speak with my uncle. Please call up and tell him I'm on my way."

Leonard frowned. "Dr. Kensington's at his office. He won't be back until after two."

She stared Leonard down. He wasn't going to deter her—not this time. "He can't be at his office. I've been standing across the street all this time watching the apartment. I never saw him leave."

"He left at seven-thirty. That was before you got here the first time."

"But you told me my father went up to see Dr. Kensing . . ." Victoria broke off, awareness exploding in her head like fireworks.

Dr. Kensington . . . *Clarissa?*

My God, that had never occurred to her. Not in this case. Normally, she always clarified which Dr. Kensington Leonard was referring to. But in connection with her father? Never. He scarcely acknowledged his brother's wife, other than to exchange niceties at family gatherings. She was an accepted appendage to a brother with whom he already had a strained relationship—a relationship that had become even more strained when Clarissa joined the family. As it was, Jim almost always took Victoria's side. Once Clarissa was added to the balance, Walter's hold on his daughter became even more tenuous.

The thought of Clarissa and her father doing business together was crazy . . .

"Miss Kensington?" Leonard asked anxiously. "Are you all right?"

She forced herself to focus. "Leonard, when you said my father demanded to see Dr. Kensington, did you mean my *aunt?*"

The doorman became totally flustered. "I thought you knew that. Yes, it was your aunt he insisted on seeing. But please, Miss Kensington, don't jump to conclusions," he begged, shaken by Victoria's mortified expression. "It really was about business. Your father isn't *involved* with Dr. Kensington. I know that for a fact." He mopped his brow, frantically searching for a way to console her.

The irony of Leonard's claim made her insides clench. "I wish you were right," she managed in a tight, bitter voice.

Her tangible distress seemed to push him over the edge. "I promise you, there's nothing going on between them," he blurted, divulging a truth he assumed would be far less unpalatable than the one she was contemplating. "Your father almost never comes by here unless your uncle's home, and when he does, he only stays a few minutes. It's that other, younger fellow Dr. Kensington's having a fling with—the one who's been upstairs with her since before your father got here."

All the noise in Victoria's head converged into a pinpoint of silence. "What younger fellow?"

She was on overdrive when she left her aunt and uncle's apartment. Automatically, she crossed the street and walked down to the park entrance. True, she wasn't dressed for a run. But a walk would do her a world of good. She needed to clear her head and plan her strategy.

She went straight to her familiar path and strode briskly around the reservoir, the events of the past few hours darting around in her head like stray bullets.

Especially Leonard's revelations.

He hadn't been happy about divulging the information, not about Clarissa Kensington. But once Victoria explained that her focus wasn't on her aunt's sexual indiscretions, but on something bigger, something criminal and dangerous that might impact her aunt, he relented, willingly telling Victoria what she wanted to know.

She was well aware she'd misled him into thinking he was helping Clarissa rather than incriminating her. But whatever guilt that realization elicited was minimal, compared to the urgency of getting at the truth.

Well, now she had that truth.

The question was, what was she going to do about it?

From a legal perspective, Clarissa's role as the Hope Institute CEO was, in itself, still speculation. Victoria had nothing to go on but circumstantial evidence: her father's urgent trip to the penthouse and the telling reference he'd made to Leonard about the business matter he and Dr. Kensington were involved in that was about to blow up.

On the other hand, combined with the rest of what Leonard had told her—the affair Clarissa was having, the detailed, incriminating description of her lover, the snatches of conversation he could recall the two of them having—it should be enough for Meyer to bring them in for questioning. After which, the FBI could quickly find the proof they needed. Search warrants would be issued. Her father's records and those of the Hope Institute would be confiscated.

So would those of that other slimy bastard. And his records would probably be the most telling of all.

Victoria's fists clenched at her sides. She should have realized another lawyer at Waters, Kensington, Tatem & Calder had picked up where her father had left off, taking over the Institute's legal affairs. It explained her father's shock that the drugs the Institute was administering weren't really proprietary combinations developed in-house. It also explained his shock at finding out how the Institute was committing fraud, collecting money from relatives who believed their loved ones were still alive. *And* it explained why her reference to the FBI seemed to come at him out of left field. If Miss Evans *had* called Waters, Kensington, Tatem & Calder to alert them to the FBI's unsettling preliminary visit, that call had obviously been routed to a different desk.

Walter Kensington was uninformed and, at least currently, uninvolved. There were too many holes, too many things he didn't know that he should have—*if* he were the Institute's active legal counsel.

No, he definitely wasn't pulling the strings.

That didn't diminish his culpability. Not with his signature on every document.

In short, he was being shafted, big-time.

Did he know about Clarissa's lover? Did he know who he was, how deeply involved he was with her criminal activities, how profoundly his guilt impacted Waters, Kensington, Tatem & Calder?

If not, he was about to.

It was up to her to open her father's eyes. That, if nothing else, would convince him to turn over what he had and help the feds. It would mobilize the damage control he'd be desperate to provide for his law firm. And as a result, it would soften his punishment and accelerate the FBI's investigation by leaps and bounds.

She had to go that route. First her father. Then the FBI. For his sake, and for hers. The more concrete evidence she had, the stronger the FBI's case would be.

She made her way to the park's East Seventy-ninth Street exit.

Her apartment was just a few blocks away. She'd go there and see if, by some chance, her father had called. If not, she'd call him. The deadline had changed. Everything had changed. She'd give him one shot, hoping he'd believe her and fill in all the missing pieces. But even if he refused, her next step was to call Meyer and tell him everything. Confirmation or not, the FBI had to charge into the Hope Institute and make arrests—now, before Clarissa reacted to what she'd been confronted with.

Victoria reached her building, glancing around as she climbed the steps. Abruptly, she recalled Zach's advice to stay close to the hotel and away from places that would make her a walking target for Mr. Cigar. Taking a jaunt around Central Park had been a pretty stupid idea. Still, he wouldn't think to look for her there. She hadn't taken her morning run since he started following her. Having lost her in a taxi heading north on Park, he'd probably check out her office, Zach's hotel . . .

And her apartment.

Her fingers trembled a little as she groped for her keys, forcing herself not to turn and scrutinize the area. Okay, fine. He might be out here, waiting to see if she came by. It was up to her to make it look as if she were stopping home for a change of clothes before returning to her love nest. As for the phone calls she'd make in the process, he and his audio friend would never know about them. She'd use her secure cell phone.

Feigning composure, she let herself in, heaving a huge sigh of relief when she was up the stairs and inside her apartment, the door locked behind her.

She went straight to the answering machine. Nothing yet. Then again, her father had a lot to digest. He was probably back at his desk, trying to decide the best way to handle things so he and his law firm would be protected.

Well, she was about to influence his decision.

She opened her purse, yanked out her cell phone, and began punching in the number as she headed for the living room sofa.

"Hang up. Now."

Victoria froze, her finger on the fourth digit of her father's private line. Reflexively, she turned, her eyes widening as she saw the gun aimed at her head. Without a word, she pressed End and lowered her arm to her side.

"Good. Now put the phone on the end table—the one next to you."

She complied. By that time, her shock had diminished, and she leveled a cool, appraising stare at her assailant. "Do they teach breaking and entering at Harvard?"

Ian's smile was as flawless as ever. "Some skills you learn outside the classroom."

"And the gun?"

"That's for protection. Besides, I don't plan on using it. I won't need to. Not that it isn't loaded—it is. But, in this case, it's just a little motivation to keep your attention while I explain what's at stake. Once you understand the options, I can put the gun away."

"Cocky as ever. Tell me, how did you know where I was?"

"Leaman. He's like Santa Claus. He *always* knows where you are."

"Leaman." Victoria arched a brow. "Ah, Mr. Cigar has a name."

Ian chuckled. "I'm sure he has several. Leaman's the only one he's shared with me. We don't exactly travel in the same social circles. In any case, you thought you lost him, but he's pretty effective. He caught up with you outside your aunt's apartment. As luck would have it, he also heard bits and pieces of both your chats with Leonard. It was enough to make me realize you knew about Clarissa and me. So when you went on your stroll through the park, I hung around. I had a feeling you'd be stopping by to give your father a call. Leaman confirmed you were headed in this direction. I just beat you here."

Victoria thought about that, grimly dismissing the notion that help would be forthcoming. Even if Atkins was nearby and had seen Ian go into her building, it wouldn't raise any red flags. Ian looked like a walking ad for Brooks Brothers. Hardly a threat.

So she was on her own.

Fine. First, she had to find out just what Ian thought she knew, and how much of it was accurate.

"You made your point," she acknowledged, wishing he'd put down the damned gun. "I'm all ears. Tell me where things stand and what my options are."

He gestured toward the living room. "To begin with, I want you far away from the door and the phone. Let's have a seat on the sofa. There's no reason we can't be comfortable while we talk. We'll be leaving soon enough." A quick glance around. "You have a charming place here."

"Glad you approve." She shot a sideways look at the end table and the cell phone lying on it. Talk about a double-edged sword. She needed that phone, especially since Ian obviously planned on moving her somewhere. On the other hand, she couldn't take it. And not only because Ian would stop her, but also because she'd couldn't risk him finding out it wasn't her regular cell. If he did, the entire plot she, Zach, and the FBI had concocted would be at risk, and Zach would be in the Hope Institute without a lifeline.

So that avenue of escape was out.

She had to find another.

Slowly, she followed Ian's instructions, walking into the living room ahead of him. As she neared the sofa, her gaze fell on her left hand and, impulsively, she tugged off her engagement ring and slipped it in her blazer pocket. Yesterday Ian had asked an awful lot of questions about her relationship with Zach. Whatever he had in mind for her, he probably wanted her as un-tied-down as possible so she wouldn't be missed—except maybe in bed. What's more, if he knew she and Zach were engaged, he might start wondering how deeply involved Zach had been in helping her check out the Hope Institute. And that was the last thing she wanted. Right now, Zach needed a low profile. Because, right now, he was David Karr.

She sank down on the sofa and crossed her legs. "Okay. No door. No phone. I'd offer you a drink, but it's kind of hard to be a good hostess while being held at gunpoint."

"True." Amusement flashed in Ian's eyes as he lowered himself to the loveseat across from her, angling himself so he could effectively block any attempt she made to run by. "I'm not a violent man, Victoria. But, I'm also not one who lets anything stand in the way of something I want. As you know, I want a senior partnership at Waters, Kensington, Tatem and Calder—*badly*. I intend to have it. I'll do whatever I have to to make sure of that."

"That much I know. The nonviolent part I have to question—at least at this particular moment." She cast an uneasy glance at his weapon.

"Fair enough." With a nod, he reached in his pocket and whipped out a cell phone. "Let's get rid of the need for the gun, shall we?" He indicated the phone, then placed it on the cushion beside him. "I have the number for the Hope Institute punched in. With one press of the send button, I can ring through and arrange for medication to be administered to any particular patient—including a patient who needs something permanent to ease his—or her—suffering. Granted, those medications are usually reserved for the terminally ill. But in this case, they could find their way into your sister's room." He stopped, letting the impact of his words sink in.

Victoria shot to the edge of the sofa, her features taut, stunned. "You're threatening to kill Audrey?"

"I'm suggesting you don't make me do anything rash. As of now, your sister is on the mend. Oh, she's weak and she's scared. She's also disoriented—a slight side effect that can't be helped. But she's totally unaware of anything that might or might not be going on in the Institute—other than a few unsubstantiated qualms you could easily explain away as the result of her medication; you know, her mind playing tricks on her."

A slight side effect that can't be helped?

"You're keeping her drugged," Victoria realized aloud, unsurprised but sickened. "You and my aunt. You're making sure she doesn't find out anything, or try calling me again. Does my father know?"

Ian gazed steadily at her, those startling blue eyes sharp and unrepentant. "No. Actually, there's a lot your father's not aware of these days. He assigned the Hope Institute to me several years ago. I've been instrumental in making it prosper. Let's say I'm willing to push a few boundaries he won't. Then again, that's as it should be. Your father's where he wants to be. I'm just getting there. As for Audrey, she's only sedated when she becomes overly agitated and tries foolish things like making phone calls. Even then, it's only in limited doses. That's Clarissa's doing. She's very tender-hearted when it comes to you and your sister. Believe me, the sedation is a lot healthier than the potential trouble Audrey could get into. Bottom line? Cooperate with me, and your sister will leave the Institute in far better shape than when she arrived. Otherwise, she might take a sudden turn for the worse."

Frantically, Victoria tried to size him up. How believable was his threat? Would he actually go through with it? He wasn't a killer. On the other hand, he'd never been backed so far into a corner. How he would fight his way out at this point was anyone's guess.

She couldn't take the risk.

"I get it," she said in a tight, controlled voice. "You win. I won't budge. Now put away the gun."

"With pleasure." Ian slipped it in his jacket pocket. "Now, let's talk frankly. You and I both know you have some random theories about the Hope Institute being involved in drug smuggling and fraudulent scams with patients' families. We also know you've led your father to believe the FBI shares your suspicions and are, in fact, ready to make arrests." One dark brow rose. "You're very convincing. You're also lying about the authorities being involved. Leaman has assured me you've made no visits to the FBI field office, or even to the local police precinct. Nor have you called either of them."

Wrong, you son of a bitch, Victoria shot back silently, thinking how effective she and Zach had been as Catherine Hughes and David Karr. Well, that was Ian's loss and her trump card.

In the meantime, she had to play along. "And how would you know that?"

His answer was just what she'd hoped it would be. "Because we've had your phones tapped, here and at your office. Surprised? Don't be. We're thorough. Anyway, no FBI means no immediate threat. So, here's the situation. Suppose for the moment you're right. Suppose we really have been doing all the illegal things you think we have. I'd need a few days to clean up the Institute and get it ready for the authorities, just in case you eventually persuaded the FBI that your suspicions had merit. During those few days, I'd need to keep an eye on you, to be sure you didn't do anything to undermine me. The only way to accomplish that would be to take you with me."

Bingo. If Ian meant what she thought he meant, she'd found her avenue of escape. She wouldn't need her cell phone. She'd have Zach. "Take me with you—where?" she asked, feigning a measured tone that sounded like a front for apprehension.

His ironic smile told her she'd succeeded. "You wanted to get into the Hope Institute so badly? Now's your chance. You can spend the whole weekend there. Monday, too. That's all the time I'll need. After that, if you're a good girl, I'll send you on your way. You can take Audrey with you. Oh, and if you still want to visit the feds, go right ahead."

"Right. By that time, the wiretap on my phones will have vanished as completely and untraceably as your drugs. I'll look like a lunatic and you'll look like a squeaky-clean Park Avenue attorney."

"Exactly. What's more, don't count on any help from your father. I've had him summoned to the Institute for an emergency meeting. He's probably there by now, waiting for me. By the time I've finished presenting my case, he'll believe I've been kept as much in the dark about the drugs as he. We'll be on a joint mission to protect our firm—which will *always* be his top priority. He's not going to be too happy with you once I mention you fabricated the FBI's knowledge of all this. I'm sure he'll agree with my decision to keep you at the Institute as a weekend guest while we do our cleanup. He can stop by your room, if you like. I don't think it will be a pleasant visit."

"You're so sure he'll take your word over mine?"

"There's no proof I lied. There's plenty you did. However, here's a little incentive for you. If you succeed in discrediting me with your father, I'll go to the other senior partners at Waters, Kensington, Tatem and Calder and plead my case. Remember who the official attorney of record for the Hope Institute is. By the time I'm through talking, they'll think your father masterminded everything and set me up to take the fall. He'll be out, his office will be vacant, and I'll get my senior partnership that much sooner." A warning gleam flashed in Ian's eyes. "I don't want it that way, Victoria. I respect your father. He's done a great deal for me. But I'll do it if you force my hand. Is that what you want?"

Victoria gave an amazed shake of her head. "Is there anything you haven't thought of? You're screwing my father out of his partnership. You're screwing Waters, Kensington, Tatem and Calder out of its respectability and its reputation. And you're screwing the families of the Hope Institute patients out of millions of dollars. And, oh yes, my aunt. Her, you're just screwing."

Ian's jaw clenched. "Don't go there, Victoria. My feelings for Clarissa have nothing to do with—"

"With what? With power? With the rush of sleeping with the Institute's CEO? With—pardon my pun—the thrill of being on top?" Victoria's laugh was as humorless as her words. "Save it, Ian. If you're about to tell me how deeply in love with Clarissa you are, don't. You don't know what love is. Evidently, neither does she. That's not my problem. It's yours."

His eyes narrowed. "And your uncle—is it his problem, too?"

"Are you asking if I plan to tell him?"

"Do you?"

"And if I do?" Her chin came up. "Will you come after me again? Kidnap me? Shoot me?"

That chiseled smile again. "None of the above. I'll just watch their marriage fall apart, after which I won't have to talk my way past that pain in the ass, Leonard. You might just be doing me a favor."

"Good. Because I'd be doing one for my uncle, too." Victoria came to her feet. "Can we go now? I want to see my sister."

"Not just yet." Ian rose, blocking her path. "I need you to make two calls. One to your office, the other to the Plaza Athénée. What did you tell Hamilton when you left his suite this morning?"

Ah, she was being grilled about Zach's expectations. No problem. It was good she'd taken off her engagement ring.

"I told him I had some work to take care of at Waters, Kensington, Tatem and Calder."

"And?"

"And what? I'm not in the habit of explaining myself, Ian. Not even to the men I sleep with."

Apparently, her little charade was believable. "Good," Ian replied. "That works out nicely. Still, he'll expect you back at the hotel later today, and your partners will expect you to show up at work on Monday." He gestured toward the end table and her cell phone. "Call them—first Hamilton, then your partners. Keep it brief if they answer. Leave a message if they don't. Say you're tied up in a huge merger at Waters, Kensington, Tatem and Calder—one that sucked you in the minute you made the mistake of walking in on a Saturday morning. You're racing the clock—your meals being delivered, no sleep till the deal's done—you know the drill. Oh, and you're behind closed doors. You can't be reached until Monday afternoon at the earliest. You'll call in if you possibly can. And, Victoria—make it convincing."

Making it convincing wasn't the problem, she mused silently. Making the calls on the phone he was pointing to was. It was the secure cell phone. Her lines were supposed to be tapped. That phone wasn't. Which meant her call to Zach's hotel wouldn't record on Mr. Audio's equipment. Warning one to the Hope Institute. Warning two was worse. Her call to her office—which *was* bugged—*would* record. And if they somehow managed to trace that call . . .

She couldn't let it happen.

"Fine." She shifted uncomfortably. "I'll make the calls. But first, can I use the bathroom?"

Ian studied her, his expression contemplative.

"You're free to check out the bathroom if it will make you feel better," Victoria invited wryly, pointing in that direction. "There are no phones, and the window's too narrow to climb through."

Ian seemed to decide that that level of caution was uncalled for, because he nodded. "Go ahead." He followed

Victoria down the hall, positioning himself between the bathroom and the bedrooms. "I'll wait right here."

"Suit yourself." She went in and shut the door. Taking a few deep breaths, she used the toilet, then washed up, splashing some cold water on her face to recharge her senses. Last, she gathered up a few toiletries and zipped them into a makeup case.

She opened the door, stepped out, and gave Ian a quizzical look. "I assume it's all right if I pack a few things. I didn't think you'd insist on my spending the weekend dirty and in the same clothes."

Again, he nodded, and she crossed over to her bedroom, where she tossed a few pairs of jeans, a couple of sweaters, and some underwear in a bag, along with the makeup case. She heard Ian's footsteps, felt his presence in her doorway.

Good.

She glanced up. "I'm ready. I'll make those calls now, and we can go." She picked up the bedroom telephone, zipping up her suitcase as she did.

She dialed the Plaza Athénée, asked for Zach's room, and got the voice mail she was expecting. She left the message precisely as Ian had said. Then she called her office and did the same.

"Nicely done," Ian commended.

"I aim to please." Victoria wondered if Atkins would find it curious that she was leaving her apartment with a stranger and a suitcase. Maybe. Maybe not. He might just assume Ian was giving her a ride somewhere. It didn't matter. Soon she'd be right where she wanted to be—inside the Hope Institute.

"Shall we?" Ian inquired, as genteel as if he were taking her out to dinner rather than kidnapping her.

"By all means."

34

Walter Kensington was pacing around Conference Room C when Ian walked in twenty minutes later.

"Finally." Walter halted in his tracks, his hazel stare as biting as his tone. "I was in the office. I checked to see if you were in. You weren't. I left a message on your home machine. I was just about to try your cell phone when I got word from Harper."

"I asked him to get in touch with you and suggest we meet here immediately. This situation is explosive." Ian shut the door, anxiety creasing his forehead as he walked over and pressed his palms flat on the large oval table. "As for why you couldn't find me, I was meeting with Clarissa. She called me right after you left. She sounded overwrought. Now I understand why."

"Did you know those drugs she's administering are illegal? That they're being smuggled into the country?" Walter fired out.

"Of course not." Ian's denial was instantaneous. "I believed the same thing you did—that they were legitimate, proprietary medications. I proceeded that way from the start. First I did some patent searches for Clarissa. After that, I recommended a few law firms that specialize in intellectual property. I assumed she took it from there. By now, I expected that the applications had been filed. None of this ever occurred to me."

Walter's expression never changed. "Our only priority is to extricate Waters, Kensington, Tatem and Calder from this mess—now. The FBI is about to make arrests. If we go to them first, it will help us legally and preserve our firm's reputation. I've already advised Clarissa of where I stand on this. To hell with any conflict of interest. I told her to get a criminal lawyer."

"Walter, wait." Ian held up a detaining hand, keeping his tone respectful. "We don't have to panic. We have time. You're wrong about the FBI; they don't know anything about this. Not yet. And by the time they do, we'll be ready for them."

A dark scowl appeared between Walter's brows. "Who told you that—Clarissa? You're a fool if you believe—"

"This isn't about Clarissa. It's about Victoria." Ian pressed his lips together, apology written all over his face. "You're not going to like this. Unfortunately, it's the truth. To begin with, I know you got all your information from Victoria. Leaman saw her go into the office this morning, and he chased her down when she followed you to Clarissa's apartment. Clearly, your daughter pieced together the truth about the drugs and the fraud, and she's trying to protect you by convincing you to disclose privileged information. But in trying to persuade you, she lied. The FBI isn't involved. She's never been in touch with them, much less participated in some covert investigation."

"And just how do you know that?"

"Because Leaman's been following Victoria day and night." A heartbeat of a pause. "And because Harper had her phones bugged."

Again, Walter's hard stare remained unchanged. "The Institute bugged my daughter's phones."

"Yes. It was a precaution, a worthwhile one as it turns out. Harper's the head of security. Clarissa was nervous about what Victoria might know, what Audrey might have told her when she called. So she had Harper put a tap on Victoria's home and office phones. I wasn't any happier than you when I heard about it—which was only a few minutes ago, by the way. The bottom line is, Victoria lied about being in contact with the FBI. She admitted it to me herself."

"You spoke to her?"

"Right after I left Clarissa. I went straight to her apartment."

"I see. And did she happen to tell you how she 'pieced together the truth,' as you put it, without any professional help?"

"She didn't exactly confide in me, so no, I haven't a clue as to how she got her information. But we both know your daughter is incredibly bright and intuitive, not to mention being like a dog with a bone when it comes to getting answers. We also know she's been uneasy about the Institute from the day she saw Audrey in Central Park. Maybe she confided in Clarissa and your brother. Maybe something Clarissa said made her suspicious. I don't know. I'm just speculating. But however Victoria got her facts, I'm grateful as hell she got them. Now—before anyone else did. She saved our firm from ruin and us from prison."

Walter's lips thinned into a tight line. "You sound very confident. How is it you plan on buying us this time you're alluding to and saving us from all criminal implications?"

"I plan to make sure the Institute is totally cleaned up, until there's not a single medication or paper trail that's not a hundred percent aboveboard. I'll personally oversee it. It'll take a couple of days, but all the damning evidence Clarissa's managed to accumulate—from the drugs to whatever discrepancies exist on the dates of patients' deaths versus the dates their families were notified—all of it's going to be destroyed, erased as if it never existed. Clarissa's agreed to cooperate. Not that she has much choice. The alternative is prison for herself and the end of the Hope Institute and everything she's worked for." Ian's palm sliced the air, his tone ringing with certainty. "Once we've finished our overhaul, the FBI is welcome to scrutinize the Institute from top to bottom. They won't find anything."

"A couple of days, you said. Well, you're damned right about that. It'll take at least that long to do what you're suggesting. And during those couple of days, do you honestly believe Victoria is going to sit by and do nothing—with or without FBI contacts? If so, you're a fool. She's probably trying to reach me right now, to get my answer as to whether or not I'll cooperate. After that, she'll decide her conscience is clear. She'll have met her family obligations, given me a chance to minimize my culpability. Her next stop will be the authorities. She's not going to ignore criminal activities to spare me, my reputation, or my firm."

"You're right. She's not." Ian steeled himself, looked Walter straight in the eye. "That's why I brought her here with me."

Walter started. "Here? To the Institute?"

"Yes." Ian didn't avert his gaze. "It was the only logical solution. It buys us the time we need, and it keeps Victoria from doing anything stupid." A pause. "By that I mean anything that might incriminate the Institute and, as a result, get Victoria into trouble." Ian cleared his throat uncomfortably. "I realize that sounds ominous. It's probably an overreaction on my part. After all, Clarissa loves your daughter very much. I doubt she'd ever do anything to harm her. Still, that's under normal conditions. Right now, she's livid. She feels betrayed, as if Victoria's turned on her family and manipulated you by lying about the FBI. She's also coming apart at the seams. You know how much this Institute means to her. It's her life. Honestly, I can't vouch for what she'd do if Victoria managed to get through to the authorities when the Institute was still vulnerable."

"I understand your concern—and Clarissa's distress," Walter replied stiffly. His expression became grim, as if he were about to broach a matter he found thoroughly distasteful. "Where is Victoria now?"

"At the moment, she's in the lounge on the third floor. Harper is keeping an eye on her while the attendants set up her bed. Obviously, I want her to be made as comfortable as possible. Since the Institute has no available rooms, I had Audrey's room converted into a double. The idea seemed to appeal to Victoria. She calmed down a bit when I suggested it."

"That's not a surprise. She's been trying to find a way to see Audrey. Now she'll have that chance."

Fleetingly, Ian gauged Walter's reaction, trying to determine just how angry with Victoria he was. He was outwardly controlled, but Ian could sense that, beneath the surface, he was sizzling.

As expected.

"I'm sure you want to speak with your daughter," Ian said carefully. A quick gesture toward the door. "Go right ahead. I'll get our cleanup under way."

"On the contrary," Walter replied in clipped tones. "I'm not feeling very conversational at the moment. I need to settle down before my daughter and I exchange words. An argument between us would only upset Audrey. The last thing I want is for her to suffer a setback. I want her well and out of this place. Let her have her reunion with her sister. It will do her good. As for Victoria, she'll adapt to her situation. She always does. You've clearly gone out of your way to minimize her inconvenience." He headed toward the door. "I'm getting some air. I'll be back later. Get busy with this cleanup of yours."

"I intend to." Ian shot his mentor a sympathetic look. "I'm sorry about all this. But don't worry. In a few days, it will all be over. And Waters, Kensington, Tatem and Calder will come through this as strong as ever."

"I'm counting on it." Walter brushed by him and stalked out.

Alone in the room, Ian smiled. Everything was going like clockwork.

*   *   *

Walter headed down Seventy-eighth Street, his mind racing. He had to act immediately, before Ian made a trip to the office. So far he hadn't been there. He'd gone straight from his apartment to Clarissa's, then to Victoria's, and finally, to the Institute. Which meant the cleanup efforts hadn't had a chance to extend to Waters, Kensington, Tatem & Calder.

That bought Walter the few hours he needed.

Swiftly, he glanced at his watch. Eleven-thirty.

He paused at the corner, whipped out his cell phone, and punched in Miss Hatterman's home number, thankful that she lived in midtown.

"Hello?"

"Miss Hatterman, it's me. I need you in the office."

"Of course." Crisply efficient as ever, his secretary didn't miss a beat. She was used to sporadic weekend fire drills. "When?"

"Now. It's an emergency. Drop whatever you're doing and leave. But first, call that computer person . . . Lake or Lakes, I think it is. Tell him I need him in, too."

"Lakeman. He lives in Manhattan, so he can get to the office right away—*if* he's home."

"If he's not, find him. Pull his personnel file if you have to. Call his family, his neighbors, whoever. Just get him to the office within the hour. Tell him he'll be well compensated for the inconvenience."

"I'll take care of it." Miss Hatterman cleared her throat. She'd never heard her employer so unsettled. "Mr. Kensington, is everything all right?"

Walter was already on the move, marching to the curb to hail a cab. "No, Miss Hatterman. It's not."

Frank Harper caught the hospital attendant's eye, nodding when he saw him signal from the doorway of the TV room. He turned to Victoria, who was perched stiffly at the edge of her chair, impatience emanating from every pore of her body.

"Okay, Miss Kensington. We can go now."

She jumped to her feet, itching to see Audrey. Hearing Zach's reassurance that she was okay had been wonderful. Seeing it for herself would be better.

"Your room's ready," the burly guard announced.

Victoria arched a derisive brow at him. "Don't you mean *our* room—mine, my sister's, and yours?"

Harper frowned. "No. I told you, the room's hers and yours. I'm just keeping an eye on you. From the hallway."

"Ah, a nanny. How touching."

"Look, lady." He crossed his arms over his chest, his jaw setting in annoyance. "Don't make this any harder than it has to be. I'm not any happier with this arrangement than you are. I've got better things to do than baby-sit a testy broad all weekend. But that's what I've been told to do. You've been bugging me to see your sister for the last half hour. Now I'm saying okay. Do you want to go to your room or not?"

Biting back another flippant reply, Victoria nodded. She might dislike this man and loathe the idea of his guarding her like a common criminal, but antagonizing him would be stupid. She wanted to see Audrey. And she had an agenda— one in which time was of the essence. Harper could be either a mere nuisance—one that could be skirted with minimal effort—or a full-scale pain in the ass who planted himself in her face and made things very difficult for her.

It was up to her to ensure he turned out to be the former.

Keeping her mouth shut, she followed Harper out of the lounge, around the bend, down the corridor, and past the nurse's station. He went two rooms farther, then stopped outside an open door, gesturing for her to go in.

"And before you start bitching about privacy and harassment and whatever else you were spouting before, I'm not coming in," he informed her. "I don't give a damn what you and your sister talk about or if you walk around stark naked. As long as you stay in that room, do what you want. Okay?"

"Fine." Victoria hurried by him, her mind already on the kind of state she'd find Audrey in.

Her gaze flickered from the bed that had been set up for her to the one adjacent to it—the one that held her sister. At last. After two long, apprehensive weeks, she was going to see Audrey, get firsthand proof that she was all right.

What she saw was better than what she'd expected.

Audrey's bed was elevated so she was raised into a half-sitting position. Her dark hair was neatly brushed, and it fanned across the pillow beneath her head. The sheet was drawn to her waist, exposing the upper half of her torso, which was clad in the familiar yellow hospital gown. Even through the shapeless gown, Victoria could see that her sister's breathing was slow and even, and that most of her previous bloating had gone down. Her body looked close to normal, as did the color in her cheeks. And there was no intravenous tube—in fact, no tubes of any kind—attached to her. Whatever medication she was receiving, albeit illegal, she was able to ingest it on her own.

Thank God.

"Audrey," Victoria murmured, moving to her sister's bedside.

Audrey turned her head at the sound of Victoria's voice, her eyelids fluttering open. Seeing her sister, her entire face lit in a weak but thankful smile, her relief as acute as if she'd been thrown a lifeline. "They said you were here. I thought maybe I'd dreamed it."

"Well, you didn't." Victoria's voice trembled as she perched on the edge of the bed and brushed Audrey's hair off her forehead. "I came the minute they let me." She leaned over, hugged her sister, and felt tears sting her eyes. Funny, she'd gone months on end without seeing Audrey, yet this two-week separation was the longest of her life. "How are you, sweetie?"

"Better." Audrey hugged her back. Her motions were sluggish, as was her speech. Victoria wasn't surprised. Clearly, it was the effects of whatever Ian and Clarissa were giving her—not for the bulimia, but to keep her sedated. "I'm still tired. But I'm eating." She paused, wet her lips. "Father visits a lot. He actually seems worried about me. Oh, he's also furious. But that's par for the course when it comes to me."

Audrey frowned, rolling her head from side to side as if to clear it. "I called you. This place is weird. I can't explain it. It's like they want me well, but until I am, they're keeping me drugged up. I'm always so out of it. I sound paranoid, I know. Maybe I am. They say it's the effects of the medicine. It probably is. But when I say I don't need it, they say I do. And Miss Rivers, the one who administers the stuff, she gives me the creeps. I told Father that. He got annoyed at me, of course, for bugging him again. But he did ask them to assign me different nurses, not her. They went along with the request. I like the other nurses much better. Especially Miss Groves, who's incredibly sweet and caring. Miss Rivers still comes in, but now it's just at medicine time."

Audrey paused, wet her lips again. "I always feel so groggy after my medicine. So out of it. I hate that."

Victoria's grip on her sister tightened. "But you're okay otherwise? In between the medicine, I mean. You're feeling stronger?"

"Yes. Much." Audrey swallowed hard. "I'm sorry, Victoria. I didn't mean to screw up again. I was doing so well, painting, feeling like I'd found myself, found where I belonged. Then I met Rolando, and everything just fell apart." Another hard swallow, as she battled her self-pitying impulses. "I became a victim all over again."

"Audrey, listen to me." Victoria drew back, noting the strength Audrey was striving for—a new and promising effort. Normally, she ran from her problems. This time, she seemed ready to face them.

Maybe something good had come from this ordeal after all.

"Sweetie, you're not a victim, not in the way you mean."

Victoria restrained herself from blurting out the whole ugly truth about the Hope Institute, knowing this wasn't the time. "It could be you needed the fiasco with Rolando to make you realize how strong you are. Maybe you had to go through all this to see how much you have to live for, and to be willing to fight for it." Victoria squeezed her sister's hands. "Everything's going to be fine," she assured her, meaning it now more than ever. "It's going to happen a lot sooner than you think. I can't explain now, but you have to trust me. We're going to get you out of here, get you settled where you'll be happy. You'll start seeing Dr. Osborne again. He can help you—without all this medicine."

"Yes, he can. And I can, too." Audrey's jaw set. Even in her weakened state, it was obvious she meant every word. "This time I'm going to get well. Not just for a while, for good. I'm determined."

"So am I." Victoria smiled. "We'll take this on together."

But first I have to get to Zach, she thought for the hundredth time since Ian had ushered her from her apartment. *I have to. The clock is ticking.*

As if in answer to her prayers, the door opened and a slim young nurse entered the room, carrying two lunch trays. "You must be Audrey's sister," she greeted Victoria. "I've heard glowing stories about you. I'm Miss Simmons."

Victoria rose, went over to relieve the nurse of one tray. "It's a pleasure, Miss Simmons. Audrey was just telling me how wonderful you've all been to her. I can't thank you enough." She placed the tray beside her bed, turning as Miss Simmons settled the other tray on Audrey's stand and swiveled it around so her patient could reach it easily.

"Audrey's a delightful patient." The nurse's lips quirked. "Except when she scares us to death by dragging herself out of bed and disappearing."

"I wanted to reach Victoria," Audrey replied, her forehead creased in rueful apology. "I didn't go far—just to the phone. I felt terrible about scaring you."

"All that matters is that you weren't hurt. And now there's no need to jeopardize your health again. Your sister is right here with you." Miss Simmons turned to give Victoria a genuine smile.

"Yes, I am." Victoria trusted her instincts and acted. "While we're on the subject, I'd really like to personally thank some of the other nurses who've cared for Audrey. I've spotted a few of them, but I can't seem to find Miss Groves. And Audrey speaks so highly of her."

A nod. "Beatrice is one of our best. She's an amazing nurse, with a heart of gold. Normally, you'd have no trouble finding her. She drops in on each patient at least once a day. This week and next are a little different. She's been assigned to one specific patient during that time. That explains why you haven't seen her."

"Really." Victoria feigned concern. "That poor person must be terribly ill to require a private nurse. I can imagine how busy Miss Groves must be. Still, I'd like to stop by and thank her, even if it's only for a minute. I promise not to keep her."

Miss Simmons was adjusting Audrey's bed so she was in a comfortable position to eat. "That shouldn't be a problem. She's on the second floor. Room 214. Just get her attention from the doorway. No one is permitted in Mr. Karr's room but Beatrice."

Room 214. That's where she'd find Zach.

"I'll do that. Thank you, Miss Simmons." Victoria forced herself to sit down and eat. Actually, she realized with some surprise, her insides were actually gnawing with hunger. She'd hadn't had a thing all day, other than the two cups of coffee she'd downed right before Zach's crack-of-dawn phone call. It wouldn't help for her to faint in the corridor. She needed every bit of her strength to get through the next few hours.

She'd eaten half her turkey and green beans when Miss Simmons excused herself and left the room, saying she'd be back in a half hour to collect the trays.

Victoria's gaze followed her exit, and she frowned as she spied Frank Harper lounging against the wall across from their room.

He was her next obstacle.

She stood and went over to Audrey, relieved to see her sister had eaten almost everything on her plate.

"The food here's better than at most hotels," Audrey declared, noting Victoria's scrutiny. A look of grateful comprehension flickered across her face. "I'm holding everything down. Stop worrying."

Victoria grinned. "That's going to be a tough habit to break. I've been worrying about you since we were kids. It's an older sister's right." She edged a glance at the door.

Audrey's lighthearted mood vanished, and dread filled her eyes. "You're not leaving already? You just got here."

The panic in her sister's voice tore at her heart. "No, sweetie, I'm not leaving." *And when I do, you'll be with me,* she added silently. "But I'd like to find Miss Groves now, while I know where she is. If it's lunchtime, she and the patient she's assigned to will be in his room."

A reluctant nod. "But you'll come back."

"By the time you've eaten your last crumb of banana cream pie and washed it down with milk," Victoria assured her teasingly.

A soft laugh escaped Audrey's lips as she recognized a promise Victoria used to make in their childhood. The laugh was music to Victoria's ears, as was the hope in her sister's eyes. In just thirty minutes, Audrey already looked better than when Victoria had walked in. Her color was rosier, her strength improved. The sooner she got out of this place, the faster she'd heal.

That prompted another concern.

"Audrey, when is your next dose of medicine due?"

"Not until three o'clock." She rolled her eyes. "I'm in no hurry."

"I don't blame you."

Three o'clock. That gave her plenty of time. There'd be no more sedatives if Victoria had her way. "Okay, sweetie, you eat up," she urged. "I'll be back soon."

She headed for the door.

Time to bulldoze her way around Frank Harper.

The guard looked up when she stepped into the hall. "Need something?"

In this case, direct was best. The less said, the less chance there was of arousing suspicion.

"Actually, yes," Victoria replied, an announcement rather than a request. If she asked, the answer might be no. "There's a nurse I need to see. She was especially kind to my sister. She's assigned to Room 214. I'm going downstairs to thank her personally."

He shrugged. "Yeah, okay. But I'm going with you. Oh, and you can't walk inside that particular room. Doctor's orders. I'll have to catch the nurse's eye and ask her to come out."

"Fair enough."

They took the elevator down. The ride was silent, partly because Harper wanted nothing to do with her, and partly because Victoria's mind was racing. There were so many potential snags to this plan. First, Zach and Beatrice had to be in the room. Assuming they were, Harper planned to rap on the door to get Beatrice's attention—which meant Victoria had to find a way to camouflage Beatrice's reaction when she came face-to-face with her. The woman was doing a fantastic job of helping them. But she wasn't a professional actress. She was bound to look startled when she saw Victoria standing there. And startled wouldn't do, not when, supposedly, she and Victoria had never met. As if that weren't enough, Victoria would then have to get permission to enter David Karr's room. The only one who could give her that was the reclusive Mr. Karr himself. Which meant praying Zach could come up with something brilliantly resourceful without a moment's planning time.

The *if*'s were limitless. She couldn't let herself think about them. She simply *had* to make it happen.

The elevator stopped. The doors slid open.

"It's this way," Harper said, pointing.

"Thanks." Victoria walked ahead of him, counting the numbers above the doors until she reached her goal.

She peeked through the glass pane on Room 214's door. Beatrice and Zach were both inside.

They were sitting near the windows, eating lunch at a small round table. Beatrice was smiling and chatting, and Zach—or rather, David Karr—was staring broodingly into his food, pushing it around as if he were angry with it.

Victoria took advantage of the few seconds of impulse time she had to act.

Even as she heard Harper's "Remember, no one's allowed . . ." she pushed open the door, and poked her head in the room.

"Excuse me, are you Miss Groves?" she blurted out before Beatrice could look up, much less react. "If so, may I speak with you for a moment? I'm Audrey Kensington's sister."

"Hey." Harper grabbed her arm and yanked her away from the door. "I told you not to go in there. Sorry, Miss Groves," he apologized, glaring at Victoria. "This visitor has trouble following instructions."

"That's all right." Beatrice rose, Victoria's diversionary tactics having given her ample time to compose herself. "Audrey's sister, did you say?" She headed toward the door, a questioning look on her face.

"She's very pretty," David Karr commented, inclining his head in their direction. "Who is she, Mother? And who's she visiting?"

Beatrice paused. "Her name is Ms. Kensington. She's visiting her sister."

"Then why is she in my room?"

"To talk to me. Only for a minute," Beatrice added hastily. "I'll be right back to finish our lunch."

David Karr frowned. "Why does she want to talk just to you? Did Miss Rivers tell her I'm crazy? Because I'm not. The doctors said so when they sent me here."

Victoria took Zach's cue. "Of course I don't think you're crazy," she assured him, tugging her arm free of Harper's grasp and taking a step into the room. "I just thought you wanted your privacy. I didn't want to disturb you. So I was going to talk to Miss Groves out here. I apologize if I've offended you."

"You're very polite. Most people are nosy and rude. That's why I don't want them around me. *You* can come in." He gestured at his tray. "Did you eat lunch yet?"

"Yes, I did." Victoria didn't dare lie. Not with Harper breathing down her neck. Her gaze skimmed Zach's lunch tray. "But I didn't have time for coffee. Maybe I could have a cup with you and Miss Groves before I go back to my sister's room."

A pleased nod. "Yes, that would be good." He scowled in Harper's direction. "I don't want him in here."

Victoria inclined her head at the guard. "It seems Mr. Karr and I have something in common. Neither of us likes you."

Harper shot her a lethal look. "Lady, you are one colossal pain in the ass." He waved her away. "Go ahead in. Do whatever you want. I can't wait till you're out of my hair altogether."

"I second that," Victoria replied sweetly. She went into the room and shut the door, accompanying Beatrice back to the low table by the windows. As she walked, she expressed her thanks to Beatrice, clearly and audibly, for the excellent care she'd taken of Audrey—just in case her voice carried into the hall.

The area by the windows was definitely out of earshot.

With feigned calm, knowing they were probably being observed, Victoria pulled over another chair, positioning it at the table so her back was to the door. She was going to be doing most of the talking, and she didn't want her lips read.

She waited until Beatrice had joined them to begin.

"Thanks, both of you. You were unbelievably quick on your feet—"

"Are you all right?" Zach interrupted to mutter.

"Fine," she assured him as Beatrice poured three cups of coffee.

"What the hell are you doing at the Institute?"

"I was brought here." Victoria took the cup. "I'll talk. You listen. I'm not in any immediate danger. I'm being held at the clinic for insurance purposes. I know too much. They want me under their thumb until they've finished destroying all the evidence you ran by me this morning. They're doing that now, even as we speak." She sipped her coffee. "I'll supply facts now, and save details for later. My aunt Clarissa's the Hope Institute's CEO. She buys drugs from the syndicate as a kind of self-appointed vigilante for her clinic—you know, a last hope for despondent patients. My father had no idea she was smuggling illegal drugs into the country. He thought the medications were legal. He's totally out of the loop when it comes to the Institute. It's been years since he handled their legal affairs."

"Then who's taken over?"

"Ian Block. He's running the whole show. He broke into my apartment, held me at gunpoint, and told me he'd have Audrey killed if I didn't come with him to the Institute. He's getting rid of anything that's incriminating over the next few days, so the place is clean if the FBI arrives. He and his cronies are probably in the crematorium right now, burning containers and floppy disks." She angled her head from Beatrice to Zach and smiled, as if they were chatting. "But, we've got an ace. Ian thinks I'm lying about working with the feds."

"Because Mr. Cigar and the phone bugs turned up nothing," Zach confirmed.

"Right. Which means you have to call Meyer right away. Get him in here before Ian's managed to flush or incinerate the evidence."

Zach nodded, taking a bite of turkey and chewing it thoroughly. "The rooms here are all filled. Where did Block put you?"

"In Audrey's room. My sister doesn't know anything about what's going on here. She only knows that the place is weird. As for my showing up, she thinks I'm just here for a visit."

"It's better that way for now." Zach leaned forward to add some milk to his coffee, effectively hiding his face from view. "Go back to her room. I'll call Meyer. He's going to need at least an hour to get the warrants. That means I'll have to slow down Block's cleanup by throwing a monkey wrench in his plans."

"How?"

"Let's not waste time on explanations. If I accomplish what I intend to, you'll see for yourself in a few minutes. Trust me. In the meantime, stay put. Get Audrey ready to leave. Tell her you've arranged for her to go home with you. That'll keep her calm. I know where her room is. I'll come get you both." Zach gave Victoria one long searching look. "You're sure you're okay? That son of a bitch didn't hurt you?"

A wry smile tugged at Victoria's lips. "Which son of a bitch are you referring to? Ian? Or that lug who's guarding me?"

Zach didn't smile back. "Don't push Harper, Victoria. He's obviously part of Block's inner circle, just like Mr. Cigar. Only Harper's more dangerous. My gut tells me so. In fact, I wouldn't be surprised if he's the one who shoved us off the road."

Victoria started. On the verge of firing questions, she caught Zach's eye and fell silent. Later. They'd fill each other in on the missing pieces then. For now, she nodded. "Okay. And to answer your question, I'm fine. No one's done anything worse than threaten me. But, Zach, Harper's outside my door like a doberman. So be careful when you show up." She set down her cup. "I'd better get back." She patted Beatrice's hand. "You've been sensational," she murmured. "It's almost over."

Beatrice's sigh was shaky. "I'll be very relieved when it is."

Coming to her feet, Victoria said aloud, "I'd better see how my sister is doing. It was nice to meet you, Mr. Karr. And, Miss Groves, thank you again for your sensitivity where Audrey is concerned. Her condition is very fragile. You made all the difference."

With a cordial smile, she left the room. Frank Harper, who'd been hovering just outside the door, straightened when she emerged. Giving her a dark look, he escorted her back to the elevator.

Zach watched them go, slicing and chewing another bite of his turkey. Then he met Beatrice's gaze, jerking his head in the direction of his private bathroom. "I'm going in there to call Meyer. I'll need a minute. Keep your eye on the door to my room, although I doubt anyone will come by. And get my wheelchair ready. I'll be taking a little jaunt."

Beatrice picked up her napkin and dabbed at the corners of her mouth. "Where to?"

"The basement."

35

"There you go, sir. You're in." Harvey Lakeman, the network administrator at Waters, Kensington, Tatem & Calder, stepped away from the computer in Ian's office, gesturing for Walter Kensington to take over. "You should be able to access whatever it is of Mr. Block's that you need."

Walter nodded, stepping forward and staring at the screen. His gaze lifted, moved from Lakeman to Miss Hatterman and back. "Listen to me, both of you. I want you to go out to the secretarial area and wait. No one is to come near this office. No one. That includes Mr. Block. Those are my orders, and I take full responsibility for whatever you have to do to carry them out. Further, what's going on here today stays among the three of us. It's not to be discussed—not with anyone. It's highly confidential, even within the firm. Is that understood?"

"Of course," Miss Hatterman acknowledged, curious but unquestioning.

Lakeman murmured his agreement, as well.

"Good. Then, if you'll both excuse me, I have work to do."

His two employees bid a hasty retreat.

Walter stalked over, locked the door behind them.

Then he returned to the computer. Bending over the screen, he scowled, one hand gripping the mouse, the other accessing the keyboard. He had to dig up the facts. *All* the facts.

He'd been on the verge of calling Victoria to supply

Clarissa's name when Harper's call had come through, instructing him to go straight to the Institute. He'd hoped the meeting with Ian would supply him with answers. Instead, it only raised more questions.

Then again, perhaps those questions *were* the answers.

He could read Ian Block like a book. Maybe because he reminded him so much of himself at that age. He'd seen Ian's extraordinary potential, and had been instrumental in hiring him. Like Walter, Ian was shrewd, ambitious, Harvard-educated. His mind was a steel trap, his instincts keen. He had everything necessary to make senior partner some day. He was a first-class, brilliant attorney.

Too brilliant to be oblivious to his clients' activities. Especially a client as important as Clarissa.

On the other hand, maybe he wasn't so brilliant after all. Maybe his ego had overtaken his intellect. Because he'd underestimated the very man who had trained him, the man whose mind was one step ahead of his.

He was a fool if he thought Walter had bought his story. He hadn't.

Poring over the files, Walter searched for any applicable patent searches Ian might have conducted and saved over the past six or seven years. Nothing. Next, he scanned the archived correspondence, looking for a note, letter, or e-mail Ian might have exchanged with some of Manhattan's most prominent intellectual-property law firms—one in which they discussed Ian's referral of the Hope Institute to them. Again, nothing. He even went so far as to check for patent filings or drafts of patent applications showing the specific drug combinations the Hope Institute was filing for, or even memoranda of invention.

No such forms or correspondence had been forwarded to the patent office.

When he finally did find a Hope Institute–related file he didn't recognize, he opened it immediately. And what he saw made his stomach turn.

A permit application made out to the Centers for Disease Control in the name of the Hope Institute, requesting consent to import body fluids from South America. And with it, a letter to some South American drug company, clearly meant to accompany the CDC's accepted application. It began, "Enclosed are copies of the CDC form for importation of agreed-upon medical specimens," and went on to instruct the drug company how to append the forms to their shipments to avoid problems at U.S. customs.

Walter stared at the evidence for one long, sickened moment.

Then he seized the mouse, selected the incriminating pages, and clicked on the print function. While the printer did its job, he leaned over and punched the intercom feature on Ian's telephone. "Miss Hatterman, are you out there?"

"Of course, Mr. Kensington," she responded from the secretarial area.

"Good. Get Charlie Boughman on the phone."

"The DA? Certainly."

"Tell him this isn't about rescheduling our golf game. It's business—urgent business. I need to meet with him. *Right now.*"

Victoria found Audrey sitting up in bed, drawing in a sketchpad. It was amazing, she noted with a renewed surge of anger, how much stronger and more coherent her sister was when her medication—*and* that damned sedative—had started wearing off.

Well, this time they were wearing off for good.

Audrey spotted her and put down the pad, smiling and beckoning her in.

"You're drawing," Victoria observed, shutting the door carefully behind her—a tangible barrier between her and Frank Harper.

"Um-hum. It's nothing great, just some pencil sketches. That's all I have strength for now. But it's a start."

"It sure is." Victoria pulled a chair over to the bed. She had to handle this just right, give Audrey enough of the truth so she'd comply without divulging anything to anyone, but not so much that it scared her to death. "Sweetie, I've got a few things to talk to you about."

Audrey squirmed onto her elbows, the effort taxing her more than Victoria would have liked. "What kind of things?" she asked warily.

"Good things." Abruptly, Victoria knew the tactic she'd take. She stuck her hand in her blazer pocket, her fingers closing around her engagement ring. "You remember Zachary Hamilton?"

Audrey nodded. "You went out with him the year before I left for Europe. He's the only guy I've ever seen you lose your cool over. Not that I blamed you. He oozed sex appeal, with those brooding eyes and hard, dark good looks. He was definitely the kind that sends shivers up your spine. It surprised me when you broke up after all those months. Why? Are you seeing him again?"

"Actually, I'm marrying him." Victoria extracted the ring, held it out for Audrey's inspection.

A sharp intake of breath. "Oh, Victoria." She touched the stone gently. "It's beautiful." Gathering up her strength, she leaned forward to hug her sister. "I'm thrilled for you."

"Me, too." Victoria felt tears sting her eyes. She hadn't realized how good it would feel to share this with her sister. "I love him so much it's scary."

"No, it's not. It's wonderful." Audrey eased back, her expression puzzled. "Why aren't you wearing the ring? Why is it in your pocket?"

Victoria stared at the stone. "Several reasons. Mostly because I wanted to tell Mother and Father the same way I'm telling you—before they saw the ring and figured it out for themselves. And second . . ." She swallowed, meeting her sister's gaze. "I wanted you out of here. Which you're going to be, within the hour."

Audrey blinked. "What do you mean?"

"I've arranged for your release. But, Audrey," she added quickly, seeing the elation erupt on her sister's face, "you can't tell anyone about this, not while we're still in the Institute. I'll explain why later. Just trust me. Zach will be here soon. You won't recognize him, not until later. I'll explain that part, too. The important thing for right now is that we get you ready—casually, so no one notices. You're weak, so tell me what you need and I'll pack it. Take only what you absolutely must. We'll send for the rest. Okay?"

Throughout her explanation, Audrey had remained silent. Now, she leaned back against the pillow, scrutinizing Victoria's face. "I was right about this place, wasn't I? Something weird is going on."

"Yes. But not for long." Victoria glanced over her shoulder, saw Harper perched in the hall. "Now hurry."

The second floor was relatively quiet.

Beatrice pushed Zach's wheelchair toward the stairwell, smiling cordially at the one or two medical attendants they passed along the way.

She stopped when they reached the ladies' room nearest the staircase. The area was deserted.

"The maintenance staff must be busy with the cleanup," Zach muttered quietly. "Every available person is probably down in the room that's got the cryogenic medical containers. I don't know what Block told them—maybe that the supply is contaminated—but they'll be frantically collecting stuff that needs to be destroyed. Block and his inside technicians will be flushing drugs down the toilets and burning containers in the crematorium."

"The room with the drugs and the crematorium are both in the basement," Beatrice reminded him in a whisper. "You've got to be careful."

"They're at the opposite end of the building from where I'm going, but don't worry, I will be." Zach edged a glance around. "You go into the bathroom, as planned. Stall. Don't come out until the lights go out and the panic starts. I'll be on my way up by then."

"But—"

"Do as I say. If I'm spotted, I've got to be by myself. It's the only chance I have of talking my way out of it. You know, David Karr, nut case. If you're with me, there'll be no explanation for why you're standing by and letting me roam the basement. Besides, your white uniform will stick out in the dark like a sore thumb. I'm in street clothes, since I threw such a fit about wearing those hospital gowns. I won't be spotted. Now go."

Beatrice nodded. "Good luck." With one last glance around, she walked into the ladies' room.

Zach stayed utterly still for a moment, making sure no one came by.

No one did.

He acted.

Jumping out of the wheelchair, he covered the short distance to the stairwell. He pushed open the door, slipped in, and sprinted down to the basement. Reaching the bottom level, he eased open the door and peeked out.

He could hear people scurrying about, as well as terse snatches of conversation. But all the activity was coming from the corridor where the crematorium was. The immediate area was deserted.

He stepped out, made his way down the hall in the opposite direction. He reached the locked door marked Utility Room: Authorized Personnel Only.

Groping in his pocket, he yanked out the set of lock-picking tools Meyer had provided in Zach's crash course at the FBI field office.

Two minutes later, he was inside the utility room.

He pocketed the tools, flipped on the light, and shut the door behind him.

Quickly, he scanned the walls of the cavernous room for

the main electrical box, the one that distributed power throughout the Hope Institute. There. A large gray panel with a red *Danger, High Voltage* sticker affixed to the front cover. Next to it was a smaller panel connected to the main box. A conduit ran from the smaller panel to a diesel generator situated in the corner of the room. Excellent. Just as he'd expected—and prayed. The Hope Institute had a backup generator that powered a special set of electrical circuits for life-support equipment. Now he could implement his plan without jeopardizing the lives of those patients who were critically ill.

Okay, first he needed some basic tools, those typically found in utility rooms. He scanned the room until he saw a workbench, beside which was a large tool chest, a supply cabinet, and a ladder. He went to the tool chest and tugged at the lid. Locked. Again he reached for his lock-picking implements. In less than a minute he was greeted with a click as the padlock sprang free. He raised the lid, found what he needed: two screwdrivers, a pair of electrician's pliers, a crowbar, a hammer, and some nails.

He took a long nail and, placing it in a machinist's vise located on the workbench, he twisted off the head. Using the pliers, he bent it into a U-shape. That done, he rummaged through the supply cabinet until he found some old cord.

Clutching his materials, he grabbed the ladder and returned to the electrical box. He climbed the ladder, then proceeded to drive the nail into a ceiling beam directly above the box, leaving enough space for the cord to slide freely through his makeshift U-bolt. He threaded one end of the cord through, leaving ample length at the opposite end so he could manipulate it. Climbing back down, he seized the pliers. He snipped off a separate, shorter piece of cord, tying the center of it to the longer cord where it hovered just above the electrical box. Then he tied each end of the shorter piece to the respective ends of the crowbar, rigging it so that it was parallel to the ground and perfectly balanced above the box.

He'd only get one chance.

Meticulously, he practiced lowering the crowbar with the cord. Satisfied with the crudely crafted mechanism, he tied his end of the cord to a rung on the ladder and moved the ladder away from the box, raising the crowbar so it hung at the precise spot he wanted it—just above the top of the electrical box.

He returned to the heavy tool chest and wheeled it toward the electrical box, positioning it between the box and the door. It would provide a sheltering barrier from what could be an explosion. Plucking out a pair of safety goggles from the tool tray, he donned them. He reached for a screwdriver and turned to remove the screws securing the protective cover of the electrical box. That accomplished, he found the two bus bars that supplied all the power to the box.

One small mistake and he'd be barbecued in an instant.

With that thought in mind, he groped in his pocket, this time yanking out the rubber gloves he'd stolen earlier from the janitor's cart near his room. He tugged them on. Preparation complete.

He grabbed the two screwdrivers, wedging them into the left and right copper bus bars respectively, carefully ensuring they were perfectly aligned with each other. He cocked his head, double-checking their alignment with the crowbar. Perfect.

It was show time.

With a steadying breath, Zach untied the cord from the ladder. Grasping it in his hand, he walked behind the tool chest and squatted. Slowly he manipulated the cord, lowering the crowbar, inching it closer to the two screwdrivers and the impending short circuit.

The crowbar made contact.

The room exploded in a fury of light and sparks. Zach dropped down behind the chest. Whipping around so his back was to the spewing electrical box, he scrambled toward the door and flung it open.

The utility room and hallway were now bathed in the eerie glow of emergency lights.

The last thing Zach heard as he closed the door behind him was the sound of the diesel generator starting up.

Victoria bolted to attention the instant the power died.

Zach, she realized, grinning in spite of the tension gripping her every muscle. What a brilliant maneuver. Shorting out the electrical system would shut down the crematorium, the computers, anything Ian needed for destroying evidence. The only move still available to him would be flushing drugs down the toilet by the glow of emergency lights.

Perfect.

Pandemonium broke loose in the halls, nurses and attendants darting back and forth, checking on patients and calming them down, while they themselves were trying to determine what had happened.

Audrey sat up in bed. "Is that our cue?"

"No." Victoria stood up, headed for the door. "Zach is our cue. We don't budge till he gets here."

A spark of realization lit Audrey's eyes. "He did this, didn't he? I remember he had a lot of degrees. Electrical engineering was one of them."

"Yup." Victoria pressed a warning forefinger to her lips. "Remember, not a word." She yanked open the door and stepped outside. "What's going on?" she demanded of Harper. "Is there a blackout?"

He was tight as a drum, looking torn between manning his post and bolting to help resolve the problem. "I don't know," he snapped. "I'm here, guarding you, remember?"

"What about the patients on life support?" Victoria pressed. "Will they be okay?"

"They'll be fine. We've got a backup generator for that." Harper's head whipped around, and he gave Victoria a blistering look. "Get back inside. I've got more to worry about than answering your stupid questions."

"Really? Then why are you still standing here?"

She'd pushed him too far. She saw the furious sparks glint in his eyes just as he reached out and grabbed her, his fingers biting into her arms. "Listen, you annoying bitch. Either get back into that room or I'm going to beat the—"

"Mr. Harper!"

It was Beatrice who interrupted him. She rushed down the hall, waving her arm and calling his name. "Mr. Block wants you in the basement right away," she said breathlessly. "The entire power system is gone. You've got to get to the utility room and see what you can do. He told me to stay with Audrey Kensington and her sister."

"Done." It was all Harper needed. He released Victoria and took off without a backward glance.

"Nice job, Beatrice." Zach appeared out of nowhere. "Take Audrey's things," he instructed. "I'll carry her." He paused to caress Victoria's cheek and give her a crooked grin. "Hi."

"Hi, yourself. You're a genius."

"And you're lousy at choosing targets to bulldoze. Stick with me. I'm safer." He strode into the room and went straight to Audrey's bed.

Audrey stared at him and blinked. "Either you've aged really badly or that's a disguise."

He chuckled, scooped her into his arms. "Both. Now hold on. We're getting you out of here."

He led the way, Victoria and Beatrice following close behind. The hall was virtually deserted as, by this time, the entire staff was either dealing with patients or relegated to the basement for repairs. The one or two orderlies they passed looked either dazed or frantic, and didn't spare them a second glance.

They took the stairs, hurrying down the three floors quickly but cautiously, pausing at each landing to listen for voices or footsteps—anything that would indicate they weren't alone.

The stairwell was silent.

Finally, they emerged on the main level.

Zach turned his head as they neared the front of the Institute, and called over his shoulder to Victoria and Beatrice. "I'll be able to open the heavy glass doors manually. That'll take us to the reception area. If, for any reason, Miss Evans is still at her desk, just ignore her. Don't stop, no matter what she says or threatens. We'll be outside in a minute. I ordered a taxi. It should be double-parked at the corner. The driver will pull up when he sees us."

God bless Zach. He'd thought of everything.

They reached the doors. Sheltering Audrey from the impact, Zach slammed his weight against the electronically operated door, applying pressure until it swung open.

They exploded into the reception area.

Miss Evans was at her desk, frantically trying to resuscitate her computer. She started when they rushed by, and did a double take as she recognized the unlikely foursome.

"Where are you going?" she demanded. "Mr. Karr, why are you carrying Miss Kensington? Why is her sister with you? Beatrice! My God, Beatrice, has Mr. Karr snapped? Does he have a weapon? What's happening? Are you being kidnapped?" Reflexively, she pressed a panic button on her desk, but, thanks to the power failure, no one from inside the Institute responded.

With a frustrated oath, she ran forward, but the small group ignored her, sprinting toward the door as fast as they could. "Stop! Stop right now!" she commanded.

Zach shoved the front door open, blowing by the doorman and dashing down the steps to the street.

Close behind, Victoria shaded her eyes, peered toward the corner, and spotted the cab. She raised her arm and waved.

The taxi surged forward, stopping in front of the Institute.

Zach yanked open the door, depositing Audrey on the

seat behind the driver as Victoria and Beatrice hurried around and climbed in on the other side.

Slamming the door shut, Zach zipped around and opened the front door on the passenger side.

He was about to jump in when three unmarked cars pulled up behind them and a team of FBI agents leaped out.

Meyer's gaze met Zach's. He paused long enough to wave the warrants in the air and give him a thumbs-up. Then he darted toward the Institute to shut down this tributary of the drug-smuggling syndicate—a tributary that would, hopefully, lead them to the source they'd been seeking for fifteen years.

36

"So where do things stand?" Zach asked Meyer, crossing one leg over the other.

The special agent skimmed his notes, then looked up, gazing from Zach to Victoria and back again. "We've got everything we need and then some," he assured them. "We've got the medical containers, the vials of drugs, the tapes, even an urn or two from that steel cabinet still filled with the ashes of supposedly living patients. Believe me, we're not missing anything. We've also got all the pertinent incriminating data we pulled off the computer, and Dr. Kensington's private medical journal, which she kept locked in the file cabinet in her private office where she and Block used to meet for their romps on the couch." Abruptly realizing what he'd said, he cleared his throat self-consciously and shot Victoria an apologetic look. "Sorry, Ms. Kensington."

"Don't be," Victoria replied quietly. "I know my aunt was sleeping with Ian Block. It paled in comparison to the rest of her offenses. By the way, I appreciate the sensitive way you handled things, letting Clarissa talk to my uncle alone before you did what you had to. She had a lot to confess, and he had a lot to absorb. It was very decent of you to give him the privacy he needed."

A terse nod. "I met your uncle when we went over and checked out the apartment. He seems like a decent guy. How's he holding up?"

"Fine." Victoria swallowed, remembering her uncle's stunned, lost expression when she'd first seen him, minutes after Clarissa had been taken away. He'd been positively gray, his normal composure shattered to bits. She'd sat with him for an hour, just talking, sharing a glass of wine, trying to sort things out, to understand how they'd both missed whatever vibes Clarissa might have given off—anything to hint at what she was involved in, or with whom. There were no answers, only questions. Questions, shock, and betrayal.

Later, Victoria had fixed her uncle something to eat and watered Clarissa's plants, making a mental note to move them to her apartment first thing the next day. Her uncle needed no reminders of his wife's passion for sustaining life. Besides, it would give Victoria a good excuse to come back and check on him.

She'd hung around until she sensed he needed time to himself. Then, she'd lightly mentioned her plan to come by tomorrow and collect the plants, gotten his promise to call her as soon as he woke up the next morning, and left.

It felt good to return a little of the strength and support he'd offered her for so many years.

Uncle Jim would be okay. He was already showing signs of improvement—agreeing, without hesitation and with sincere pleasure, to be Zach's best man, returning to his practice and patients, easing Audrey back into counseling with Dr. Osborne. Yes, Uncle Jim would be fine. With a little time and perspective, he'd get his life in order. Victoria would make sure of it.

She felt Zach reach over, enfold her hand in his, and squeeze it.

She smiled. "My uncle's a survivor. All the Kensingtons are. He'll come through this with flying colors." She inclined her head quizzically at Meyer. "You said you found my aunt's private journal. What did it say?"

"A lot of what we already knew—her goals for the Hope Institute, the lives she wanted to save and how. It also provided us with a nice list of her inner circle, a group she referred to as the 'disinfection team.' We've rounded them up, gotten statements from them all."

"Who are they?"

"No surprises, just the concrete proof we needed to haul the appropriate asses in." Meyer counted off on his fingers. "Dr. Kensington herself, Ian Block, Gloria Rivers, Leaman—who, incidentally, not only followed you around, but checked your mail on a daily basis—and a few key technicians: the one who operated the crematorium, the one who did the electronics work, and a computer hacker who tapped into your PCs and laptop. Oh, and Frank Harper. You were right about him. Block hired him to run you off the road."

"That part was in my aunt's notes?" Victoria breathed painfully.

"No. Actually, that was one venture Block took upon himself and kept from your aunt. He didn't think she'd go along with it. I got it straight from the horse's mouth. Harper spilled his guts in exchange for a lighter sentence. He wasn't supposed to kill you, just scare you away. He was pissed as hell that it didn't work." A slight grin. "He doesn't like you much."

"The feeling's mutual," Victoria retorted, feeling an inexplicable sense of relief that her aunt hadn't been part of that plan. It was just as Ian had said. Clarissa hadn't wanted to hurt her, or Audrey, either. She'd just wanted to preserve life, despite her inexcusable methods for doing so. In some odd way, that was comforting. It didn't lessen the gravity of her crimes but, after eight years of family closeness, it did wonders for Victoria's psyche.

"A few other fascinating tidbits we got from your aunt's journal," Meyer continued. "Remember those mandatory outpatient visits specified in the legal documents you found? The visits provided for all those lucky patients well enough to go home, and which were required to take place solely at the Hope Institute? Well, according to Dr.

Kensington's notes, they consisted of injections of the 'non-FDA-approved drugs,' as she calls them, and a take-home regimen of follow-up pills. Guess what those pills were? Placebos. No more life-sustaining than M and M's. But an excellent source of capital for the Hope Institute and, according to your aunt, a mental balm for the patients. Another of her twisted blend of crime and compassion. Inject the patients with the periodic doses of medicine they need, and send them home with sugar pills they believe in and pay for, but that don't do anything. *And* that can't incriminate the Institute if someone else happens to find them. Remember, inside the Institute's walls, the drugs are accounted for and cautiously dispensed. Dr. Kensington couldn't have her outpatients walking around with illegal drugs in their pockets." Meyer shook his head. "Either she, or Block, or both of them, are geniuses."

Victoria was beginning to feel sick again. "Anything else?"

Meyer glanced down at the file. "Only one other thing I think you'll find interesting. You know those photos in the reception area showing the happy patients recuperating at the Hope Institute? All actors. Not that the patients weren't happy. The ones we've interviewed these past few days had been more than satisfied—until now. But to protect everyone's privacy, Clarissa Kensington hired actors to pose for those shots. That way, no patients, past or present, could be recognized. I tell you, she thought of everything."

He turned over the last page of the file. "Anyway, the Hope Institute's now officially shut down. The assets will be liquidated, and the funds set aside. That cash pool will be used to pay off the millions of dollars in lawsuits they're sure to face. There are a lot of angry families out there who were defrauded and lied to. The remaining patients have already been transferred to the hospitals of their choice. That didn't take much arm-twisting; they weren't too eager to stay in a place that was using them as human guinea pigs."

"No, I'd imagine not." Victoria was relieved that Meyer had completed his Hope Institute report. The list of her aunt's crimes was already appalling enough. She wasn't sure she could stomach any more.

"What about the syndicate?" Zach demanded, changing gears to address the bigger picture.

Triumph glittered in Meyer's eyes. "We've got names and places now—Colombia, Mexico, and a few other key locations. Interpol has already been brought in and is mobilizing as we speak. Give us a week, two at the most. The whole damn syndicate will be blown apart."

"I want you to keep me posted," Zach informed him. "I want to know when the arrests are made. I want progress reports on extradition proceedings. And I want to know when the scum running this syndicate go on trial in the U.S. I plan to be there to watch them pay for what they did."

Meyer didn't hesitate. "You've got it. It's the least I can do." He gazed steadily at Zach. "And then, it'll finally be over."

"Yeah," Zach agreed roughly, letting it sink in that the retribution he'd craved for his father's murder was finally at hand. "Thank God."

Victoria looked at him, sensing his emotions and experiencing an acute surge of relief. At last, Zach would have his closure. His parents could rest in peace. He could let go of the past. And the nightmare would finally, *finally*, be at an end.

"Yes, thank God," she echoed, reciprocating Zach's loving support by squeezing his hand as he had hers. No one but the two of them understood quite how much this meant to him. More so since they were together—sharing the closing of this chapter, poised on the brink of a new and wonderful one.

Zach's fingers tightened around hers.

"So that's that?" Victoria asked Meyer.

The agent took her cue. He shut the file and leaned forward, propping his elbows on his desk and nodding. "Yup. That's that. Case closed, at least from this end. Think you can go back to enjoying a mundane life with just one identity apiece?"

"We'll manage," Zach assured him dryly. "Besides, I doubt our life will be mundane."

"Yeah." Meyer's gaze flickered to the engagement ring on Victoria's left hand. "I doubt it, too. When's the wedding?"

"In two weeks," Victoria replied. "I wanted my sister to be a little stronger. She's my maid of honor." A brief pause. "I also wanted to make sure my father would be free to give me away."

Meyer eyed her thoughtfully. "I take it that's a question. All right, here's my answer. Your father crossed a helluva lot of ethical lines."

"We're not discussing ethics. We're discussing the law."

"I was getting to that." Meyer frowned in Zach's direction. "Does she ever let you finish a thought?"

Zach's lips twitched. "Occasionally."

"Right." Meyer sounded decidedly skeptical. "Anyway, according to the DA, your father's pretty much in the clear. He had no knowledge of the drug smuggling or the fraud, and no direct part in aiding and abetting Block and Dr. Kensington. He also had no idea they were keeping your sister sedated for their own protection rather than hers. His judgment sucks, as do his morals. But he did provide vital evidence. In fact, I got a call from the DA before I got yours, Hamilton. Which means Walter Kensington freely gave over those pages that put the final nail in Block's coffin and made our job a lot easier. Granted, he did it to save his own skin, and his law firm's, but he did it nonetheless. My guess is he'll get a strong slap on the wrist and a warning from the Bar Association, then be sent home to deal with the lawsuits Waters, Kensington, Tatem and Calder are going to be fielding." A hint of warmth softened Meyer's tone. "So, Ms.

Kensington, I think it's safe to say you can plan on your father walking you down the aisle."

"Thank you." Victoria cleared her throat. "And the others?"

"If you mean your aunt, she won't be doing any more medical research, not at Mount Sinai or anywhere else. My guess is she'll be spending a fair amount of time in prison. Drug smuggling and trafficking is a serious offense, whether or not it's for humane purposes." Meyer shrugged. "But I'm sure your father will hook her up with a good criminal lawyer. She'll survive."

"And Block?"

Whatever traces of leniency Meyer had been feeling vanished. "He's scum—the classic seeker of power and wealth at all costs. No altruistic motives there, and no conscience, either. He'll be disbarred and sent away for a long, long time."

"I guess that means the senior partnership at Waters, Kensington, Tatem and Calder is out," Zach put in dryly.

"I'd say that was a certainty." Meyer pushed back his chair and rose. "I think it's time you two got on with your lives. Thanks, from the FBI—and me personally—for everything you've done." He extended his hand to Victoria. "You're a smart, gutsy woman, Ms. Kensington."

"Even if I am a bulldozer," Victoria reminded him, smiling as she shook his hand.

"Yeah, even so." A broad grin. "I wish you and Hamilton a long, happy life together." He turned to Zach, gave him the same firm handshake. "Then again, I think that one's in the bag. I knew it from the start. The minute I saw the way you looked at her."

"That morning in your office?" Victoria asked in surprise. "But we were delivering evidence. We were too riled up to—"

"Not that time. The time before."

She paused, totally mystified. "You and I never met before that day."

"Maybe not, but I caught the expression on Hamilton's face when he first recognized you on our surveillance tape. Take it from a happily married man, your happiness is a done deal."

"A done deal, huh?" Victoria murmured, lying naked in Zach's arms. They were in his hotel suite, which was a mile closer to the field office than her apartment and had therefore become the destination of choice.

A wise decision, since they'd never made it to the bed. In fact, Victoria had already finished unbuttoning Zach's shirt and was kissing her way down his chest, unfastening the belt on his pants as she did, by the time he groped behind him to throw the bolt on the suite door.

They made love the first time right there where they stood, Zach lifting her against the wall and driving into her hard and fast, bracing his arms on either side of her to cushion her from the force of his thrusts. He brought her to an instant, violent climax then, seconds later, spurted into her as his own orgasm slammed through him.

Still shuddering with aftershocks, he'd carried her to the bed, lowered himself onto her, into her, that heated intensity still burning in his eyes. Their lovemaking had resumed, as fervent and consuming as it had been since they'd escaped from the Hope Institute six days ago.

Maybe that was because they were more aware than ever how fragile life was, how lucky they were to have found each other again, to be safe and alive, and in each other's arms.

And maybe it was because they never intended to forget that.

Now, cradling her against him, Zach smiled, the lazy, possessive smile of a very happy, very sated man. "Yeah. A done deal. And happiness is too tame a word. How about elation? Or euphoria? I think those are far more fitting terms for our future." He sifted her hair through his fingers. "Wouldn't you agree?"

"Oh, without question." Victoria smiled back, feeling more joy, more bone-deep contentment than she'd ever imagined. She draped her thigh over his and rubbed the arch of her foot against his calf. "Let's spend two weeks in this bed."

He chuckled, his fingertips caressing her spine in teasing, seductive motions. "We have dinner with your uncle tonight. Tomorrow we have a morning of house hunting with the Realtor and an afternoon appointment with the Jack Russell breeder. And Sunday we have brunch at your parents' house. Or did you forget?"

She kissed his neck, her own fingers gliding down his body with a distinct goal in mind. "I forget everything when you're inside me," she whispered.

He groaned, shifting to give her better access. "So do I." A hard shudder racked his body as she found and stroked his erection. "We'll call and cancel," he ground out, teeth clenched. "The dinner, the Realtor, the breeder, the brunch—all of it."

"We can't do that," she murmured, drawing out her caresses in a way that pushed him dangerously close. "My uncle's looking forward to showing you his sound system. I'm looking forward to finding the perfect house and the perfect Jackson puppy. And Audrey's looking forward to showing off her progress. She's eating three square meals a day. She's also seeing Dr. Osborne and, believe it or not, trying to start a civil, relatively healthy relationship with my father. What's happened seems to have mellowed him a little. Even my mother's noticed. She's cut down on her antidepressants. So you see, we can't cancel our plans. Things in Greenwich are definitely looking up."

She bent over, her lips and tongue following the path her fingers had taken. "Speaking of looking up . . ."

That did it.

With a muffled curse, Zach rolled her to her back, wedged himself between her thighs, and thrust into her. She was wet, already aroused by their foreplay. He hooked her legs over his arms, angled her so he could penetrate her as deeply as possible, and began a relentless rhythm that had them both unraveling in seconds.

Afterward, Zach propped himself on his elbows, stroking damp strands of hair off her face. "I'm insatiable when it comes to you. How do you expect me to let you out of this bed?"

She smiled, looping her arms around his neck. "I don't. When I said let's spend two weeks in this bed, I meant our honeymoon."

That didn't seem to please him. "Yeah, right. Some honeymoon. We're going to Europe, jumping from country to country to get my business affairs in order."

"Correction. We're going to Europe, but not for business. And not to jump from country to country. In fact, we're not even going to the Europe you're expecting."

"You lost me."

Her eyes danced with mischief. "You're not the only one who's overbearing. I like running the show, too, remember?"

A corner of his mouth lifted. "I remember. What did you have in mind?"

"I contacted a vice president at each international location of Hamilton Enterprises. They were very cooperative when they heard our predicament. They say congratulations, by the way. They're already getting your affairs in order. Everything you need—from files, to bank accounts, to your suits and ties—is being put together and shipped. It'll be delivered to my apartment next week. Our plane tickets have been cashed in, and our hotel reservations canceled—both of which facts are being held in the strictest confidence. As far as the world's concerned, we're going to Europe."

"Really?" Zach was openly grinning now. "And where will we be instead?"

"I told you—this bed." Victoria patted the mattress. "Our

own private taste of Europe. The place we first made love, and where we fell in love all over again. The Plaza Athénée. I know you planned on checking out this week. But I convinced the management to find other accommodations for the businessman they were assigning this suite to. I explained to them that it was our honeymoon, that Suite 1010 had particular significance to us, and that it would mean the world to us if they'd cater to our sentimentality. I was *very* convincing and *very* persistent. Anyway, the suite's ours until June third. Surprise."

Zach stared at her for one flabbergasted minute. Then he began to laugh. "You really are a bulldozer. An amazing one, but a bulldozer nonetheless."

"But you love me anyway."

"More than life itself."

"Then you like my arrangements?" she asked with mock innocence, arching her hips to draw him deeper inside her.

His gaze darkened, and he lowered his mouth to hers. "What do you think?"

Also available from

ANDREA KANE

The Black Diamond

Dream Castle

Echoes in the Mist

Emerald Garden

The Gold Coin

The Last Duke

Legacy of the Diamond

Masque of Betrayal

The Music Box

My Heart's Desire

Samantha

The Silver Coin

The Theft

Wishes in the Wind

Visit
❖ Pocket Books ❖
online at

....

www.SimonSays.com

....

Keep up on the latest new
releases from your favorite
authors, as well as author
appearances, news, chats,
special offers and more.

SIMON & SCHUSTER
A VIACOM COMPANY
www.SimonSays.com

Pocket
Books

2381-01

**Visit the Simon & Schuster
romance Web site:**

---

www.SimonSaysLove.com

**and sign up for our
romance e-mail updates!**

Keep up on the latest
new romance releases,
author appearances, news, chats,
special offers, and more!
We'll deliver the information
right to your inbox—if it's new,
you'll know about it.

POCKET BOOKS